Mary,
Enjoy the
family stories
in old Cape Cod
+ New Cape Cod.
Love,
Marianne
aka:
Mrs Shafer

A CAPE COD FAMILY SAGA

# THE HOUSE ON CROOKED POND

M. L. SHAFER

# THE HOUSE ON CROOKED POND
## A CAPE COD FAMILY SAGA

*iUniverse books may be ordered through booksellers or by contacting:*

*iUniverse*
*1663 Liberty Drive*
*Bloomington, IN 47403*
*www.iuniverse.com*
*1-800-Authors (1-800-288-4677)*

*Because of the dynamic nature of the Internet, any web addresses or links contained in this book may have changed since publication and may no longer be valid. The views expressed in this work are solely those of the author and do not necessarily reflect the views of the publisher, and the publisher hereby disclaims any responsibility for them.*

*Any people depicted in stock imagery provided by Thinkstock are models, and such images are being used for illustrative purposes only. Certain stock imagery © Thinkstock.*

*ISBN: 978-1-5320-0863-4 (sc)*
*ISBN: 978-1-5320-0862-7 (e)*

*Library of Congress Control Number: 2016918785*

*Print information available on the last page.*

*iUniverse rev. date: 1/25/2017*

# Contents

# Acknowledgments

My greatest sources of inspiration for this story are the historic half houses of Cape Cod—those half saltboxes, half colonials, and half Capes whose unique architecture supplies a large part of the charming character of this land surrounded by the sea.

I combined my love of these old houses with information gained about local history through research with the aid of Mary Sicchio, former archivist at both the Falmouth Historical Society and the Cape Cod Community College Nickerson Archives. I am grateful for her help.

Gwenn Friss of the *Cape Cod Times* is to be thanked for giving me a tour of the paper's facility in Hyannis and providing information on the assignments of journalists.

I would especially like to thank the members of my critique group— Pat Mullaly, Gail Nickerson, and Ann Specht—as well as my two beta readers, Denise Jacobson and Cornelia Costello, for their valuable suggestions and contributions. With their interest in my project, my journey through this storytelling process has been one amazing adventure.

Another special thanks goes to my cousin, John Lockwood, for his information on the German weapons of war.

Without the Cape Cod Writers Center summer conferences, this book would not have been possible. I send my sincere thanks to its leadership and the numerous guest faculty members who, over a period of many summers, offered me insights into all aspects of the writing craft. The connections I made at the CCWC with authors Carol Smilgin and Arlene Kay have proved invaluable. Their support and suggestions are truly appreciated.

Thanks also to Dorene Sykes Photography for my portrait as seen on the back cover.

I would finally like to thank my family for understanding the true meaning of family.

# Author's Note

I have used my imagination to enhance the historical facts that play important roles in this story. Crooked Pond does exist in Falmouth, but the village of Herringville, the house, and the Lyman family exist only within the pages of this book. To lend Cape Cod flavor to the story, I have used surnames frequently seen on the Cape both in the past and present. My characters have no relation to persons with these names, living or dead. Lyman is not one of these common Cape names, but the surname has been in my family for centuries. The Lymans in the story are purely fictional and not based on any of my relatives.

Twenty-first-century advances in DNA testing play an important role in the life of "The Collector," the first part of our story, which takes place in 2014. The fictional *Cape Cod Evening Star*, billed in the story as the largest newspaper on the Cape, is not intended to bear any resemblance to existing media outlets.

In *The House on Crooked Pond*'s second part, "The Farrier's Daughter," Quaker Tacy Swift's first name is pronounced to rhyme with Stacey. In the 1880s and '90s, a Quaker blacksmith by the name of Daniel Swift operated a forge in West Falmouth, and his building is still there. The Quaker blacksmith of 1712 in my story is purely fictional.

During the War of 1812, houses on Shore Street in Falmouth were damaged by cannonballs from the British ship *Nimrod* in January 1814. It was common practice to move whole houses intact from one location to another at that time. In the third part of the book, "The Matriarch," this detail is a focal point.

Guano from birds on islands in the Pacific and the Caribbean was shipped to Woods Hole by the Pacific Guano Company, who operated a fertilizer factory there from 1863 to 1889. To meet the needs of this industry, the railroad was extended to Woods Hole in 1872. The rail extension also made it easier for visitors to travel to this part of the Cape, and by the late 1890s Falmouth had become a popular summer resort. Railroad travel from Falmouth to Boston, Providence, and New York also offered more opportunities for people to travel to the gold mines of the far West, as reflected in *The House on Crooked Pond's* fourth part, "The Adventurer," set in 1912.

*For we are the same things our fathers have been;*
*We see the same sights our fathers have seen;*
*We drink the same stream, we feel the same sun,*
*And run the same course our fathers have run.*

*—William Knox, 1789–1825*

# Prologue

Be careful what you say as you walk through the forests of Cape Cod. The trees are listening. If this were not true, they'd have nothing to whisper about as they swayed in the gentle salt breezes that caressed their pine needles and oak leaves with tender affection.

Cape Cod, that great spit of sand, boulders, and marshlands left behind thousands of years ago by the retreating glaciers of the last ice age, has a long history. The first people to come to this land called themselves "People of the Dawn," or "Wampanoag."

Their stories taught respect for every living thing. When they made their way through the forest in their silent moccasins, they gently pushed aside the lower branches, taking care not to disturb the countless creatures and plants that called the forest home. They wondered when the strange men they had heard about, men with white faces, would come to this land of theirs. They called it Suckanessett. It is now called Falmouth.

In 1685, the first white-faced men stomped along in their heavy boots, trampled down the underbrush, and slashed their way through the forest. Hezekiah Lyman; his sons, Charles and Jabez; and four other sturdy men from Plimoth, with axes slung over their shoulders, drove a pair of locked-together, snorting oxen right up to the irregular shoreline of a pond. They cut down several oaks and pines and had their oxen drag the logs a short distance to the top of a hill to a relatively flat place, where tangles of cat's-claw briars and spring-flowering rhododendrons grew. There the Englishmen began to strip the bark off the logs, cut them into beams and planks, and assemble them into the form of a large house.

The house was two and a half stories high in the front, with the back roof slanting sharply down to cover one story in the back. It had the shape of a common saltbox, those wooden containers built to carry salt from the evaporating vats near the sea to parts inland whose steep, sloping lids were designed to let the rain slide easily off. This became known as a saltbox style house.

The largest and strongest beam inside the house had to support the center of the ceiling in what was called the keeping room, now the library. One end rests on the large stone fireplace they built on the side of the house just inside the front door, and the other end rests on the opposite wall. The Englishmen called it the "summer beam," a term that comes from the French *sommier*, meaning "beast of burden."

The house holds many tales of the generations of Lymans who have lived there since it was built. The first mistress counted as she thrust her hand into the beehive oven at the back of the great fireplace to test if it was hot enough to bake her rabbit pie. Her moans of sexual pleasure, as well as her cries at the births of her ten children, happened there. Five of these children were buried down the hill in the family plot next to the pond.

For centuries, the family, sitting around the same fireplace, told stories on various subjects, from witches to wristwatches, cannonballs to computers. Puppies ran through the house, and one angry master kicked one of them until it yelped no longer.

Four of the many tales of fourteen generations of this Lyman family, who all lived in the house on Crooked Pond, take place in the years 1712, 1814, 1912, and 2014. The first account begins with the start of the most current year.

# Part I

# The Collector—Winter 2014

*I love acting. It is so much more real than life.*

—*Oscar Wilde, 1854–1900*

In January 2014 the snow from the first of many blizzards to harass the Cape this year has just about disappeared. The ground has not yet taken on its hard winter freeze. Crooked Pond is covered with a sheet of ice so thin that, this afternoon, when five squawking canvasback ducks glided in to land on the ice to rest, they found themselves surprised to be cracking through to float on the water.

However, this story does not begin here on Crooked Pond, in the village of Herringville, in the town of Falmouth. It begins about forty miles east in another Cape Cod town, Chatham.

# Chapter 1

## THE POEM

*She never had a mother.*
*As far as she was concerned, she simply always existed*
*In the vast, windswept marshlands,*
*The forests of oak and pine,*
*The sea at the bottom of the dune.*
*These were the ones she could talk to.*

—*Abby Jenkins*

Abby printed out a copy of her poem, slid it into her file drawer, and locked it so her mother wouldn't find it. She finished writing up her book reviews for the local Chatham newspaper and went downstairs to sit at the bay window in the dark dining room. She tried to decide which was worse—the harsh odor of garlic and onions left over from her mother's cooking or the blaring sounds coming from the TV her parents were watching in the living room. She peered into the night, impatient as she waited to hear the characteristic rumblings and see the first glimmers of the headlights of Jeff's Porsche announcing his arrival as he rounded the bend of her long driveway.

"Are you still waiting for that Fredericks man with the fancy car?" Her mother padded through the dining room in black fleece slippers on her way to the kitchen for another glass of Pinot Noir. "You're foolish," she said as she pulled on Abby's scarf in an attempt to straighten it. "He's too old for you." She pushed back what she believed to be an unruly lock of Abby's long brown hair. "You should know by now that he's not going to come." With a wave of her hand, she dismissed her daughter. "It's ten o'clock. Go to bed."

"Oh let her be, Gladys," her father called from his recliner in the living room.

Abby turned back to the window, took a deep breath, exhaled, and redirected her exasperated feelings to more pleasant ones. How she loved her father for always being on her side. For as long as she could remember, whenever her mother complained about some minor thing Abby did, her father would wink at her in reassurance that everything would turn out all right.

If he hadn't had a stroke last summer, she would not be living here. His need for care had postponed her plans for a career working in Boston as a journalist. Immediately after receiving her master's degree, she had taken a position as one of the junior editors of a midsize publishing company there, but she'd left after three years when her father had taken ill.

Her mother's position as principal of the Chatham Country Day School left little time for her to spend at home caring for her husband. Abby had returned to the Cape to work at home, reviewing books for her local Chatham newspaper, freelancing by submitting articles to magazines, and caring for her father. She hadn't, for a minute, given up her dream to eventually move back to Boston; this was, she was certain, but a short interruption in her professional life.

Now that her father's recovery had progressed to the point where he could speak with ease and walk around the house with the aid of a cane, Abby had begun to plan once more for a life away from her childhood home—especially since Jeff Fredericks had come into her life.

A professor of English at Boston University, Fredericks was about to celebrate his fortieth birthday. His wife had divorced him two years ago, and he and Abby had been seeing each other for weekends on the Cape for the past three months. Her thoughts now drifted to memories of last weekend. She ran her fingertips through her hair and began to smile.

She recalled sitting with Jeff on the sofa beside the crackling fire and sparkling white lights from the Christmas tree in his Chatham house. Two thick columns of Bayberry candles on the mantel provided the only other light in the room. Their aroma, mingling with the heady scent of the balsam fir tree, was as seductive to Abby as the man sitting beside her.

"You know," he said as he drew back a little, his eyes skimming over her entire form, "I really admire your L.L.Bean sense of fashion."

She laughed, shook her head, and made a gesture that encompassed his crew neck sweater, button-down shirt, and black corduroy slacks. "That's because you're an English professor clinging to the preppy look." Then she leaned in toward him, her blue eyes teasing. "So what else do you admire about me?"

"Well, I really do love these." He fondled her large breasts. Then he drew her even closer, caressed her ear with his lips, and whispered, "You are one delicious woman."

The intense sex that followed had left Abby no longer questioning her feelings for this charming man. He had a peaceful, settled, clean look about him; she loved the velvety smoothness of his voice; and the sex was great each time they slept together. The fact that he was an English professor with a house also in Wellesley, one inherited from wealthy parents, rendered him interesting enough to fit into her plan to eventually find a man whose company she could enjoy, without becoming too emotionally attached.

After her first love was killed in a car accident while they were still in high school, Abby refused to be so devastated again. At that age, she had not been equipped to handle the confusion and grief that overpowered her. With no more comfort and understanding than a "You'll get over it" from her mother, Abby slowly learned to push her feelings aside. She was now determined that the man she would live the rest of her life with would be smart, interesting, and pleasant, but would never be another great love.

Or, might Jeff Fredericks be the one man who could add love to these other requirements?

———•———

Her cell phone chimed to announce a call from Jeff, bringing her back to the reality of the evening. She ran upstairs to her room.

"Guess what?"

"You had a flat tire, and that's why you're two hours late?"

"Oh? Oh, I'm sorry. No, I didn't have a flat tire. I have decided I want to get married."

*Oh my God, is this the way English professors propose?* She shook her head as though trying to unscramble her thoughts. Was she ready for this? She felt the best response was to be coy. "Well … um … who's the lucky girl?"

"Remember I told you about an old girlfriend of mine, the one from Japan who teaches at BU and was on sabbatical? Well …"

She sat down on her bed.

"She has just returned and decided …"

Abby closed her eyes and pinched the bridge of her nose.

"And so we are going to …"

She thought she must have misheard him. "Wait a minute, Jeff. I thought we had a date tonight. And now you're telling me you're going to marry an old girlfriend next week?"

"Abby, honey, you didn't think anything between us was serious, did you?"

———————

Within ten days Abby had applied for and was offered the job as assistant to the editor of the books and lifestyles section with the largest newspaper on the Cape, the *Cape Cod Evening Star*, in Falmouth. Since it was early January and off-season, it was easy to rent an affordable studio apartment there, on the top floor of a house on a hill. The small deck outside her room offered a magnificent view of the Great Sippewissett Marsh and sunsets over Buzzards Bay.

She gave a tearful hug to her father and promised to call at least once a week. She also hugged her mother, but without either tears or promises. She was on her way.

Although this was not quite the Boston assignment she'd dreamed of having one day, Abby knew it was her first step in the right direction. Staying focused on her career would be easy now. She would no longer have to waste her time musing on the charms of Jeff Fredericks, she would be free of the constant criticisms of her mother, and she would be only an hour's drive from Chatham if her father needed further care. Best of all, she would be only an hour's drive from the city life in Boston. She could not wait to begin her new job.

# Chapter 2

## The Journalist

Abby's first month at the *Star* had been productive but more stressful than she had expected. While working at the town's weekly edition in Chatham, she had only to go online to check the wire services for book reviews. For the daily editions of the *Cape Cod Evening Star*, she had to correspond with other reviewers in nationwide newspapers, interview Cape Cod authors when their books were first released, and keep up with any Cape events that might capture the attention of subscribers interested in the lifestyles section. The fact that she had her own cubicle in a newsroom of twenty-four others almost made up for the stress, for she loved feeling that she was a part of something so vibrant.

Weekly phone calls to her father provided his constant assurance that he was well and pleased with her move. The interest he took in her new position contributed greatly to her confidence in believing she had made the right decision, even though her mother, as usual, thought differently.

On the thirteenth of February, the newspaper's executive editor, Bruce Crowell, called Abby into his glass-walled office directly off the newsroom and shut the door behind her. "Now sit down and listen to this!" He pointed to the chair that faced his desk and returned to his seat at his computer. When he continued, his voice was hushed, as though he didn't want anyone else to hear him, but Abby also noticed that he was quite keyed up.

"It's an e-mail from John Linton! You remember him—that actor who suddenly disappeared from the face of the earth in the early eighties?"

Abby was about to say she had not heard much about this man, but Crowell, cutting her short, said, "I was a big fan of his. He wants to give an exclusive interview to the *Star*! Listen." He turned to his computer and read the e-mail out loud: "'I have a remarkable collection of memorabilia from before the Revolutionary War up to the about the first half of the twentieth century. I would like to share this with the public, and I want to have a specific member of your staff, Abigail Jenkins'"—Crowell paused and looked at Abby, his dark, bushy eyebrows raised—"to write up the story and take a few photos.'"

Abby's eyes lit up with the idea, but she wondered why this has-been actor had asked for her specifically. "Why just me? I can see it going in the lifestyles section, but why can't we also send our staff photographer?"

"I have no idea. Maybe he saw your story on the Winter Art and Book Show at Highfield Hall. You did take several great photos there, and they printed out well in our Sunday edition."

She started to ask more about this man Crowell was so interested in, but he silenced her with a wave of his hand. "Listen! Linton says, 'Please contact me by writing in care of Harry Norman.' Then he gives the Herringville post office address. Can you imagine? John Linton knows crazy old Harry Norman! Well, I'll be damned!" He sat back in his chair, looking happily exhausted.

"Who is this 'crazy old Harry Norman' you're supposed to contact Linton through?" Abby had not been in Falmouth long enough to have heard about all of its colorful characters.

"Oh, Norman lives like a hermit in the run-down Lyman house on Crooked Pond, but that's not important." He shook his head and scowled as if annoyed by her question. "What's important is Linton has made it clear that only you can be the one to interview him. And you are going to do this."

"Well ..." Abby began.

"Let me continue." Crowell looked down at his computer. "Linton says, 'Once I receive notice that you are interested, I will disclose further necessary information. I will be in town for a few weeks, but I must insist on my privacy. If I discover that reporters, or anyone else other than you or Ms. Jenkins, are trying to contact me, there will be no story. Also, Ms. Jenkins can take my photograph and write about only my collection, nothing about my personal life. And if any news of my whereabouts should leak to the public before I am ready to release it, there will be no story.'"

Crowell sat back, clasped his hands behind his neck, and gave a broad grin to Abby. "So? What do you think?"

She took a deep breath and collected her thoughts. Glancing to her right, she could see through the glass wall that the oldest member of the staff, Marcia Wentworth, was standing close by, appearing to be intent on shuffling some papers, but obviously trying to listen. Abby returned her attention back to her editor.

"This sounds like an exciting assignment, and I'm looking forward to researching this actor you said was so famous. But if he was, why do I only vaguely remember hearing about him? I watch the classic movie channel, and I can't say that I can recall even one of his movies."

"You would have heard a lot more if you were a little older." Crowell frowned. "He was big for a short time in the sixties and seventies, before you were even born."

He placed both hands on his desk, stood up, and leaned toward her. "John Linton totally removed himself from public view in 1980 after a short movie career characterized by booze, numerous affairs, and an Oscar nomination. Disappeared! Completely! At first, people joked that he had been shot by an irate husband and buried in a landfill, but his fans still tried to track him down. Reports of sightings were never confirmed. Now, no one knows if this man is still alive. But there are plenty of former fans of his who would love to find out that he is."

Crowell beamed. "Abby, you are going to resurrect my former screen idol. You're going to get a story about John Linton, even if it is to be only about his collection."

Abby's insides took leaps as she considered the possibility that, if this story were to create the interest Crowell believed it would, it could be her chance to make a name for herself. She did publish articles in magazines, and the stories of the literary world that she covered in the time she had been with the *Star* were well written and had prompted a few admiring letters to the editor. Still, they were not big-city news. This assignment might be the opportunity she had been waiting for so she could move up—up and back to Boston. Her sense of adventure began to take hold.

"Okay. I'll check the press files on him right now."

"Good," said Crowell. "But believe me, as one of his avid fans, I've tried. You're only going to find some pictures of him in his prime and some stories about his disappearance years ago."

"You're sure it'll create enough interest?"

"Absolutely." Crowell began to pace the floor behind his desk, gesturing wildly as he spoke. "Just the fact that he has turned up alive is going to make this story go viral. It will be all over the Internet. The *Globe* will be after it and maybe even the *New York Times.* It'll go to *People* magazine, Hollywood will go crazy, and who knows what else! Do a good job on this and you, as well as our little old *Cape Cod Evening Star* will be making it big time." He stopped and tapped her shoulder and added, "You just might be able to extract a story out of him about where he's been for the last thirty years."

That convinced her. She would love this assignment.

As she was leaving the room, he cautioned her. "Abby, I'm not going to risk losing this story. I'll come up with a fake assignment to cover your absence from the building when you go to interview him. Remember that you're to tell no one about this—not your best friend, not your family, and especially no one on the staff. Got it? No one."

As she closed the door behind her, his words echoed in her ears, and she thought about Marcia Wentworth standing so close to the glass wall of Crowell's office. Marcia most certainly had heard what was going on. She would have to confront her, and she would have to do it right away, before Marcia had a chance to go for a coffee break. She looked around and found that the gossipy little lady was nowhere to be seen. She decided to check the woman's lavatory and found her at the sink.

"Hi there, Marcia," she said, checking under the stalls to be sure no one else was there.

Before Abby could say a word, Marcia finished rubbing her hands under the noisy dryer and turned to Abby, grabbing her upper arms and shaking her. "Oh, Abby! This is the most exciting thing I've heard in years! You are going to interview John Linton!"

"So you *were* listening! Marcia, this is supposed to be confidential. Linton insisted—"

She could not finish her sentence, as her coworker hugged her more tightly than Abby thought the frail old woman was capable of.

"Oh, I know, I know. How wonderful!"

Then Marcia grabbed Abby's hands and squeezed them, telling her how lucky she was and that she would give anything to be in Abby's shoes. Then she declared how she had once practically worshipped John Linton. "In my younger days, I would have run off with him at the drop of a hat."

"Was he that good-looking?"

"Oh my, yes. Some compared him jokingly to Orson Wells, but taller. I agreed. I thought him handsome in a wicked sort of way, especially around the eyes."

Just as Abby was getting drawn in to Marcia's impressions, the cleaning lady arrived with her mop and pail. To stop Marcia from saying anything else, Abby put a finger to her lips.

"I'd love to hear your stories because I know so little about this man," she said, "but not now." She nodded in the direction of the cleaning lady who had just entered the first stall to begin her task.

As she and Marcia left the lavatory and walked down the long hall to the newsroom, Abby whispered, "Please remember this assignment is to be completely confidential."

"Oh yes, I won't tell a soul."

---

At two o'clock, Bill Lambert, the sports editor, leaned over the four-foot-high partition to Abby's cubical and whispered with an excitement she could only imagine him exhibit after the Red Sox had won a World Series, or at least as much as might be generated if a runner from Cape Cod actually won the annual Falmouth Road Race. "Don't tell Crowell

12

I said this, but I heard you don't know much about this Linton guy, so I thought you might want to know that he acted with Brando as well as Pacino. He had a supporting role in *Apocalypse Now*, and—"

Abby had to cut him off. "Please, Bill, I appreciate your willingness to help, but this is supposed to be just between Crowell, Linton, and myself."

"Sure. I know. But it's such a big deal that I couldn't help myself. I had to tell you. Good luck meeting with that great guy."

At half past three, the arts and entertainment editor, Jud Parker, leaned over, eager to whisper to her that Linton had made one great picture as a leading man, his dramatic role in *Rains of Summer*, which had won him an Academy Awards nomination.

After thanking him for the information, Abby grabbed hold of his shirt collar and pulled his face down close to hers, whispering with the hiss of a snake, "Listen! My assignment here is supposed to be confidential. Do you understand what that means?"

"Sure, Abby, sure. I was only trying to help." He wiggled out of her grasp and quickly left.

Abby held her head in her hands, wondering how many others Marcia had told. She got up, went directly to Marcia's desk, and threatened to tell Crowell that Marcia had been listening to their conversation if she told anyone else about Linton.

Looking down at her keyboard and not making eye contact with Abby, Marcia promised.

＊＊＊

The wind was howling that afternoon as she left the office after work. She had all she could do to pull her car door closed. Once she did, she saw Stan Kelley, the *Star*'s thirtysomething, talented photographer, battling the wind that was attempting to rip off his scarf as he fought his way across the parking lot to catch up with her.

"Hey, Abby! Can you give me a lift to Starbucks?"

"Sure." She didn't know Stan very well, but she did know he was one of those good-looking guys who always sported what looked like a two days' growth of beard, much like the men she saw in her L.L.Bean catalogs. Except for one thing. She believed that Stan's sandy brown hair would look better if it were five inches shorter. She lifted her black leather tote bag from the passenger seat and tossed it into the back as he climbed in.

"So, what's wrong with your car?" She threw her car into reverse, checked the backup screen on her dashboard, and began to back out of her parking space.

"Well," he said, "my car has a very big problem." He frowned, looked down at his knees, and scratched the stubble of beard on his chin. He shook his head as if he thought he would never drive his car again, and then he turned to look at her. "My car is worried about a certain young lady who might be getting herself into trouble."

"Trouble? What kind of trouble?" She didn't want to hear the answer she knew would be forthcoming.

"You know, the John Linton thing."

"Oh my God. So you have heard too?" She pulled back into the parking space and turned off the engine.

"Yes. I know Crowell doesn't want anyone to know about your assignment, but I really want to talk to you, and I thought Starbucks would be a good place to do just that."

"I appreciate your concern, but you don't have to ... I mean ... *your car* does not have to worry." She rolled her eyes at his attempt at humor. "I can take care of myself."

"Listen. If I say *if* you have to interview this Linton guy at the old Lyman place, let me take you. I'll drop you off where my car can't be seen from the house and stay nearby in the car. Tell Linton you have just one hour before your 'driver' comes back to pick you up. That way I'll be handy, just in case."

"Just in case of what? We don't even know yet where this interview is to take place. Anyway, what is it about the old Lyman place that makes you feel you would have to protect me?"

Stan leaned back and tugged on his scarf. "Did Crowell tell you that Linton was known to be an alcoholic? And that he was once issued a protective order to stay away from his first wife because he threatened her?"

"No."

"How about the time he had to be restrained from physically attacking a female reporter because she insisted on asking him questions he didn't want to answer? Did Crowell tell you about that?"

She just stared ahead.

"And did he tell you that the old Lyman place was in danger of being condemned a few years ago? And that it's so isolated that no one can see if any of it has been improved since then?"

"No."

"Well, I suggest you check with town hall to see if any permits were issued in the last few years. If not, you'd better be prepared to wear a helmet, in case the place collapses while you're there."

"Sure." Abby turned the key in the ignition, pulled out of the lot, and headed for Starbucks.

When they got there, instead of parking, she headed for the drive-through window.

After the barista took their order, she reached into the back to retrieve her wallet from her leather tote, and had to yank it out of his hands as he insisted "the drinks" were on him. Their almost playful tug-of-war ended when they saw the barista at the window with their order. Before Abby could open her purse, Stan unbuckled his seat belt, leaned across, and thrust a twenty-dollar bill into the extended hand, whose owner was beginning to look impatient. As he did so, his closeness, offering up the scent of a men's cologne she had never encountered before, unnerved her. She reluctantly admitted to herself that she liked it.

Taking the two lattes, Abby handed one to Stan and put hers down in the cup holder. She pulled the car into an available parking spot, left the engine running, and then turned to face him.

"Okay. Listen. Even if I hear that I'll be doing the interview at the Lyman house, I will go alone. I can take care of myself. Now, is that clear?"

Abby saw him studying her face intently. He finally turned away to stare out the window.

He took one sip of his latte. "Sure."

Abby drove out onto the street and headed back to the office in the late-afternoon darkness, to drop him off at his car. Neither of them said another word.

———◆———

Upon arriving at her place, Abby picked up the mail and climbed the stairs to her apartment. Flinging the mail down on the kitchen counter, she patted the head of her cat, Mr. Darcy, fed him two kitty treats to keep him from howling, and turned to the bathroom for a long soak in her tub. As she did so, she noticed an envelope sticking out from among the catalogs and magazines. A glance told her this was not a bill.

Only two initials were on the return address—J. L. Snatching the letter from the pile, Abby sat down on her sofa. Studying the outside of the envelope, she saw that her address had been handwritten in black ink. The return address was Harry Norman's post office box in Herringville. *Oh my God. He didn't even wait for Crowell's reply!*

Opening the envelope, she found a formal invitation card, also handwritten:

Dear Ms. Jenkins,

You are cordially invited to come to the home of my friend, Harry Norman, at the old Lyman house, 23 Pond Road, Herringville, on Wednesday, the twenty-sixth of February, at one o'clock in the afternoon.

At this time, I will grant you an exclusive interview, and you may photograph my collection of historic objects. Please remember this invitation is for you only.

Most sincerely yours,
John Linton
RSVP

Included was a self-addressed stamped envelope holding a card for her reply, to J. L. in care of Harry Norman.

She had two weeks to do her research, and, given Stan's warnings, she wanted to find out about the Lyman house where the interview was to take place, as well as more about the troublesome actor, John Linton. Caressing the fine, vellum, cream-colored stationery, she smiled.

After checking off the "will attend" box and signing her name, she licked and sealed the envelope and set it on the table to go out with the morning mail.

———•—•———

Abby had always appreciated how these centuries-old houses were referred to by the name of their first owner, no matter how many other families had lived there. By checking the town records on the Lyman house, she found it was originally surrounded by 110 acres of property and that it had been in the Lyman family for about three hundred years. The house was a south-facing, steep-roofed saltbox with smaller half Cape wings attached to the east and west sides. Having lived in Chatham most of her life, she knew these two distinctive house styles. They had dotted the Cape Cod countryside since the first settlers built in the 1600s.

She found that, in the mid-1980s, someone from New York named David Norman had purchased the property, and then in 1989, he'd donated all but ten acres to the town of Falmouth for conservation. Although the house belonged to David Norman, his brother, Harry Norman lived there alone.

By inquiring of some locals at the market in West Falmouth, she found that no one except caretaker Uriah Bates ever saw Harry, and Uriah was adamant about not revealing any information, except that Harry was a hermit. The woman behind the counter at the market told her she knew Uriah used to drive his truck to the shabby house each Wednesday with groceries from her store and mail from Harry's PO box, but he hadn't been seen lately.

No one could recall ever having met the owner, David Norman.

But he paid his taxes and utilities bills promptly. The townspeople, glad that the property was well out of sight, respected the no trespassing signs posted on the chain-link fence that surrounded its ten acres. In the manner of true New Englanders, they let things be.

In checking on the elusive John Linton, Abby found information to support Stan's stories and warnings. Not one of the accusations was ever proven, but this additional information now left more than a splinter of apprehension sticking in her mind. She was able to find one account where a woman Linton had been seen arguing with had never been heard of since. She also found two previously unpublished accounts, which turned up in the back files of a Hollywood gossip column. Both were incidents occurring just before Linton disappeared. Both involved the mistreatment of women.

# Chapter 3

## THE HOUSE

At a quarter to one on the cold and clear afternoon of the interview, Abby got ready to leave her apartment. She slung her camera and tripod bags over one shoulder and picked up her soft, black leather tote. This reminded her of the conversation she'd had in the car with Stan at Starbucks. She tried to push his nay-saying out of her mind but then smiled at herself for having liked the scent of his cologne. Since then, she and Stan had spoken only when necessary at work and not once about the interview she was about to do. She was not going to tell him about the unpublished material she had found.

As the time grew closer to interview day, she sensed that Stan was watching her closely. Some gals, she thought, would be flattered, for he was pretty good-looking. Did he really believe she was going to be in trouble? Or was his ego getting in the way because he had not been asked to take the photos?

After finding out about Linton's alleged abuse of women, she knew she had the choice to back out of the assignment or insist that she not go alone. But she had never backed away from a challenge before, and a challenge was exactly how she saw John Linton. Abby was determined to meet this challenge head-on.

She stuffed her wallet, cell phone, laptop, and recorder into her black bag. Into one of the zippered compartments on the outside, she tucked a small metallic blue tube of what looked like lipstick. It was, in fact, a tube of pepper spray. "Damn you, Stan Kelley," she said, as she climbed into her Honda CR-V.

⸻◆⸻

After checking the address on MapQuest and Google Earth, Abby knew it would not take more than ten minutes of driving to arrive at the entrance to the Lyman property. She also saw how deep into the forest the house was located. As curious as she was about how her meeting would go with John Linton, she was looking forward to seeing the three-hundred-year-old Lyman house. As she turned into the narrow dirt driveway, she could see car tracks that had been recently worn into the light covering of snow, exposing patches of dried sticks and copper-colored oak leaves.

About twenty yards in and at the bottom of a small hill, the road took a sharp turn, and Abby found herself confronted by a closed metal gate obscured from the street by a cluster of rhododendrons. A large no trespassing sign hung on the gate, which stretched between two posts attached to a chain-link fence that disappeared to the left and right of the gate, well into the woods. She barely had time to register this before the gate slowly swung open, allowing her to pass. As soon as she drove through, she looked back to see it swinging closed behind her and locking, with a double click she could hear even though all the windows of her Honda were tightly closed.

She thought about the accusations against Linton and scanned the property, wondering if the only way out was through the gate. *What if he does turn out to be a misogynist?*

Then, with an appreciative pat to her CR-V's steering wheel, she knew what she would do if worse came to worst. She would just step on the gas and plow right through the gates. *Just like in the movies. Dear God, please don't let it come to that.*

Abby had learned early in life that the way to push unwanted thoughts out of her mind was to mentally shove them into a room and then slam the door shut. Slamming the door shut now on her concerns, she continued on.

The driveway wound up and down through a dense overgrowth of pitch pine, juniper, and oak trees; leafless chokecherry; and the dried, shriveled vines of poison ivy. Her car held well to the rutted road, skidding only a few times on the obstinate remains of last Saturday's blizzard.

Finally, she saw the house stretched along the top of a small hill, mostly obscured from view by a forest of tall pine trees and the twisting branches of a huge winter-bare oak tree splattered with tufts of pale green lichen.

As Abby drove closer, she saw that most of the first floor of the structure was hidden from view by a high stockade fence that seemed to grow out of the space where a half Cape was attached to the eastern side of the house. A tangled mass of dead grasses, weeds, and indistinguishable shrubbery choked the yard. Rhododendrons with shrunken leaves grew up to the eves of the half Cape, almost hiding two windows that tried to peer out from the left side of the door. More dense rhododendrons, in three large wooden planters, shivered in the cold as they huddled tightly together up against the fence.

As soon as Abby stopped the car and got out, she began to wish she hadn't come alone. *Maybe Stan was right.* Everything was so still, so silent, so neglected. She quickly checked to be sure her cell phone was turned on and in the vibrate mode and then tucked it into the pocket of her coat. As she looked around, it was one of the few times her emotional side took control of the rational side, and she had to fight the urge to get back into the car, crash through the gates, and head for home.

To regain confidence, she tried to imagine the place with soft gray shingles and neat wooden shakes on the roof, covered with vines of pink roses, like other aged but cared-for houses that graced the winding old roads of Cape Cod. But the shabby nature of this structure quickly overcame her fantasy.

To her right, she saw a detached barn with one side partially collapsed. A tiny cottage seemed to be peeking over the ruin, looking as if it needed little encouragement to fall apart at any moment. A rusty pickup truck languished in front of the barn, its hood yawning open over a flat tire. Its engine rested on a set of cement blocks, partially covered with a torn, blue tarp, which flapped in the light wind.

Looking up to her left, all she could see of the saltbox were five double-hung windows with twelve panes over twelve, evenly spaced across the second floor. Their shutters hung askew, with most of the slats either broken or missing. Dead leaves and needles from the massive oak and pines choked a rotted, paint-weary gutter that ran across the top of the house. Detached from its downspout, it promised to fall off with the slightest breeze. The first-floor windows were completely hidden behind the stockade fence.

To the right of the fence, the small half Cape appeared to grow sadly but bravely out from the side of the larger house. Lichen crept under the rotting roof shingles, forcing them to curl up as if begging for release from their impossible job of protecting the house. A planked, windowless door stood to the right of the two windows, only about two feet from the eastern end of the small house. Abby could see that the stockade fence gave her no choice but to enter through this door.

Taking a deep breath and gathering her tote and camera equipment, she approached the entrance. The sudden strangled cry of three black crows swooping overhead startled her.

"Damn it," she said softly. *Get a grip.*

As Abby was about to knock, she heard a window opening somewhere around the corner of the house. A man's voice called, "Please come in. The door is open. I shall be right down as soon as I put on my shoes."

Abby opened the door and walked in. She found herself immediately facing a narrow, steep staircase. In an instant, she was reminded of the time when she was ten and Maureen McDonald had locked her in a toolshed during an "innocent" game of hide-and-seek. The grown-ups had not found her for three hours, and since then, Abby had been pretty sure she was claustrophobic. The Lyman house was confirming her suspicion, with all the suddenness of a quick punch to the stomach.

She had no choice but to turn left, her sense of foreboding growing stronger with each passing second. Taking a deep breath, she stepped into what looked like a living room, lit only by a single lamp and a sliver of light that entered through an open doorway in the back of the room.

Heavy brown curtains covered the only two windows in the room, barely letting in what light the overgrown shrubbery outside let pass through. The fireplace smelled of wet ashes, as though flakes of the last blizzard had fallen down the chimney to rest on the hearth. Two worn sofas stood at right angles in one corner.

Illuminated by the single lamp, a black, lacquered Chinese screen stood behind one of the sofas, nearly reaching the ceiling. Its four panels, painted and inlaid with what appeared to be ivory and jade figures of graceful women, trees, and pagodas, were so beautiful that the screen seemed out of place in the rest of the room.

Both sofas were piled with army-green, rectangular, canvas boxes of different sizes. A section of one sofa had been left clear, possibly to sit on. Abby could not imagine anyone ever wanting to sit in this room, as she realized the nature of John Linton's collection. She could barely move without stepping on or bumping into implements of warfare. She felt as if she were in a cramped storage unit filled with weapons of destruction.

In front of the brick fireplace stood two wooden sawhorses, about four feet high, which appeared to be specifically made for supporting saddles. They were indeed covered with two worn leather army saddles, leather rifle cases, saddlebags, and myriad cavalry artifacts. Three pairs of high, leather riding boots stood to the left, their insides braced anachronistically with thin sheets of stiff white plastic. As she looked around she counted at least seven rifles of varying shapes and lengths stacked in three corners of the room.

*So this is Mr. Movie Star's important memorabilia collection.* She felt suddenly grateful that Harry the hermit wasn't going to be here. Meeting just one strange man in a room full of weapons was quite enough.

She made her way deeper into the back of the room, where a tall oak cabinet partially blocked the way to what she could now see was the brightly lit kitchen. The cabinet's glass doors revealed even more weapons—battered shell cases; swords, both in and out of their scabbards; knives; bayonets; and ammunition. Peering through the glass, she could see that most of the labels on the instruments were written in German.

23

As she walked into the kitchen, a life-size mannequin dressed in a German Imperial Military uniform, which she recognized from her undergraduate history classes, confronted her. Each brass button on its jacket boasted a shiny crown, inviting her to draw closer. But the lifeless stare in its eyes sent a chill through her body. She backed away slowly and bumped into another sawhorse draped with two more saddles.

Light from the afternoon sun, shining through the glass of a sliding door leading to a deck, illuminated the kitchen. There, more objects of warfare hung haphazardly on three of the walls. The countertops held binoculars, tripods, and other optical instruments she could not identify. The fourth wall displayed framed cases of German Iron Crosses and two framed, black-and-white photos of dead, blood-covered soldiers.

To Abby, the entire setting reeked of violence, fear, and death. But before she could dwell on this, she heard slow, heavy footsteps coming down the stairs by the front door, each step followed by grunts of heavy breathing. She was about to meet this former idol of the silver screen.

The grunting stopped, and she heard John Linton moving slowly through the room she had just left. Then he appeared. Far from the handsome actor whose pictures she had seen on Google, here was a four-hundred-pound old man, well over six feet tall. His tan chinos were held up by a pair of red suspenders, forming a sharp contrast to the white dress shirt with buttons down the front that seemed at the point of popping from the strain they endured. Abby could see why Marcia Wentworth, years ago, had thought his face reminded her of Orson Wells.

He wore a gray cardigan sweater that almost coordinated with the bushy gray beard that covered his round face and hung down to at least a foot below his chin. A crop of thick, gray-black hair was pulled to the back of his head and then fell twisting in a fat braid halfway down his back.

"How do you do, Ms. Jenkins? I am John Linton." His voice was deep, hollow, and melodic. "It is a pleasure to meet you, and I thank you for agreeing to come here today." He leaned toward her and studied her face. "Remarkable," he said as he extended a puffed, wrinkled, age-spotted hand.

Abby took his hand hesitantly. "Thank you for your invitation, Mr. Linton." She wondered what he found to be remarkable. Searching his face for signs of possible evil intentions, she believed she found none.

Her immediate impression of the yard and rooms had caused her to think she was definitely in the wrong place at the wrong time, but now her sense of curiosity took control. Once Linton began to speak, she regained her confidence and prepared to settle into her usual inquisitive journalistic mode.

He indicated a chair at the table. "Please, put your things down here while I escort you on a tour of just part of my collection."

Abby put down her camera equipment and was about to set her black leather tote next to it when she thought of the pepper spray, her safety measure. Stan's words rang in her ears. *Just in case.*

She hiked the straps of the purse over her shoulder, only to have Linton abruptly pull the purse from her and lay it next to the camera and tripod. Was she wrong in detecting a flash of anger as he did so?

"Oh no, my dear." He smiled. "This looks much too cumbersome to carry around in these tight quarters."

She thought quickly. "Well, I'd like to tape the information you give me before I photograph your collection, so I can identify everything correctly. May I just take out my recorder? It's very unobtrusive."

"That will not be necessary. I have a printout of information on the entire collection, which I will give to you before you leave. Now, let's begin here."

To her great surprise, he actually bowed in a courtly manner, smiled again, and extended his hand to direct her back to where she had first entered the kitchen—toward the two saddles she had almost knocked to the floor.

At the entrance to the living room, he flipped on a switch. Suddenly the room was illuminated by lights recessed in the thick overhead beam that ran from the top of the fireplace to the top of the opposite wall. Abby looked up at the beam, where she could barely make out what appeared to be a date carved into its side—1712.

Noticing her attention there, Linton said, "Oh yes, the year this small part of the house was built. It was actually built at the end of Shore Street in town and then moved here about two hundred years ago."

John Linton's collection consisted of hundreds of objects, covering wars from the Revolutionary War through Vietnam.

"I must apologize for the crowded conditions here for my illustrious collection of war memorabilia," he told her. "I am currently renovating part of the inside of the barn, where this collection will be held until I can find a worthy museum for its final resting place."

He looked pleased when Abby asked about the importance of the two saddles near the mannequin. "How nice of you to show an interest. A man named George B. McClellan noticed the foreign designs of the British and French army saddles during McClellan's time in the Crimean War … I mean the first Crimean War, not the one that's being shouted all over the news today, the one that lasted from 1853 to 1856. These two represented the changes in his original saddle design, changes that took place between 1904 and World War II."

As he told of their history, Linton caressed each saddle as though he were petting a favorite dog, speaking softly. Yet he never took his eyes off Abby. She felt he was constantly studying her face, as if to find the answer to something deeper than the topic at hand.

"I'm sorry," Abby broke in. "I'm not too familiar with that Crimean War."

"What?" he shouted, startling her. "You never heard of Tennyson's *Charge of the Light Brigade*?"

"Well, yes I have, but—"

He stormed across the living room with a burst of energy unusual for a man of his size, reached up to a wooden bookcase filled with old volumes, and took down a small tan one from the top shelf. When he showed it to her, Abby could see it was a beautiful little book of Tennyson's poems. Half of the front cover was embossed with a silver design and the other half was a floral design behind a painting of a house surrounded by a snowy field.

Flipping quickly through the worn pages, he stopped and read aloud: "Theirs not to reason why, theirs but to do or die. Into the valley of death rode the six hundred." He slapped the little book closed and waved it into her face. She smelled its musty odor.

"One of the Lymans from this house actually fought in this battle. You've never heard of it?" His eyes bulged as though they were going to leap from their sockets.

"Actually, I … I have heard those words, but I didn't remember they were from that war." She felt uncomfortable with him standing so close. In defiance, she held up her chin and stepped away.

Her behavior appeared to have no effect on him. "Here!" He thrust the book toward her. "I no longer need it." He held the book out and would not lower his hand until she took it from him. "Read up on Tennyson. You will learn a lot from him."

He continued on about the saddles without a pause, his voice growing more excited by the minute. "Now, I suppose you have also never heard of Black Jack Pershing and his army chasing Pancho Villa across the Mexican border in 1916? These McClellan saddles were used by his men. Really, Abigail, I find your education in history quite lacking. What kind of schooling did you have anyway?"

This vacillation between kindness and anger was throwing Abby off. She had to calm him down, get just enough information for a story, and then make a graceful exit. She smiled. "Please, Mr. Linton, this is not about me. Let's go on with your collection."

"Of course. My apologies for that outburst. You have to forgive me. Sometimes I forget myself. I did take many drama lessons, you know. And whenever the occasion arises, I … rise to the occasion." Linton directed Abby's attention back to the kitchen.

A three-foot-long, narrow, wooden box stretched along one countertop. He opened it to reveal what looked to Abby like a pair of binocular eyepieces, with two attached tubular extensions stretching out for about fifteen inches on either side.

"Ahhhh," he said quietly, his face shining as he stroked the instrument, "my favorite. The epitome of German optical precision. It's the EM36 Stereoscopic 1-meter Rangefinder. It was to be used either with a shoulder harness or mounted on a tripod. And look." He pointed to a photograph of a German soldier with the shoulder harness supporting the Rangefinder. "Those Germans were unsurpassed in the optical technology of the day." His tone was almost reverential.

He picked up more binoculars to show her, becoming excited again each time he gathered the next bunch into his arms. "Three World War II Flackfernrohr 1080s. Wonderful!" He snatched up more. "And look here, two excellent Sherenfernrohrs. These beauties were called rabbit ears and were used to look up and over the sides of trenches. Marvelous, don't you think?"

"I do think so. But how did you come across so many of these German weapons?"

"Money can buy anything, my dear. That is"—he paused—"almost anything."

Abby never stopped being aware that all the time he was describing his treasures, he was looking directly at her, as if studying her every move.

Linton was now beaming with pride as he moved back and forth between the joys of his collection. He took a deep breath and sighed. "There is more to see. But first, let's sit down here in the kitchen for a little while, where you may begin your interview."

# Chapter 4

## THE FOREST

On the afternoon Abby was to interview John Linton, Stan Kelley grabbed his SLR 35 millimeter digital camera, stuffed it into his backpack, and left the *Star*, saying he was going to take pictures of the local fabric store that had just been damaged by fire. In reality, and without telling anyone, especially Abby, he was going to take a trail through the woods to approach the Lyman house undetected. He would remain hidden nearby, just in case she needed help. He did not trust that Linton guy. And if he were to make a move to harm her, Stan knew Abby would let out with a yell.

Hopping into his Jeep, he took down the sign announcing him as a member of the press that was dangling from his rearview mirror and whipped out a map of the Crooked Pond Reservation Trail. He studied it to determine the best way to get onto the property undetected. He wanted to approach the house from the pond side in the back, to avoid being seen by anyone inside, especially John Linton.

Stan hadn't gotten to know Abby very well yet. She'd been on the staff at the *Star* for only a short time. He liked the way she'd insisted on being independent in this assignment, and he'd enjoyed that tussle over who was going to pay the bill at Starbucks. But he still couldn't quite put his finger on why he felt so strongly that he needed to be available if she should want help. She is a good-looking gal, he reasoned with himself, with those sexy blue eyes. But that alone couldn't be it.

Recently, the few times they had spoken to each other, he'd had to work to prevent his attention from being drawn back and forth between her eyes and the lovely, interesting way her lips moved when she spoke. He couldn't believe he had the urge to touch her mouth. He found himself covertly watching her as she walked around the newsroom, admiring her athletic stride. He was glad he had devised a plan that would place him in a position to help her, if necessary.

Parking the Jeep at the trailhead and hopping out, Stan slung his backpack over his shoulder and headed into the woods. Although motorized vehicles were banned from the trail, mountain bikers had worn it down considerably as they peddled, bumped, and raced up and down over the hilly paths, exposing roots and rocks, which long believed they would be hidden forever.

These same roots and rocks were almost completely covered now with the remains of the last snowfall, which was why Stan never saw the root he tripped over. He plunged forward, using his hands to avoid planting his face in the middle of the rocky, snow-spattered path.

"Shit!" He sat up slowly and then began the task of picking the small pebbles and sand out of his scratched and bloody hands. As he dabbed away with his handkerchief, he heard footsteps rushing up behind him.

"Are you all right, sir? Here, let me help you."

Stan looked up and saw a tall, skinny teenager, whose short spikes of blond hair seemed like they were desperately trying to escape the poor kid's red, pockmarked face. Stan couldn't decide whether the kid looked like a neo-Nazi punk from the '70s or a modern-day computer geek from MIT.

"Yes, yes, I'm fine. And thank you," he said. "But I really don't need any help." *Thank you. Now get the hell out of here and leave me alone. I'm about to do some serious trespassing, maybe worse, and I don't want a witness*, he thought.

"Really, I'd be glad to help, sir. Are you sure you don't want me to walk along with you for a while? You took quite a fall."

"No! I said I was fine, so just go along on your way and ..." He paused, realizing that he was sounding rather churlish. "Have a nice day."

Stan wasn't sure if he was more upset with himself for letting his mind wander in the woods or at this kid for calling him "sir."

"Sure, Pops, you too." The boy leaned over, grinned, patted Stan on the shoulder, and then sauntered off.

Trying to stifle his irritation, Stan stood up, brushed the sand and snow from his jeans, finished wiping his bloody hands, and checked the GPS on his wristwatch. He saw that he was close to the point where he should leave the trail, and swore under his breath. Now he would have to let the shuffling kid get far enough ahead to not notice where Stan would turn off. He imagined the scruffy blond, tearing into the woods after him. *Hey, sir! Do you know that you left the trail back there?* Sometimes good Samaritans could be a royal pain in the ass.

Cautiously rounding a curve in the path to make sure the kid was gone, Stan came upon a rough-hewn bridge made up of logs. Once across, Stan knew that all he had to do now was turn off the path, head into the woods, and follow the stream until he came to the pond. Once he rounded the pond, the house would not be very far away. The blue sky was beginning to cloud over, obscuring the sun and sending more of a chill to the day.

John Linton led Abby to the kitchen table, where she pushed her camera equipment to one side and hung her purse over the back of her chair, glad to be close to it once more. Three woven placemats covered a fringed tablecloth, all looking like they needed a good shaking to rid them of crumbs.

He held out one of the chairs for her. Once she was seated, he pulled on a cord to fully open a curtain that hung over the sliding glass door behind her. She could see a deck covered with snow, twigs, and small fallen branches. Then he locked the door.

He dropped his enormous body into the single chair opposite and leaned toward her. "You may use your laptop." He smiled as he motioned to the black leather tote she had draped over the back of her chair.

As if his simple act of locking the door behind her wasn't enough to jangle her nerves, the fact that he knew she carried a small laptop took her by surprise. How could he see it? Or was he really smarter than he looked? She hoped he couldn't also know about the pepper spray.

She fumbled in her bag to take out the laptop and swore to herself when her recorder, comb, and pen suddenly clattered to the floor.

"Oh, I'm so sorry," she said as she bent over to retrieve the items.

"Not at all," he said. "My manners insist that I pick up these items for you. But, as I am sure you are well aware, my dear, my immense girth does not allow me to do this very gracefully. Please accept *my* apologies."

"Thank you," was all she could think of to say.

The combination of his overly mannerly speech; his erratic behavior; and the depressing, cluttered surroundings was beginning to take its toll on her. Even though the room was cold, beads of perspiration lurked under the collar of her turtleneck sweater. She turned on her recorder and laptop and then looked over the questions she had prepared.

Linton smiled, leaned forward, and tilted his head to one side. His blue eyes pierced hers, and his brow lowered in what she hoped was a friendly frown. "Come now, Ms. Jenkins, do you really need to refer to a list? Can you not just come up with some questions of your own? What are your reactions upon first coming here? What is the most important question you can think of to ask me?"

"Okay," she said. "But do you mind if my first questions aren't about the specific nature and history of the items in your collection?"

"I expected as much," he said. "But just remember, I will have the final say as to what you actually print. I'm sure your editor informed you of this?"

She noticed again how his voice could be calm and soothing, almost seductive. She could almost see why, two hundred pounds and thirty years ago, he could have been considered a handsome leading man.

"Of course," she said. And then, without wanting to, she had to clear her throat and swallow. "Well," she began, "I guess the first questions that come to me concern your connection with Harry Norman—why is your collection here in his house and not in some museum somewhere?"

John Linton laughed and slapped his heavy right hand down flat on the table, causing Abby to jump in her seat. "I knew it! I knew these would be your first questions!"

He leaned across the table, clasped his hands together as if in prayer, gathered his thoughts, and suddenly became very serious. "My connection with Harry Norman, my dear Abigail, is one you will find hard to believe."

———•———

Now that Stan was off the trail, tearing quickly through thickets of rough and thorny underbrush was not an easy task. His already sore hands were beginning to feel the pain of having to rip aside the labyrinth of twisted grapevines and branches. He swore at himself for not wearing leather gloves. Climbing over felled trees and uprooted stumps, his greatest challenge was breaking through the cat's-claw briar, whose tendrils of claw-shaped thorns tore at his every piece of clothing. A few giant Norway spruce trees, their thick branches spreading out horizontally before shooting up to the sky, were forcing him to take more turns than he wanted to.

He finally reached Crooked Pond. Finding himself at the edge of the water, he could barely make out the back of a house, obscured by tall pines, on a hill across the pond. Checking his GPS, he then took a pair of small binoculars out of the pocket of his fleece vest, and looked again. It had to be the Lyman house—not only because of his GPS location but also because he could see the long, slanting back roof of its saltbox design.

He knelt down, cracked a hole in the thin ice, took out his blood-soaked handkerchief, and swished it around to rinse it. At the pond, he knew he needed only about another ten minutes to circle around and reach the house. He'd already lost too much time.

Standing up to leave, he heard a rustle in the woods. He stopped to listen. Emerging on to the sandy shore, a scrawny coyote, eyed him warily. Drawn by the smell of blood, the creature lowered its head. Stan backed very slowly away, keeping his eye on the animal. He figured if he could just get to the tree that stood about three feet away, he could jump up out of reach. The coyote hunched down as if ready to spring. Stan immediately leaped on to one of the lower branches of the tree and hauled himself up. As he did, the coyote lunged at him, snarling, snapping, and missing his leg by inches. Counting himself lucky, Stan broke off a branch and shook it, as well as the tree, hoping to scare the animal away.

"Beat it! Scram! Get the hell out of here!"

Just as the beast turned tail and ran into the woods, Stan saw a black object fall out of the tree he'd been shaking and smash to the ground. Checking to see that the coast was clear, he hopped down to take a look. It was a remote video camera.

# Chapter 5

## THE TRAP

John Linton began to tell Abby his tale of Harry Norman. "For years I had enjoyed the ego-boosting and pocket-filling fruits of stardom when suddenly, my career plummeted due to one bad picture and a few scurrilous rumors."

A sharp beeping sound prompted him to excuse himself, push away from the table, and walk over to the kitchen sink. He reached up and tapped a button mounted under the cabinet above the sink, causing a small video screen to slide down.

"Oh. I daresay it appears we have a visitor. Come. Have a look. Anybody you know?"

Abby couldn't believe that such a run-down house could hold such high-tech equipment, but then she remembered the gate at the entrance to the property. She got up and walked over to stand beside Linton and felt herself going weak at the knees as she watched the video of Stan looking across the pond and then meeting with the coyote. Right after that, the screen went black.

"I have no idea who he is."

"Come, now, Abigail, You are obviously not very good at falsehoods. I have done some investigating, you know. This is Stan Kelley who works with you every day at the *Cape Cod Evening Star.*" His voice was rising, his eyes narrowing, displaying once more his intense glare. "I thought I explicitly stated that you were to come alone." He was no longer looking at her with the interest and curiosity he had shown before. He leaned over her, his entire body growing more threatening by the second.

She sat down in her chair again and gathered her tote to her lap. She placed her hand on the zipper; with one movement, she would have access to the pepper spray. "All right, all right," she said. "I do know Stan Kelley, but what makes you think he's coming here? He's probably just out hiking in the woods."

"Hiking off the trails, and using binoculars to see across the pond to spy on this house? What a coincidence! Are you sure he didn't know you were coming here?"

"I did not tell anyone about my assignment, and I know Bruce Crowell didn't either. Stan must have overheard Crowell and me talking." She found herself searching for excuses. "He must have been curious to see the place where a former movie star was visiting. He probably wondered why he was not asked to do the photos of your collection. Then again, maybe he knew about the isolation of this place and was worried."

He spun around to face her, his eyes flashing. "So, why didn't you worry?"

She thought for a moment, gathering her wits. "Because I wanted to hear your story. From what I was able to find, you were a man who had everything money could buy. Why did you practically disappear from the face of the earth? And why show up now, asking for *me* to report the story of your unusual collection?"

Without responding, Linton snatched a down-filled parka from a peg on the wall and shrugged it on. Then he walked around behind her, unlocked the door to the deck, and slid it open with a violent thrust, disregarding the cold gust of wind that rushed into the kitchen. He stepped out, his eyes searching the woods across the pond.

Abby stood up, zippered her coat, and joined him on the deck, noticing with relief that a set of stairs led down to the backyard.

He continued looking out. He did not answer her questions.

"Mr. Linton?"

Still no response.

Finally, "Ms. Jenkins, I am not going to answer your questions right now." Then, cupping his hands to his mouth, he called out into the woods, his deep voice booming off the trees and across the pond. "Stan Kelley! Are you still there?"

Abby clutched her collar closer around her neck, not knowing whether she wanted Stan to reply or not.

"No need to worry, Mr. Kelley," the voice boomed again. "Just come right along. I will be glad to welcome you here."

Stan called out, "Abby, are you all right?"

Linton grabbed her arm and clenched it, staring closely into her face, his eyes bulging. *"Are* you all right, my dear?" With a sweep of his other hand, he gestured toward the sound of Stan's voice.

"It's okay, Stan. Come on, it's okay." Abby was surprised at how shaky her own voice sounded; she was certain that now she desperately wanted Stan to join her.

Linton smiled as he let go of her arm and then patted her on her shoulder. Thrusting his hands into his pockets, he walked to the side of the deck, where he waited and watched. He then shifted his gaze from Abby to Stan as the photographer approached and climbed the wooden stairs. But before he reached the top step, Linton suddenly moved to prevent him from coming on to the deck. Leaning down, with all his obesity looming over Stan, he offered his hand. "How do you do, Mr. Kelley? I am John Linton."

Before Stan could respond, the door from the kitchen slid open. "Are you all right, Mr. Linton, sir? I saw a strange car in the driveway and——" The voice broke off as its owner charged out onto the deck. He was a scrawny kid with spiked blond hair and a pockmarked face. He became speechless as he came eye-to-eye with the guy he had called 'Pops'.

For a few seconds, no one moved or said a word. Finally, Linton, looking from Stan to the young man and back again and noticing the sparks of recognition between them, asked, "How do you two know each other?"

"We met on the path," said Stan, moving across the deck to stand next to Abby, who was giving him troubled looks.

The young man apologized. "I … I'm sorry, Mr. Linton. I had no idea Pops here was a friend of yours. I—"

Linton cut him off with a snap, "He is *not* a friend. He is an *intruder*. Never mind that now. I will address that issue later."

Immediately Linton's demeanor changed. "But, where are my manners? Please let me formally introduce you." Then, with a bow, he said, "Abigail Jenkins, may I present Nils Swanson. Nils is a friend of mine. Nils, may I present Abigail Jenkins. Ms. Jenkins has been invited here to photograph my collection and *possibly* write a story about my whereabouts these last thirty years."

Abby extended her hand to Nils, surprised to hear Linton say he was considering telling her about his past. The e-mail Crowell had read her had made it clear that the interview would be about only his collection. At this point, she felt she would be lucky to get any story from this unpredictable man.

"Nils Swanson, friend, may I present Stan Kelley, intruder." Linton looked at Stan and emphasized his displeasure by practically spitting out Stan's last name. "Mr. *Kelley* works on the same newspaper as Ms. Jenkins but has *not* been invited here to cover my story. In fact, no *Kelley* has been invited here for decades."

"Please," Stan said in an overly polite sarcastic imitation of the obese man, offering his hand to Nils. "Please feel free to call me Stan."

"Sure, Pop … I mean, Stan."

"And Mr. Linton, *sir*," Stan said, in imitation of the pock-marked kid, "I believe this is your camera." He reached into his backpack and handed the smashed item to Linton.

"You are correct," Linton said, staring into Stan's face as he accepted it. "One cannot be too cautious these days. The woods are full of trespassers, you know. Thank goodness for the marvels of modern technology. You would not believe the sights I've seen."

Linton then put his arm around Nils's shoulders and prepared to lead him back to the kitchen. "You'll have to excuse us for just a moment. Nils and I have some business to discuss. I shall return shortly. Please, make yourselves comfortable." He gestured to a pair of once-white plastic deck chairs, their seats covered with a greenish tinge that was almost hidden by piles of dead leaves soaked in snowmelt.

"Thank you," said Stan and Abby at the same time, both glad to be left alone for even a minute.

"Oh, I forgot,' said Linton. He walked to the head of the stairway and slid closed a gate, pushing a button hidden under the deck railing to lock it. "I would not want you to fall down the stairs." He smiled as he joined Nils at the kitchen door. The two disappeared into the house.

Stan waited for the door to slide closed. "Is this guy as weird as I think he is? Does he think that gate will keep us from leaving? Anybody could climb over that."

"But—"

Abby was just beginning to object when they heard what sounded like a door from under the deck slide open. Within seconds, two large, muscular, brown dogs of unknown pedigree bounded out and charged up the stairs barking, sniveling, and growling, and then chewing on the top of the gate.

Linton quickly returned to the deck and, ignoring Abby and Stan, walked to his animals, speaking softly. "Oh, my darlings, no need to be so angry. You will be fed shortly." Then he put out his right hand in the universal dog sign language and said, "Stay."

The dogs immediately quieted.

Linton pointed down the stairs. "Go."

The dogs, tails between their legs, retreated whimpering to the bottom of the stairs.

"Down."

They lay there, heads on paws, looking up at their master with eyes that suggested they felt they had just been deprived of a great treasure.

"Stay."

Without another word, John Linton turned and went back into the house.

Stan thrust his hands into the pockets of his vest and nodded to Abby in the direction of the opposite end of the deck, away from where the kitchen and the dogs were located. They both stood at the rail with their backs to the small house. Stan's voice was low and seething. "Are you thinking what I'm thinking?"

Without turning to face him, she countered, "I was thinking that maybe he's just a rude, self-important eccentric. And I hope you know you've ruined *everything*."

"You're telling me everything was just lovely before I showed up?"

"I'm telling you I was handling the situation well enough before you met that damned coyote. We saw you on the screen in the kitchen. Actually, it was rather a comic scene watching you jump up onto the tree."

"Not one of my better moments." He pretended to frown at her.

Abby was not going to grace that remark with a smile. "What in the world were you thinking by coming here? I thought I told you to stay away. Now you're here, and we're trapped on the deck of this rotting, old house with that vicious dog duet licking their chops waiting for us to make a wrong move."

Abby put both her hands to her head and ran her fingers through her hair in pure frustration over their situation. Shaking her head, she continued. "Well, I guess that's it for my story. I could have turned this assignment into my chance to get off the Cape and take a job in a more civilized place. Thank you for ruining things."

"Look ..." He put his hand on her shoulder.

"Bug off!" She turned her back to him, shrugging off his touch.

Just then, the kitchen door opened, and Linton walked over to them. "Oh my," he said, with an obvious lack of concern. "Have I interrupted something? A lover's quarrel perhaps?"

"By no means," said Abby. And then, calling upon her characteristic honesty, she turned directly to face Linton. "We were trying to decide whether or not we thought your story was worth the tension it's producing."

Linton walked over to Abby and stood there a moment, regarding her with a tilt of his head. "You know, my dear, you are absolutely right. I apologize for all these interruptions, even though some of them were not of my doing." He threw a disparaging look at Stan and then, turning back sweetly to Abby, said, "I do want you to hear my story. So please, let me show you both more of my collection." He turned and led them back into the house.

Stan closed his eyes, shook his head, and followed Abby into the kitchen, where, in compliance with Linton's directions, she dropped her coat on the table. She picked up her tote, and carefully tucked Tennyson's lovely volume into it. Studying the collection of war objects on the walls and countertops, Stan was momentarily unable to say a word as he took out his digital camera and set his backpack on the table.

Reaching to the top of the refrigerator Linton took down a fat manila envelope and handed it to Abby. "This is full documentation of my entire war collection—at least the part I'm willing to share—everything you can see in this room and the living room."

Then he turned to Stan. "Mr. Kelley, I see you have brought your camera. If you wish, you may photograph now."

Stan began to work his way slowly around the kitchen taking pictures as Abby read from the list that described each article, Linton correcting her each time she stumbled over a German word.

He then led them through to the arms-cluttered living room, where Stan became visibly excited about seeing even more weapons. After he finished taking the photos, he began to pack up his camera.

Linton held up his hand. "Wait. We are not finished."

The big man picked his way through the clutter to where the two sofas met. Grabbing the arm of the one that stood in front of the lacquered screen, he easily rolled it out on casters that Abby had not noticed before. Then he snapped the four panels of the screen aside to reveal a door that Abby realized must lead to the large saltbox section of the house.

"Be careful," Linton said, turning around to face them. "There is a step up into this part of the house. When they attached the small house to this large one, they didn't quite get the levels of the floors to match."

41

# Chapter 6

## THE OFFER

Abby and Stan both stared in amazement as they stepped into the 1685 saltbox. This immaculate room was as different as possible from the dingy half Cape. It took only seconds for them to absorb its elegance. The first things Abby noticed were the aroma and gleam of care not found in the small house. She felt she was in a completely different place, far away from the weapons-cluttered house on Crooked Pond. The room was sparkling clean and exquisitely furnished as a library, with floor-to-ceiling, oak bookcases filling three of the walls. The bottom third of the bookcases each held a series of three drawers with shining brass handles just begging to be pulled.

She skimmed her fingers lightly along a gleaming mahogany table, which stood to one side on thick, carved legs. Two bronze lamps with green glass shades cast halos of light on the dark wood. The six oak armchairs at the table boasted green leather backs and matching leather seats, all studded with brass tacks. A brown leather sofa, with its back to the table, faced the fireplace, flanked by two matching wingback chairs.

Abby glanced down at the shining planked and pegged pine floor, partially covered with an oriental carpet. Then her attention shifted to the brick-and-wood-paneled walk-in fireplace, with its fieldstone hearth; the crackling of a hearty fire released the aroma of apple wood to blend with that of furniture polish and floor wax.

The fireplace surround was covered with plaster the color of rich cream. Over the thick oak mantel hung a long antique rifle and, above that, a portrait of a man with a patch over his left eye, the entire left side of his face a mass of scar tissue. Abby was about to ask who this unfortunate individual might be when her attention was drawn to the front wall of the house.

Under the two windows, two narrow oak trestle tables ran twenty feet along this wall and held three printers, a fax machine, a couple of external hard drives, large plastic boxes filled with folders, and three computers. At the middle computer sat Nils Swanson.

"Mr. Linton," said Nils, swinging around in his chair and pointing to the computer. "Oh, I'm sorry, sir. I thought your guests might have left." He quickly turned back to the computer; closed the screen; and stood, clasping his hands together. Abby could swear he made a slight bow to Linton.

"Do you want to know—"

"Stop." Linton cut him off. "Just tell me in one word. Yes or no."

"Not yet."

A visibly disappointed Linton walked over to the young man. "So be it. For now, continue your work on the 1712 findings. We will talk later."

He turned to his guests. "Please excuse me." He cleared his throat. Swaggering to the middle of the room, Linton held out both arms as if he were a tour guide showing off the glories of the Sistine Chapel. "My dear Abigail, you are now standing in the library of the family of Hezekiah Lyman, the first of his family to come to this country in 1639 from Essex, England. His son, Hezekiah II, and grandsons, Jabez and Charles, were all born in this country. They were the men who built this magnificent saltbox house in 1685. It is the unfortunately disfigured grandson, Jabez, whose portrait you see here over the fireplace."

Abigail was still amazed at the contrast between the small part of the house and the contents of this magnificent room. Stan was also visibly appreciative of the room and its furnishings. He held his camera up, ready to take a few shots, but Linton grabbed his arm, nearly knocking the camera to the floor, and shouted, "No!"

"What the hell—?" Stan began but was interrupted.

"Not yet!" Linton shouted again, his eyes aflame as he held his hand up in Stan's face. Then, composing himself, he smiled, his voice once more smooth and melodic. "Do not worry. You will be given time to take more photos."

Abby decided that a few compliments might lessen the big man's chances of flying off the handle again. "This is beautiful, Mr. Linton." She walked around the room, marveling at the structural elements. "Is that the original summer beam?" She looked up, admiring the handsome, thick oak beam that ran from the top of the fireplace to the opposite wall. "Is that a beehive oven inside this enormous fireplace? And most of all, why has Mr. Norman let the other sections of the house fall apart while this one is so very well maintained?"

"To answer your questions, yes, that is the original summer beam, and yes that is a beehive oven. As for your interest in why only part of the house has been maintained, David Norman"—Linton stopped for a moment and cleared his throat—"wanted no one to know of the fine treasures contained within these walls, so he kept this restored section closed to the prying eyes of those who must be let onto the property. All they would see is the crumbling barn and cottage, the wrecked truck, the decaying small section of the house, and the second-story shutters falling off this tall section of the house."

He chuckled, rubbing his hands together. "I do believe he set the stage very nicely for his little deception. One would think he had worked in the theater as a stagehand. I do like the mystery of it, the challenge of playing two opposites against each other—the rundown, small house and this elegant home. Opposition is one of the great elements of art, you know."

He caressed the oak mantelpiece; held his hand out, palm open, to silence any forthcoming comments; and continued. "All repairs, new construction, restoration, and decorating has been handled by outside sources from off Cape who have been well compensated to remain silent about their work here. As far as anyone in the town knows, this property is not worth looking at."

He cleared his throat again. "Now, let me show you the second part of my collection, the part which is stored in this room. I don't collect only war material you know."

"Well that's good news," Abby muttered to Stan.

The heat from the logs blazing in the fireplace, combined with his excitement, caused Linton to whip out his white handkerchief and mop his brow. "I am about to show you the letters, diaries, multivolume journals, accounts, ledgers, deeds, wills, maps, clothing, and other artifacts of the Lyman family, some of which David Norman, when he bought the house, found hidden in the walls, stored in boxes and chests in the attic, and perfectly preserved in sand-filled barrels in the cellar under this room." The pace of his voice increased along with its volume and the flushing of his face.

*Here he goes again*, said Abby to herself.

He turned to the wall of shelves behind him and pulled open one of the brass-handled drawers. "Look!" Then, without stopping, he moved excitedly around the room, flinging open drawers and doors to reveal shelves of books and letters, along with a gathering of pewter plates, mugs, and candlesticks; an old brass pot; and a wooden trencher.

"Look!" He slid open more drawers and whipped out articles of what appeared to be eighteenth-century clothing. "This once-white Quaker bonnet must have belonged to the only Quaker ever to be part of this family, Tacy Lyman." Then he pulled out a homespun coat of wool. "A Bounty Coat! Titus Lyman's Revolutionary War coat, made by a woman from Newbury who sheered the sheep, carded and spun the wool, wove the fabric, and then sewed the coat."

Placing the coat carefully back in the drawer, Linton picked out a pair of old riding boots. "No right or left to these early eighteenth-century dandies." He pointed to initials on the top cuff of one of the boots. "See here? See the E. L.? These belonged to Edmund Lyman. Made while he was in England."

Linton brandished an ebony-and-brass walking stick with a fox head handle. He flourished a buckskin jacket with fringed sleeves. "When I first found this jacket, there was gold dust in the pockets."

From the very back of another drawer he drew out a small pistol with a carved ivory handle; looked at it; and, without a word, returned it to its place.

"There are such treasures here! Let me show you my favorite." He pulled open still another drawer and lifted out a large cannonball. "Fired on Falmouth in January 1814 by the British ship *Nimrod* during the War of 1812. A thirty-two-pounder, it is! Fortunately, it was not one designed to explode." Linton laughed, gasping for breath. "Here," he said, hefting it over to Stan. "How would you like to have one of these fall out of the sky into your house?"

Without answering, Stan carried the ball of iron back to the drawer from which Linton had taken it.

The big man wiped his brow once more and continued. He pulled out yards of lace trim, two identical broad-brimmed hats, and folds of linen tablecloths and napkins, spreading them out and draping them haphazardly over the mahogany table and chairs.

Abby's mind was spinning, trying to find a connection between this erratic man and the Lyman family memorabilia. She had to slow him down. "Excuse me, Mr. Linton, but how did you come across this collection? Are you related to the current owners of this house, the Normans? Are you related to the Lymans?"

"Related? My dear girl!" He picked up a worn and faded quilt and tossed it like a cape around his shoulders. Then he moved up and struck a dramatic pose so close to Abby she could smell the sweat now pouring off his face. "Related? Ha!" He jerked his head back and laughed.

"I, the great John Linton, famed Hollywood star? You ask if I am related to the Normans? No, my dear, I am not *related* to the Normans. I *am* David Norman." He spun a complete circle. "You ask if I am related to the Lymans? No, my dear, I am not *related* to the Lymans. I *am* Joshua Lyman—Joshua Benjamin Lyman, the thirteenth generation of Cape Cod Lymans, beginning with the sons of Jabez Lyman, the unfortunate gentleman you see here." He gestured to the gold-framed portrait over the fireplace and then took a deep bow.

"Now there's a lucky number for you," whispered Stan, raising his eyebrows as he glanced at Abby.

Linton continued. "This is my family home, a home I was once forbidden to enter. But now it and all contents belong to me."

As if she didn't have enough evidence before, Abby was convinced she was dealing with a very unstable man. *In Psych 101, I'm pretty sure we called this kind of thing multiple personality disorder. Has this guy's career as an actor affected him so long that he doesn't even know who he is anymore?* She looked at Stan, whose expression said that his thoughts were traveling along the same path as hers. He nodded and, pointing his finger to his temple, whirled it in a circle.

Shrugging the quilt from his body to the floor, Linton reached into his pocket and pulled out a set of keys and a pair of white cotton gloves. Unlocking a glass door on one of the bookcases, he put on the gloves and then, one by one, carefully lifted out three worn books. "My pet volumes." He placed them on top of the linens on the table. He picked up the smallest one. "The oldest. Cotton Mather's *Good Lessons for Children in Verse.*"

Next he displayed a thin volume with a tattered, brown leather cover. As he opened it Abby could see that the entire book was handwritten.

"The diary of Tacy Swift Lyman, meticulously crafted between the years 1709 and 1722—a remarkable chronology of the times. She was the Quaker, you know."

"May I …?" Abby was about to pick it up, but Linton held up his hand.

"No, no, my dear. No one must touch these with bare hands. You will have time later to inspect the books. Actually, there are more diaries here—all kept over the years by women of the Lyman family. You will have time to read them … but not now."

Then he lifted the last and reverently announced its title. "*Aristotle's Masterpiece.* This edition was published in 1759. Have you heard of it?"

"Greek philosophy?" asked Abby.

"No … What do you think, Mr. *Kelley?*"

"No idea." Stan shook his head as though certain that whatever answer he gave would be the wrong one.

Linton beamed with delight. "It is a … sex manual!" He practically shouted the words.

"Sure it is," said Stan. "And it was written by the thirteenth great-grandfather of Aristotle Onassis."

"No, yet it was not written by the ancient philosopher Aristotle. Rather, it was written much later and given that title to masquerade the sexual content of the book. Look here." He opened the cover and carefully turned through the pages.

Abby could not believe a book originally written over two hundred years ago could contain such explicit accounts of sexual intercourse, with woodcuts of naked males and females, their reproductive body parts highlighted, their functions fully explained. She had a difficult time trying not to squirm as she stood shoulder to shoulder with Stan looking at Linton's little sex treasure.

Stan said, "Well, how interesting ... uh ... I think we really have to be going now. Don't you agree, Abby?"

Before he could move, Linton put a hand on his shoulder, his voice resuming its quietly smooth, patient tone. "Now, now, don't be embarrassed. You see, this book was used mainly as a guide for midwives and to instruct newlyweds. Look here at the pictures of birthing. And look at these woodcuts of monster births. Back in the old days, everyone believed that witchcraft was the cause of such abnormalities."

Suddenly Linton snapped the book closed and clapped his hands twice, causing Abby to jump out of her thoughts of monster births and witches and the young man engrossed in his work on the computer to jump up out of his chair. "Nils! Bring us some wine!"

"Yes, sir, Mr. Linton." Nils quickly crossed the room. Sliding open two wide, dark oak pocket doors on the back wall of the room, the young man disappeared into what was revealed to be an upscale kitchen.

A cooler the size of two large refrigerators was filled with about a hundred bottles of wine, visible through its glass doors.

"Nice collection," Stan said. He stood with his hands in his pockets, looking around with pursed lips as though getting ready to whistle in admiration.

"Oh, yes," Linton agreed, puffing out his already puffed out chest. "I also keep an excellent wine cellar in a shaft beneath the west wing, with about a hundred bottles. One can never have too much wine, you know." Then he licked his lips, rubbed his stomach, and smiled.

Abby, imagining what this man was going to be like after a glass of wine, or two or three, said, "Mr. Linton, I'm sorry but we'll have to refuse your generous hospitality. I'm on assignment, and we're not to drink while at work."

"Oh, don't be ridiculous," Linton snarled. "How boring! You can't have a glass of wine at three in the afternoon? I've never heard of such nonsense. What are you? Underage? Mormons? Muslims?" He began pacing the floor, throwing his hands to the ceiling. "How many business deals have been completed over three-martini lunches? This is a glass of wine, for God's sake. I insist." Then, turning with more annoyance to face the open doors, he snapped, "Nils, where the hell are you?"

Composing himself once more, Linton said, "Come, Abigail, Mr. Kelley, sit. It's time for you to hear my story." He directed them to the brown leather sofa. Pulling up one of the wingback chairs, he angled it so he could more easily stretch his legs toward the fire. His heavy breathing continued but at a slower rate, as he dropped into the chair.

Nils returned with a large silver tray, placing it carefully on the coffee table. On the tray were a Cabernet Sauvignon wrapped in a white linen towel and a Pinot Grigio nestled in a black marble wine chiller. Crystal glasses stood at attention next to three ivory linen cocktail napkins embroidered with the initials JL. A cobalt-blue-and-white Wedgwood nut bowl brimmed with shelled cashews. Nils first lifted the Cabernet for Linton to inspect the label.

"Yes, yes, that's fine."

Then the Pinot Grigio.

"No. This California white was a gift from a man who obviously knew nothing about wine and everything about being cheap. It's a damn good thing you don't have to earn a living being a sommelier. Now, take this back and bring out the 2012 Blanc Neuf."

After the wines had been poured, Nils left the bottles on the coffee table and walked out of the room, quietly sliding the doors behind him.

Abby took her small recorder from her pocket, placed it on the table, and turned it on. "May I?" she asked, thinking how she'd love to have proof of this man's wild behavior but wishing she had been able to record things earlier.

"Of course."

Linton raised his glass to the light, swished the wine around,

49

tested the aroma, took a sip, swirled it around in his mouth, and then swallowed with a pleased and thoughtful look on his face. Then he raised it once more.

"To Abigail Jenkins, who is about to be presented with an offer she will not refuse."

"Really?" said Abby as she raised her glass. "We'll see."

Linton leaned forward and clinked their glasses with a flourish that left a fine Waterford chime ringing throughout the room. Then he took another sniff and a sip.

"This is a fine one," he said. "I shall show you the wine shaft later." Linton placed his glass on the table, took a deep breath, and exhaled slowly. Then he leaned forward, his eyes looking deeply into Abby's, his voice becoming once again smooth and soft.

"Now, listen carefully to what I am about to propose. I had originally asked you here to write about my weapons collection, but I have had a change of plans. As you see, I have not only a wartime collection, but also a collection of my Lyman family memorabilia, plus two more collections, which you have yet to see. My proposal is this. I would like to give you, Abigail, my full authorization to come here to this house and write not just a simple article about my collection but a piece on the entire Lyman family history, from the time of the life of Jabez Lyman over there on the wall up to and including the life of yours truly, Joshua Lyman."

With the mention of his own name, he covered his heart with both hands and looked to the heavens as if in wonder at his own glory.

"But, Mr. Linton—"

"Do not interrupt. You will have your chance in a minute. Listen first. Our young friend Nils Swanson has already completed much of the research. He has chronologically listed and organized according to ownership all original documents and other goods that are here in this room, plus the more valuable ones stored in a vault downstairs. As I mentioned before, ever since the early 1700s, the Lyman women here kept diaries and journals. These, which Nils has yet to study, should be especially valuable. It is my hope that we shall be able to learn something of our present from their past. You will have access to everything you need." He paused to look up at the ceiling and then returned his gaze to Abby.

"This will be a book of a family who lived through significant times in American history. Upon completion, the book will be published by a major New York company, with whom I already have, in utmost confidence, a contract. Now, your questions?" He raised his hands palms up, tilted his head, and raised his eyebrows as if there could not possibly be any questions.

"Mr. Linton, I truly appreciate your offer, but I can't do this. First of all, I have a full-time position as a journalist. I am neither a biographer nor a writer of historical nonfiction. I have never written a book. I agreed to come here today to gather information for a newspaper article."

"Those are unacceptable reasons," Linton snapped. He rose and began to pace, the thumb of his left hand hooked on one of his red suspenders, his right hand flailing in the air. "I have seen your work. This assignment is well within your area of expertise. You will still have your little story for the *Star*. But after that is done, you will leave your newspaper position to work here."

At that, Stan interrupted. "You mean she's going to come here every day from nine to five and not have to worry about the guns and ammunition in the other room or the mad dogs in your cellar? What an opportunity!"

Stan's sarcasm went right over Linton's head. He laughed. "Oh, those darlings? Once I properly introduce you to them and they lick your hands, they will obey you as surely as they do me."

"I still don't think Abby should be coming out here." Stan rose, put his empty glass on the table, and stood as if ready to leave.

Linton looked sharply at Stan. "Who are you, a *Kelley*, to question the integrity of a Lyman? I know all about you *Kelleys*." Again, he spat out Stan's last name.

Stan turned his back on the man, folded his arms across his chest, and stood looking up at the portrait of Jabez Lyman.

"Wait, Stan," said Abby. "I think I agree with you that we should leave."

Then she addressed the actor. "Mr. Linton, surely you can find a well-recognized author to do this for you. I mean, what if I accept your offer and then it turns out my writing is not the quality your publisher expects?" She couldn't believe she sounded as if she were actually considering the offer. She was determined not to have come this far only to have him throw her out of the house without any story at all.

"Believe me, my dear, I daresay the New York publisher will not complain."

"Well ... what if we moved all of this documentation to my place so I can work from home?"

"I will not allow it to be moved. Anyway, this will be your home, rent-free, for as long as you wish ... to ... ah ... complete the assignment."

At this, Stan faced Linton once more. "Oh no. Abby's not living here. Abby, you can't seriously be considering this. Come on, I think this interview is finished."

Just as she was about to open her mouth to answer, Linton held up his hand. "You will be paid $250,000 for starting this project and another $250,000 upon publication."

"What?" Abby leaned forward toward him, certain she must have misheard. "Why would you ever want to pay me that much money?"

Stan walked to the other side of the room, shaking his head in disbelief.

Linton turned his head away without answering.

She felt there must be some hidden reason lurking behind his offer—a reason she felt was somehow not honorable. *Is this man a liar? Why is he always touching my arm? Is he a pervert paying me to live in his house?* With this last thought, she remembered the unpublished articles she'd found about his having abused women. Her safety would have to somehow be guaranteed. She would need more time to consider all the ramifications. This consideration would have to include input from Stan and from Bruce Crowell. And since it was such a major decision, she felt she must consult her father in Chatham. Once she heard their ideas, she would make her own decision.

"May I think this over, Mr. Linton ... or ... Mr. Lyman, whoever you really are?"

"Or Mr. Norman," Stan said, looking down at his shoes.

Linton ignored the remark. "You may call me John Linton for now. That's the name I will use for the article on my military collection. And you must reveal to no one my true identity as Joshua Lyman. That will happen when I give you my written permission. And yes, you may think it over. Of course. In fact, I do want the two of you to come back tomorrow to see my other two collections. Perhaps it will help in finalizing your decision. Mr. *Kelley* may take more photographs then. Shall we say ... around one in the afternoon?"

Linton reached over the coffee table, picked up Abby's recorder, turned it off, and slid it into his shirt pocket. "You will not need this until tomorrow. Our interview is concluded until then."

With difficulty, he pulled himself out of the chair, stood up, and bowed slightly. And with a wave of his hand, he indicated the door that led back through the small part of the house.

As the trio stepped out into the driveway, a cold stiff breeze picked up, sending dried brown forest litter, leaves, and flakes of snow flying into their faces. Abby and Stan quickly took refuge in her car, the wind slamming Stan's door shut seconds after he pulled his leg in.

Linton motioned to Abby to lower her window. Leaning on the roof of the car with both hands and glancing up over his shoulder at the gathering clouds, he had to shout to be heard over the rush of the coming storm. "Oh, and one other thing, my dear Abigail. Just in case you were worrying about living here, you have my word that you will have the place all to yourself. I have given a comfortable retirement to my caretaker, Uriah Bates. Of course, you will have to feed and care for the dogs, but you will have complete freedom of the place and may ask anyone you wish to stay with you. There are four lovely bedrooms upstairs, each with its own bath en suite, and you will be quite comfortable. Good day."

He turned abruptly and then, called over his shoulder, as if an afterthought, "Oh, by the way, wear sturdy shoes tomorrow and dress warmly. We are going for a hike in the woods."

Linton then walked back to his house.

"Great," said Stan as they drove away. "But if he's going to be carrying one of his guns and a big shovel, I'm not going."

As she pulled out of the yard and headed down the long, rutted driveway to take Stan to his car, he lowered his side window, tilted his head out, and looked up.

"Shut the window," Abby snapped. "It's cold!"

"Sorry, just trying to count how many more surveillance cameras we need to go through before reaching the gate." He pulled his head back in and gave her an exaggerated wink.

Abby shook her head and, for the first time in two weeks, smiled at him. "So, smart aleck," she said," how do you expect to tell our esteemed editor you found out about my secret assignment and followed me to Linton's?"

"Well, if I follow the wishes of our esteemed-movie-hero-gone-berserk and don't reveal anything that happened today, I guess you'll have to tell Crowell you persuaded Linton to let me join you tomorrow to take pictures. Before I left the office today, I told him I was going to do a photo shoot of the fire at the fabric place and wouldn't be back."

"You do think of everything, don't you?"

"Yes, my dear Abigail," he said, mocking Linton. "I daresay I do."

As they approached the gate near the end of Linton's driveway, she stopped and waited while it slowly swung open.

"My," said Stan, "what a great guy this Linton is, allowing us to leave with a mere click on his home alert system."

Abby let Stan off at his car and was about to drive away when he stopped her. "Say, why don't we have dinner together tonight at Chappy's so we can talk about just what happened today?"

She surprised herself at how quickly she responded. "Okay. I'll meet you there at seven."

"I can pick you up."

"No thanks. See you there."

Somehow she felt it would be more like a date if he picked her up, and she was not yet ready to think about starting to date again, such a short time after Jeff had broken her heart. She did feel grateful to Stan for showing up and for his sarcastic attempts at humor, which made her feel more at ease, yet she was not ready to think of a new relationship. Abby was determined to concentrate on her career. If she drove herself, she could consider the dinner to be nothing more than a business meeting.

# Chapter 7

## The Meeting

As Abby was about to leave her place that evening, she wondered if she should have talked to her father about the offer immediately but realized she wanted to talk to Stan first. She knew her father would call her tomorrow night on her birthday. That would be soon enough to discuss this strange turn of events with him.

Tonight she would wear the ring her parents had given her years ago on her eighteenth birthday. The pink-and-white fiery opal was cradled in a finely woven, fluted basket of gold and perched atop a gold filigree band. She considered it the most precious gift she had ever received. Every time she wore it she felt the love of her parents, mostly her father.

Abby arrived at the grill before Stan and felt lucky to get seated next to the stone fireplace, for the room was crowded. A cold and blustery winter's night was the perfect time for locals to go out for a good wood-fired brick-oven pizza or some fine Mediterranean cuisine. She peered over the top of the menu to see him walking to her table.

Stan greeted her with a wink. "Hey there, gorgeous! You must be my date!" He draped his jacket over the back of the chair, loosened his wool scarf, and then sat down across from her.

"Stan." She gave him a look that she hoped told him he was not being funny. But she couldn't help smiling just a little. "This is not a date. We're here to talk about today."

"My dear Abigail, I daresay you are right." He cleared his throat and stole a few glances around the room.

The foursome at the next table had caught the humor in the stuffy formality of his tone of voice and was grinning at him. With a nod and a smile to them, he returned his attention to Abby. Leaning across the table he spoke in a hushed, conspiratorial tone. "One thing I thought of on the way here. We can't let anyone overhear our conversation. So, because the place is crowded"—he turned to smile again at one of the foursome, who was obviously attempting to overhear their conversation—"we'll have to speak in code."

"Really, don't you think you're being a little overly dramatic? I believe Linton's—"

"Shhhh. Don't say his name. This is exactly what I mean. If we're to keep his information from the public until he authorizes it, then we can't talk about him in a close place like this."

"So why did you suggest coming here?"

"Because I love their penne alla vodka, and I'm hungry. I know. We'll call him by another name … um … how about … Dracula?"

Just then, Stan noticed the server standing right behind him. "Say, do you guys know the count personally?" Her eyes were as bright as her smile.

"Oh, we do. In fact we spoke to him just today." Stan looked at the waitress with such seriousness that, for a split second, he thought she almost believed him. "I'll have a Bloody Mary." Then he winked at her and ordered his usual Chivas Regal.

The waitress was bubbling with giggles as she left the table and then returned with the scotch and a glass of Pinot Grigio. Then she took their dinner orders and left once more.

"Okay. So what do you think I should do about … Dracula's offer?"

"Whoa! Hold on, Miss All-Business. Let's relax a little before we get into the deep stuff. Let's pretend we really are on a first date and just try to get to know more about each other. I never see you at the office very much, with you being on the privileged first floor and me usually out of the office on assignment or on the second floor. Where were you born? Where did you grow up? All I know is that you came here from Chatham and that, according to our esteemed editor, you're more than a quarter of a century old."

"Great. You would remember that part. That could mean I'm anywhere between twenty-five and fifty."

"I noticed it because I'm already into my thirties. How far away from thirty are you, anyway. And on what side of thirty?"

"Really." She shook her head but could not help but smile again. She thought she was beginning to like him, but reminded herself he was not her type: too scruffy, with hair a bit too long and unruly.

"Come on. I have to know if I'm out with an older woman."

"You're not *out* with me. We're having a business dinner meeting. And speaking of that, let's get down to business. Let's talk about Dracula."

He sat back and hugged his elbows. "Not until you let me know if I'm having a business dinner meeting with an older woman."

She pretended to frown at his playful persistence. "Okay. I'll be twenty-eight tomorrow. There. Now can we get on with the Dracula thing?"

"Tomorrow? Well, this calls for a toast. Happy birthday to a woman who is younger than I am. Now"—he paused, gazed furtively around, leaned forward, and whispered—"don't tell anyone, for this is my deepest secret." He lowered his brow and scowled. "I hate having business dinner meetings with older women."

She had to laugh.

He held up his hand to stop her. "Wait. Now you must tell me your deepest secret."

"Never!"

They both laughed, clinked glasses, and took sips.

That was when he noticed the ring. He reached out his hand to take hers so he could get a better look at it. "That's one lovely opal. Never seen a setting like that."

"Thanks. There are actually some interesting stories about opals. For one thing—"

"You mean you're actually going to loosen up and talk to me about something other than our darling Count Dracula?"

She looked at him and reluctantly admitted to herself how much she did enjoy his company. She also reluctantly admitted she felt the need to find out if he was wearing that same scent she had inhaled during their tussle at Starbucks. She quickly put that thought out of her mind.

He spoke again before she could reply. "So, is this an engagement ring?"

"No. It was a birthday present from my parents when I turned eighteen. It is definitely not an engagement ring. I was almost engaged once, and I'm not in any hurry to ever become engaged again."

Stan raised his eyebrows at that statement but decided, instead, to inquire about the opal. "So, what can you tell me about the ring?"

"I wrote a magazine article on opals a few months ago, before I joined the *Star*, and the information I found in the research on the subject was absolutely fascinating." She took another sip and leaned toward him, her hands clasped, resting on the table. "It seems opals are surrounded by many myths and beliefs. The ancients believed them to be symbolic of fidelity, luck, optimism, and purity. Yet it was said that witches would point a black opal at someone to cause him or her harm."

"Oh no! Be careful." He grabbed both her hands and leaned across the table, whispering, "There's an evil woman over there pointing her black opal at you!" He nodded his head in the direction of a woman who sat at the bar with her back to them, totally ignorant of their presence. He then positioned his fingers to make a cross to ward off the evil.

"That doesn't work against witches, you fool." She laughed. "Only against vampires."

"I know, I know. I was just practicing for tomorrow's meeting with Dracula. Do you think you should wear a necklace of garlic? That works too."

"Speaking of Dracula ..."

"No, no. I want to hear more about opals first."

"Well." She was glad he wanted to hear more of her story. "Mark Antony wanted to buy one for Cleopatra; Napoleon gave one to Josephine; Queen Victoria loved them; and in medieval times, people thought they had strange powers—to give great insight and even to make the wearer invisible."

"Okay. Stop right there. Your decision is made. You will take Dracula's offer. And you will wear your ring. Your invisibility will make it impossible for the mad dogs and the crazy fat man to harm you while you live in his haunted mansion and write his boring family story."

Abby gave him a look of exasperation and then laughed again. "Can't you ever be serious?"

"Sure I can. Seriously, since that awesome ring means so much to you, why not consider it to be a kind of talisman, like a good luck charm."

"You believe in good luck charms?"

"Not really, but isn't it fun to think something as small as your ring could have a huge effect on your life?"

"Okay, how about that scarf you always wear? Is that your talisman?"

"Uh ... well ..."

"Tell me, are you really superstitious?"

"Who me? Nah." With a flourish of his hand, Stan appeared to accidentally knock over the saltshaker. "Oops!" Then he picked it up and tossed a sprinkle over his shoulder, with a wink and a grin.

"That's enough." She shook her head and laughed. "Let's get to work."

Just then, their dinners arrived. As they began eating, Stan said, "You begin. Tell me all the reasons why you think you should take the offer and all the reasons why you should not."

"Okay. There are a few reasons why Linton's offer is slowly becoming more attractive to me, including the challenge of writing a book, which I guess I always had in the back of my mind. Maybe I'll even try doing some experimenting with a fictional account, filling in the gaps where his collections and Nil's research have not told all. I am curious about the Lyman family with those artifacts. And then there's the money."

Stan leaned back and crossed his arms. "I agree those are all good reasons to take his offer. But let's see if I agree with your reasons not to take the proposal. And I hope the number-one reason is that Sir Dracula is loony."

"Yes. He does come across as being quite unstable. He's always smiling one minute and then shouting the next. And I guess you know that I don't want to be so isolated, living in that house is the middle of nowhere." She thought about telling him about the woman Linton had been seen arguing with who had then disappeared but changed her mind.

"All right. If those are your concerns, here's what we'll do." Stan thought for a moment and then said, "We'll make a list of conditions for him to meet before you consider moving in there."

# Chapter 8

## THE LABYRINTH

At exactly one o'clock the next afternoon, Abby and Stan pulled into Linton's driveway. He was standing right outside the door of the shabby half Cape, and if it weren't for his shape, they would not have recognized him. He was clean-shaven, the immense beard no more than a memory, and his long, thick braid had been replaced by a crop of short white hair that curled in the wind around his wool cap. Dressed in a green tweed hunting jacket with a brown suede collar and elbow patches, Linton looked every bit the English country gentleman out for a walk on the moors of old Yorkshire. As his Burberry scarf flapped in the wind, Linton held on to his cap and relied on a tall, carved wooden walking stick to waddle slowly over to greet them.

"What's with the shave and haircut?" Stan shook his head at Linton's strange new appearance.

"Oh, that wig and fake beard are just one of my disguises. Quite effective, no? I have decided I no longer need that look." He laughed and seemed to congratulate himself at getting the exact reaction he had hoped for and then, with a slight bow to Abby, continued. "Good morning, my dear! Welcome once again to the House of Oaks. We have a bit of a chilly breeze today, so it is good to see you are clothed adequately for this walk."

"Oh we're prepared, all right," said Abby, fascinated by the change in his appearance. She snapped up her black L.L.Bean storm coat and tightened the scarf around her neck. Then she adjusted the glove on her right hand to make it fit more comfortably over the opal ring she had decided to wear for her birthday. "Mr. Linton, I have to tell you that I'm not quite ready to make my decision. I hope that's all right with you. I'd like to hear a little more about you, for instance—"

"All in due time, my dear," Linton interrupted. "All in due time. First we must take our little walk. Mr. Kelley, I wonder if you could do me the favor of rolling aside those rhododendrons you see in the planters in front of the fence here." He pointed with his stick. "I have no one here to help me today."

"Sure." Stan set to work.

Once the boxes were moved, he and Abby could see the thick mass of rhododendrons had been hiding a gate in the stockade fence, a gate wide enough to let a car pass through.

From a pocket, Linton produced a remote that he pointed at the gate, which obligingly slid open. "Follow me, please."

The crushed-clamshell driveway continued through the gate and along the front of the rest of the house. Attached to the west end of the saltbox was another half Cape, the same size as the shabby one Abby had entered the day before. But instead of two windows to one side of its door, a large, many-paned window gleamed in the sunshine. Everything on this side of the tall fence was in immaculate condition, the yard perfectly landscaped. More bushes, rhododendrons, junipers, a small lawn, and a now-frozen koi pond all offered a sharp contrast to the sad exterior of the second story of the house, the only part visible from the approaching driveway.

At the end of this inner driveway sat a sleek white Mercedes coupe. Stan whispered to Abby, "Sweet Christ, that's a Maybach Cruiserio. Mercedes used to make them for the Saudi royal family. They've been discontinued, but I'm pretty sure one of these babies sold at auction last year for over a million bucks." He shot a look at Linton, who was squeezing his bulk behind the wheel of a golf cart. "Maybe the old bastard really can pay you half a million for writing about his damn family."

"Come," said Linton as he started the engine. "Abigail, you sit here beside me, and Mr. Kelley, I am afraid you will have to ride standing up on the back, caddy style."

Having never sat in a golf cart, Abby was looking around with curiosity and just beginning to feel comfortable when she saw the small sign on the dashboard that read, "Danger! Falling off or rolling over can cause death." *Oh great. I wonder if this warning's on all golf carts or just on Linton's.*

"Is everyone ready?" Without waiting for an answer, Linton lurched out of the driveway and into the woods, following a trail with two well-traveled tracks that were just wide enough for the golf cart. Holding on for dear life, Abby found herself shouting to make herself heard above the chugging of the gasoline engine as they twisted and turned along the way. "Mr. Linton, could you please slow down!"

"Aha!" He laughed. "Afraid you'll fall out? Just wait until we get to the hill! Here it comes!" A moment later, he roared, "Hold on, Mr. Kelley!"

Stan braced himself, gripped the sides of the roof, and hunkered down to avoid being swept away by the low, leafless branches. Linton drove the rutted path down the hill with the assurance of a man who had done this before, delighting in his own skill as he pulled to the left and then to the right to keep the cart barely in balance.

Near the foot of the hill, the ground leveled off and Linton let the golf cart coast to a stop. They were at the bottom of a wide, round hollow filled with a cluster of more of the massive rhododendrons.

As she felt her heartbeat return to something close to normal, Abby said, "Mr. Linton, your driving is *totally* irresponsible. Don't you have any concern for others? We might have been injured ... even killed!"

"Irresponsible? Well, my dear you are not the first to call me that. In fact, I have grown rather fond of the title."

He huffed himself out of the cart and said, "Follow me," as he struck out straight into the greenery. He parted the rhododendron branches and shriveled leaves with his walking stick, forcing Abby and Stan to follow as best they could.

After struggling through about a dozen feet of wild vegetation, they came to a wide clearing—a flat section of land surrounded on three sides by more of the same bushes and, on the fourth, by the wind-churned waters of Crooked Pond. A chain-link fence with a locked gate separated the land from the water and then disappeared right and left into the tangle of woodland. Abby and Stan stopped in their tracks as they saw the area was filled with the gravestones of an old cemetery.

At first, Abby thought the stones were arranged in a series of circles, but upon closer inspection, she could make out the form of a labyrinth. The path, paved with irregularly shaped, multicolored pieces of slate, was bordered every now and then with a gravestone. At the center, standing with her back to them, loomed a larger-than-life white marble angel.

Without a word, Linton led them halfway around the outside of the labyrinth. As they followed, bending into the chilling wind, neither Abby nor Stan could take their eyes off the white angel. With intricately carved feathers detailing her outspread wings and wearing a draped gown, she stood on a pink granite plinth. As they finally came around to face her, they saw the name "Lyman" in raised letters on a bronze plate attached to the base of the statue. The angel was leaning forward, looking down to one side, and clasping to her breast the stone stems of a bouquet of roses, the carved blossoms pointing toward the ground.

Linton paused for a moment and stood as though transfixed. For an instant, Abby almost thought she saw him bow his head, but then he became animated once more.

"Ah, my white angel. Do you like her? She was my addition to the family plot, you know. Brought her over from Italy. What do you think?"

"She's beautiful, Mr. Linton," Abby said in honest admiration.

Stan was visibly impressed with the labyrinth. Entering the opening to look at the names on the first two gravestones, he suddenly felt Linton's hand grab his arm. "Not yet!" Linton shouted, pulling Stan roughly back to the outside of the circle, and then, suddenly in a hush, "We will enter the labyrinth *when I say so.*"

"Sure, whatever," said Stan. "It's your party."

Abby shook her head. Why did Stan always know how to defuse a potentially volatile situation?

Linton ignored his comment. "Now, let us sit for a while." He indicated a black wrought iron bench behind them. It faced the front of the angel and was situated between a small, rocky outcrop and a narrow path barely cut into the dense confines of tall junipers.

Linton moved to the bench, where he indicated Abby was to sit beside him. "Now, my dear Abigail." He searched in the pocket of his tweed jacket, pulled out Abby's recorder, pressed the record button, and handed it to her.

She checked to see if anything more had been recorded or erased since he'd taken it from her the day before, but the settings remained the same.

Stan sat himself on the rocks on Abby's side of the bench and leaned toward her, wrapping his arm onto the back of the bench behind her as she said, "Mr. Linton, my first questions, of course, now have to do with this beautiful family cemetery."

"Ah yes," Linton interrupted. "I was hoping this would come up first. I am pleased you find it beautiful. I designed the labyrinth myself."

"You designed it? The first stone here at the entrance to the path dates from the late 1600s," said Stan.

"Oh yes, originally the first fifty-three graves were laid out in five straight rows, but I thought it to be a more dramatic arrangement if—" He suddenly stopped and yanked the recorder from Abby's hand, turning it off. He put it in his pocket and continued. "It would be a more dramatic arrangement if I were to dig up the remains and rebury some of them in the pattern of a labyrinth. Tell me, Abigail, has your education ever introduced you to the significance of the magnificent labyrinth?"

Abby adjusted her gloves. "I do know that a labyrinth is not the same as a maze and that the ancient Greeks had a legend about one. A Minotaur was said to preside over the labyrinth ... and something about this monster devouring the bones?"

"Bravo, my dear! You are absolutely correct. A maze is intended to get you lost. A labyrinth is intended to help you find yourself. Actually, I had originally planned to put a Minotaur chewing on bones at the center but could not resist the white angel."

"Oh, what a kind gesture," said Stan. "But let's get back to the part where you were digging up the fifty-three graves to make the labyrinth. And I assume that's why you don't want this recorded? You dug them up yourself?"

"Certainly not. As David Norman, I had a lot of help. You must remember that money can buy anything, even the silence of people willing to dig up bodies and relocate some. All I had to do then was pay someone to arrange the headstones into the labyrinth pattern I wanted and lay the slate between to designate the path."

Abby needed to know more. "So, we have here a labyrinth design with some bodies replanted. What happened to the other bodies?"

"Well. That is where my third collection comes in."

She shook her head as though she could not believe what she had just heard. She was not looking forward to seeing this third collection.

Linton rose from the bench and started on a narrow path away from the labyrinth to his right, a path cut between more of the fortress of greenery. "Come."

# Chapter 9

## THE OSSUARY

Abby and Stan followed Linton single file along the narrow path. Abby clasped her collar tighter around her neck against the howling wind. The path led directly to a stone crypt dug into the side of the hill. An arched, planked, wooden door stood between large blocks of a pink granite facade. Over the door they saw the name "Lyman" engraved in a bronze plaque set in the granite.

A thick tangle of crisp, brown ivy guarded the top of the crypt, its vines almost seeming to hold the stones in place. Its dry leaves crackled as they trembled in the wind.

"Here it is," said Linton, pulling out his keychain and unlocking the sturdy door to the crypt, "my third collection." Straining to pull open the door against a sudden chilling gust, he finally succeeded. Kicking a rock in place to hold it open, he whipped a small LED flashlight out of his pocket, shining it into the gloom. Arches of brickwork could barely be seen.

Peering in, Abby's fear of closed spaces swept over her. She backed away and covered her nose and mouth with her hand as the dank, stale odor assaulted her, its musty smell hitting her as if she had been slapped in the face with a much-used dishcloth. It seemed as if the crypt had not been opened in years. She coughed, clearing her throat of the stale air.

"Oh, I am sorry," said Linton. Shining his light on the wall to the left of the door, he reached over to flip on two switches, one to barely illuminate the room from a chandelier with only four of its eight bulbs lit, the other to activate a fan. Instantly, they heard a whirring sound and felt the rush of cold, fresh air pulled in behind them from the outside. "I try to keep the winter temperature in here at about fifty degrees, but we do have to let in the fresh air once in a while ... and ... well, you'll get used to it."

A short, narrow passage opened onto a room about fifteen feet wide, stretching close to twice that distance into the back of the hillside. Five large, square brick columns stood out from the walls on either side of the room, supporting brick arches, each arch delineating an area with shelves lining its back walls. The shelves were filled with boxes that seemed to Abby to be made of some kind of green metal. At the far end of the room, a semicircular brick structure filled half of the back wall and rose from the floor to disappear into the ceiling. Attached to it, a staircase led to an iron-studded door at the top.

Linton stood in the middle of the room under the chandelier. Its light washed over the brick arches, sending dark shadows onto the shelves. He turned abruptly to face them, threw open his arms, and proclaimed, "Welcome to the Lyman family ossuary! Herein are contained the bones of many generations of Lymans. I got the idea from a letter I read that my grandfather had written after visiting one on a trip to Rome. Come in, come in."

"An ossuary," Abby repeated, letting the idea slowly sink in.

"Isn't it beautiful? It was originally designed as a wine cellar about a hundred years ago. The only part I now actually use for wine is located in the shaft that leads up from the stairs over there"—he gestured to the brick structure at the far end of the room—"to a trap door in the west wing of the house. I thought this section would be put to better use as a place to hold the bones of all the Lymans." He slowly turned away from them to admire his creation.

"How nice," said Stan. Leaning toward Abby, he whispered, covering his words with his hand, "Do you think maybe he really is a Minotaur, and he actually cleaned the bones with his very own teeth?"

Abby was too distracted to reply. She pulled on Stan's arm to lead him to join Linton at the center of the room, all the while turning every which way to take in the full effects of the area. She noticed moisture oozing from the ceiling. She shivered at the dampness. She brushed away threads of a cobweb that caught in her hair.

Stan put his arm around her shoulders and whispered, "I wonder if this is where he keeps his cask of Amontillado?"

Apparently, he'd whispered more loudly than he thought, for Linton replied, "No, Mr. Kelley. Although, I am surprised that you have actually read Poe, my favorite author. I can assure you both that no live bodies have been sealed up behind these brick walls," he paused for effect and then added, "at least not to my knowledge."

The fresco on the ceiling held faded images of cherubs and angels floating among puffed clouds of white in a sky of pale blue. One angel caught Abby's attention. It appeared to be wearing a ring that looked strangely similar to the opal she was wearing. *Why would an angel be wearing a ring?* Then, to divert her attention from this strange vision, she looked down. The stone floor was of a colorful mosaic, reminiscent of the ruins of Pompeii she had visited years ago.

"Now, look at this." Linton pointed to the inside of the first arched space, where they could see two rows of the green metal boxes, tightly packed together, their lids strapped shut with leather belts and metal buckles. As they moved closer, they could see, attached to the front of each box, a brass plate engraved with the name and dates of birth and death of the deceased.

"Come closer." He motioned for them to join him as he slid one of the boxes out of its niche and placed it on a small but heavy oak table.

Abby found her practical journalistic side fighting her emotional side. Was this interesting or creepy? Creepy won. "I'm sorry," she said. "I'll just stand here."

"Oh, don't be such a fool," he snapped. "There is nothing to fear. These are just bones."

Stan took her hand and squeezed it. Together they moved over to where Linton was beginning to unstrap the box. The thought of looking at a pile of human skeletal remains, which had been broken down and stuffed into a box no bigger than her carry-on luggage made Abby want to run from the place. But her curiosity got the better of her. She grabbed Stan's arm, clenched it to her body, and focused on the box.

While Linton fumbled around, the bones clacked against one another, as if in protest against once again being disturbed. Then he pulled out the skull, leaving its lower jaw still nestled among the other bones. "See? This is Daniel Joshua Lyman, my grandfather. He is rumored to have had multiple identities also. I never knew him, but the one thing I remember my father telling me about him—what fascinated me most as a young child—was that, whenever my grandfather would laugh, you could see flashes of gold inside his mouth. Look!" With one hand, he tipped the skull up so they could see two gold molars set in the upper jaw, glimmering in the light from the chandelier.

Patting the top of the skull and running his hand over it as if to smooth down some long lost, unruly hair, Linton slid his finger into a hole in the skull. "Such a waste," he said. Then he held it up close to his face and cooed, "Dear Grandfather Lyman, time to go back into your box." Returning the skull carefully on top of its mandible and reclosing the box, he slid it back into place in the wall.

"How ... um ... touching," Stan said.

Abby jabbed him in the ribs with her elbow.

Linton continued his story. "The gravestones were, of course, left on the outside," Linton said. "It was about ten years ago that I decided to add my own ideas to the cemetery, arrange the stones into the shape of a labyrinth, and contain the bones here. I do have a well-developed sense of artistic drama, you know."

"Yes, I can see that," said Abby. "So, all of these boxes contain the bones of your ancestors who were first buried in the cemetery outside?"

"That is true. And some of the family is still buried outside—those who have not yet been deceased for fifty years. It takes time, you know, for the flesh to fall off the bones."

"Oh, I'm sure of it," Stan said, his expression giving no hint of whatever he may have been feeling. "And when the flesh has, as you say, *fallen* from the bones," he continued, "you will dig them up, clean off any remaining ... um ... tidbits, and place them in their very own boxes here."

"Of course I will, if I am still here. If not ..." Linton paused, as if thinking of something he wanted to say and then said simply, "Come. Take your photographs, and out we go."

As Stan set up his tripod and began to shoot, the flash of the camera starkly lit up the staircase at the back of the room. In the light, Abby could now see, over the top of the arched door, a curved iron dragon. She walked closer and saw that surrounding the shining, silver eye of the dragon was a small, intricately fashioned, woven, fluted basket, remarkably similar in design to that of the opal ring on Abby's finger. *First on the angel and now on the dragon over the door.* She clasped her gloved hand to be sure it was still on her finger.

She shook her head to clear her thoughts and found her voice. She pointed to the door. "So that's the way to your current wine cellar?"

"Yes."

"May we see it?" She was hoping the sight of something else might calm her and help her forget her internal questions about the eye of the dragon.

"Not now. I will show it to you at another time. It is indeed a beautiful work of architecture. I have yet to contract a crew to come in to dig down from the bottom of the shaft. I want the floor of the shaft to come out even with the floor here, which will make room for more wine."

Linton paused as if considering something and then continued. "Actually, I hate the thought of digging up the present base of the shaft. There are three initials carved into the cement—R. I. H. I originally thought they belonged to the man who designed the wine cellar, but I believe his name was Luigi Landucci."

He motioned to Stan. "Come now. Finish up with the photos. You may return tomorrow, if you need to take more."

Shooing Abby and Stan out the door in front of him as if he were directing a couple of schoolchildren, Linton turned off the light and fan, closed and locked the heavy door, and led them back to the entrance to the labyrinth.

# Chapter 10

## THE GRAVESTONES

"If I'm correct," Abby said to Linton, "you would like me to write a story about your Lyman family, using your four collections—the three you've shown us and one we've yet to see. And you want to pay me a great deal of money to do so."

"Yes, that is what I desire."

"If I may ask, why are you doing this? Why have you decided to expose yourself to the public this way? How do you expect to maintain your privacy once the information about your collections is out there for everyone to see?"

Instead of answering her, Linton walked toward the entrance to the labyrinth. "Come." He beckoned to her. "My dear, I know you have seen a few things here that may have upset you. I have put this off until I was sure of some other things. Now that I am sure, I want you to follow me through the labyrinth."

Abby could think of nothing worse than being alone with this man as they followed the serpentine pathway he had created by digging up his ancestors' bones. She took Stan's hand once more.

Linton's face tightened. "No! Not you, Mr. Kelley, just Abigail."

Realizing this was probably the only way to get her story, Abby nodded at Stan to show that she was okay with the arrangement. As Stan sat down on the bench, she stepped into the opening of the labyrinth.

Linton pointed to the first stone. "We begin here with the son of our grand patriarch, Hezekiah Lyman I. It is the gravestone of Hezekiah

Lyman II, who, along with his sons Jabez and Charles, built the house in 1685."

The rough, worn stone had a carved top enclosing a miserable-looking, winged cherub. Abby read the inscription aloud: "As I am now, so you shall be. Prepare for death, and follow me."

She shot a glance at Stan, who spread his hands as if to say, "It's your choice."

"Yes, they were quite grim in those days." Linton's voice drifted off as they moved along.

Although the labyrinth was about eighty feet in diameter, Abby could see she would be in Stan's sight all the way. Unlike the grand English labyrinths of tall, closely trimmed evergreens, where you could not see more than a few feet ahead of you as you rounded the curves, the gravestones were neither high enough nor close enough together to hide her from his view.

"You see, my dear," Linton said, "the point of a labyrinth is to stretch your soul, to make you see clearly, and to help you take courageous challenges. Legend has it that, once you enter, you can only go forward. When you reach the center, you are exactly where you are meant to be. And when you return to the beginning, you have become *transformed*." As he slowly spoke the last word, he looked intently at Abby.

Approaching the white angel in the center, she could see that the last ten or so gravestones were of a newer material, the polished pink granite flashing in the sunlight to illuminate the twentieth-century dates of birth and death.

Linton continued. "My mother, Mary Birdsall Lyman, and my father, Elijah Joshua Lyman—they died together in the airliner that exploded in midair and crashed near Lockerbie, Scotland, in 1988. Their remains were two of the few recovered relatively intact."

"Oh, I am—'

"You may spare your condolences, especially where my late father is concerned. Excuse me for saying so, but he was an unforgiving bastard. He threw me out of the house when I was eighteen because he could not bear the thought that a son of his could ever want to embrace what he thought of as the lowly, degrading occupation of an actor. Once I made clear that I would not be dissuaded, he disinherited me by allocating all my inheritance to my older brother. Then he gave me a hundred thousand dollars in return for my promise to disappear and never to return home again."

Linton's voice rose, and he began to pace back and forth, flailing his arms as the words rushed out. "He said he hoped I would rot in hell. Well, I hope that is where he is *right now*. Thank God, I will not be around in twenty-four years to move his bones into the ossuary. He can stay right here. Let the coyotes dig him up and eat his putrid remains, for all I care."

"I am so sorry," Abby said.

"*Sorry?* It is a good thing you never knew him. He would have thrown you to the dogs!"

"*What?* Why?"

"I … I don't mean that. Please excuse me, Abigail. I get carried away." He stood for several moments, regaining his breath. "Please, let us move on."

The next stone was marked with the name Elijah Joshua Lyman II.

"Your older brother?" Abby asked, catching her breath as she saw the date of death, only one month ago.

Linton nodded. "Lijah came out of Vietnam in a bad way. He suffered from what they now call post-traumatic stress disorder. He could take care of himself with help but was also rendered impotent from the exploding booby trap that he was unlucky enough to step on. He lived for years in Brookline with our parents, but could never shake himself of the terrors of war. Then he began to exhibit symptoms of early onset Alzheimer's. My parents had refused to acknowledge their younger son, and now the elder son could not carry on the name."

Linton stood with his hands grasping the lapels of his tweed jacket. Abby could see that telling this story was affecting him deeply, and she dared not interrupt.

"In 1987, one year before our parents died, I found that the house and property here on Crooked Pond were for sale. They had left it to ruin while they lived in Brookline and had no interest in restoring it. Knowing they would never let me, their disgraced son, live here again, I bought it under the name of David Norman, the name I assumed when I first disappeared from public life back in 1980." He stopped and drew a deep breath.

"After my parents died in the Lockerbie plane crash, the family fortune went to Lijah. As his next of kin, Joshua Lyman, I bargained with him. Now that our parents were no longer around to care for him, I told him I would, after he turned his entire inheritance over to me. He agreed. After that, I changed his name to Harry Norman, moved him here, and continued my masquerade as his brother David."

"After your parents died, what was the need to remain as David and Harry Norman and not return to your so-called original name of Lyman?" Abby was having a hard time understanding this grand, almost psychotic plan of deception.

"There were two reasons. In his mental state, it was only a matter of weeks before Lijah actually believed his name was Harry Norman, never remembering this house as being the one he grew up in."

The big man paused, shook his head, and continued. "The second reason? There were a few of my Hollywood friends from long, long ago who might have been able to connect my screen name, John Linton, with my original name, Joshua Lyman. At that time, I was not eager for anyone to remember my failure as an actor after those few disastrous movies." He paused and looked up at the face of the white angel.

"Yes, Harry Norman was my brother—David Norman's brother, that is. With help from a well-paid man, Uriah Bates, our caretaker, Lijah did all right. Then two months ago, while back with me in New York, he had a massive heart attack. I had him cremated, and Uriah and I buried his ashes here beside my goddamned father."

"If you so detested the … your Lyman family, why are you now so interested in having the story told?"

"Come." He led her along the path to the last two gravestones, close together, huddled directly under the gaze of the white angel. Abby could see the first stone was one for a child. It was smaller, with a resting lamb carved into the top. The stone read, "Stillborn Son of Joshua Benjamin Lyman and Sarah Beaufort Lyman."

"My son, stillborn and, therefore, not even able to be graced with a name. He was to be Elijah Joshua Lyman III. And sometimes, when I come down here, I call him Little Eli."

Abby looked at the gravestone next to the one of the child and saw the name Sarah Beaufort Lyman. There were fresh flowers in front of the stone. "Your wife," Abby said quietly.

"Yes. My wife and son died in South Carolina. But since I'd had them cremated, it was easy to bury their urns here just last year."

She read on. "Died in childbirth."

"I'm so sorry," she said, touching Linton's arm. "Did she die giving birth to Eli?"

"No, my dear. Look again at Eli's date, October 21, 1983. After Eli died, the doctors told us she should have no more children. But I, the great John Linton, insisted we try again for a male heir. She was willing. We both felt she was strong enough to deliver again, but apparently the doctors were correct. Now, look at the date of Sarah's death."

The engravings on Sarah's stone were done in a richly curved script, making it difficult for Abby to read the exact dates, but when she did, she straightened up in surprise. "That's interesting," she said. "She died on February 28 … That's tomorrow. So that's why you have the flowers here. What a lovely gesture."

"Yes, but read on. Read the year."

"Let's see, she died on … February 28, 1986. Oh. That's just one day after the day I was born."

"Exactly. If only I could have wished you many happy birthdays, Abigail. But you see, your birth was the cause of Sarah's death, and Sarah's death was the beginning of my descent into hell."

"What do you mean?" Abby felt she was on the brink of being overtaken by a tsunami of accusation. Was Linton saying she was responsible for his wife's death and his misery? She was now convinced the man was crazy. Her heart pounded. She began to back away.

"Mr. Linton, I'm sorry, but I have no idea what you're talking about. I'll have to leave now."

Before she could move any farther, her grabbed both of her arms and began to shake her, shouting, his face inches away from hers. "You *must* listen to me! You must! *It's true!*"

In less than a second, Stan was on his feet and running in as straight a path as possible to the white angel. As he saw Stan approaching, Linton let go. He leaned back against the statue and slumped down to sit on its granite plinth. Suddenly calm, he shook his head, took a deep breath, raised both hands to the sky, and then let them fall with a slap to his thighs. "Damn it. I wish ... Abigail, I wanted this to be a private moment between us, but now the chance for that is gone."

Abby felt the man was shrinking before her eyes, yet she felt no sympathy for him.

"What the hell is going on here?" Stan was panting as he came up and wrapped his arms around Abby, pulling her close.

"All right, Mr. Kelley. You may as well know. You have spoiled a precious moment. I was just about to tell Abigail that I am her biological father."

Abby stared at the buttons on Stan's shirt, frowning, speechless in shocked disbelief.

"What the hell are you *talking* about?" Stan asked.

"Look." Abby found her equilibrium returning. She shrugged out of Stan's arms and pointed to Sarah's grave. "His wife died exactly twenty-eight years ago tomorrow. Today is my twenty-eighth birthday."

She turned to Linton. "You're telling me that, not only are you my biological father, but that my mother is Sarah Beaufort Lyman and she died a day after giving birth to me?" She took two steps closer to him and could feel an uncontrollable urge to hurt him. "I cannot accept this. I will *never* accept this. You're a goddamned liar!" She lunged toward Linton, but Stan stopped her.

Linton barely flinched. "It's true."

Suddenly, Abby could see all of Linton's energy seem to melt away, as if he had finally relieved himself of a great burden. *Could he have possibly thought this would be a wonderful moment when he would reclaim me as his daughter? Didn't he ever consider that I might not want him for a father?*

"Now wait a minute," said Stan. "This whole thing has just gone too far. I think we have to go. This is totally unbelievable and ... well, we just have to go." He took Abby's arm to lead her to the path.

Instead of going along, Abby pulled away and swung back to face Linton, her eyes wild, her voice breaking. "Why do you expect me to believe this? *Why?*"

"Abby, this is ridiculous," Stan said. "The guy is obviously making this all up. Why, I have no idea." Then, turning to Linton, he said, "How do we even know you're really Joshua Lyman? To say nothing of the claim that you're her father. Abby, let's get out of here."

"I have proof," Linton said. His head dropped to his chest.

"Proof? What proof could you possibly have?" Abby asked. "I have a birth certificate that says my parents are Gladys and Thomas Jenkins."

"That certificate is a fake. I had it printed and forged the seal and signatures, after you were formally adopted in South Carolina by the Jenkinses. They both agreed. They had their own reasons for not wanting anyone to believe you were adopted. Ask them. Your real birth certificate is in a safe up there in my house, along with other proof."

"Other proof?" asked Stan.

"Yes. You will see. Come back to the house, and I will show you my fourth collection—legal documents."

Linton got up and began tracing the path back to the beginning of the labyrinth. Stan motioned silently to Abby to join him in walking in a straight line back to the bench, disregarding the labyrinth's pattern. But she frowned at him and shook her head. She grabbed his hand and led him along the labyrinth's path through three centuries of Lyman gravestones.

Once back at the bench, Linton led them around the outside of the clump of rhododendrons instead of fighting their way through the way they had come. Just as they were within sight of the golf cart, he stopped.

"You may either ride back with me or take the stairs there to your left." He gestured to a partially hidden, wooden staircase that zigzagged up the side of the hill through the brush. "One hundred steps," he said. "Too many for me."

"We'll take the stairs," said Abby.

"Fine. They will lead you to the back lawn. I will meet you there."

79

# Chapter 11

## THE PROOF

They waited for Linton to turn the golf cart around and watched as he slowly drove up the hill, the noisy gasoline engine coughing its noxious fumes into their faces. Then they began the climb.

"So," Stan said, twisting around to face her on the landing at the first turn in the steps, "What kind of proof do you think your daddy has?"

"Oh, stop it. He is *not* my father. He's just ... I don't know. I don't know what to think. Why would he say all this if he didn't believe it? And if he believes it, then is he *truly* crazy?"

"The better question is," said Stan, "if he is truly crazy, how could you even consider his offer to stay here and write his story? Oh, I just thought of a great title for your book—*My Dad the Lunatic.*"

"You're not being very helpful."

"Helpful?" He swung around to face her again. "You want helpful? I'll give you helpful. Let's get the hell out of here." He flung his arms skyward as if to throw the whole situation to the wind.

"Your daddy claims to be David Norman and Joshua Lyman as well as himself, John Linton. He hides surveillance cameras around his fenced-in property, keeps vicious dogs in his cellar, violated I don't know what kind of local health laws by burying his so-called brother within one hundred feet of a freshwater pond. He's dug up the bones of his so-called family and forged your birth certificate. How can you believe anything this man says? He's going to show you some proof? Sure. Another forged document. Maybe he has a framed signed Act of

Congress up there in that schizophrenic house of his stating that you are indeed his daughter."

"He's not my father! For God's sake, stop harping on that. Now *you're* beginning to sound like the lunatic. I'm actually curious to see what proof he claims to have. Let's do that before we make any other decisions."

"Like deciding never to come back here again, I hope. Abby, this guy is a chameleon if I ever saw one. Really, you have to be sensible about this. I don't care how much money he offers you."

"But you have to admit it will make one hell of a story."

"Sure. If you ever live to write it."

<hr>

As Abby and Stan came to the top of the stairs and out of the woods, the ground leveled. They found themselves looking at the backside of the house. At first, they thought they might have reached the wrong place. The entire width of the saltbox had a semicircular deck curving outward toward them with a white railing supported by four-foot-high imitations of slender Grecian columns. A wide set of stairs led down to where they stood on the winter-brown lawn. At the top of the stairs, their host greeted them with a wave.

Linton led them through a pair of French doors into a stunning dining room, its center of attraction a Queen Anne–style table of solid cherrywood surrounded by eight matching armchairs. White, painted chair rails ran the perimeter of the room, along the top of a matching wainscoting that reached a third of the way up the walls.

They followed him through to a living room the same size as the library on the other side of the central chimney. Instead of bookcases on all walls, the walls in the living room were of a simple white plaster, offering a dramatic contrast to the large, dark, wooden beams that held up the ceiling.

Three walls were hung with gold-framed portraits of generations of people Abby assumed to be Lymans, grimly staring out with eyes that followed her across the room. Abby stood admiring an early oil painting of a woman in a fine gown. Linton rushed to her side.

"That is one of our more famous family portraits, a Copley, painted in Boston when dear old Olivia Lyman lived there. All the portraits you see here were brought from the family home in Brookline when I acquired this property. And"—he pointed to a large portrait of a handsome man with a stern look—"this is a photograph of my father, the bastard. I would have burned it long ago, but it was taken by the great Yousuf Karsh."

Without stopping to take a breath, he continued. "Now, look here." He directed their attention to an antique upright piano, its panels painted with scenes from Greek mythology. It graced the wall between two windows that looked out over the front yard.

Centered over the piano hung a huge, framed document. Richly colored on parchment paper, its vibrant reds, blues, and greens combined with gold leaf to form an inner frame composed of the complex design motifs of Celtic knots, spirals, and mythological animals. It reminded Abby of a seventh-century illuminated manuscript she had once seen on a PBS presentation of Anglo-Saxon art. This intricate frame surrounded what appeared to be a grand tree with a fat, gnarled trunk. Drawn to examine it closer, Abby could see that it was not just a tree but a family tree—a genealogical record of the Lyman family.

"If you look carefully, I hope you will appreciate that this Lyman tree begins in the year 1066, the year of the Norman conquest. But you will have time to examine it later. Right now, I would like to direct your attention to this." Linton swept his arm in the direction of the fireplace where a welcoming fire blazed.

Abby looked above the fireplace to see a painting of a slender young man standing in front of a tapestry-draped table. He was dressed in a knee-length, pale blue, heavily embroidered coat that appeared to be made of silk.

"Ah yes," Linton said, noticing her appreciative gaze. "This is the first Hezekiah Lyman. The painting was done when he was a young man in Essex, England, before sailing here. He's the one who came over during the Great Migration period in 1639, with his wife, and four servants."

When she looked into the blue eyes of the young man in the portrait, she had an eerie feeling he was trying to tell her something. As she moved to one side, his eyes seemed to follow her. Was he warning her to stay away? Or welcoming her into a family she never knew?

As Abby and Stan removed their coats and gloves, Linton motioned them to a soft, floral chintz patterned sofa and two matching armchairs, forming a comfortable seating area in front of the fire. On a low, white wicker table in front of the sofa sat a leather-covered box ten inches high with dimensions about the size of a half-folded newspaper. Linton sat across from them and lightly placed his hands on top of the box.

"I must warn you, my dear. This is going to be difficult for you, but ... well ... you will see. I hope this last collection will convince you to believe me." He leaned over and gently lifted the lid. As he did so, the front side of the box flapped down, revealing a pile of documents each encased in its own envelope of archival preservation paper. He handed the first one to Stan. "Please, read it aloud."

Stan glanced at the document. "Legal Name Change, State of California, September 5, 1960. Joshua Benjamin Lyman to John Linton."

"That's when my career began. I wanted to change my birth name legally because I no longer wanted to be associated with the family that had disowned me. I also totally changed my appearance by dying my hair black and growing a short beard and mustache."

He handed the next document to Stan. "Read."

"State of South Carolina, Common Law Change of Name, December 17, 1980, John Linton to David Norman."

"This is the name I used to hide my identity as a bad actor. While running away from everything, I met my dear Sarah on Hilton Head, Mr. Kelley. In '82, we were married. But I used my Lyman name for the marriage, and since she wished to continue to live in the South, and I was no longer welcomed in my family home in the North, I agreed. In '83, our son was born and died there. Then, three years later, you were born, and my Sarah died.

"As I told you before, in '87, one year before my parents died at Lockerbie, they decided to sell this house. Oh yes. I knew they would never let me live in this house again, and since my brother, Lijah, was being taken care of by them in Brookline"—Linton stood up and began pacing back and forth in front of the fireplace—"I bought the house under the Norman name."

Linton continued. "After the Lockerbie incident, my brother sold the house in Brookline under my direction and came to live in the house now owned by David Norman." He handed Stan another name-change document dated 1989.

Stan read, "Elijah Joshua Lyman II to Harold Norman."

"Many of these family treasures came from the house in Brookline which Lijah inherited after our parents died."

Abby quietly tried to digest all this.

Linton continued. "When Sarah passed away the day after you were born in '86, Abigail, it was more than I could bear. Rejected by my father and my public and now deserted by the one person on earth who loved and believed in me, I began my life of despair. I could not bring myself to look upon the face of my sweet little girl, and so I gave you up for adoption. Now I feel I abandoned you."

Linton dropped back into his chair. "It was not until after finding the old family treasures in this house that I began to wish I had never let you go. Four years ago, I went back to South Carolina where you were born and started to search for you."

"How did you find me?"

"I had just about given up all hope. The Jenkinses had covered their tracks well, most likely to be sure I would not come to look for you. Imagine my surprise when I googled your name and found an article in *Fine Gems* magazine about opals, written a few months ago by one Abby Jenkins from Chatham. It showed a photo of your opal ring. You were quite easy to track down after that."

Stan looked at Abby, who was sinking lower into the cushions of the sofa. He picked up the last of the three documents. "Commonwealth of Massachusetts, Barnstable County Probate and Family Court, Petition for Change of Name, February 28, 2014. David Norman to Joshua Benjamin Lyman."

"Yes, I will drive to the Barnstable County Courthouse in two days to file the petition."

Abby stood up and walked to the French doors. No one said a word as she stood there. Finally she turned back to Linton. "And my birth certificate?"

Linton reached into the box of documents, pulling out a fat folder labeled "Birth Records." From this, he selected one and handed it to Abby.

She read it slowly, wrinkling her brow as if that would prevent any unwelcomed knowledge to be gleaned from the report. "It's from the State of South Carolina. Abigail Sarah Lyman, born, February 27, 1986. Father, Joshua Benjamin Lyman. Mother, Sarah Beaufort Lyman." Abby was still skeptical. "How do I know this is not a forgery? How do I know this is me?"

"Be patient." Linton removed another paper from a folder labeled "Death Certificates" and handed it to her to read.

"Certificate of Death. State of South Carolina. Sarah Beaufort Lyman. Cause of death: Complications due to childbirth. Date of Death: February 28, 1986."

Abby looked up at Linton, unable to say a word.

He drew out a nine-by-twelve, full-color photo. "My Sarah lived just long enough to have our picture taken with our child."

Stan let out a low, slow whistle as they looked at the picture of a young, slender, and handsome John Linton seated on a hospital bed, one arm holding a yawning newborn infant wrapped in a pink blanket. Only one name on the baby's identification wristband could be read— "Abigail." Baby Abigail's father's other arm was around the shoulders of a woman who looked almost exactly like a very pale and tired Abby Jenkins, the brown hair and blue eyes startlingly similar. On the right hand of the new mother, Abby could see an opal ring, the stone encased in a delicately woven basket of gold. Holding her own opal ring up to the picture, she could see the rings were identical.

When Linton saw Abby's ring, he sat up sharply. He reached out to touch it lightly. "Yes, it is the same ring. It has been in the family since the 1700s, as you will notice when you look carefully at some of the portraits on the walls here."

"But *my father* gave me this ring as a token of his love for me."

"Yes, a token of a father's love for his daughter. But I gave it to the Jenkinses for them to give to you on your eighteenth birthday. It was a token of my love for you. And not just *my* love."

He pointed to the photo. "Abigail, this was a mother who was consumed with love for you, albeit for only one day. In that one day, I believe she felt more care for you than some mothers feel in a lifetime."

Abby frowned and pressed her fingers to her lips as if forbidding them to utter words she might have no control over.

Linton sat back in his chair and folded his hands across his lap. "Yes, there we are—the happy family. How foolish I was. I dearly loved my Sarah, yet, with my characteristic distrust of everyone and everything, I needed proof that the child was mine."

"So?"

"DNA paternity testing was just coming into use. I had the child tested. She was mine."

Abby unease was growing. "That still does not prove I'm that child," she said, scrambling to keep all that she was learning straight in her head. "Sure, your Sarah does bear some resemblance to me, but that proves nothing. What makes you so sure that child is me?"

"Two things. First, there is this." He handed Abby a copy of her adoption papers showing her name and the names of Gladys and Thomas Jenkins. Abby looked at the papers and then laid them aside. She covered her face with her hands.

Dropping her hands abruptly, she said, "Do you realize, Mr. Linton, that if what you say is true, this will be a terrible shock to my parents, having you show up and confront them, after all these years?"

"They are not your parents!" he shouted, startling both Abby and Stan.

"Well, as far as I'm concerned, they are!" she shouted back, trying to suppress the tears that threatened to pour from her eyes.

Immediately, Linton calmed down. "Wait, my dear Abigail, that is not all. Do you remember two weeks ago when I sent you that invitation in the mail to come here, with self-addressed envelope for an RSVP?"

All she could do was nod her head in affirmation.

"Recent advances in DNA can compare a woman's saliva from a licked envelope with a lock of her mother's hair." Linton reached into his pocket and pulled out a small, round silver case. Opening it, he revealed the remainder of a lock of his dear Sarah's hair. "I have carried this with me since the day your mother passed away."

Returning the case to his pocket, he continued. "Here is the official report, which I received just after you left yesterday, with the results, a photograph of your envelope, and your signature on the RSVP. This, my dear, is absolute proof of who your parents really are. You are my daughter, the youngest surviving member of the Hezekiah Lyman family … as far as I know, that is."

Abby let that last qualifier pass, for she was not yet ready to give in. "What is family, Mr. Linton? Is it some names out of the past or people who loved and cared for you? If what you say is true, you're not talking about family; you're talking about a spiral of molecules, a string of DNA."

"You are right, my dear. Family is not just a string of DNA. It is a group of people who feel they belong to each other. And I am sincerely hoping that, eventually, you will consider yourself to be part of my Lyman family. Abigail, I have lost my career, my parents, my wife, my son, and my brother. I have long regretted that I abandoned you for adoption. Now you are all I have left."

Abby started to speak, but Linton held up his hand to stop her.

"Please, let me finish." He shifted uncomfortably in his chair. "Next week, I am going to celebrate my seventy-sixth birthday. I am tired of running and hiding and pretending and lying and changing my name. But most of all, for all my posturing and bravado, I am consumed with guilt over abandoning you so I could pursue my selfish pleasures."

"And how do you think I feel having to relate all this to the people I love? How do you think they will feel?" Her mind was clouding over with images she could not bring herself to be a part of. "You know what, Mr. Linton? I cannot do this to them."

Stan looked at her in surprise.

She went on. "I will do your article for the *Star,* but I will not take all the money in the world to write your Lyman story if it means destroying the family I grew up with. I refuse to tell them any of this."

Without a word, the big man got up, clasped his hands behind his back, and walked to the fireplace. He looked up at the ceiling and then down at the floor. He mumbled something neither Abby nor Stan could make out.

"What did you say? Turn around and speak up, damn it." Stan started to get up off the sofa, but Abby held him back. She wasn't sure she could bear hearing anything more from this man who wanted to destroy everything she thought she knew about herself and her family.

"I said"—Linton faced his daughter, pronouncing each word slowly and distinctly—"you do not have to tell them anything. I already have."

"You ... what?" Abby could not believe what she just heard.

"What are you saying? Or is this another one of your lies?" Stan demanded.

Linton returned to his seat. "Right after you left yesterday afternoon, I received word from Nils confirming the DNA from the saliva on your envelope. I immediately had him drive me to the address of the only Thomas Jenkins's house in Chatham to be found in the phone book, where I revealed my intentions."

"I don't believe you. They would have called me immediately."

"I persuaded them not to. As angry, shocked, and devastated as they were to see me show up again, I was able to convince them to let me break the news to you. And when I guaranteed them they would have the exact same access to you as they have always had and told them what I was offering you to write the Lyman story, they finally resigned themselves and accepted the fact."

Abby whipped out her cell phone and began to call home.

"No need for that, my dear. Gladys and Tom are most likely on the road right now and will be here for dinner at seven." He went to grab the phone out of her hands, but she snatched it back and called again, this time her Dad's cell phone.

As soon as she heard her father's voice, she felt herself falling apart. "Dad! This is not true! Please tell me that this man is lying!"

There was a pause at the other end and then, "Abby, sweetheart, I am so sorry, so very, very sorry."

"How could you not tell me? Why—"

He interrupted her. "Please, Abby. We'll be there soon, and I'll explain everything."

"But—"

"Look, sweetheart, I can't talk now while driving. We'll see you at dinner at the Lyman house at seven. Please. You have to believe I'm sorry."

Just before he hung up, Abby heard her mother from the passenger side say, "It's about time she found out."

Abby stared at the phone as if she had no idea what it was. Stan went to her and wrapped his arms around her, pulling her close.

As though nothing had happened, Linton said to Abby, "It is your birthday, you know. I thought it an appropriate time for this revelation." Then, turning to Stan, he said, "I do hope you will also be my dinner guest tonight. And at that time, I will be glad to answer any questions you or Gladys or Tom might have."

---

Driving away from the house on Crooked Pond, Stan asked, "Are you sure you want me to join you tonight? I mean, I'd like to be there to offer my support, but I don't have to go unless you really want me to."

She slowed the car down as they approached the gate and waited for it to open. "I do want you to be there with me," she said. "Even though I barely know you, you're the only one I have any faith in right now."

He looked at her as though waiting for her to say something more, but she could not. They passed through the gate and got to the very end of the driveway, where she had to stop before pulling out on to the main road. Then she spoke.

"I still don't trust him. They say he was once a great actor. What if he still is? He said that, for years, he blamed me for his wife's death. What if he still does?"

# Chapter 12

## THE DINNER

The night was black as tar when Tom and Gladys Jenkins entered through the automatic gate and drove up to the house on Crooked Pond. They pulled in through the opened stockade fence and parked between Abby's CR-V and the Maybach. At the far end of the drive sat a green van with the words "Cape Cod Caterers" splashed across its side in bold black letters. As they got out of the car, they heard dogs barking from around the side of the house.

Then they heard a voice. "Stop! Stay!"

All was quiet again except for the crunch of their steps on the clamshell driveway.

What they could clearly see of the house was the renovated first floor, each window dimly lit with an electric candle, giving off a soft glow. The front door was barely illuminated by two wrought iron lamps. But the broken shutters and windows on the darkened second floor did not go completely unnoticed by Gladys.

"Oh for God's sake, Tom. Look at this place." She pointed to the upper level. "It's falling apart!"

Before Tom could reply, the door was flung open by the man who, before yesterday, they had not seen in twenty-eight years—the man they had never wished to see again.

"Welcome! Welcome!" With an expansive smile that almost matched the width of his outstretched arms, he greeted them. "How good of you to come here, and I know this will be difficult for you, but—"

Tom Jenkins roughly pushed him aside with his cane. "Where is my daughter?" He limped into the living room, where Abby stood like a sculpture of ice. When he wrapped his arms around her and drew her close, she melted into a flood of tears. All he had to do was hold her, and she was reminded of all his years as her father, when he had lovingly comforted her. As angry as she was, she knew now she would always love him.

Gladys walked up to them and tapped Abby on the back. "Now, now, it all had to come out sooner or later."

"Please, make yourselves comfortable," their host said, indicating the sofa and chairs that surrounded a coffee table set with red and white wine, pâté, a bunch of grapes, and a selection of cheeses and crackers.

When Abby pulled away from her father's arms, Stan walked over to her and offered her his handkerchief. She wiped her eyes and tucked the handkerchief back into his jacket pocket. Taking a deep breath and exhaling slowly, she introduced him to the Jenkinses. Then, with one hand still holding Stan's, she took hold of Tom's with the other and led them both to sit beside her on the sofa.

"Well now," Linton said. He settled into one of the wingback chairs, clasped his hands together, and smiled broadly. "Which wine may I serve you this evening, Gladys?"

"Why, how charming you are, kind sir! I would like—"

"Stop it!" Abby shouted. "Stop being so goddamned pleasant to each other! This is not a picnic!" She turned to Linton. "You have torn my life apart, and now all you can think of is what kind of wine to have? Can't we just … can't you …?" Abby could not continue.

She got up as though to leave but then sat down again, facing Tom. "I want to know, and I want to know right now, why didn't you tell me?"

Tom leaned forward and held his head in his hands. Then he patted her knee. "Okay, sweetheart. Hold on. First of all, I want you to know how badly I feel that this had to be revealed to you this way." He looked at Linton, who sat opposite him, expressionless.

"I want you to know how upsetting it was to us to have this man"—he indicated Linton by lifting both hands, palms up toward him—"show up at our house yesterday, and tell us what his plans were for reuniting with you as his daughter."

Abby could now see that her father was as upset with Linton as she was.

Linton said, "Tom and I had it all out at their house last night. Actually it almost came to blows." He gave a little laugh. "But we restrained ourselves. I told them about my miserable life up until now and the offer I have made you to write the Lyman story."

"Believe me, sweetie, from the time we first adopted you, we loved you. And that's why Mom and I thought it would be better for you if you didn't know. But Mom's parents, who lived in Savannah, insisted that, when you turned ten, we should tell you. They knew that Mom had never been pregnant and felt that you weren't really their granddaughter. We refused. Then they threatened to tell you anyway."

Gladys broke in. "Yes, it was my parents' fault, of course." She gave her husband a dark look.

Without a glance in his wife's direction, Tom continued. "I began to think it would be even worse if you heard it from them. So when you were still an infant, I moved the three of us from South Carolina up here to the Cape."

"Much to my displeasure," added Gladys. Then she turned to Linton. "I'll have a glass of the red." She reached for a cracker and spread it with cheese.

As he poured a glass for Gladys and for himself, Linton said, "Of course, Tom and Gladys had no idea I had ever lived here. And living up in Chatham, they had no chance to have heard about this old Lyman house."

"And if we had," Tom said, "we certainly would have moved away again."

Abby sat there, looking from Tom to Linton, considering whether her life would have been any different had she grown up knowing she'd been adopted. Would she have felt less loved? There was no way of telling. But now, what about her present life and her future? She looked to Stan, as if he could read the questions that were thrashing about in her mind.

"You don't have to choose between them, you know," he said. "Tom and Gladys will still continue to be the parents who love you and raised you, and Linton—"

"I am your biological father!" Linton slammed his hand on the table. "And you will live here as my daughter!" He got up. "Now we are going to have dinner!"

"Slow down, man, slow down," said Stan.

He and Tom both stood up and gripped Linton's flailing arms.

"Wait a minute!" Abby was beginning to understand what it would be like with him as a father.

"I said we are going to have dinner. Now." He struggled out of Tom and Stan's grip, pointed to the dining room, walked in, and stood behind his chair at the head of the table. As his guests slowly filed in, he directed everyone as to where he or she should sit.

Gladys took one look at the exquisite decor of the room and the table setting, raised her hand to her throat, and settled into her chair with a satisfied smile.

Two men from a catering service came in from the kitchen and dished out a steaming hot cup of chowder to each of them.

Once the servers left the room, Abby spoke up. "Mr. Linton—"

"If you can't call me Father, then at least call me Joshua, here, in private. Outside of this house, you will address me as Mr. Linton until after you write the story of John Linton's war collection. Then you may forget my screen name. And that goes for the rest of you too."

"All right, Joshua. I'm not sure if I can live here, as your daughter, or even at all. There would have to be some changes."

"Many changes as far as I can see," Stan said with a nod in Joshua's direction.

As the host and guests began dipping into their cups of chowder, no one said a word. After a few minutes, Tom said, "Although the rooms we've seen are beautiful, the second-floor exterior of this place is really run-down. I don't think Abby should even consider living here until you do something about that."

"You are absolutely correct." Joshua shook his head in agreement.

"And construction workers are coming in on Monday. By the first of April, she should be able to live here in comfort."

The dinner guests let this all sink in as they finished their first course, and then the servers cleared the chowder cups and served the entrée of Cornish game hens and fresh garden vegetables.

"And where will you be living?" Abby asked, hoping she could believe his answer.

"Yes. What about you? Where will you be living?" Tom was still concerned for his daughter's well-being.

"After the construction has been completed, and if Abby agrees to write our Lyman family story, I will remain at my New York home and come here only upon her invitation." Then he looked at Abby. "I do hope you will invite me here from time to time, so we may become better acquainted."

Abby countered, "How can I be sure you won't come here uninvited?"

Joshua's head dropped to his chest. He closed his eyes as if in deep sadness at the thought that his daughter did not trust him.

Stan quickly offered a suggestion. "How about you pay for a guard to be sure no one comes here uninvited while Abby lives here?"

Then Tom added, "Yes. That is, a guard of Abby's choice, not yours. And she will also need a caretaker and housekeeper—of her choice."

"If you feel that is all necessary, then so be it."

"And you're going to have to take the dogs with you," Abby added.

"We will discuss that after you've had time see them again, tomorrow."

Abby looked at Gladys and Tom. "What are your thoughts?"

Gladys looked at Tom for his response.

"It's up to you, sweetheart," Tom said. "Would you be comfortable living here under those conditions?"

"We'll need a complete physical tour of the entire house, the outbuildings, and the property," she replied.

"Of course." Joshua agreed without a blink.

Stan leaned over to Abby and whispered, "What about the mental tour?"

95

Ignoring him, Abby asked, "May Stan and I come here to do the tour tomorrow morning?"

"Yes. At nine." The big man sat up straight in his chair and smiled around the table at three concerned faces. Gladys was smiling into her glass of wine.

Abby directed her attention to Tom. "Dad, I do want to talk with you privately, sometime within the next few days, about other concerns I may have."

Joshua scowled at her.

"That will certainly be welcomed, sweetie," said Tom.

"So, are we all in agreement?"

"Joshua, I'm not sure I can believe any of these promises you've made, and there's still something troubling me, something you said yesterday."

"Now whatever is that?" He sighed with obvious impatience.

"You said you held me responsible for the death of your wife."

"Your *mother's* death! Can't you get that into your head? Sarah Lyman was your *mother*!" His face became red as the words stormed out of his mouth.

"Calm down!" She found herself shouting at him. "I *can* get it into my head, but it's going to take time, damn it!"

Tom pushed back his chair and stood. "Joshua, I had enough of this kind of bickering last night. Don't try to start it all over again, with my daughter. She needs time. We all need time to get used to this, so—"

"Thanks, Dad," Abby broke in. "Now," she turned to Joshua, "if you'll let me finish. I can see it's true that Sarah died giving birth to me. And for that, I am sorry. But there are many possible complications that go along with childbirth. It's the chance two people take. After all, aren't you also responsible? She didn't become pregnant all by herself, you know."

Joshua stared down at his two hands that were now gripping the edge of the table as though he were hanging on to the edge of a cliff. After a few moments he spoke in a low voice. "This dinner is over. All of you will please leave now. I shall see Abigail and Mr. Kelley for the tour tomorrow at nine."

He got up, took his glass of wine and began to leave the room but stopped and said, "Abigail, I would like you to start immediately on the article on my ... on John Linton's war collection. And none of you must say anything of our family connection or the offer I made to write the Lyman story until you, Abigail, decide to live here as my daughter."

"After Stan and I come here tomorrow, I'll want at least two weeks to think this over."

"Fine." Then he added, "Oh, and Mr. Kelley ... Stan ... you might have a good reason to convince my daughter to do as I wish. I suggest you go on Ancestry.com to look up your Kelley family tree. You will find that your great-great uncle, Ian Kelley, had a connection to the family here."

He walked slowly back to the table to stand beside Abby, rested his hand on her shoulder, and said, "I sincerely wish you will let me back into your life. Once I have left the area, I will only return upon an invitation directly from you. Please believe me." With a nod to each of them, he left the dining room, quietly closing the door behind him.

After a few moments of silence, when no one could think of anything to say, Gladys spoke up. "Well!" She picked the napkin up from her lap, folded it, and slapped it down on the table. "I haven't even finished my game hen, and we're asked to leave?"

"What's more important now is the decision Abby has to make," Tom countered. Then he turned to his daughter. "Please, sweetie, take all the time you need. And come up to Chatham so we can talk more about it."

"I will. Right now I just want to go home—wherever that is."

———•———

That night Abby couldn't sleep. She had no idea how she would make the decision she faced—a decision that could change her life.

# Part II

# The Farrier's Daughter—
# Spring 1712

*Let us then try what love can do to mend a broken world.*

*—William Penn, 1644–1718*

Early eighteenth-century Cape Cod was a time and place of relative security for the Quakers. They had once been whipped and branded, had their ears cut off and tongues pierced with branding irons, and been imprisoned in Boston for what the Puritans called heretical practices. By 1712, a group of these peace-loving Friends had moved away from those terrors, first to Sandwich and then farther south on the Cape. There they established a successful settlement in the western section of the town of Falmouth, which had been incorporated in 1686. Here they were free to practice their own beliefs, meeting at each other's houses for worship.

Still looked upon with suspicion by the Puritan Congregationalists in the surrounding area, they led their gentle lives as pacifists, believing that the spirit of God was to be found within each human being and that all are responsible for the welfare of others. They therefore refused to fight in Queen Anne's War, which had erupted in the colonies between the governing British and the French and Spanish, who wanted control over large areas of the new land.

For years, the colonial men and boys had to fight the French from as far away as Newfoundland to the British frontier in western

Massachusetts. By refusing to fight, the Quakers gained even more disdain from those who had lost sons, fathers, and husbands in the war. As the wounded returned, some were even more hostile toward those who stayed safely at home. But then again, there were those who were made stronger and more forgiving.

This story opens in a blacksmith shop in the Quaker settlement of what is now known as West Falmouth. The roar of the fire is in heavy competition with the sound of the smithy's hammer.

# Chapter 13

## THE STRANGER

Tacy Swift grasped the horns of Goodman Barlow's ox and planted her feet wide apart on the dirt floor of her father's shop. She tried to keep the huge animal from thrashing about and swaying as it hung, suspended by heavy ropes in a wide leather sling. This sling allowed the blacksmith to hold the ox just high enough to take weight off its feet. Unlike a horse, which could stand on three legs while being shoed, the ox's weight required all fours to be on the ground or it would lose its balance.

She looked into the animal's dark, round, fear-filled eyes and smiled, speaking words of comfort even as it pitched and bellowed. "Oh, my dear Apple, thou needs not worry so much. All will be over soon and thou will be safely back on all fours." Tacy knew the actual bonding and then nailing of the shoe did not hurt the ox, but she also knew it was terrified at being suspended this way.

Her father pressed the half-moon-shaped, hot iron ox-shoe into half of its left rear hoof. As the smithy seared and bonded hoof and metal, a column of odorous smoke rose to the rafters of his shop. He turned his head to avoid it and winked at his daughter. "Thou art fortunate to be standing at that end of this beast. And I am sure he is thankful for thy comfort."

Tacy's deep sensitivity to animals was looked upon as an excess by her fellow Quakers. At the same time, they appreciated the expert care she and her father administered to their livestock, so the village folk usually kept those thoughts to themselves. They also frowned upon her outspoken and sometimes contrary ways, yet they never questioned the idea of a young woman working in a blacksmith shop. Since Samuel Swift had lost his only son, it was natural that one of his five daughters would take his son's place, and Tacy loved working with the animals.

Samuel finished nailing the bonded shoe onto the other half of the hoof. Straightening up and adjusting the leather apron surrounding his considerable girth, he then loosened the thick rope hanging from a pulley attached to the high beam, which ran between two stone walls of his shop.

"Good boy! Here thou goes now." He patted the ox on its rump, with a hearty laugh at the snorts of the animal as he lowered it to once again stand on all fours. "Oh, great beast, that was not so bad, was it? There, there, thou will be fine."

He turned to his daughter of twenty-one years. "I am now going to see what I can do for the Nickerson's unfortunate pig," he told her. "I shall be back shortly. If anyone comes and is in need of immediate attention, please see what thou can do. And if thou cannot help them, ask them to please wait."

"Yes, Father. And do not rush. Thou knows I can take care of things here."

"How well I know, my dear." He laid both hands on her shoulders and smiled at her. "And how thankful I am for thy help, now that our apprentice has left and our William can no longer be here. May God forgive him for failing to live as he should." He turned quickly and left the forge.

It had been seven years since Tacy had witnessed the horrible death of her older brother, a vivid memory that would never leave her. Even then she knew William had been wrong to taunt and tease the animals her father cared for as town farrier, and violence against any farm animal was not tolerated, even by their Puritan neighbors. She knew William's temper, an inclination toward rage that was so unusual in their small, peace-loving Quaker village, would one day get him into trouble. How she wished she could have reached him in time to prevent him from kicking repeatedly at the pregnant belly of the cow.

"No! William! Stop!" she had screamed as she'd run toward him across the wide field.

"This animal just butted me with her head," he'd shouted back over his shoulder as he continued kicking. "She deserves to be punished!" Then he'd stopped kicking and turned to his sister as she'd approached. "Get thyself home! Now!"

The last word was barely out of his mouth when the injured cow had reared up on its front legs and, with one great kick knocked him to the ground, where he'd smashed his head against one of the many fieldstones that littered Goodman Barlow's pasture. Tacy would never forget that sound. She had watched, paralyzed with horror as her brother's blood and gray matter slowly oozed down the side of the rock and soaked into the grass below. She had run, screaming to the house to get help, although she had known it would not save him.

She wished she had not called out to William, causing him to turn his back on the animal, leaving open the opportunity for the cow to defend itself. This was a part of the account of William's death she could never bear to share with anyone. When asked about how it had happened, all she could say was that William had been kicking the cow.

On that terrible day when her father and Uncle Robert had come to the field to carry William away, she had begged them to allow her to stay behind to assure the safe delivery of the calf, the cow's premature labor being brought on by the angry kicks of her brother. She could already see two small front legs emerging from the cow as they lifted William on to a wooden plank to carry his lifeless body home. They'd let her stay.

She had never delivered a calf before by herself but had witnessed the process many times. She knew that, if the cow took too long to expel the calf, she would be forced to reach in and pull. Tacy Swift, at the age of fourteen, had helped deliver not one but two calves that day before Goodman Barlow was able to send someone to help her.

Twin calves were such a rarity that, when word of their birth got around to the neighboring Puritans, they'd raised their eyebrows at the girl's abilities. To some, the Quakers, who called themselves Friends, would always be suspected of witchcraft because Quakers professed to not believe in the devil. Therefore, the Puritans reasoned, surely they must be in league with the Evil One. Some also believed William's death was a punishment from God because William had refused to bear arms against the French. Now that the Friends had their own village in the western section of Falmouth, daily tensions had ceased, but tongues still wagged when unusual things happened.

It was on the day she delivered the two calves that Tacy Swift had vowed to do everything in her power to become a farrier like her father, taking care of the health of all animals. Her four younger sisters at home with her mother would care for the female chores of running a household, at least until they married. They were the ones who would bake the bread, brew the beer, make the candles, wash the clothes, cook, tend the garden, milk the cow, and clean the house. Tacy joined her father at the shop, working alongside the new apprentice hired to take William's place.

However, since the apprentice had left after serving his term, the blacksmith business was beginning to suffer. A new shop had opened to the south of the Quaker settlement, and bog iron was becoming more and more difficult to obtain.

Now, not wanting to dwell on the tragic loss of her brother, Tacy grabbed the rope that was tied around the neck of Goodman Barlow's ox and gently tugged on it to help the huge creature step out of the heavy leather sling. She then walked the ox out of the heat and smoke of the shop to the pen outside, where it would await the return of its owner in the fresh sunshine of a lovely day late in the month of May.

"Dearest Apple, that was not so bad, was it?" she said, patting the side of the ox's hairy face.

Apple tossed his head and in doing so would have thrown her to the ground had she not let go of the rope in time. Tacy laughed, giving the animal a playful hug and a pat to its side. Apple was one of her two best friends.

Since she had saved the lives of not only the two calves but also the injured cow, in gratitude, Goodman Barlow had allowed her to name the two calves. And when they reached four years of age, he'd promised, she could be the one to train them to the yoke as oxen. She had chosen the names Apple and Pie after her favorite sweet. A strong bond of trust had been building steadily these last three years, and she knew neither Apple nor Pie would ever object to her playfulness.

Once he was in the pen, Tacy danced around Apple. "So, thou thinks to get rid of me? Just wait until thou needs another shoe. Who will comfort thee then?" She grabbed Apple by his horns and planted a kiss on the warm broad softness between his eyes.

"Do you always talk thus to animals?"

Being so absorbed in playing with Apple, she had not noticed the approach of the rider on a horse, just outside the pen. Neatly dressed in a broad-brimmed hat, a dark brown jacket with matching knee breeches, and a white shirt, the man in shining leather boots appeared to be a natural extension of the magnificent brown-and-white horse upon which he sat.

"Oh, I am sorry. I did not know anyone was here. May I help thee?" She wiped her hands on her apron and tucked a stray golden hair into place under her cap as she approached the fence.

"I do not think so, unless you are the village blacksmith." As though pleased with his own humor and almost smiling, the man eased his horse closer, where it poked its head over the top railing of the pen. "I have come on business to the shop of Samuel Swift. When I looked inside not a soul was there. Do you know where I may find him?"

"Oh, certainly, I do. He shall return shortly."

"Pray, tell me, mistress, what is your position here, aside from dancing around large animals?" He looked her up and down, seemingly amused at the way she appeared to be boldly appraising him.

"I am the daughter of Samuel Swift, and I assist him both as farrier and in the shop."

"You work there at the blacksmith shop?" He nodded in the direction of the low stone building, its broad chimney releasing a thin stream of smoke into the sky. "What could you do in a blacksmith shop? 'Tis man's work."

"It does not take a man to carry in the firewood and carry out the ashes." She looked away. "Our blacksmith business has been not so frequent now that the new shop has opened just south of here, but I am almost as good as my brother was if I do need to work the bellows."

"And where is your brother now?"

Tacy looked at the man for a moment but did not answer him. Instead she said, "Please, rest and refresh thy horse." She pointed to the large, granite watering trough in the back of the yard near a huge pile of firewood. "And now, while thou waits, would it please thee for me to wipe down thy steed?"

"You want to wipe down Traveler?"

"Most certainly." Tacy reached up to pat the horse, running her hand along the broad white patch that ran down its face. The horse tossed his head and snorted with pleasure.

"As the farrier's daughter, I am well trained in caring for the needs of all farm animals. And if I may say so, Traveler here has gotten into quite a lather. He looks like he's been hard-ridden and could use a short walk to calm him down, some water to drink, and a good grooming."

"Are you accusing me of being careless with my horse?" He studied the young woman as if in wonderment that anyone would question his abilities.

"Oh, no. Not at all," Tacy said as she tugged open the gate, hurried through, and slammed it closed, causing a dozen chickens in the yard to cluck and flutter about.

She moved quickly up to the horse and grasped hold of both sides of the beast's face. "But I am certain thou can see in his eyes, as sure as sunlight streams through the trees above us, that Traveler is uncomfortable. Get thee down and look." She gently stroked the horse's head.

Muttering as though not being at all used to having people tell him what to do, especially an outspoken country girl, the man dismounted. In one quick motion Tacy snatched the reins from his hands and wrapped them around the fence. "Come now, see the eyes?" She tugged on the stranger's arm and pointed. "Can thee not tell by looking at his eyes that thy steed is in need of care?"

As she encouraged him to look at Traveler's eyes, she could not help but notice the bright blue eyes of the man himself, eyes that presented a sharp contrast to the rich dark brown of his wavy hair. Without waiting for his response, she once more took the reins and began to lead the horse to the trough. Looking back she could see he was following her with a scowl on his face.

"And what did thou say thy business was with my father?" she asked as Traveler dipped his head to drink. "Judging by his steady gait, it does not appear that thy horse is in need of a shoeing." Snatching a sheepskin cloth, which she kept hanging on a nearby tree for such purposes, she began to wipe down the hot and thirsty horse. As she did so, she noticed that the stranger now seemed to be admiring her every move. When their eyes met, they both looked away.

He cleared his throat with a little cough before answering. "I am here with a few requests. First, I would like the farrier to visit my farm to inspect the new flock of sheep I have just had driven down from Plimoth. In addition, I have a bent and broken wagon wheel, which he must pick up to repair. And I have also brought a list of tools and other ironware that I would like your father to make."

"My father will be grateful for thy business."

"Our farm has been neglected these last few years, and I have recently come from London—that is in England you know, across the sea to the east—to restore the farm to its original state of usefulness." He reached into his breast pocket and pulled out a stiff piece of paper on which the list was written in fine, flourishing script.

"Why does thou think thou needs tell me that London is in England and that England is across the sea to the east? My father has three whole books—one with maps and charts, one New England Primer, and ..." She paused for a moment, wondering whether she should mention the almanac her father kept hidden in a chest. Quakers discouraged influence by non-Quaker knowledge of the world. She decided not to tell him. "And other printed material. I have read all of it."

"I am sorry. Please excuse my thoughtlessness. In London, we were told that few here in the colonies have ever been educated in the art of reading and that many have no knowledge whatsoever of geography, mathematics, or the philosophical sciences. Where did you learn to read and write?"

"We had an apprentice living with us here while he worked at the shop to learn the blacksmith trade from my father. My mother felt it best to teach him so he could better make his way in the world. I and two of my sisters were permitted to observe the lessons. I have kept a diary for the last three years."

As if to prove her point, Tacy snatched the list from his hand, and as she read each of the articles aloud, she paused and looked up at him as if waiting for her skill to be confirmed. There was no reaction from the man.

"Well, thou needs not tarry here any longer among the ... uneducated, for I will give the list to my father, who can also read the Queen's English. Judging by the kinds and number of tools thou requires, they will be ready in one week's time, at a total cost of ... let me see"—she quickly added up the items—"two pounds, two. The farrier fee will amount to ..."—this time, she quickly sized up the arrogant horseman and decided, by the cut of his clothes, that he was wealthy—"one pound, six. That comes to a total of three pounds eight. He will price thy wagon wheel when he sees it. If thou would prefer to pay the price in trade, thou may discuss this with my father when he sees what goods thou has to offer."

With a slightly amused look, the man asked, "Would it be possible for your father to deliver the ironware to my farm and, while there, to take a look at my sheep?"

"Certainly." She now looked boldly at him and flashed a smile. "Thy tools could be delivered next Fourth Day around midday, but only if thou lets me know to which farm they should be delivered."

"Fourth Day?"

"Yes, the fourth day of next week. We do not use thy pagan names for days of the week."

"Of course, I see. Please permit me to introduce myself. I am Edmund Lyman, son of Jabez Lyman, nephew of Benjamin and Charles, brother of Thomas." He ever so slightly bowed his head. "We own the land over the hill to the east on Crooked Pond. Do you know of it?"

"I have heard of its reputation for once having the best crop of corn in these parts, but I thought the Lyman farmland was going to be sold."

"'Tis no longer for sale. This is the farm on which I spent my childhood. The war took the lives of two of my brothers and maimed another, so the farm has deteriorated somewhat. I have been abroad these past nineteen years but now have returned to improve it so it will once again be productive."

"I am sorry to hear of the loss of thy brothers, but I do believe a productive farm must be in need of a new wagon wheel, healthy sheep, and sturdy tools. When my father delivers thy ironware, he will take a look to see what other needs thou may have that he could assist thee with."

"Very good, Mistress Swift."

"I trust thy other animals are all in good condition? Cows ready to calve, sheep in need of dipping and shearing, oxen ready to be trained to the yoke, no injuries in want of care?"

"That is all yet to be discovered. I have only been here one week." His voice rose, betraying his irritation that she seemed to know more than he about the condition of his farm.

"And how is thy father? I have heard he is bedridden and in need of special care. Is someone there to see to his comfort? Is he in need of any herbal remedies?" Tacy Swift was not going to let him off too easily after his remarks about uneducated colonists.

"So, you not only care for animals, but you also cure the ailments of humans? My, what talents you possess."

Edmund climbed into the saddle. "Please see to it that your father has the list. I will expect him with the goods at Crooked Pond next … Wednesday midday." Without even a nod to her, he turned his horse and galloped away.

Tacy climbed over the fence back into the pen where Apple munched contently on salt marsh hay. She hugged his neck. "Apple, the man is quite rude, yet he is also quite handsome."

When Apple nodded, she knew her dear friend was in complete agreement.

———◦———

Edmund Lyman returned to his house on Crooked Pond. Deep in thought, he walked slowly up the steep and narrow staircase to the room where his father lay sleeping. Pulling aside the damask curtains, which hung from the top of the four-poster bed, he leaned over and whispered, "Wake up, Father. Wake up."

"Water! Get some water! No! No!" Jabez Lyman, startled out of a recurring nightmare, awoke flailing his arms about his face.

Edmund sat on the bed, grabbed his father by the shoulders, and drew him close. "'Tis all right, Father. 'Tis just your dream. You are fine. I'm with you now. Look, we are in your room here on Crooked Pond. There is no fire except the small one over there on the hearth. You probably smelled the smoke." He held his father away and gently stroked the scar tissue that made up the entire left side of his face. A black patch covered his father's left eye.

Having heard Jabez screaming, their two-hundred-pound, forty-five-year-old servant, Biddy Doane, rushed in. Edmund put out his hand to stop her from coming closer. "He is all right now, Biddy. Go back to your work. I'm here. It was just his dream."

The old man's nightmare was of the Boston fire of 1679, exactly one month after his wedding day. His resulting gross disfigurement and the loss of his left eye were why, in 1685, he moved with his father, his wife, and his brother Charles, from Boston to the relative isolation of Cape Cod. There, Jabez and Charles had built the house on Crooked Pond. After the house had been built, Charles returned to Boston to work with another brother in the family shipping business. It was on Crooked Pond that four sons of Jabez Lyman were born, and four daughters were born and died.

As Biddy closed the door, Jabez pulled away from his son's embrace. The haggard-looking man shook his head, and as his wild white hair fell back into place, his frail body fell back onto the pillows. He slowly returned to the present.

"Edmund," he finally said, as if by acknowledging the presence of his son he was assuring himself that he was once more functioning in the reality of the day. "Did you place the order with the new blacksmith in town?"

"In truth, Father, I went instead to the Quaker blacksmith to the west, and all has been taken care of. The tools will be delivered Wednesday midday."

"Why did you go there when I told you to go to the new one in town?"

"One of the men who herded our sheep down from Plimoth told me to go there for a better price. He said the Quaker is in need of more business, so I thought I would give him ours."

Jabez snorted. "The reason I told you to go to the town blacksmith is because I do not approve of those Quakers. I still resent their refusal to fight in the Queen's War. Maybe if some of them had joined our men ..." The old man dropped his head to his chest and sank deeper into his pillow. Then, he added, "I'm sorry. You are a good son. You do not know the comfort you bring to me by coming home to take over the running of the farm."

At the mention of this, Edmund looked away, but Jabez continued. "Since we lost Robert and David to the French, your worthless brother has let the place go to ruin."

"Do not be so hard on Thomas, Father. He is still young."

"Young? He has twenty years!" Jabez sat up, struggling to adjust his rumpled sheets. "You were not here when he returned from the war and had lost two fingers on his right hand. I, when just a few years older, after losing my left eye, was cutting trees, pulling stumps, and hauling rocks from this land so it could be put to pasture. Now, with barely enough livestock to keep us alive, the only thing we grow well is corn." He shifted his position, grimacing as a pain shot through his back.

"Please, Father." Edmund tried to calm him.

"Be quiet and listen to me. All Thomas wants to do is work on building things ... that blasted addition to the barn. What good does a barn do if we have no animals to keep in it? Thomas could care less for animals! Look at the disgust he showed when those dirty sheep arrived yesterday." Jabez threw up his arms and lay back, crossing his bony hands over his sunken chest, panting, exhausted from his long speech.

Edmund patted the old man's arm. "Father, I know Thomas can be difficult to deal with. But you may rest assured that we will bring the farm back to where you would like it to be. We will succeed. I promise you."

"And just where and when are you going to start?" Jabez's voice was now weak and gravelly.

"Actually, that's what I came in here to tell you. I have found a wife."

"A wife? You have found a wife?" Smiling, Jabez Lyman sat up straight in bed, energized by the idea. "I thought you said you would never marry again after losing your dear Catherine in London. Is this some fine gentlewoman you have been planning to import from your European connections? How wonderful, Edmund. Pray, tell me more"

"I am going to marry the daughter of the farrier, Samuel Swift"

"What? Which daughter? I have heard Samuel has five."

"The one who helps him at the blacksmith shop."

"You have spent one morning at the blacksmith's and now you come home to tell me you are going to marry his daughter?"

"Yes."

The old man slumped down, the brief surge of energy lost in his disappointment. "So you are going to marry a Quaker. You know my opinion of those people. They want peace but are unwilling to fight for it." He shifted his position on the bed. "I sent you to school in England so you could possibly someday become an Anglican priest in Boston, not to marry a damned Quaker. No Lyman has ever married a Quaker!"

"Father, that was years ago. That has all changed." Edmund turned his back on his father and hugged his elbows, dreading what he was about to reveal.

"There is something I have never told you because I knew of your disappointment over my not entering the clergy. I was pleased when you wrote saying you were so proud of my being made a member of the Royal Society. What I didn't tell you is that a man I had considered my friend, Newton, had me thrown out of the society for backing his rival. That is the only reason I came back. I came back in disgrace. Did you ever think I came here because I wanted to be a farmer?"

Without giving his father a chance to answer, he swung abruptly around to face him, his voice rising. "I am here now because this isolated, forsaken farm is about as far removed as possible from the life I wanted to live but could not. I am here now because this farm is also as far removed as possible from the disgrace I suffered. Remember, Father, you left Boston to hide your disfigurement. Well, I am here to forget my past, to purge from my mind the humiliation I had to endure in London."

"So, you were disgraced, rejected by your peers. And now you want to disgrace your father by marrying the daughter of a blacksmith—and a Quaker, no less! A Lyman will not marry any daughter of a blacksmith. Do you not know that, to marry a Quaker, you would have to embrace their faith? I will not have it!"

Edmund walked back to his father's bed, towering over the old man. "I am afraid, Father, that you will have nothing to say about it," he said quietly. "And as for becoming a Quaker, I cannot think of anything easier to do in order to further my plans."

As Edmund turned to leave the room, the old man raised himself from his bed. "Wait, Edmund. What is her name? Has she so quickly accepted your proposal?"

"I don't know her name. It does not matter. Nothing matters about her except that she'll be an asset to the farm. She knows more about the care of animals than you, me, and Thomas put together. She can read. She is no stranger to hard work and will be able to labor in our fields for hours. Her strong body will also produce many sons." He paused for a moment and then added, "Another thing, Father. Please do not mention any of this to Thomas, or anyone else."

"What is the need for such secrecy?"

"Because I have not yet said a word of this to the young woman. But believe me, I know of a way to offer her a proposal she will not reject. I'm going to put part of my inheritance from Uncle Benjamin to good use by offering her father a substantial amount of money for his daughter, which I will cleverly disguise as an investment in the blacksmith shop. It will include a steady supply of pig iron plus the guarantee of the lifetime services of an accomplished blacksmith, a well-recognized farrier from Boston."

"Edmund, this is all wrong," the frail man continued, shaking his head. "Do not make such a hasty decision. Your dear Catherine passed away just two months ago."

"I have no intention of ever forgetting my love for Catherine. I do not have to love this young countrywoman. She is outspoken, has not a polite thing about her, and dances around oxen with the abandonment of a gypsy."

Edmund walked as far as the bedroom door before he stopped and turned back. "No, Father, I will never love her. But I will put her to good use."

# Chapter 14

## THE BROTHER

Tacy Swift sat beside her father in their horse-drawn wagon, as it carried them bumping along the road to the Lyman farm. The day was exceptionally warm, and bright sunshine flashed like tiny mirrors through the wispy, newborn oak leaves above them. Now and then, her father turned to smile at her, ducking as the lower branches of white pine and sassafras brushed against the sides of the wagon, releasing their heady aroma.

Few people on Cape Cod owned horses; most used oxen for their transportation and farm needs. But Samuel Swift was fortunate in having been able to obtain his two, three years ago, by trading a large volume of his blacksmithing work at a time when he was the only blacksmith in the area. He was forever thankful for this. The trips he made to neighboring farms were much faster now than they'd been in the past when he'd had to rely on the plodding oxen.

Leather harnesses on the two horses, Sand and Rust, produced the semblance of musical harmony with the clop-clopping of the hoofs. Jostling up and down in the back of the wagon, newly formed farm tools scratched against each other, while three bog iron pots, two kettles, a spider-legged trivet, and a long-handled journey cake maker nestled protectively in a pile of straw. This order had used up almost all of Samuel's iron supply, and he worried when more could be found.

The wagon creaked slowly through the uneven terrain. The narrow road, once an Indian footpath, led east out of the Quaker settlement, immediately climbing a steep hill, which slowed them down considerably. It would take the farrier and his daughter over an hour to make the trip.

At a level and smooth section of the road, Samuel leaned over and patted his daughter's knee. "Now, Tacy, do not fret. I know thou art unhappy to accompany me, but I do need thy help at the Lyman farm. If I were to go alone, by the time I'd arrived, assessed the farm's further needs, looked at his new flock of sheep, and seen what he might want to offer in trade, it would be dark before I could return home."

Days earlier, when her father had first proposed that she accompany him to the Lyman farm, she had raised an objection, saying, "But what if someone comes to the forge while we are gone? How can we afford to not be available to our closest neighbors in their time of need? Thou knows the shop is in need of more business if it is to succeed."

That was what she had said, but deep down inside, she had wondered if this was the real reason she did not want to go. She was unsure of how she would react to facing once again the handsome man on the brown-and-white horse.

"There have been other days when I have had to close the forge, usually for lack of iron or lack of business," Father had told her. "Since our shop has suffered for want of customers, one day's closing will be no different. Our close neighbors are patient, understanding people. They will surely not condemn me for attending to the needs of other settlers, our distant neighbors, the Lymans."

Now they were on their way and had been for some time. "Just how far away is this farm?" Tacy asked. "This is the longest I can ever remember traveling in our wagon. It seems we have been riding forever."

"Thou art too young to remember our long rides years ago to Spring Hill Road in Sandwich to attend Quarterly Meeting. Now we need only ride to a neighbor's house to worship, and soon we will have a meeting house of our own."

"Nothing could have been as lengthy a ride as this." Tacy tugged on her apron, tucked her golden curls under her cap, and leaned forward to stretch her back.

"We should not be too long now, if I remember correctly. I have been to their farm only once, about ten years ago. It was quite a large place, and I thought to ride over one day to arrange to do business with them, but Jabez Lyman refused to deal with Quakers. In fact he refused to even come out of the house to meet with me, telling one of his farm hands to inform me that his smithy work was being done elsewhere. I am greatly pleased that his older son, who has recently returned to the farm, has decided to trade with us. What did thou say he is called, Edmund?"

At the sound of his name, Tacy readjusted her position on the wooden bench of the wagon. In the week since the man had come to the forge, she had not been able to put him out of her mind. How arrogant he was. How rude and self-assured and inconsiderate of the needs of his horse. Yet, as much as he had irritated her, Tacy could not erase the memory she had of the handsome face; the penetrating blue eyes; and the lean, manly figure of Edmund Lyman seated atop his horse.

As they approached a sharp turn in the road, the sound of hammering came echoing through the deep woods. "Ah, we must be near now." Samuel clicked his tongue and flicked the reins gently to the backs of the horses to get them moving along at a faster pace.

Rounding the bend, they came to a clearing where the only building they could see was a large, new barn, close to completion. Newly furrowed, open fields were dotted with men bending down to plant seeds they pulled from sacks slung over their shoulders. "I believe they are the Praying Indians, converts to Christianity from Marshpee that Goodman Barlow told me about," said Samuel. "They plant fish in with the corn, and that is why they say that Goodman Lyman's corn is the best in these parts."

As they drew closer, chickens and geese wandered about, pecking here and there at the ground. A sty off to the side offered up the stench of five grunting pigs, and within seconds, a black-and-white dog ran barking to meet them, startling the horses, and causing Samuel to pull up on the reins. "Whoa! Whoa! Easy now!" He stopped the wagon.

A ladder leaned up against the south wall of the barn, and Tacy saw at its top a young, shirtless man hammering away in the sunshine, attaching wide-planked, vertical siding. Hearing the commotion, the man turned, a clutch of nails sticking out from his mouth like quills on a porcupine. Tacy could not help but laugh at the sight as the man spit the nails to the ground with a sputtering sound and quickly descended to grab his shirt from a peg on the barn wall.

"P-Please," he stammered, a blush of shame rushing to his cheeks, "please excuse me for my lack of proper dress. I had no idea a lady would be present." As he buttoned his shirt, he made an awkward bow to Tacy.

"Thy apologies are accepted." Samuel smiled. "Thou must be Thomas, the younger son. May I introduce my daughter, Tacy Swift? Tacy has joined me today to see how many of thy sheep are in need of care. Tacy, please greet Thomas Lyman."

As the young man brushed back his hair and moved closer to greet her, Tacy was momentarily startled when she saw that the first two fingers of his right hand were missing, but this was soon overlooked when she noticed how much he resembled his brother. Both had penetrating, sky-blue eyes and handsome, angular facial features. Yet, where Edmund had thick, dark brown hair, Thomas's hair was the exact golden color of her own.

"It is a pleasure to meet you, Mistress Swift. And welcome, to you and your father, to Crooked Pond."

Tacy immediately noticed one more difference between the Lyman brothers. This one liked to smile.

"Please, let me take you to the house. My father and brother will be glad to see you are here. But first … excuse me for a moment." He turned and walked up to a small opening cut into the side of the barn and shouted. "Caleb! Take care of the wagon and horses!"

A few seconds later, a huge man came out from the barn. "Yes, Master Thomas."

At the sight of him, Tacy stared in disbelief. Caleb was close to seven feet tall. His rolled-up sleeves revealed arms that were even more muscular than her father's. Noticing their surprised looks, Thomas was quick to let them know that Caleb and his wife, Biddy, who worked in the house, had been with them for six years now as their highly trusted servants.

Samuel knew all about the seven-year indentures. "Does that mean thou has but one year left in thy indenture and will be leaving in another year?"

"Well." Caleb smiled. "The Lymans have been very good to us. It will be difficult to leave. My wife has grown quite fond of the elder Goodman Lyman."

"And my father of her as well." Thomas smiled. "Come now," he said, beckoning to the two visitors. "Let me take you to the house."

After just a few steps, the trio rounded the side of the barn to where the house became visible for the first time, and its sight stopped Tacy in her tracks. It was the largest house she had ever seen. As she gazed at it in open admiration, she looked at Thomas, who returned her look with a broad grin.

"This is the only house I've ever lived in." He moved closer to her and stood looking at the house with his hands on his hips. "I know it is sinful to take pride in a possession, but I do admire the place. It was first built in 1685 and then added onto in 1690," he said. "I finished off some of the inside two years ago when I was discharged from my duties in the militia. I wanted to make things more comfortable for my father. He is an invalid, you know. Took a bad fall a year ago and has not been able to get out of bed since."

"Yes. I have heard. I am sorry."

"And now that my brother Edmund has come home, I'm adding two extra rooms in the barn to house some of the new help. We now have quarters there for Caleb and Biddy, and soon there will be a room for the two men who have just herded fifty sheep down from Plimoth. Edmund has big plans for the farm. We are blessed that he has chosen to use his inheritance from Uncle Benjamin this way."

Once again, the mention of Edmund's name distracted Tacy, but only momentarily before the front door of the house opened and Edmund himself came out. No longer dressed in the fine brown jacket and polished boots he had worn a week ago, he now appeared in a great white shirt, open at the throat and hanging loosely about his frame, nearly to the top of his knees. The polished leather boots were now replaced by thick shoes, out of which a pair of woolen socks stretched up to close-fitted knee breeches with buttons at the sides. He frowned at his brother.

"Thomas! Why did you not tell me we had guests? And who are—" He stopped midsentence as he suddenly recognized the young Swift woman, which meant the man with her must be her father, the blacksmith. Momentarily taken aback by her unexpected presence, it was all Edmund could do to come up with a weak, "Of course. How do you do, Goodman Swift and Mistress Swift?"

Samuel stepped up and offered his hand for a hearty shake.

"And how art thee, Edmund Lyman? Do call me Samuel. And this is my daughter, Tacy, one of the best farriers in these parts, who I believe thou hast already met. I have asked Tacy to join me because we heard thou had a new delivery of sheep and felt some of these new animals might need looking at while I attempt to assess the problem with thy wagon wheel."

Tacy and Thomas smiled at each other. Then he said, "Please, come into the house to refresh yourselves and then we may carry on the business you came to attend to here. Would you—"

"You must excuse the condition of our home at this time," Edmund frowned as he interrupted his brother. "We've not yet been able to unpack my recently delivered goods from London."

Tacy said nothing. Trying hard to avoid the blue eyes of the older brother, she found herself looking instead at the way his loose-fitting shirt moved about his body in the warm spring breeze. Embarrassed by her thoughts, she looked completely away, almost tripping on the granite step. Edmund caught her waist, holding on for just a moment before letting go as quickly as if he had touched a hot coal.

"Are you all right?"

"Yes, yes, I'm fine. I thank thee." She hurried in, shaken by his touch.

She was immediately welcomed by a steep and narrow staircase just opposite the planked, nail-studded front door. It rose quickly away from the door in five tall steps and then curved sharply to disappear upward into what she assumed was the second story. She couldn't help but compare these stairs to the ladder she climbed every night to sleep with her sisters in the loft above her family's keeping room. Tacy wondered what the upper level of this grand house could possibly look like as Thomas and Edmund led her and her father into the great room.

Wooden packing boxes and barrels filled the dimly lit interior. A huge spinning wheel, off to one side, was surrounded by more barrels. Tacy made her way to the wheel. Running her hands over the smooth wood, she marveled at the size and complexity of its construction compared to the wheel her sister Elizabeth worked at home.

A small casement window had been pulled open to let in as much light as possible. This was on the shady side of the house, where sunlight was overpowered by a spruce tree rising not far from the window, its scent carried by the breeze into the room. Two identical windows on the front wall also pulled open into the room. Tacy was fascinated with the rippled texture and shape of the glass panes. She touched one, running her fingers lightly over the metal parts that separated each of the diamond-shaped panes.

Pleased with her curious attention, Thomas said, "The glass is held together with strips of lead. And the windows are few and small due to the 'light tax' imposed on us at the time of the new King James when this house was first built. He also taxed the number of risers in the stairs, which is why Father had to make them so steep, to reduce the number of steps it takes to get to the upper level."

"Oh we Quakers know well the royal taxes," Samuel said, sadly nodding his head. "About thirty years ago, my father had to give up two of our three cows to pay them." He raised a finger and, with a twinkle in his eye, poked it playfully at Edmund's chest. "Fortunately we no longer need to also pay taxes to thee Puritans to keep thy ministers fed, because we do not attend thy services."

Edmund gave a short laugh. "Oh do not call them *our* ministers. As Anglicans, we are well aware of having been forced to pay without attending."

Samuel looked closely at Edmund. "Thou art Anglican? I did not know there be any of the Anglican faith this far south of Boston. But, if so, then it appears we now have a common enemy in those Puritans."

He laughed and clapped Edmund on the back, causing him to skip a step with the force of Samuel's large hand.

"Indeed." Edmund smiled broadly. He beckoned to the Quaker and his daughter, directing them toward the keeping room. "Please, come, have some refreshments. Step carefully."

Tacy, surprised to see this pleasant side of Edmund, was still curious about the contents of the room. "I will join thee in a moment," she said, lingering behind, and picking her way around the boxes and barrels as Edmund and Samuel left the room.

She looked at the rough-hewn, wide horizontal siding on the walls, which was similar to that on the walls of her own house. She took interest in a section of the wall surrounding the fireplace. This part seemed to be covered with a thin coating of a hard, white material, almost smooth to her touch. A long, thick beam directly above and running the entire length of the opening of the fireplace displayed a series of white, clay pipes hanging to either end of a polished rifle.

Looking to her left and right, she could see that some of the containers filling the room had been pried open, the wooden lids hanging over at odd angles. One open box revealed a large collection of books. Tacy immediately estimated there must be close to one hundred, and she had to resist inspecting each and every one. Glimmerings of silver and pewter poked out from the protective English oak acorns that filled other boxes. The acorns spilled out and scattered over the floor. When unavoidably stepped upon, they filled the room with their nutty aroma, especially noticeable from having been contained so long in transit.

"Please be careful of the acorns," said Thomas, moving up to take her arm and help her through the clutter and on into the keeping room. "This is a bit of a muddle right now, but Biddy will soon have everything in order. Edmund purposely had some of the goods he brought over packed in acorns gathered from his estate near London. He wants to plant them here to try to grow some giant English oaks. Right now, they are nothing but a hazard."

"I do agree with thee," Tacy said, picking up her skirts to watch more carefully where she was stepping, after nearly slipping on one.

As they entered the keeping room, Tacy immediately saw her father and Edmund deep in conversation at the far end of the room. Then she noticed how warm sunshine, let in from the open back door and two windows, danced across the wide, planked flooring. A narrow table with long benches huddling to its sides stretched along the middle of the room. An ornate, tall, wooden chair with polished arms commanded the head of the table. And at the other end, a smaller, slender chair with no arms seemed to shrink away, as though apologizing for having to be so far removed.

A child's potty-chair, carved with grooves for tying the child there with rope, stood to one side. A wiggling, smiling, gurgling toddler sat tied to the chair. The rope served two purposes—it kept him away from both the fireplace and from wandering out into the yard, where wolves might decide he was a good candidate for dinner. Immediately, a girl of about seven years rushed out of a small room to the side of the fireplace, untied the boy, carried him back to the room, and kicked shut the door behind her, causing the child to let out a loud wail.

"Our servant's children," said Thomas. "The older girl does not speak, yet she is quite adept at helping her mother with the child care and with cheese and candle making."

Tacy was immediately drawn to the enormous fireplace, big enough for her to walk into without having to duck her head. She admired the broad expanse of soot-covered bricks forming the interior of the fireplace; the arched, brick baking oven built into its back; and the flat stone hearth. Iron utensils and pots stood and hung everywhere around the hearth, causing her to wonder why Edmund Lyman needed to order more.

The fireplace was lit, over which a kettle of water, steam puffing from its spout, hung on an iron hook attached to a wooden pole stretched high above the flames. With just one quick sniff, Tacy could tell that beneath it and to the side was a rabbit stew bubbling away in the black pot that sat over a bed of coals on a trivet leaning precariously over its one short leg.

"So here is the reason thee ordered a new trivet," she said cheerily to Edmund, hoping to get some kind of pleasant reaction from him.

"Yes."

Ignoring his lack of reaction, she looked about. Near a door that led to the room into which the young girl and baby had disappeared, she saw a dresser holding a pile of wooden trenchers, seven pewter drinking mugs, and four colorfully painted Dutch ceramic plates, the likes of which she had read about many times in one of her father's books.

Edmund called for refreshments. "Biddy, bring some cool sassafras beer for our guests."

He gestured for everyone to sit at the long table. He sat at the head in the elaborate chair, Thomas on the bench to his left and Samuel directly on his right, with his daughter next to him. The slender, carved chair at the other end of the table remained empty and seemed to be waiting for someone to sit there.

Out from the side door Biddy appeared, dressed in a white apron and white cap. Her sturdy appearance convinced Tacy that this woman was strong enough to not take any back talk from her big husband, Caleb.

Opening the door to the side room and directing her daughter to carry the baby outside, Biddy greeted the guests with a broad smile. Tacy and Samuel, firm in their Quaker belief in the equality of all persons, rose and held out their hands to the servant. Biddy fidgeted with her fingers on her apron but, nodding to them, declined to reach out. She then walked to the far side of the room, bent over, and pulled up on an iron ring that was attached to a hatch in the floor. Descending a ladder, she disappeared into the cellar, only to come up moments later with a small cask of beer, pushing it up onto the floor as she climbed up.

Tacy jumped to her feet. "Please, let me help."

"That is not necessary, Mistress Swift. Please sit down. Biddy knows perfectly well how to bring a cask up from the cellar." Edmund's harsh tone caused Tacy to return quietly to her place on the bench.

An awkward silence filled the room until the sound of the hatch slamming closed startled everyone but Edmund.

As Biddy Doane poured beer into the pewter mugs, Samuel, noticing his daughter's discomfort at the way she had just been admonished, pointed over her shoulder. "Well, look over there, my dear. I have not seen one of these in ages!" He was admiring an extra-long wooden bench that stood against the far wall of the room.

"A bachelor's bench! One more way to foil the royals! Splendid!" Samuel clapped his hands.

"Yes," Edmund was quick to answer. "My grandfather built this." Then noticing Tacy's puzzled look, he asked, "Have you not seen one of these?" His incredulity was obvious.

Feeling he was again attacking her lack of knowledge and experience, she hesitated, "Well, I ..."

Her father interrupted. "Oh, my Tacy is much too young to have ever seen a bachelor's bench." He patted her hand and then continued. "There are none in our village now, but I remember them from some of the larger houses when I lived in Sandwich."

Samuel hoisted his muscular form up from the table and moved closer to the bench, bending down to unhinge the small latches on the sides. "Look, my daughter, look at this." He released the latches and pulled out on the board. Two hinged legs, tucked under the seat and hidden by the board, swung down to the floor for support, making the bench wide enough for a man to sleep upon.

"Two small flicks of the thumb and this bench becomes a bed—a hidden bed that the king's men could not count in their assessments because they were not allowed to touch or move any object while making their rounds. I heartily approve!" Samuel once again clapped Edmund on the back, this time causing him to spill a bit of his beer.

"Yes," added Thomas grinning, "and this is where I, the poor bachelor, must sleep until I finish building the third bedroom upstairs, or until I marry. And that is something I must do soon, for as far as the local Puritans are concerned, a bachelor is looked upon as hardly better than a criminal."

He directed Tacy's attention to a broad ladder leading to a loft above, where she could see piles of wool waiting to be spun. "One day, this will be a true staircase, and I will have a room of my own on the second level, just as my brother and father have now."

Tacy could not help but smile at Thomas for his exuberance. "How nice for thee."

Then she immediately registered the thought that perhaps Edmund was not a bachelor. *If not, where is his wife? And if he has a wife, why should I care?* She took a final swallow of the beer. "And how fares thy father?"

"Thank you for inquiring," Thomas answered. "He's not well enough to leave his room but still shows great interest in the care of our farm. You see—"

Edmund abruptly slapped both hands on the table, pushed back his chair, and stood. "Excuse me, Thomas, but we must now conduct our business." Then, directing his attention to Samuel, he said, "Shall we go to your wagon so I may inspect the goods you have brought? After that, I will show you our damaged wheel. And then you may look after our new flock."

Before Samuel could answer, Tacy spoke up. "But should I not be going out to inspect the sheep now? It will save time, for we want to be home before dark."

"Yes, of course," Samuel agreed. "There is no need for thee to be present while we talk business." He then turned. "Thomas, will thou please show my daughter to thy sheep so that she may attend to their needs?"

"Gladly," said Thomas, grinning eagerly. "Please, Mistress Swift, follow me." He led her through the open back door.

# Chapter 15

## The Decision

As she stepped outside, Tacy looked around. Biddy's children were nowhere to be seen, and she saw how different this back part of the house was from the tall front. The view of the steeply slanted roof from where she stood made clear its broad expanse. But she had no time to admire the house.

Off to one side, she saw the new flock of sheep Edmund had ordered driven down from Plimoth. They were grazing contentedly in the pasture, and she smiled at the gentle sound of their bleating. Two men were tending the flock, trying to keep them away from the brush-covered bank, which sloped steeply down to a large pond with a very irregular shoreline. Thomas hailed them, beckoning, "Richard! John!"

Then to Tacy, he said, "'Tis time for you to meet the flock, and our two new hired hands."

As farrier, Tacy had administered to pigs, goats, horses, cows, and oxen, but sheep and lambs were her favorites. As the flock was directed away from the bank and toward the two young people, Tacy could not stop herself from smiling. Impulsively she ran out to meet the wooly mass. To be surrounded by these animals and their funny, playful babies was one of her greatest joys. Once in the middle of the flock, she knelt to the ground, embracing as many as she could. "Oh, what dear, dear creatures!"

Remembering that she was not there to hug sheep, she quickly stood up, wiped her hands on her apron, adjusted her cap, and directed a question to Thomas. "Is there not a small pen where I may confine a few at a time to see if they are in need of any special attention?"

"Yes, of course." He pointed to an area at the back of the barn where a low stone wall enclosed what Thomas called their sheep pen. "Caleb and I just repaired it. Years ago, my father had many sheep here. They were sold off when I was but a child."

"And thou art learning to care for sheep for the first time, with the arrival of this flock?"

"Yes, well, that is, the help will be taking care of them. We are looking to find enough help to take care of all the livestock Edmund hopes to bring here. I do know that sheep must be washed before shearing, and he believes the pond is a good place to do just that. Aside from the Praying Indians who come down from Marshpee every day, we also have these two more farmhands to help. I would like you to meet them."

He waved to the two men to come closer, and Tacy immediately noticed the dramatic difference in their heights. Looking down on the shorter man, she saw he wore a big smile, revealing a wide gap where his two front teeth used to be.

The thin, taller one had curly red hair and a long beard. When he kept scratching his face, she assumed there were lice in his beard. On the back of his right hand, she could barely make out some kind of mark. A branding, perhaps?

Tacy walked closer, and without waiting to be introduced, took the hand, seeing more clearly that there was the letter H burned into his skin. "Could thou possibly be Quaker?" she asked the tall man, gently covering the scar with her other hand.

"Years ago, in Boston, my Quaker beliefs resulted in my branding as a heretic. But I don't want to talk about it." He scowled at her, snatched his hand away, and hid it behind his back. His companion gave a loud laugh.

Thomas spoke. "Mistress Swift, this is Richard Crowell and John Banks. They will be staying with us on the farm now to help with the livestock, the corn, and our other crops. Men, this is Mistress Swift, one of the best farriers in these parts. We may need to call on her if any of our animals appear to have problems."

"This little woman? A farrier who will come here to help us?" John, the short one, laughed. "How fortunate we are." He looked at Richard as if to suggest something lewd, his bushy eyebrows raised.

Richard ignored him, becoming at once very polite. "Pleased to make thy acquaintance, Mistress Swift. As Thomas well knows, John and I can herd fifty sheep all the way from Plimoth, through swamps, briars, wolves, and Indians. But when it comes to knowing what ails them ..." His voice trailed off as he smiled and shook his head.

John grunted in agreement.

"Well, it does look as though thou did a fine job in getting them here safely." Then, directing her request to Thomas, Tacy said, "I'd like to start now. Please have the men bring the sheep to the pen." She immediately walked to where she would inspect the flock.

As she did so, a pair of osprey circled overhead, their sharp cries calling to her as if in need of her attention. "Are they nesting nearby?" she asked Thomas.

He was glad to reply. "I just last month found a new nest down by the pond atop a bare tree and soon the nest will be this big"—he held his arms out in a large circle—"and this tall." He turned his arms to indicate a height of about two feet. "Would you like to see it?"

"Oh yes! I've seen their nests near the marsh by my house, and I always love to see more of them." Then, remembering her purpose here was to take care of the sheep, she quickly added, "But not just now. First I must attend to thy flock."

"Well, I promise I will show the osprey nest to you the next time you return."

She smiled at him, glad to think of their next meeting. "And I will hold thee to thy promise."

Asking John and Richard to let in two sheep at a time, she immediately found a few of the flock in need of care, with ailments such as torn ears, wounds on legs and bodies, and one with an injured eye.

"I shall return in two weeks to check on the well-being of these six and to wash them at that time. For now, keep the injured ones separate, here in the pen, for me to tend to more thoroughly."

As the men gathered the healthy animals of the flock and proceeded to drive them back toward the pasture, Thomas walked over to Tacy and took both of her hands in his.

Startled by his intimate gesture, she started to pull away, but then she saw his deformed right hand. "I am so sorry," she said, drawing his hands closer. "Whatever happened?"

"It was the war. But learning to deal with this has been a bit of a blessing. It's opened my eyes to seeing the more beautiful things in life and not taking them for granted." He paused and then said, "The way I once did my fingers."

She gave his hands a gentle squeeze. "Thou certainly has the light of God within thee."

Shaking his head as if he could not believe the capabilities of this lovely young woman, he moved closer. "Mistress Swift, I cannot thank you enough. You have brought a well-needed sense of promise to this farm." His blue eyes sparkled. "Thank you." Thomas Lyman drew her hands to his lips and kissed them.

Such an outward display of affection was not ever allowed in her community of Friends. Yet Tacy had to secretly admit she liked the way it made her feel. She drew back her hands and clasped them together, as if to keep Thomas's kiss from escaping. After a brief look into his eyes, she turned and went back to tending the sheep in the pen beside the barn.

———————

After having thoroughly inspected the farm tools and ironware in the smithy's wagon, Edmund pronounced it all to be of superior quality, gladly paying Samuel in coin half the amount Tacy had determined, and then promising the other half in bags of ground corn, in the fall, a payment Samuel appreciated more than the currency. Not many traded in coin these days.

"I thank thee, Edmund Lyman," said Samuel. "But I must inquire as to the health of thy father. Is he at all able to meet a neighbor who appreciates his business?"

Edmund was not sure how to react. He did not think this was the right time for Samuel to meet his father and was not sure at all if his father wanted to meet Samuel.

But Samuel persisted. "Please, take me to thy house and let me meet him," he said. "I understand how it was important to him to not want to deal with Quakers years ago, but now thou must understand how grateful I am to him for finally allowing us to help with the care of this farm."

"Well ..." Edmund hesitated. "I think you might want to take a look at our wagon wheel first. It is badly in need of repair."

"All right then," said Samuel, tucking his thumbs into his belt and raising his chin to look up as if to gain some advice from the fluffy, white clouds overhead, "I'll look at thy wagon wheel only *after* thee lets me meet thy father. 'Tis only fitting that I thank him for allowing me to gain thy business." He looked at Edmund with a tilt of his head and winked.

His broad smile could not help but erase Edmund's reluctance. "You win," he said with a small laugh. "To the house first and then to the wheel."

Back at the house, Edmund stopped at the foot of the stairs. "I must tell you that my father has met with a terrible accident."

"I heard he was not well."

"He recently fell and injured his back, rendering him bedridden. But years ago, before moving here, when the family lived in Boston, he lost his left eye and had that side of his face badly burned in a great fire. His disfigurement is rather shocking for one to see, so I thought to warn you."

"If thy father is at peace with his Maker, no disfigurement will matter."

"Thank you, Samuel. Come."

They climbed the steep, narrow staircase that turned sharply before landing directly at the bedside of the quietly snoring Jabez Lyman.

Edmund touched his father's arm gently. "Wake, up, Father. Our new blacksmith is here."

It did not take the congenial blacksmith long to win the reluctant yet respectful attention of Edmund's father. As the two older men discussed the plans Jabez had for the farm, Edmund walked to the window and opened it to let in some of the warm May sunshine to cheer up the room.

As he did so, he looked down on the yard to the side of the barn, just in time to see his younger brother kiss the fingers of the woman he himself intended to marry. Edmund looked long enough to see them gaze briefly into each other's eyes and then move apart. In those few seconds, he made a decision. Thomas could no longer live in the house on Crooked Pond.

He walked back to the bed. "Excuse me, Father, but I believe Samuel has yet to see what needs to be done to repair our wagon wheel." He waved his hand toward the stairs, clearly indicating to Samuel that his conversation with Jabez was over.

"In due time, my son, in due time." Jabez was sitting up taller in the bed than he had in a long time, his voice stronger, his one good eye flashing about, indicating an energy Edmund had not seen since his arrival two weeks ago.

"Our kind smithy here has already pointed out some valuable issues we must attend to if we're going to bring this place back to a productive life," Jabez said. "You go down and see how Mistress Swift judges the health of our flock. Samuel will meet you in the barn shortly."

Samuel cheerily agreed. "Go along now and leave us two old men to tell each other our stories."

Edmund could not believe he was being dismissed. "Yes, enjoy your stories," he snapped. "But remember, Father, before you make any agreements as to the care of this farm, I will have the final say." He paused for a second and then added, "And also, Father, remember our agreement about my private plans." He had to be sure his father would not disclose any information about his interest in making the farrier's daughter his wife until he himself was ready to do so. With a nod to

Samuel, he went slowly down the stairs, hoping it would look like he was leaving on his own accord and not being dismissed.

Walking across the front yard to the barn, he kicked at the sand beneath his feet to scatter the chickens, ducks, and geese, who objected in a chorus of squawks. "Get out of my way, you disgusting creatures!"

Entering the barn, Edmund looked around at its heavy beams and vast openness. There were six stalls for the horses and oxen, yet more stalls would have to be built to accommodate the livestock he would soon add. Edmund admired the fine carriage he had arrived in from Boston, which was parked off to one side. He ran his hand over the wooden seat of the haymow. He grunted with contempt as he looked at the crude farm wagon standing beside it, a block of wood holding up the axle where the broken wheel used to be. He wondered if he could ever get used to this life, which was now to be his.

Samuel Swift's newly wrought farm tools leaned against the wall where Caleb had placed them, next to the broken wagon wheel. Edmund looked across from the stalls at the two small rooms, which provided living quarters for Caleb, Biddy, and their children. In the back of the barn, a fresh collection of hay marked the area where Richard and John slept, two worn quilts hanging on pegs revealing the men's only comfort against chilly spring nights. The blankets would not be needed this night, Edmund thought, wiping his brow. He inhaled deeply the scent of horse and hay and, for a second, almost found himself relaxing.

Thomas had built the barn with help from a few Suckanessett men who were too old to fight for the crown, but willing to aid any neighbor who was not a Quaker. Edmund had to admit it was well built and would probably last a long time. He admired his brother's workmanship. In these past two weeks, he had come to be quite fond of this younger brother, whom he'd only previously heard about in the lengthy weekly letters his father had sent to London. But now he looked upon Thomas in a different light—as a rival. Edmund's plans were beginning to take shape, and he would allow no obstacle, not even one posed by his brother, to block his way.

He walked to the back of the barn, where a large sliding door stood slightly opened to the pasture and the sheep pen. Edmund could tell by the sounds of her voice, now laughing, now soothing amid the bleating of the sheep, that Tacy was there, examining them. Moving to the door and without sliding it open any farther, he looked out, watching undetected, registering her skill and calculating the benefits he could see adding up like so many gold coins being dropped, one by one, into a jar.

"Edmund?"

Startled out of his thoughts, Edmund whirled around to see Samuel standing on the other side of the barn, at the entrance. "Yes, oh, the wagon wheel. There, leaning up against the wall."

The iron rim had come apart in pieces from the cracked wheel. Samuel picked it up. "However did this happen?"

Suddenly impatient, Edmund gave a curt answer. "That does not matter now. I heard you were also a wheelwright. Can you fix it or build me a new one?"

"Surely, I can make thee a new wheel. But I will have to see thy wagon first and—"

Before he could finish, Edmund interrupted. "How long will it take you to do this?"

Samuel walked slowly toward Edmund and quietly answered, "If I may take one of the good wheels from thy wagon, I will return both to thee in one week. And I thank thee for thy business. But tell me, Edmund, have I offended thee in any way? If so—"

Realizing that he had been treating the visitor like one of his own servants, Edmund now took a conciliatory tone. "I am sorry, Samuel. I've been unduly anxious over the plans for the farm. Please, 'tis no fault of yours."

Remembering he had better be on his best behavior, since he was soon to make an offer to this man for the hand of his daughter, he put his arm around Samuel's shoulder. "Come." He smiled. "Take a look out here."

He slid the barn door wide open, and they both walked out to the pen, where Tacy had just finished tending the wounds of the last sheep.

All that night, Edmund had lain awake trying to decide upon a suitable plan. Several possibilities had raced through his weary mind as he punched his goose-feather pillow into what he hoped would be a more comfortable position. How could he possibly get his brother to willingly leave the house? Thomas had been born and raised in this house. He had invested long hours cutting down trees and then sawing and hammering boards to add on rooms, a new roof, and a barn. In this house, Thomas had witnessed the lives, deaths, and burials of his uncle; an aunt; four cousins; three sisters; two brothers; and, most devastatingly, just a year ago, his mother.

Edmund had to come up with a plan that would make his brother leap at the chance to move away. Or, if Thomas wouldn't leap, then perhaps Edmund would have to push him. The memory of Thomas kissing Tacy's hands slashed through his mind, almost to the point of reaching his heart.

Finally, as the birds were beginning their predawn songs, he had an idea. Early in the morning, Edmund rode east until he found the road south to Falmouth.

The road from Crooked Pond passed several smaller ponds. As he rode, Edmund went over in his mind the plan he had finally settled on. He could not help but acknowledge his gratitude that Thomas had held the farm together these last few years. Edmund had sent money from London to pay for its upkeep, but now things had changed. Today he was going to arrange the purchase of land for Thomas a good five miles away, near the shore. He would finance the building of a small house for his brother's future use. And to guarantee that Thomas and Tacy should not want to form any bonds in the future, he would make it clear to him that he was never to return to the house on Crooked Pond.

Tomorrow Edmund was going to ride to Barnstable Harbor to dispatch a letter by packet to his Uncle Charles in Boston. He would apply what he had read in his father's letters about Thomas's boyhood dreams by respectfully requesting that his uncle enlist Thomas's services as a seaman in his fleet of merchant ships.

Within a week or two, younger brother would be sailing out.

# Chapter 16

## THE UNEXPECTED

Two weeks later, on Fourth Day, the farrier and his daughter returned to the house on Crooked Pond. This time the wagon held the new wheel Samuel had made, plus the old one he had taken from Edmund's wagon and used as a guide. Dangling from the back of the wagon was a brace of rabbits, Samuel's gift for his new friend, Jabez Lyman. Tacy had been looking forward to this return ever since they'd left. She did not want to admit it to herself, but she was looking forward to seeing Thomas Lyman again.

Her father quietly hummed, whistled, and sang to Sand and Rust, making up the tunes and words as the two aptly named mares struggled to pull the wagon along the muddy road. She knew this gay singing would be frowned upon in the village. But out here in the woods, as her father had said many times on their trips to aid the neighbor's animals, "Only thee, my dear daughter, and the Good Lord can hear me, and I do not think either will object."

Hugging her father's arm and resting her head on his shoulder, she looked away into the trees, memory racing back to her first meeting with Edmund. How grand and handsome he had looked seated so upright upon Traveler. What fun she'd had in showing him that she was not the uneducated colonial he thought she must be. Immediately, her thoughts changed, and she smiled, remembering her first meeting with the shirtless Thomas. She saw the image of him up on the ladder, spitting nails and rushing down to grab his shirt. And immediately after that, she recalled Edmund's long, white, loose shirt that had seemed to dance around and caress his body the first time she had seen him at his farm. Yet, how rude and thoughtless he seemed to be. And then there was the image of Thomas again, boldly kissing her fingers. As she had often done in the past week, she raised them to her lips, closed her eyes, drew a deep breath, and kissed him back.

Her father interrupted her thoughts, startling her. "So what makes thee smile so much today? Surely 'tis not my singing."

She immediately wiped her hands on her apron, tucked them under her skirts, and sat upon them. "Oh, no, Father, although thy singing always makes me happy. I was just thinking of the sheep I will be washing today. Thou knows how I love the sheep."

Samuel looked closely at his daughter. He had never seen her blush before. "Art thee sure thou was thinking of the sheep?"

As if reacting to the word *sheep*, a wolf sent up an eerie howl from somewhere in the forest quite close by. Sand and Rust reared up and took off, racing along the uneven road.

"Whoa! Whoa!" Samuel pulled on the reins with all his might but could not stop the horses from bolting in fear. "Hold on! Tacy! Hold on! The wolf must have caught scent of the rabbits."

Gripping the iron bar on the side of the wagon seat with one hand, Tacy grabbed her father's arm with the other and turned to look back. The wolf was sprinting along after the wagon, its tongue hanging out in anticipation of some freshly killed rabbit meat. Just as the wolf was about to catch up to its prey, a gunshot rang out.

The wolf dropped to lie motionless on the road as the wagon continued to be pulled along, almost out of control, by the frightened horses. Then, sensing there was no more danger, Sand and Rust slowly allowed Samuel to pull them to a halt. Tacy looked back down the road. She could just make out the figure of Edmund Lyman in his wide-brimmed hat and shining leather boots, seated on Traveler. The horse was bent over, sniffing at the dead wolf. Catching her eye, Edmund raised his hand, holding up a rifle as though offering her a toast.

Samuel gave the reins to Tacy, climbed down, and walked back to

Edmund, who had dismounted and was now poking at the dead animal with his boot.

"I do thank the Lord and thee for this, Edmund."

"Yes, we must thank the Lord that I happened to be out looking for quail," he replied, warmly welcoming Samuel with a handshake and a clasp to the blacksmith's shoulder. But Tacy detected a shift in Edmund's eyes, as though he were not quite telling the truth. She wondered why he felt he had to conceal something.

"Does thee know there is a bounty for the hide of this creature?" Samuel asked Edmund, pointing at the carcass that lay on the ground. "Wolves have been destroying many of the sheep in these parts."

"I had heard there was trouble with them up in Sandwich, but not here."

"Take this wolf to the town proprietors, and thou will be rewarded handsomely," said Samuel, kneeling down and turning the animal over to be sure it was dead.

"Oh no," Edmund said. "You must claim the bounty. After all, it was most likely the brace of rabbits you have hanging from the back of your wagon that the wolf was after."

"But I was bringing the rabbits to thy father, so the bounty must be thine!"

The two men looked at each other and laughed.

Edmund picked up the wolf by its two front legs and carried it to the wagon.

"Good morning, Mistress Swift." Flashing his warmest smile, he added, "I'm afraid this wolf must have given you quite a scare."

"Oh, it did indeed frighten Sand and Rust. But I knew Father would gain control and lead us out of harm's way. I never felt we were in a state of danger. In another minute, I would have taken the reins, and Father would have taken his shotgun and performed the same feat you did."

Then, seeing the stern look on her father's face and a nod of his head toward Edmund, she realized she must thank the man who did shoot the wolf. "But, I do thank thee, Edmund Lyman, for thy kindly deed."

Samuel walked to the back of the wagon, let down the gate, and then he and Edmund hefted the wolf up and into the wagon, being careful not to let its bloody hide touch Edmund's newly forged goods. As soon as the gate was closed, Edmund took his leave, saying he had some business to take care of before they arrived at Crooked Pond.

"You are less than an hour away from the house now. I shall see you soon."

As he galloped away, Tacy scolded herself for not having been a little more pleasant to him. After all, the Quaker teaching that guided her life required that one must speak with kindness at all times. She surprised herself at how excited she had been by the way he'd looked, dressed once more as a gentleman in his broad-brimmed hat and fine jacket. She had even noticed that his initials, EL, were tooled into the cuff of his boot. Most men in these parts wore only farmer's clothing, except for on Meeting Day when they would all dress in their one fine set of clothes. So she was also surprised at seeing Edmund in a different jacket, breeches, hat, and boots than he had worn when she'd first met him only two weeks ago.

Although Quakers frowned upon such frivolous thoughts, she still felt how nice it was to see a well-dressed man on a day other than the Sabbath. What's more, he had smiled at her for the first time. Noticing the way Edmund's straight back moved up and down as it adjusted to the gallop of his horse left her with a pleasurable inner feeling, almost like the one she had experienced when Thomas had kissed her fingers.

At last, three barking dogs, along with the usual geese, ducks, and chickens, greeted Samuel and Tacy as they pulled up in front of the barn. Caleb rushed out.

"Just leave everything to me, Goodman Swift," he said. "I will see to it that your horses are cared for, and I will unload the wagon. I hear my master shot a wolf." He ran around to the back of the wagon, leaned over the side rail, and peered in. "Oh, this will fetch the bounty for sure!"

Samuel untied the brace of rabbits from the back of the wagon and held them up for Caleb to see. "These are for my new friend, Jabez Lyman. He told me how fond he was of rabbit stew, so I thought I would bring a couple along."

"Yes, they are fine," Edmund agreed, coming out the front door. "Father will be greatly pleased."

After welcoming the Quakers, he turned to Caleb. "Take these to Biddy and—"

"But no!" Samuel interrupted, holding high the furry animals. "I must show them to Jabez myself. Please. Then Biddy may take them. They have already been bled and their insides cleaned."

"All right," Edmund agreed, "Father will be glad to see you again. Go on in. You know where to find him. And when you are ready, come back to the barn so we can work on replacing the wagon wheel."

Samuel went into the house, Caleb led the horses away, and Tacy and Edmund were left standing in the yard, the three dogs yipping around their legs. She bent down to pick up the youngest, a squiggling mass of black-and-white puppy fur.

"How sweet!" She twirled in a circle as she cuddled the pup. "Are these dogs a new addition to thy farm? I saw but one dog here before."

"Yes. The bitch and whelp arrived earlier in the week. I thought a few good hunting dogs would help. But now, Mistress Swift, you must get to your sheep, so please put down the dog and follow me."

"Oh yes, I must get to my sheep" she said, hoping he would notice the annoyed tone of her voice and wondering what had happened to his smile. "But tell me, please, does thee never find time to enjoy the beautiful things in life, like the feel of a soft puppy in thy arms?" She hugged the pup even closer, rocking it back and forth and kissing it as though it were a baby.

Edmund stopped walking. "This young dog is to be trained as a working animal, not to be coddled, not to be picked up and petted as if it were one of the queen's spaniels."

He reached over and roughly snatched the animal from her hands, releasing it not too gently to the ground, where it let out a yelp. "Quiet!" Edmund slid his boot under the pup and, with a small kick, lifted it off the ground, sending it tumbling.

Tacy immediately ran to the whimpering dog and picked it up, looking defiantly at Edmund. "How can thee be so rough with this little animal? Surely it has never hurt thee, and even if it had ..." Her voice trailed off as images came to her of her brother William, lying dead in the pasture, kicked by the cow he had been abusing. She quickly turned her back on Edmund, hugging the dog and blinking away the tears gathering in her eyes. She gave it a brief going over to be sure it was not injured. Carrying it over to the side of the barn, she set it down, well out of Edmund's reach.

"All right then," she said in a tone of impatience. "Show me the way to thy sheep."

She was suddenly looking forward to seeing the animals, certain that Thomas would be there to help.

Edmund led her to the cart path that wound down the hill to the pond. After walking about halfway, he stopped and pointed to an opening in the trees to the side of the pond where the flock was waiting to be washed. Richard was adjusting the makeshift pen of thick branches, which held the six she was to tend to.

"You may continue on your own," Edmund said. "When you have finished, Mistress Swift, please come back to the house." Edmund began to leave.

"But wait." She grabbed his arm and then immediately let go. "Is only Richard here to help? I thought Thomas would be here. He said he would be, and he promised to show me the osprey nest."

"Thomas cannot be here. He has moved away. He will not return. Anything Thomas has promised, I will take care of." Then he added, "Anything." And with no further explanation, Edmund headed up the path.

Tacy stood in disbelief, staring at Edmund as he walked away. *How can this be?* She couldn't understand why Thomas would just move away in two weeks. He had talked about building additions to the house and barn. He had said nothing about leaving. *Will I truly never see him again?* As stunned as she was by this news, she was just as surprised at her own reaction. She now knew she had taken more of an interest in Thomas than she was willing to admit.

Pulling her attention away from Edmund's retreating back, she started slowly down the hill, walking toward the sheep, her body chilled with a feeling of emptiness. Just then, two ospreys circled above. Looking up, she wondered if their plaintive call was a question or a warning. As she came to the level ground where the sheep grazed, the smell of their damp, curly wool as they milled about was, for once, of little comfort.

Shaking thoughts of Thomas out of her head and wiping her hands on her apron, she quickly put herself to the task at hand. If Thomas could not be there, she was glad it was Richard, and not the other hired man, that she was to work with. The fact that Richard had been physically branded with an H on his hand as a heretic Quaker somehow made her trust him.

Richard led one sheep at a time from the wooden pen down to the shore. Tacy removed her shoes and hose and stood in the pleasantly cool waters of the pond, coaxing the injured animal in until its feet were no longer touching the muddy bottom and it was beginning to float. There, with Richard trying to hold it still, Tacy gently spoke to the animal while she rubbed its wool, carefully pulling out briars and twigs and being especially careful around the injured areas. As each sheep's turn came up, she and Richard moved to a clearer section of water along the shore, leaving behind a pale yellow oil slick with tangles of floating debris that had once clung to the wool. Although the washing process took only a short time, each wooly creature was noticeably relieved when finally allowed to climb back to the grass and shake its coat.

Richard admired her expert care of the animals. "Now we will know how to do this chore the right way!" he said, laughing, to Tacy. "John is on an errand right now, but as soon as he returns, we will finish washing the rest of the flock."

"Why wait? I can help thee begin right now."

"No. I have been given orders to send you back to the house as soon as you finish with these six. John should be here very soon."

Tacy did not have to ask who gave the orders.

# Chapter 17

## THE PROPOSAL

Her job accomplished, Tacy left Richard behind with the flock and climbed the hill to the house. Going first to her father's wagon, she took her Meeting Day petticoat, skirt, apron, and stockings from where she had stashed them under the seat that morning. As she was wondering how and where she should change from her muddy, dripping things, the front door opened. A thin woman, with hair as white and wispy as the clouds overhead, came out onto the granite step.

"Come in, come in, dear," she called, waving both arms toward her flat bosom. "Biddy and the children are out gathering fiddleheads."

The woman approached Tacy. "I am here to do some spinning. But first we must get you out of those clothes." Before Tacy could utter a word, the spinster continued. "You may not enter the great room in such a condition. Please, dear, follow me around back to the keeping room. There we will get you properly cleaned up." She took hold of Tacy's hand and pulled her around to the back of the house. "Come along now, no stumbling. The sooner you are out of these clothes, the sooner you can come and help me with the wheel."

Tacy could not get a word in until she was standing half-naked in front of this talkative woman in the small room off to the side of the keeping room. "Please tell me thy name. We did not meet when I was here a week ago." She spoke while pulling on her dry skirts.

"Oh dear, I thought you knew. I am most sorry. You see, I know all about you, so I thought you knew all about me. You are the one who

143

was allowed to name my sister's new calves, Apple and Pie, because you assisted in their calving and saving the life of their mother."

"You are Mary Barlow?"

"Mary Harris. My sister, Rebecca, married Goodman Barlow."

"Of course. I have often spoken to thy sister's husband, and I am very grateful for being able to name Apple and Pie. But I had no idea he was related to Mary Harris, the expert spinster everyone talks about. How happy I am to finally meet thee."

"My sister's husband keeps a closed mouth about those things. We are not the kind to boast, you know. Boasting is the work of the devil."

Seeing Tacy cringe at the mention of the devil, Mary excused herself for mentioning him. "I am so sorry, my dear. I forgot for a moment that you Quakers do not like to hear the devil mentioned. My grandfather used to say that Quakers were a shock of hair of the devil himself … Yes, well …" Her voice trailed off as she fiddled uncomfortably with adjusting her skirts.

"Come, now. I must get on with my spinning, and since Goodman Lyman has told me you took an interest in the great Walking Wheel here, I think you will enjoy watching as I work. And I will show you how to use that magnificent wheel, because I hear that you don't spin but rather spend your time helping your father with the forge and the neighbors' animals."

"Oh yes. It's true that I don't spin. I prefer the higher level of activity required to help my father. Sitting and spinning? I don't think I could sit for so long. My mother and sisters have a small wheel at home, and they take care of our household needs. But I must admit I have never seen a wheel quite the size of the one in Edmund Lyman's great room."

"Well, it's about time you learned to spin. I think you'll be surprised at what I'm about to show you. Now, come dear—don't just stand there."

As she entered the great room, Tacy looked in wonder at the changes that had taken place. The large wheel still stood off to one side, but the packing boxes were gone, along with their scatterings of English acorns. A fine, intricately woven carpet now covered the gleaming floor, except for the part the wheel stood on, its deep reds and blues and greens

144

looking to Tacy to be more than soft enough to sleep upon. A carved and polished dresser stood to one side of the fireplace, its open shelves displaying dishes and bowls and spoons that beamed in a silvery delight.

She was pleased to see a chair table to one side of the fireplace. She had only seen one before and was intrigued by its design. The chair had a large, round, hinged back, which could be tilted down to rest on the arms, forming a table. When the tabletop was acting as the back of the chair, it would offer protection from the cold drafts of winter. She pictured Thomas sitting there with his feet to the fire. Was he really never to return? With a pang of sadness, she put thoughts of Thomas out of her mind.

On one wall hung a gold-framed portrait of a young man exquisitely dressed and standing next to a table that looked exactly like the one Tacy could see in a corner of the room where she stood. The young dandy posed with one hand on his hip and, with the other, was gesturing out a window, directing the viewer's attention to a ship in full sail.

"Over here." Mary called. "Come. Stand clear now, for this grand wheel requires a good deal of walking. It is the biggest wheel in these parts, you know, and a delight to work at. I can spin five skeins in a day. And by the time I have done that, I will have walked close to twenty miles. Now watch."

Walking backward beside the wheel, which was taller than she, Mary turned the wheel slowly with her right hand and then quickly switched to walking forward, spinning the wheel with her left hand as she wound the yarn onto the spindle. The hum of the wheel soon filled the room, and Tacy was impressed with the great amount of effort required by the spinster in walking back and forth, back and forth, turning every five steps or so. It was not at all like watching her sister Elizabeth at home, sitting and spinning peacefully at her small wheel.

"I am impressed," she said, "but I can only watch for a short while. I must get back to Father."

"You will do no such thing," the spinster said. "The men will return when they are ready."

The men were not ready. Replacing the wagon wheel Samuel had used as a guide for designing the new wheel was no problem. Fitting the new wheel into the existing axle of Edmund's wagon was no problem. Testing the wagon with its new wheel was no problem. The only problem lay in the offer of marriage Edmund Lyman had just made for the hand of Samuel Swift's daughter.

They sat in the barn on the back of Edmund's repaired wagon, their legs hanging over, feet brushing into some stray pieces of straw that sent up the sweet, peaceful aroma Edmund was slowly becoming attached to. It was not easy for him to forget the balls and banquets of his years in London and to accept how different his life must be from now on.

"Which part of my offer are you unwilling to accept?" Edmund struggled to believe that the farrier would not immediately jump at the chance to see his daughter make such a good match. "Let me go over them one by one, and you stop me when I get to the part you cannot accept."

A troubled Samuel agreed to listen once more.

"I have an agreement with a man to come down from Boston and work with you in your shop to take the place of any of Tacy's work, plus more. This man is fully experienced in the work you do. As well as being an excellent blacksmith, he is also well known for his abilities as a farrier. I will be paying him enough to guarantee that he will work for you in your shop as long as you live."

Nodding his head, Samuel said nothing.

"I have arranged to have your shop completely equipped with the latest tools and materials. You will be able to enlarge your forge to meet the growing needs of this area and have a steady supply of the best iron and wood to be found in the colony. Samuel, you already are known as the best blacksmith, farrier, and wheelwright around. Can you not see that my offer will only enhance your trade?"

"Go on." Samuel's voice contained no affect at all.

Edmund continued. "Well, finally, I have promised you that I will take good care of your daughter. As my wife, she will want for nothing. She will have full say about the care of the livestock here, the running of the household, and anything else that pleases her."

Samuel held up his hand. "Stop."

"Yes?"

"I ask thee, Edmund, does thee truly know what pleases my daughter?"

"Well ... I ..."

"I have witnessed thee speaking harshly to thy brother Thomas, thy father, Jabez, and even to my daughter when she tried to help thy servant, Biddy, bring up the cask from the cellar. Thou did not even notice the unpleasant effect thy words had on these three."

Samuel put his hand on the hand of the man sitting next to him, forcing him to look directly into his eyes. "Edmund, one thing that greatly pleases my daughter is kindness—kindness to people no matter what their station in life; kindness toward, tolerance of, and respect for different points of view; and kindness to animals as well."

Samuel dropped down off the back of the wagon, took a few steps, and then turned to face Edmund. "If thou cannot accept this and make this part of thy life, then I cannot, in all good conscience, give my daughter to thee in marriage, no matter what material goods thou promises to give to me or to her."

"Wait, Samuel, please." Edmund's first impulse was to deny his rude behavior, but he immediately realized that Samuel was speaking the truth. Edmund knew people saw him as rude at times. But deep inside, he felt his attitude was a logical reaction to the poor behavior of the people he happened to be dealing with. What could he possibly say now to convince Samuel to change his mind? He walked up, put his arm around the farrier's shoulder, and led him back to the wagon, all the while trying desperately to think of the best possible response.

"Samuel, you are right," he said at last. "I have appeared to be rude at times, and I am truly sorry if I have offended anyone. But I have been upset lately. Moving here from London was extremely difficult, and I am now trying to care for my father as best I can. I want to make this farm work again, but most of all ..." He paused, as if about to make a grave confession. "I must tell you the truth. Please, sit down."

They both sat at the back of the wagon once more.

Edmund drew a deep breath, exhaled, and began. "Ever since I first saw your daughter, I have realized what deeply tender feelings I have for her. Her care for all living things, the way she works to do her best at whatever task she is attempting, her laughter and the spirited way she can stand up for her own opinions have brought a long-absent sense of joy to me. Please, Samuel. I promise I will try my best to put kindness toward your daughter first in our marriage."

Edmund hoped Samuel would believe him, even though he did not completely believe himself. He had lied before to get what he wanted.

Finally Samuel spoke. "If all is as thou says, I will not object. I have only two conditions."

"They are?"

"One, thou must agree to allow Tacy to continue in the practice of her faith. This includes a Quaker wedding and your willingness to embrace our faith yourself."

Edmund knew he could brush away in a blink thirty years of Anglican upbringing. He knew it would be much easier to pretend to be a Quaker than to pretend to be an Anglican. "Of course. I look forward to learning and practicing your faith. The second condition?"

Samuel looked straight into Edmund's eyes with such compelling force that Edmund had to summon all his strength to keep from looking away. "She must agree to marry thee. She will be honest. Unlike many fathers in these parts, I will not arrange a marriage for my daughter against her will. If she has any reservations, any questions, any doubts at all, this marriage will not take place. Is that understood?"

"Yes. Thank you." Then he thought of a most important caution. "Will you promise to say nothing to Tacy until I have had the opportunity to offer her my proposal?"

"I will."

Edmund breathed a sigh of relief, offering a handshake to Samuel to seal the agreement. The most difficult part of this transaction was over.

He knew exactly what he would say to Tacy to guarantee she would accept his proposal.

———◆———

The two men entered the great room to find Tacy working at the wheel, walking backward and forward with the swiftness of an experienced spinner. Between the *clickety-clack* of the operation, the mesmerizing hum of the wheel, and the total concentration of the two women as Tacy walked back and forth, neither she nor the spinster noticed the two men standing in the doorway.

Samuel spoke first. "I have never in my life seen such work!"

Tacy, startled out of her concentration, abruptly stopped winding the yarn on to the spindle, letting the wheel slowly come to a halt. She adjusted her cap and smoothed her apron, both of which had been tossed askew with the physical effort of working the large wheel. "Oh, Father," she began.

Edmund quickly crossed the room, interrupting her. "I thank you, Goody Harris, for helping out here. For a long time now, we have neglected having our small old supply of wool spun. I do hope you will return tomorrow."

"Oh indeed, sir. I look forward to working this magnificent wheel. And I must say, my new assistant is as quick to learn as she is willing to work hard."

Tacy could do no more than modestly bow her head.

"I am sure that she is," said Edmund, bowing his head slightly toward her and smiling at Tacy in a way she had never seen him do before. Although it was a smile that washed over her entire body, it was a smile that painfully reminded her of Thomas.

Before she could say a word, Edmund added, "And now, with your leave, shall we all retire to the keeping room for some refreshment? I believe you will take delight in the cool sassafras beer Biddy has ready for us on this warm spring day. Samuel, will you please escort Goody Harris? I have a few things I would like to discuss with Mistress Swift."

As Samuel and the spinster moved into the keeping room, Edmund closed the door behind them. "Please, Mistress Swift, come and sit here." He indicated the table chair and carved wooden armchair placed facing each other in front of the fireplace. The ashes and remains of the fire that had crackled and burned well enough to take the early-morning chill off the room were now silent and cold.

"There is something I would like to ask you."

"And there is something I would like to ask thee also. Why has Thomas left so quickly? Just last week he was saying—"

"I know, I know," he cut in. "You have already made clear your thoughts about Thomas." Then, remembering his promise to Samuel, he lightened his tone. "Please let me explain," he said, in what he believed to be his kindest voice.

"You may not have been aware of this, but Thomas has a deep aversion to animals." He waited for her reaction and was pleased to see her visibly affected. He continued, choosing his words carefully. "We are not certain how he developed this, and we have prayed and prayed for guidance on how to handle his problem. Now that I am here to take care of the farm, Father and I thought it best to give Thomas the opportunity to go to sea, something he has dreamed about since he was a child."

"I had no idea. I thought Thomas loved to be here on the farm."

"Yes, he loved his work as a builder. He loved the barn, he loved the additions he made to it, but"—he paused recalling Tacy's obvious pleasure in greeting the sheep—"did you ever once see him take pleasure in the new flock of sheep we just acquired, the ... uh ... the dear goats that roam the yard? No. Because he feels they are dirty animals. He is repulsed by them. He sees them as a disgusting hardship one must endure if one is to harvest their wool, their milk, and their meat."

"I am so sorry for this affliction he must have," she said. "So thou says he has gone to sea?"

"We were able to arrange for him to leave just yesterday. He is now aboard the *Mariwin,* a trading vessel out of Barnstable that will take him to Boston. From there, he will be apprenticed on our Uncle Charles's ship, to stop in New York on its way to South America. He should be back in about three years, plenty of time for us to have a new house built for him on Suckanessett Landing. Thomas will be able to live there while waiting to leave on his next voyage. By expanding the farm here, we will be able to provide him with everything he might need during his short and … infrequent stays on land."

"Oh, I see." She broke eye contact with Edmund and lowered her head.

"Yes," said Edmund, clearing his throat. "We shall all miss him."

He pulled his chair closer and leaned over, readying himself for his plan. But as he looked at her, he suddenly realized that, for the second time in his life, he might be rejected. Being thrown out of the Royal Society for his rudeness in backing Newton's opponent was one disgrace. Having this simple young countrywoman refuse his marriage proposal, despite the approval of her father, would be even more humiliating. He stalled for time. "Mistress Swift … Oh, may I call you Tacy?"

"Yes, thou may."

"Tacy, what I want to talk to you about is … Well, the farm is in need of … I mean … I do not know very much about farm animals, having lived the academic life most of my adult years, and perhaps you could help me."

"Of course. I can come to thy farm to help whenever thy animals are in need."

"I was thinking of a more permanent arrangement. Would you be willing to …" Seeing the rise and fall of her bosom suddenly threw him off track. He shot up out of the chair, almost knocking it over. Tacy had to grab onto it to keep it from sliding into the ashes of the fireplace.

Edmund punched his fist into his hand. "Damnation!" he swore, turning his back on her, infuriated with himself for losing control of the situation. How many times had he rehearsed this proposal? It was to be one of complete practicality with absolutely no emotional involvement. He ran the fingers of both hands through his hair and looked up at the rough-hewn beams on the ceiling.

Then, remembering his pledge to her father, he said, "I am so sorry for this blasphemy. May God forgive me and not desert me in my moments of weakness."

Tacy rose quickly and went to him. "God will never desert thee. God is found inside thee. His light does not shine only within us of the Society of Friends, but within all." She gently took both of his hands in hers. "Thou has only to obey it."

He turned away.

"Please, Edmund, what troubles thee? Is it anything I have said or done? I would never intentionally offend thee. But if I have, pray, tell me, how have I done so?" She moved around to stand in front of him and once again gently took both of his hands in hers.

The kindness of her gesture after his unforgiveable cursing momentarily rendered him at a loss for words. He then regained his composure. "The permanent arrangement I was speaking of was one of marriage. I would like you to come and live here on the farm ... as my wife."

Dropping his hands, she took two steps back, and then her whole body stiffened as she stared at him, speechless.

He smiled, surprised at her lack of immediate response, and taking it to mean she was overcome with delight. He reached into his pocket and grasped the opal ring, which, just two months ago, he had slowly slid from the lifeless finger of his wife, Catherine. He took it out and held it for Tacy to see. Then, just in case she was unclear as to his intentions, he asked, "Will you do me the honor of becoming my wife?"

She took another step back.

"Tacy?" He closed the gap between them, expecting at any moment that she would fall into his arms.

"I am so sorry, Edmund. But I cannot marry thee."

He grabbed her. "What do you mean?"

"I am thankful for thy offer of marriage, but I ..."

"*What*? Whatever can be your objection?"

She struggled out of his grasp. "I cannot possibly leave my father's business at the forge to move to your farm. I am not yet ready to marry."

He felt relieved, for now he had the perfect reply. He told her of the offerings he had made to Samuel—the apprentice blacksmith, who was also an accomplished farrier, the supplies of tools, iron, and wood. On a second thought, he also told her of his commitment to allow her to continue to follow her faith and for the wedding to be a Quaker ceremony.

"Thou asked my father's permission and he agreed?"

"Yes." Edmund felt he had now sealed the agreement.

"He said nothing about my wishes?"

Edmund reluctantly admitted that Samuel told him he would need Tacy's permission.

"I cannot give thee my permission ... no matter what thee offers my father."

He returned the ring to his pocket, thrust his shoulders back, and raised his chin. "Are you so sure about this?"

"I am." She started to leave the room.

"Wait!" he commanded. "Let me tell you something."

Tacy stopped short at the door.

"If you refuse to marry me, I shall direct all my efforts into ruining your father's business. Your father will have no more access to iron. I will direct my considerable fortune into promoting the new forge south of here. Your family will be starving in a month."

He walked slowly toward her and then lifted his hand and pointed his finger in her face, shaking it as he emphasized each word. "And if you ever, ever divulge any of this conversation to anyone, including your own family, and especially your father, I will ruin his business whether you choose to marry me or not. Is that understood?"

She looked up at him. "Yes, I understand thee perfectly well. But I cannot understand how thou could be so inconsiderate of those very same people thou intends to spend thy life with—thy new family, thy new neighbors."

"You have me all wrong, Mistress Swift." He gave a little laugh. "I will only continue to be ... as you say ... *inconsiderate* if you don't follow my wishes. You see, all depends on you. If you marry me and tell no one about our little conversation here, I will be as considerate as you and your most peace-loving family and *Friends* could ever desire."

Tacy stood as if frozen in place. She frowned, bit her lip, and looked away. "Then it appears I have no choice."

"How observant of you."

She turned her back to him, clasped her hands together, and pinched her eyes shut, her chin dropped to her chest. "So be it," she said slowly. "I shall marry thee."

Without waiting for his reaction she raised her head and composed herself. She opened the door to the keeping room, where her father and Goody Harris were enjoying tankards of beer. As she walked across the room to them, she glanced out of the open back door. Hearing the gentle bleating of the new flock of sheep, she knew at least they would be able to listen to her, to comfort her. And perhaps she could bring Edmund Lyman to follow the light of God within him as she made her new life with this unpleasant man in his house on Crooked Pond.

———◆———

Since 1690, when Jabez's brother, Charles, had moved back to Boston after helping build the house on Crooked Pond, the two families had kept little contact with each other. As Charles's fortune in the shipping industry grew, he'd became involved with the best of families in Boston and would not dream of inviting those relations who were farmers of Cape Cod to their gala events. But Charles agreed to take on his nephew Thomas, the youngest son of Jabez, as a seaman apprentice, to work on his great fleet of ships that sailed around the world.

While Thomas was away, Edmund financed the construction of a small house for Thomas on Shore Street in Falmouth, close to the town landing.

In 1715, Thomas returned to the Cape. Forever banned from the house on Crooked Pond, he moved into the half Cape his brother had built for him. Soon after, he married Hanna Thatcher, even though he knew his heart lay elsewhere. Just as Charles in Boston had not wanted to communicate with those Lymans on Crooked Pond, so Edmund on Crooked Pond insisted that his family would never again communicate with those on Shore Street.

# Part III

# The Matriarch—Summer 1814

*Be mild with the mild, shrewd with the crafty … and a thunderbolt to the liar. But in all this, never be unmindful of your own dignity.*

—*John Brown, 1800–1859*

In the small house on Shore Street, Thomas and Hanna's family had grown. Their offspring had thrived for generations as seamen and shipbuilders and also as housewrights, building the houses, shops, and barns that became necessary as the population of the Cape expanded.

Of Thomas and Hanna's six grandsons, Peter, the youngest, was to continue the family building trade living at the house on the shore. Hezekiah, the oldest, was sent off to Harvard. While attending Harvard, Hezekiah Lyman met his distant cousin Olivia Lyman, Charles's great-granddaughter, at a lavish party in Boston.

On May 23, 1759, shortly after graduation, Hezekiah and Olivia were married at King's Chapel on Tremont Street. Olivia's father was a prosperous shipowner, who gladly took his son-in-law into partnership. The young couple immediately moved in with her wealthy parents, and they all lived on their country estate on the south slope of Beacon Hill. Since that day, Olivia Lyman Lyman insisted on the constant use of her maiden name along with her married name, a practice that was unheard of at that time.

Named Olivia by her father, after the female beauty of Shakespeare's

Twelfth Night, and forever admonished to remember her privileged background, she couldn't help but feel she was better than most. It was quite difficult for her to accept the fact that one of her three sons, Titus, decided to leave the Boston life and move to his Uncle Peter's house on Shore Street in Falmouth.

In 1812, the Boston Lymans' business was ruined when British ships destroyed their entire fleet in the Atlantic, confiscating all of the valuable cargo. In December 1813, Hezekiah died, and on the first of January 1814, a grieving Olivia Lyman Lyman had no choice but to endure three days of uncomfortable travel by carriage as she moved to Falmouth to live unhappily in the small house with her widowed son Titus; her grandson Benjamin; his wife, Susanna; and their two children, William and Abigail.

This house was much too confining and crowded for her, offending her sense of how she should be accommodated. Not only were the effects of the ongoing war difficult to tolerate; every day was a chore, trying to adapt to the country ways of her son and his family. The matriarch Olivia Lyman Lyman never forgot her previous life and spent most of her days on Shore Street reminding everyone how she missed the comforts, the social advantages, and the cultural enlightenment of living in the city and how she grieved for her deceased husband.

This story opens in the summer of 1814 as the war continued to place hardships on the people of Cape Cod. The price of flour rose to eighteen dollars a barrel, and sugar was unavailable because it was impossible for American ships to get to the West Indies, as the British fleet raided, blockaded, and bombarded the coast. The small house on Shore Street, located but a few hundred yards from the sea, was especially vulnerable.

# Chapter 18

## THE PREPARATION

Benjamin Lyman had no choice but to nail his grandmother's sheets to her bed as she lay between them. Even though the recently sprained ankle of her already lame foot confined her to the bed, he needed to make sure she would stay there.

He regretted the lies they had given her every day for the last two weeks. He told her the digging and hammering noises she complained about were because they had to make extra repairs to the side of the house and foundation, which had been damaged by a cannonball from the British ship *Nimrod* in January.

Her son Titus told her the creaking, tilting, and shaking of the house she complained about were because they had to raise one side of the house at a time in order to finish the repairs.

What they decided not to tell her was that, today, they were about to move the entire small house in one piece, from Shore Street to the ancestral family property on Crooked Pond and attach it to the side of the large saltbox house there. They also decided not to tell her that she'd be inside the house while they moved it.

Months ago, when they had first approached her with the idea of moving the house to connect it to the house on Crooked Pond, she had been adamantly opposed.

⟞⬥⟝

"Titus, our family and those on Crooked Pond have been separated for nearly one hundred years. This house, small as it is," she added with a sniff, "was built with the full intention of having it, and those of us who occupy it, forever remain apart from those Lymans living in that house on the pond. It is a tradition you shall not abuse. I shall not have you move it."

"But Mother—"

"Do not interrupt me when I am speaking!" She adjusted her position on the chair table by the fire to take a more assertive pose. "Living with that side of the family is something I shall never do. You cannot choose who your family members are, but you can certainly cross them off the list of those with whom you choose to associate." She raised her blue-veined hands and gently patted the white curls of her short hair.

Her son would not back down. "The strained relations between our two families have eased since those days. I see Eben at market frequently, and we all agree it would be in the best interest of the entire family."

"Family? Your father refused to call them *family*. He preferred the term *Loyalist traitors*. As I am now the head of this family, I shall choose those to whom I may grant that venerable title." She focused the gaze of her pale blue, watery eyes on the canvas ceiling of her room and drew her thin frame up to sit even straighter in her chair than her son and grandson believed to be possible.

Titus scratched his beard and thought he'd try again. "But, Mother, you will like cousin Eben's house. It's much bigger, and you'll be much more comfortable there."

She glared at her son. "I do not care how big their house is. A traitor is a traitor, and this house will remain where it was built." She looked around at the small room she was confined to. "Although I shall never understand why you choose to live in such a small house when you can well afford to add on a few more spacious rooms. All I keep hearing is how well you and Benjamin have done with building saltworks all along the shore. Why have you not built yourself a more respectable house?"

"Mother, that's not possible right now. Right now, I wish you would consider moving inland, away from the shore where we continue to be threatened. You'll soon get used to living there."

Olivia Lyman Lyman banged her walking stick on the floor. "The Lymans of Crooked Pond and the Lymans of Shore Street shall never unite under one roof. Do I make myself clear?"

———

Titus and Benjamin had honored her objections on that February night. But two weeks ago, on August 25, when news arrived that the British had burned the Capitol Building and the White House in Washington, they had decided they'd had enough of living on the shore, so close to another possible attack. They made the decision without her knowledge and immediately began to make preparations.

Benjamin's wife, Susanna, would take no part in these deceptions. Thoughts of moving left her a little sad. She would miss her sewing bees in Falmouth, but Benjamin convinced her she could invite all her friends to Crooked Pond. So, being a dutiful wife, she agreed to say nothing about these plans for relocation and chose instead to divert the old woman by reading aloud daily to her from her precious new book, Washington Irving's, *History of New York*, and her precious old volumes of the plays of Shakespeare. Susanna also agreed to keep their young son out of his great-grandmother's room until everything was done. Everyone knew that little William could not keep a secret.

Now it was time for just one last lie. Benjamin leaned over his sleepy, bedridden grandmother; touched her arm; and spoke gently. "Grandmother, we are going to have to tilt the house once more, but first you must take your medicine."

As he carefully tipped her head forward so her lips could reach the porcelain cup he was holding, she suddenly grabbed his other arm, pulled herself up, and looked around the room in anguish, demanding, "Why is everybody here? Why is Abigail taking my portrait off the wall? Susanna, stop! Where are you going with my washbowl and my comb and my mirror? Hezekiah, where are you? Stop this!"

Susanna gave a quick glance to her husband as if to say she had known this would happen. Having Grandmother speak to her dead husband was a sadness the family had been dealing with for a while now.

"It's all right, dear," she said to the quivering woman. "We just don't want anything to move around while they"—she paused to give emphasis to her last words—"work on the house."

Susanna wrapped the bowl, comb, and mirror in a linen tablecloth. Moving over to a wooden box, which was nailed to the floor, she carefully packed these items along with the old woman's precious collection of porcelain snuffboxes.

"Where is my stick? I must have my walking stick at my side at all times!"

"But, Grandmother," Benjamin said, trying to be patient, "you know you must not get up because of your ankle. You may have your stick when you can walk again."

"Benjamin, do not tell me I may not have what I want. What if the British land and break into the house? They have already done considerable damage to some of the houses here, as well as to our own house and our saltworks. They have ruined my foot, and now they are still hovering off shore. I will not be defenseless! I need my stick!"

The shining ebony walking stick, a long-ago gift from her husband Hezekiah, was topped with the brass head of a fox. She had even named it "Kiah," a term of endearment she had used for her husband when speaking to him in their most intimate of moments. She guarded it closely, along with the small, locked trunk she'd brought from Boston, which was now sitting at the foot of her bed. Just as no one was allowed to use her walking stick, no one was allowed to see the contents of her trunk, the key to which forever hung on a gold chain around her thin, white, and wrinkled neck.

Both Benjamin and his wife had to restrain her from thrashing around in the bed. Olivia Lyman Lyman was not going to let on that her foot did not hurt as much as she wanted them to believe. She preferred to stay in bed and be read to and be waited on than to have to get up and move about in what she considered to be a ridiculously small house. And she would not tolerate being without her precious stick.

"All right, all right," said Benjamin. "I'll place your stick here beside you." He gently curled her fingers around the ebony shaft, only to have her grasp it fiercely. "Now, you must promise to stay calm. And you do not have to worry about the British. We chased them away in January, and we will chase them away again if need be."

He sat down beside her on the bed. "Come now, take your medicine, and then you'll rest comfortably. Do not worry about anything."

He once again moved the cup to her lips. This time, she drank it, sinking back to her soft pillow when she was finished. He tucked both of her arms under the sheet, making sure her walking stick was also under the sheet, in her hand for comfort. She smiled at him and closed her eyes. Minutes after she'd taken her medication, Benjamin could see that she'd relaxed the tight hold she had taken on her treasured stick, as it lay by her side under the sheet.

After waiting for the drug to take full effect, Benjamin shook her shoulder. "Grandmother?"

No answer.

Then louder, "Grandmother, can you hear me?"

No answer.

With Susanna keeping the sheets as taut as possible, Benjamin nailed each end of the linens to the wooden sides of the bedstead. Then he knelt down and hammered the stout, square legs of the bed to the pine floor.

He wiped the perspiration from his brow, leaned out the window, and signaled to his father. Within the hour, as Olivia Lyman Lyman lay fast asleep inside, the small house was raised on screw jacks and then drawn up and onto a long, low, twenty-four-wheeled wagon. Enlisting the pulling power of two of their own teams of oxen plus three teams voluntarily driven by their neighbors, it would take most of the day to transport the house and its occupant from Shore Street at Falmouth Landing to the Lyman property on Crooked Pond.

In all that time, the old woman awakened only once, and that was due to a recurring dream, which she refused to acknowledge as a nightmare, based on a frightening past event.

It had occurred late last January, just over a month after newly widowed Olivia Lyman Lyman had moved into her son's house on Shore Street. At ten o'clock that morning, the British had sent the town an ultimatum—Falmouth was to surrender its cannon. If the town refused, anyone living between the shore and Main Street had two hours to evacuate, for exactly at noon, HMS *Nimrod* would begin to bombard the town.

While the militia and all able-bodied men and boys manned the trenches at the shore to prevent a landing of British troops, nervous women, children, and the elderly dressed in their warmest clothes; packed food, supplies, and small family treasures into rough sacks; and removed to the north of town.

The town administrators inspected all the houses in the area to be sure everyone had left. When the inspectors came to the Lyman house, it appeared to be empty, but it was not.

Refusing to give in to the demands of the enemy and knowing Titus and Benjamin would be away with the rest of the men defending the reinforced trenches at the shore, the sprightly Olivia Lyman Lyman had made a decision. She tied three loaves of corn bread into a cloth; made sure her family was dressed in their warmest clothes; and then herded Susanna, Abigail, and little William down the steep stair ladder into their cold, circular "bean pot" cellar. She threw a pile of blankets down after them.

Threatening them with her walking stick, she warned the frightened family to not make a sound if anyone should enter the house. Then she handed down the bread and a lantern to Susanna, who tried in vain to object to the old woman, whose word held sway over every member of the family.

"Hurry, hurry, we do not have much time!"

The old woman took the flintlock rifle and powder horn from over the mantel, handed them down to Susanna, and then struggled backward down the narrow stairs to join them. The cold of the cluttered room could not mask the smell of potatoes and onions stored there in baskets on the shelf that circled the top of the low wall surrounding the area. She shooed her family over to the west side of the cellar. Pointing to some wide planks of floorboard, which were resting on two apple barrels standing less than four feet apart, she issued a command.

"You are all to squeeze in together under there."

"But, Great-Grandmother—" Abigail began to object.

"Hush! Do as I say." Placing her hands on top of the heads of the two children she pushed them down and under the planks.

Then she turned to Susanna. "You too. Go!"

She leaned down and tucked the blankets around the three protestors to ward off the cold winter air that filled the room. Reaching into one of the barrels with both hands, she grabbed as many apples as she could and dumped them into William's lap.

"You're the man of the house now," she said to the ten-year-old. "Stop your whimpering and take charge of these. And hand them out only when necessary. We do not know how long we shall be here."

Then, turning to his fourteen-year-old sister, she ordered, "Abigail Lyman, take care of this bread."

"Yes, Great-Grandmother," Abigail said, glad to have something as comforting as a few loaves of freshly baked corn bread to clutch to her breast.

Settling down next to the apple barrel shelter on an empty, overturned, wooden box that had held sugar before the days of the embargo, the old woman rested the flintlock and her ebony stick over her knees. She scowled at her shivering, huddled family, now wrapped as one, bundled and tented in blankets.

"Remember," she admonished them, "do not move from your place and do not make a sound, no matter what you hear. And you will hear cannonballs being fired from the British ship."

Susanna had to speak up. "Are you sure you don't want to come in here with us? I'm sure we—"

"Hush, woman! I know what I am doing! You take care of your children." Olivia turned down the wick on the lantern to barely a flicker and wrapped the last blanket around herself from the top of her head to the top of her boots. Then she grasped the rifle in one hand and her stick in the other so they stood at her sides. Sitting there with her back as straight and rigid as her two weapons, she waited, as brave and determined a sentinel as ever there was.

Exactly at noon, the *Nimrod*'s thirty-two-pounders began to bombard Falmouth. Susanna cringed when she heard her china plates crashing to the floor above as vibrations from the blasts shook the house. Abigail covered her ears and cried in her mother's arms. Susanna also held William close, issuing words of comfort and trying to reassure all that they were safe. The terrifying bombardment lasted for hours, only appearing to let up as the setting sun gave way to twilight.

Then came one more roar of the big guns. Seconds later, the family was shocked as a section of the house's wall and foundation erupted into their cellar. The enclosure where the three huddled between the barrels, along with the thick layer of blankets, protected them—but not their guardian.

Splintered wood and bricks hurled through the room as the iron ball dropped to the cellar floor, rolled, ran over the old woman's foot, and then came to a stop. As determined as she was that she would remain calm no matter what happened, Olivia Lyman Lyman joined the screams and choking coughs of her family as the wood, bricks, and dust showered down around them.

"My foot! My foot! They have broken my foot!" she shrieked as an icy blast of wind howled in through the gap in the wall.

Half-chewed apples and chunks of partially eaten bread spilled onto the floor as Susanna crawled out and checked to see that her children were not injured. Directing Abigail to hold on to William, who was screaming and struggling to bolt, she threw off the quilts, shook the debris from them, and then wrapped the two together as one. Forcing them back between the barrels, she tucked a folded blanket over their heads.

Susanna stumbled toward the old woman, who was now moaning and writhing in pain. She turned up the flame of the lantern to examine her injury.

"Get back in there with your children!" the old woman yelled, dropping her stick and rifle and pointing to the barrels.

"No, I will not! The children are not hurt. I will tend to you first," said Susanna. "Now sit still!" She unhooked the boot and carefully pulled the stocking down. Examining the wound, she could see there were no broken bones but knew there would be a great swelling. Susanna threw off her wool cape, ripped the ties from her apron, wet them with cold apple cider vinegar from a nearby jug, and wrapped the ankle, knowing that this was the best remedy.

"Is Great-Grandmother going to be all right?" asked Abigail, peering with red-rimmed eyes out from under the quilts.

"Of course I will be all right," Olivia snapped. "A cannonball just rolled over my foot. That is all. Now, cover up and be quiet!"

The memory of that terrifying winter day would stay with the old woman forever, disturbing her sleep and increasing the frequency with which she would converse out loud with her deceased husband, Hezekiah.

# Chapter 19

## THE JOURNEY

Now it was near the end of summer. Goldenrod and asters offered their last bits of soft color as squirrels scampered about in search of acorns, keeping out of the way of the oxen that plodded along, pulling the great wagon holding the house from Shore Street. The house was on its way inland, carrying its sleeping passenger, unaware, to a destination she vehemently objected to. After about three hours of travel, the wagon wheels confronted a large root stretching half-exposed across the sandy road. It took ten jolts for the wagon's twenty wheels to pass over the root.

Olivia Lyman Lyman slowly awakened from her drugged sleep, where she was being fearfully reminded once again of the crash and clamor of bricks and timbers of a house that seemed to be falling down around her.

Before opening her eyes, she was dimly aware of strange sounds outside her open window. She listened carefully to see what she could make of her unusual situation as she felt unfamiliar bumps and heard unexplainable, loud creaking noises. Feeling a sense of movement and daring to slowly open her eyes, she could see she was still in her small room, staring straight up at her all too familiar ceiling with its dark oak beams.

She heard voices. In the distance, men seemed to be calling to their animals. She turned her head to the window and gasped when she saw distant trees passing by outside. Before she could figure out what this meant, she saw Susanna come close, riding on her horse outside, just under the window, with Abigail riding pillion behind her. Although he was out of sight, she could hear little William chattering along with them, complaining about having to walk while Abigail was allowed to ride. As mother and daughter turned to look in on her, she quickly closed her eyes to pretend she was still asleep.

"Good," she heard Susanna say. "Dear Grandmother is still sleeping comfortably." Then her voice faded as she and Abigail slowly rode away from the window.

Wondering if perhaps she were still dreaming, she tried to lift her hand but found all she could do was move it enough to discover her dear Kiah at her side. Grasping its comfort, she smiled as a soft breeze filled the air in her room with the warm, sweet smells of late summer. Still partially drugged, she attempted to analyze those smells. They were different. She sniffed, keeping her eyes closed to better concentrate on what she was breathing in. It was honeysuckle. But there was no honeysuckle around her son's house. And where was the acrid smell of the seaweed at low tide? Where was the salt air that had constantly permeated her every breathing moment since she had moved down from Boston into this house over half a year ago?

She suddenly became aware of how constricted she was in the bed. She could not move either arm or leg. Nor could she twist or turn her body. Raising her head ever so slightly she could see the linen sheet pulled tightly from her neck to her ankles.

"Of course, Hezekiah," she said, the sudden shocked realization of what was happening leading her once again to converse with her absent husband. "Despite my explicit wishes to stay on Shore Street, we and the house are being moved away from the British threats on the Falmouth shoreline to that distant cousin's house on Crooked Pond. Benjamin and Titus must have secretly planned this for months, despite my strenuous objections. I have been betrayed by my own son and grandson."

She realized that, now that because she was bedridden, they had decided to make the move when she could no longer object. They had put her to sleep and tied her to her bed to be moved with the house. "Hezekiah, how could you let them lie to me and humiliate me this way?"

Turning her head to face the open window, she called out, "Susanna!"

When her grandson's wife on horseback appeared at the window, she demanded, "Send my son and your husband in here immediately! Right now! I will hear of no excuses!"

As soon as the wagon slowed enough for Benjamin and Titus to climb onto it, they quickly entered her room.

Olivia Lyman Lyman glared back and forth between the two men, who did not dare to come any closer but stood at her bedside, their hats in their hands. Being bound did not diminish the fury she unleashed without even saying a word. She waited to see which of them would be first to try to apologize or explain or lie to her again, taking satisfaction in their obvious discomfort.

Titus spoke first. "So, Mother, you know."

"Know what? Say it. Tell me what it is that I know."

Benjamin went to her side and sat on the bed. "Grandmother, please—"

"You will be quiet. I want to hear what my son has to say."

"Mother, we only did it to make you more comfortable."

"Comfortable? Comfortable while you raised the four sides of the house *to repair the foundation?*" She spit out their lying words as though they were offal from a slaughtered pig.

"Mother, first of all, after generations of having our family ties severed between us and our cousins on Crooked Pond, Benjamin and I have been in touch with Eben's family and both sides agree it is time to reunite under one roof."

Benjamin then added, "We knew you didn't want to leave the house and move to Crooked Pond because you were intent upon keeping our families apart. But we strongly believe the British might attack again."

When she closed her eyes and shook her head at this, Benjamin spoke up once more. "Grandmother, we made this decision to move inland for the safety of our family."

"Father would certainly have approved, under these circumstances," Titus offered.

The old woman said nothing. She turned her head to the open window in time to see a flock of migrating birds fly overhead. She sighed as she thought that at least they were moving of their own free will. Resigned to the fact that there was nothing she could say or do to change things, she gave in.

"If you truly believe your father would approve, so be it."

"Thank you, Mother." Titus patted the top of her head and kissed her gently on her papery cheek. "We knew you would understand."

"Just do not think for one minute that I will ever forgive you for lying to me. Titus, I brought you up to be a gentleman, and gentlemen do not lie, especially to their mothers! Remember who you are and the family from whom you are descended!"

"Yes, Mother. I am truly sorry. We just believed it would be easier for you to accept if you awakened and were already there."

"Well, you were wrong."

"Grandmother, let me give you more of your medicine to help you sleep through the rest of the trip. It should not be long now."

"Absolutely not! I shall endure this trip as best I can, even though my nerves are stressed beyond repair."

"But, Grandmother, it will be much easier on your heart if you're relaxed."

"My heart? You are suddenly concerned about my heart? Why didn't you think of this before you forced me to make a major change I had no control over? Have I not been subjected enough to changes, to facing a multitude of unknowns? And now you are forcing me to live in a strange house, with people I have no respect for."

"Mother—"

"Enough! I will take no more medication until we arrive at Ebenezer's house, but I have two demands to make of you."

"Yes?"

"If you must bind me to this bed, at least let me suffer here in the heat with my arms on top of this infernal restraining sheet. And, you must let me hold on to my Kiah."

The two men agreed to this and rearranged her bindings to free her arms.

"One more thing," she said, wagging her Kiah at her son. "If I should die on the way due to stress, it will be the fault of you, my son, and you, my grandson. I may accept this abomination, but I shall never forgive you for it. You have betrayed me. You are no better than the traitorous Lymans on Crooked Pond. Now get out of here and let us proceed."

"Dear Grandmother—" Benjamin began.

"Enough! Out!" She slammed her stick on the bed.

This family was very dear to her, but she had to be careful not to let on that this was the case. She had always felt being a soft-hearted, loveable mother, grandmother, and great-grandmother would not gain her the respect she needed to train them up in the only way, the proper way, the *Boston* way. But after this, she wondered if perhaps she had failed. She resolved then and there to be stricter with her family in the future.

Making sure they all had left the room, Olivia Lyman Lyman lifted her sleek ebony walking stick. "Come, Kiah," she said.

She unscrewed the brass fox head top, and took a small, swift draught of her private store of tincture of opium. When she had first arrived in Falmouth, she had met a woman whose son had access to a large supply of the drug. The two women had become close friends, and every time she came to visit, she secretly delivered a few more ounces of it to Olivia Lyman Lyman.

Now, by denying the same medicine from her family and using her own secret store, she felt she was once again exerting her power over them. Taking a deep breath to search once more for the sweet scent of honeysuckle, she heard the men call to their oxen. The wagon, house, and oxen lurched forward. The rattling, creaking, and clattering soon fell into a rhythmic chorus, inviting sweet memories from over three-quarters of a century of her previous life to lull her to sleep.

———◆———

As the teams of oxen strained their way north, following an old Indian trail that coursed away from the sea, the land to each side of the rough road gradually opened up, where more forest had been cleared for new houses, firewood, and free grazing of farm animals. Waterfowl, swimming in the ponds and freshwater marshes, took off in a rush of excitement as the team clattered along, pulling its burden through the wetlands.

The road itself had been widened with increased travel by farmers from Falmouth driving their ox carts filled with corn to be ground at Dexter's Mill on Five Mile River, not far from the Lyman house on Crooked Pond.

The biggest challenge to be met by Titus and Benjamin as they led their teams of oxen north was navigating around a few sharp turns in the road over the course of the trip. Benjamin had traveled the entire route many times in the last month, scouting out the likely detours. Finding just the right places where the team would have to begin a wide turn off the road to travel over barren fields, he had driven stakes into the ground with strips of white linen nailed to the tops. Now it was his task, riding with his father at the head of the team, to locate those stakes and direct the oxen to begin their long wide curves away from and then back again onto the road.

When they came to the first major departure from the road, Titus said to his son, who was riding along at his side, "Benjamin, I am going to ride back to take a look in on Mother, to be sure she is not worried when she notices the sharp turn in the route."

"Do you want to stop the teams?"

"Not at all. I will just look in the window and tell her what's going on in case she's concerned. I would send you, but you're needed to lead us over this last detour."

As Titus turned his horse around to head back to the wagon, he saw Susanna galloping toward him, waving frantically, Abigail holding on to her mother with all her might.

"Come quickly!" Susanna yelled. "Something's wrong with Grandmother!"

Racing back, Titus got to the window and looked in. He could see she appeared to be asleep.

"But, Father, I called and called to her, and there was no answer!" Susanna's voice betrayed her fears.

With growing concern, he pulled his horse closer to the window, and when there was no response to calling her name, he handed the reins of his horse to Susanna and proceeded to climb onto the slowly moving wagon and then in through the window. Once at her side, he took her hand and patted her wrist.

"Mother?" He patted her cheek. "Mother, can you hear me? It's Titus. Are you all right?" He lowered his ear to her chest. All he could hear was the creaking of the wagon.

As he made this last call to her, his foot caught on something on the floor. Bending down, he picked up her walking stick. At once he was overcome with guilt. He never should have let her hold on to her precious stick with her arms outside of the linen. The wagon must have lurched, causing her to let go of it. And when the stick rolled off the bed to the floor, he reasoned, in her anxiety, her heart had failed. And now she had died. He covered his face with his hands.

Benjamin, who had seen that his father was not on his horse, stopped the teams. He rode back to climb in the window. There was his father kneeling at the bedside, his head bowed, his hands clasped in prayer, his voice weak with grief.

"Dear Lord, forgive me."

"No!" said Benjamin, understanding immediately and falling to his knees on the opposite side of the bed. "Dearest Grandmother, I am so sorry, so very, very sorry."

In their shock, grief, and guilt, both men dropped their heads, facedown, to the bed, their outstretched hands not quite touching the sides of the poor old woman.

"Well, let that be a lesson to the both of you," said Olivia Lyman Lyman, flashing open her eyes. "I have never lacked the courage to accept a challenge, and I see now that I must summon all of my courage to meet this one. Now, please hand me my stick. And let us get on with this abomination."

Titus did as he was told. As the two filled the room with profuse apologies and futile attempts to make their side of the story understood, Olivia would hear none of it and waved them away.

As they started to leave, she stopped them. "Wait! You must leave by the front door. A Lyman does not crawl through windows like a common thief."

# Chapter 20

## The Arrival

Hours later, after a strenuous pull up the long, gentle slope of a hill, the house on Crooked Pond came into sight, standing tall and solid among the vast acres of open fields.

Benjamin was the first to see it. "There it is! There's the house!"

The teamsters let out a chorus of cheers. Benjamin rode back to where William was trudging along beside the horse on which his mother and sister were riding. "Come, William, you shall be the first to greet your cousins." He reached down and pulled his son up to sit behind him, and then, tipping his hat to his wife and daughter, trotted off.

"Susanna, what is all the commotion? What is going on?" the old woman called from inside the house.

"Oh, Grandmother!" said Susanna. "We can see the house! Oh, it is a grand house. It is surrounded by vast fields of corn standing tied in shocks, and there are sheep grazing all around! You will love it!"

"Hmmm. We shall see about that." The old woman sniffed, convinced she could never love living anywhere with relatives her husband had thought of as traitors. But she would deal with it.

"Great-Grandmother, over there," said Abigail, pointing to the barn set off to one side of the house. "I can see pigs and goats and geese and a fenced-in vegetable garden and a whole orchard of apple trees, and the house is so big and fine with an enormous chimney poking out through the roof and—"

"All right, all right. I shall see it all when I can."

But Abigail was not to be stopped. "And I can see Father and William talking to two men who must be our cousins."

"They are indeed," said Susanna, straining to identify the men chatting with her husband and son while they were still a good distance away. "The older one in the top hat must be Ebenezer, Eben they call him, and the taller one his son, Joshua."

Although Benjamin and Titus had been to the cousins' house more than a dozen times to make arrangements for the move and to prepare the east wall of the Crooked Pond house to accept the addition of the Shore Street house, the rest of the family had never made the trip and had never met the cousins. Now Susanna and Abigail were pleased to see the men and little William talking and laughing together.

Abigail wanted to hurry to ride up and meet their new family members, but Susanna held the horse back. "No, we will stay with Grandmother until we are close enough to stop the wagon and help her out of our house and into our new place."

"Well, you can stay," Abigail said. "I'm going."

Before her mother could protest, she jumped down off the pillion; hoisted up her skirts; and ran toward the house, her bonnet flying, releasing a tangle of chestnut-colored curls.

As she passed the wagon and the neighbors, who continued to lead their oxen forward, one of them called out to her. "So, Abigail, our oxen are too slow for you?" He laughed.

She gave him a quick wave and a smile as she ran by. "Even our horse is too slow for me, Mister Bates!"

And then, as she passed her grandfather at the head of the snorting team, she cried, "I shall be there before you are, Grandfather!"

Titus shook his head at the behavior of his impetuous granddaughter but smiled, glad to see she was enthused about this move.

---

Even before coming within speaking distance of her father, Abigail could see his look of disapproval. But she didn't care. She knew he was thinking that she had forgotten her manners by running up here in an unladylike way, arriving panting in a complete state of dishevelment. She knew he would wonder if his grandmother's teachings about decorum and propriety had all been for naught.

"Well, Eben and Joshua, may I present my daughter, Abigail."

Ebenezer Lyman doffed his top hat, revealing the hairless top of his head. He was a tall, stout man, with blue eyes that sparkled as he spoke. "I am so pleased to meet you, Mistress Abigail." He bowed his heavy frame down to get a close look.

"And I am so happy to be here," she replied. "What a large cornfield you have! I have never seen one so big!"

Her enthusiasm immediately charmed him. "Wait until you see the whole farm. We have six cows, seven pigs, two yokes of oxen, four horses, and one hundred forty-five sheep!"

Taking his offered hand, Abigail bowed her head and then gave him a graceful curtsey, one she knew her great-grandmother would have been proud to observe.

Still beaming, Eben continued. "And this is my son, Joshua."

Joshua bowed his head and smiled in acknowledgment as Abigail curtseyed once again. She thought he was the handsomest boy she had ever seen. "Cousin Joshua," she said, "how nice to meet you."

Just then, the front door of the big house opened, and the rest of Eben's family came rushing out, all smiles except for twelve-year-old Anne, who stood by the door, frowning, her long, blond curls spilling over her shoulders. She remained there, hands clasped behind her back, looking down and kicking her shining boots into the sand.

Thirteen-year-old Harry, a rather portly youngster, ran up to William and lifted him off the ground in a bear hug. "Cousin William! At last we meet! I have heard so much about you! I am so glad you are finally here! We'll have many wonderful adventures! Let me show you to the barn where I'll tell you my innermost secrets!"

Totally overwhelmed by this attention, William hesitated, looking with wonder at his enthusiastic new cousin, and then said, "Fine!" And with a quick look back at his father for approval, he ran off with Harry to the barn.

"Welcome, welcome, dear cousins!" Eben's wife Jenny held out her arms as if to embrace the entire world. "Welcome to Crooked Pond!" She kissed Benjamin on both cheeks. Then, holding Abigail at arm's length for further inspection, she said, "Oh my, what a beauty you are! Your father said you were an exceptional daughter, but I had no idea ..." She let her voice trail off as she gave Abigail a smothering hug. "And when will the rest of your family arrive?" She searched the road to catch a glimpse of the team of oxen pulling the wagon with the house.

"My mother is staying back with the wagon because Great-Grandmother is sleeping in the house."

Abigail continued to hold on to Cousin Jenny's hands as if in thanks for making her feel so welcome. Then, looking over Cousin Jenny's shoulder, she saw the girl she had heard was called Anne.

Abigail walked over to where the girl was standing. "Hello. You must be Anne. My name is Abigail, and I am sure we will soon be good friends." She held out her hand, only to have Anne slap at it.

"We will not ever be good friends! Your family has taken away my bedroom, and I will not ever be happy again!"

Before Abigail could say a word, Anne spun around, ran to the house, and slammed the door.

"Pay no attention to the child," said her mother. "She changes her mind at the drop of a hat. She will adjust quite quickly. You will see."

Before Abigail could react, all attention was directed toward her grandfather as he trotted up on his horse. He directed the noisy, snorting team to pull past the big house and stop exactly where the wagon would be positioned to unload the small house from the back.

———•◆•———

Once the team passed and the wagon stopped, Susanna took another look in through the window to check on Grandmother. Then she rode up to the chatting family, pulled her horse to a halt, and dismounted.

"Oh," said Abigail, as her mother approached, "please excuse me. I will tend to Great-Grandmother." She curtseyed to her new cousins, ran back to the wagon, and climbed on.

"Your daughter certainly has good manners," Eben said to Benjamin.

Benjamin replied, with a nod to his wife, "Both Susanna and I do believe they are entirely due to having her great-grandmother living in the same house these past months. Abigail has slept on a pallet every night on the floor beside Grandmother's bed, and the two of them have become very close."

"Yes," said Susanna. "Grandmother has had a good influence on both William and Abigail, although her methods are quite … extraordinary. I do hope she doesn't upset your children."

"I believe our children could use a few lessons along those lines," said Jenny, with a nod back toward the house. "And how is Grandmother doing?"

"Quite well," Susanna answered, not wanting to alarm her new cousins. They would find out about Grandmother soon enough. "When I last checked on her, she shooed me away and told me not to look in on her again until the house is settled. Abigail will watch her for now."

"Fine," said Jenny. "Come with me, Susanna. Let me show you your new living quarters. We are about to set up a lovely feast for you and your kind neighbors, who helped you today. Tonight, they will sleep in the barn."

Arm in arm, the two women had just turned toward the house when suddenly the door burst open and Anne tore out, tears forgotten. She ran toward the wagon and stopped abruptly when she came within about ten feet of it. With cautious curiosity, she slowly drew closer to inspect the new house, totally oblivious of the family standing there.

Jenny put a finger to her lips as a signal to the adults to say not a word as Anne approached the front of the small house, now walking step by step, like a cat stalking a bird that might at any moment fly away.

Reaching the back of the wagon, Anne reached up to pull herself on with a burst of strength and energy. Just as she climbed halfway over the rail, the door of the small house flew open with a bang. Anne froze as Olivia Lyman Lyman came limping out onto the back of the wagon, impeccable in her favorite shining, black summer dress, every curly white hair on her head held in place by her shining, black poke bonnet. Abigail was right behind her.

Holding on to the door for support and shaking her gleaming

walking stick at the girl who sat straddling the rail in a state of paralyzed fear, she commanded, "Just one moment, young lady. What in the world do you think you are doing clambering up onto this wagon with no more modesty than a gypsy?"

Abigail took the old woman's arm, "Now, Great-Grandmother, stop threatening poor Anne. I'm sure she just wanted to meet you. Didn't you, Anne?"

All Anne could do was to nod her head in agreement before leaping down and running back to stand, embarrassed, behind her mother.

"Mother! What about your ankle?" Titus cried, rushing up to the wagon.

"Abigail, what have you done?" Benjamin frowned at his daughter.

"I had no choice, Father. She would have injured herself. She was struggling so in trying to get loose. I had to rip off the linens. And then she insisted on getting dressed. But look, she can walk with a little help!"

"If you think for one moment, Titus, that you can keep me nailed down to my bed while you all hold discourse with these new people, you are mistaken!"

Hearing all the commotion, William and Harry ran out of the barn.

"Hurrah!" cheered William. "Great-Grandmother has arrived!"

"William," the old woman admonished, "control yourself!" Then, turning to Titus and Benjamin, she said, "Now, please help me down off this infernal wagon so that I may properly meet everyone."

"Oh yes," Susanna muttered. "She has indeed arrived."

# Chapter 21

## THE MEETING

The two families stood there in the yard facing each other, and before any formal introductions could be made, the old woman made clear her preferences in such matters. "I should like to be addressed as Grandmother by all but the children, who shall address me as Great-Grandmother."

She extended her hand to Eben. "How do you do, Ebenezer?" Then she turned to his wife. "And I do believe your Christian name is Jennifer. How do you do, Jennifer?"

Eben and Jenny glanced at each other before she answered. "Yes, that is correct, Grandmother." Jenny was as short and willowy as her husband was tall and stout. "How happy we are to welcome you and to join together our two families."

Neglecting to acknowledge that last phrase, Olivia Lyman Lyman said, "It appears that these are your children." With a sweep of her hand she indicated the tall boy, his chubby brother, and his young sister. "Am I correct?"

"Yes, Joshua, Harry, and Anne are here. But we also have three other daughters and a son who are all married and living elsewhere."

Joshua stepped forward, took the frail hand in his, and bowed his head. "I am pleased to meet you, dear Great-Grandmother."

Olivia Lyman Lyman took one long look up and down at Joshua from his hair to his toes, turned to look at Abigail, and then looked back again at the young man. "Hmmmm. Yes. How do you do, Joshua?"

Then she turned to the younger boy, who was standing with his hands clasped behind his back, locks of curly, corn silk hair falling over his face. She immediately decided that this young man had to be taught to eat less. "And you must be ... Henry, correct?"

"Oh no, ma'am, I'm Harry." He tossed his head to shake away the curls, gave her a big smile, and held out to her a handful of fragrant rosemary sprigs. "Welcome!"

She accepted the gift with a slight nod of her head and a brief smile. "However, I do believe your Christian name is Henry." Then she turned to his mother. "Am I not correct, Jennifer?"

"Well, yes," Jenny replied.

And before she could go any further Harry broke in. "Everybody calls me Harry. Everybody!"

"But I shall call you Henry. Is that understood?"

"Yes, ma'am."

"And how are you to address me, Henry?"

"I mean, yes, Great-Grandmother." Harry ducked his head and stared at the ground.

Anne, her curiosity about this ancient woman banishing her shyness, gave a quick curtsey and then looked up into the wrinkled face to see pale blue eyes smiling at her.

"Why," said the old woman, "I can see you look just like my little Jane. You will enjoy playing with her." Then she turned to look about the gathered group as if searching for her little girl, who had died forty years ago.

Sensing a bit of embarrassment in the air, Jenny herded the women toward the front door, leaving the men to finish taking care of settling the small house into place.

Abigail reached out to take her great-grandmother's arm to help her across the yard and was rewarded by a pat on the hand. The old woman was not leaning on her at all. She looked down at her great-grandmother's feet and then quickly up at her face.

Olivia saw the question in the girl's eyes and immediately began to limp once more, determined not to relinquish her position on the displeasure this move was causing her.

Once inside the front door, Jenny directed everyone to the left. "Our house wasn't always this big," she said as Susanna and Abigail marveled over the size and furnishings of cousin Eben's great room.

"About a hundred years ago, my husband's great-great grandfather, Jabez, added on by completely doubling the house. There is what it looked like originally." Jenny pointed to a painting on the wall hung along with several framed portraits, all in gilded frames.

In the painting, the half saltbox stood in a field of tree stumps. Three small windows peeked out from the second story, while on the first floor, a solid-planked door stood to the left with two small windows to its right. The new clapboard siding was a pale brown, matching the color of the hand-hewn roof shingles.

"I see you have much bigger windows now," said Abigail, comparing the picture with the current double-hung windows, which had nine glass panes in the top and nine in the bottom sections.

"Yes," Jenny said. "During the last war, we were obliged to forfeit our leaded windows to make gunshot for the colonials—although I must confess, my husband's father did secretly support the king in those days. But to pretend we weren't Loyalists, we gave up the lead."

"Well!" Olivia Lyman Lyman sniffed. "My late husband Hezekiah always suspected you Lymans were traitors, and now I know he was correct. I certainly hope you do not approve of the current British attacks on our shores." She pounded her stick on the floor to make her position clear.

"Please don't concern yourself over that," Jenny told her. "We are now true to our new country. In fact, Joshua would right this minute be drilling with the militia on Falmouth Green, if he weren't exempt from service."

"And why, exactly, is that?" The old woman had a way of raising her chin and tilting her head to the side to show her skepticism.

"He works daily at the Lawrence's fulling mill over on Five Mile River. In his own way, he's contributing to our American cause by processing the woolens to clothe our fighting men."

"Hmmm. And why is he not there now?"

Jenny had had enough of this interrogation. She snapped the words out. "He is not there *now* because he wanted to be *here* to help your family move in." She shook her head to clear her impatience. "I am sorry. It is just that—"

A wave of a black stick interrupted her, coming close enough to Jenny's face to cause her to wince and draw back a step. "Apology accepted."

Then, jabbing in the air with her stick toward the picture of the old half saltbox, which was hanging ever so slightly askew, Olivia Lyman Lyman commanded, "Abigail, please straighten that picture."

She then walked along the wall of portraits, leaning close to examine each one. "Pray tell us, Jennifer, who are all these people?"

Hiding her hurt feelings that the old woman had to adjust a picture on her wall and was most likely now going to find fault with the Lyman portraits, Jenny smiled as pleasantly as she could. "There will be time for that later, dear Grandmother. Now we must attend to the food."

"You women go ahead. I do not attend to food. I wish to rest here." Glancing around the room to decide just where to sit, Olivia finally settled her thin frame down on the largest cushioned chair in the room. She planted the tip of her stick on the floor in front of her rigid body, rested both hands on top of it, and closed her eyes, waiting for the women to leave.

As soon as the door to the great room closed behind them, the matriarch got up. Driven by a curiosity to inspect the house alone, with no one there to offer comments she felt were neither important nor necessary, she stepped with a sprightly grace past the front door to see the other half of the house.

Walking into the formal dining room she was immediately drawn to the grand mahogany table with graceful, carved legs. She admired the ten matching side chairs and two armchairs upholstered in green leather with brass tacking. Not being able to resist, she ran her white handkerchief around the bases and shafts of the two silver candelabra that graced the table, to determine if they had been properly dusted. Then she had to inspect the woven silver basket filled with bright red apples to see if all the apples were fresh and had no soft spots.

"Hmmm." She reluctantly digested the possibility that things here were very well cared for. Making a further inspection of the room, she saw that, behind glass doors, on one wall of the room, shelves held rows of fine china plates, tureens, bowls, and vases. The open shelves on the other two walls were packed with leather-bound books, many of their titles embossed in gold print. Lace curtains fluttered at the windows, announcing the arrival of a welcoming breeze.

"Can it be, Kiah," she asked, clasping the brass fox head to her breast as she delighted in the smell of furniture polish, "that we have finally found a proper home?"

Immediately her skepticism set in. "But what shall I ever find to occupy myself with here? This house is even farther removed from civilization than the one on Shore Street." She shook her head, frowned, limped back to the great room, and sat down once more. Sighing deeply, she took off her bonnet, relaxed, and fell fast asleep.

———•———

In the keeping room, the bountiful feast that was being prepared greeted the other women cheerily. Being made by Jenny along with her servants, Bertha and Martha, as well as two of the Praying Indians, this feast was to celebrate the joining of the two families. It was the largest feast Susanna and Abigail had ever participated in cooking. As if to compensate the women for having to swelter in the steaming kitchen at the great fireplace, the delicious fragrances permeated every inch of the room, filling them all with a fine sense of accomplishment and belonging.

Abigail volunteered to turn the larkspit, where several quail were crackling away, dropping fat to sputter into the fire as they roasted. Susanna tended to an herbed rabbit stew, which sat simmering in a spider pot, three legs holding it above the coals on the hearth. Suspended from an iron crane and hanging directly over one side of the fire, a pot of briskly boiling carrots, onions, potatoes, and turnips chortled away, bubbles bouncing out and hissing on the burning wood.

Carefully removing the iron door from the beehive oven, Jenny reached her hand in and counted to tell if the coals had reached the correct temperature to bake her bread. She knew exactly how high she had to count before she had to withdraw her hand to reach the temperature of whatever she was cooking. For the bread Jenny was preparing, the temperature was just right. Bread was a luxury these days. Wheat flour was at a premium with the war going on, and they had no idea when they would be able to buy more.

Bertha shoveled out the coals. Jenny slid the loaves in and then attached the iron door once more. Soon the aroma of baking bread mingled with that of the roasting birds and stewing rabbit.

Outside, now that the small house was in position to be joined to the saltbox, the men were engaged in moving the long wagon away to the side of the barn where it would stay at Crooked Pond. In the coming weeks, Titus and Benjamin would dismantle it, making three ten-foot wagons from the huge one. These they would give to the three neighbors from town who had helped them move the house.

Now the men unhooked the teams and Eben's farmhands helped lead the oxen down the hill to a fenced area, next to the family cemetery by the pond. There they would be fed and watered and spend the night resting before the long trip home in the morning. The men would be treated to the fine feast before sleeping in the barn.

———◆———

While the women were in the kitchen and the men down by the pond, the two young boys were in the barn. Harry showed William a room hidden under the hay-covered floor, a room where the Loyalist Lymans had hidden some British spies before Harry was born, during the War for Independence. William could not believe what Harry told him.

"You mean you were on the side of the Redcoats? How could you ever have done that?"

"Shush, William. It's not something we are very proud of … now. Don't tell anyone I told you."

Quickly forgetting his flash of patriotism and not to be outdone, William felt he might share a secret or two with his new friend. They climbed back up the ladder from the hidden room and began to replace the floorboards. William took a deep breath and tugged on the hair that insisted on falling in front of his face, as he always did when he was unsure of himself. Should he confide in his new cousin or not?

His desire to impress Harry made up his mind for him. His eyes bulging with confidence, he blurted out, "Do you know what I did once?"

"No."

"Last fall, before the British destroyed our saltworks, me and two of the big kids in my neighborhood poked a hole in one of the hollow logs that carried seawater to the evaporating bins there."

"So? What's so good about that?"

"The salt water spouted up, up, up ... straight up into the air! It was wonderful! We ran away fast as we could and"—he finished in a whisper—"no one found out it was us!"

Harry rolled back in the hay and laughed in complete enjoyment of the prank.

"But I have another story," William continued, feeling encouraged by Harry's reaction. "My house is small compared to yours, but I must show you it holds a secret too."

They left the barn, crossed the yard, and struggled to reach the knob of the front door of the small house. The house was in place, resting on a series of logs but not yet connected to the saltbox. William led Harry into Great-Grandmother's small bedroom, the only separate room in the house. Looking around to be sure no one was in there, he closed the door.

"Look at this, Harry," he said, pointing to the locked chest at the foot of her bed. "This has never been opened—*never*—since Great-Grandmother came to live with us. We keep asking her what is in it, but she refuses to tell."

"So what good is it if we don't know what is in it?" Harry, looking totally bored, stood with his hands on his hips.

"That's exactly why I'm showing it to you." William sat on the floor. He ran his hands over the leather straps on the lacquered chest as if smoothing the hairs on a pet dog, and then, cradling the brass lock in his fingers, he looked up with raised eyebrows at his cousin. Harry settled down beside him.

William continued. "If we can get to the key, we can open the chest. But the key is always hanging around Great-Grandmother's neck—except at night, when she takes it off and puts it on the table beside her bed."

"How do you know that?"

"My sister told me. Abigail sleeps on a pallet on the floor here, right next to the chest."

"Hasn't your sister opened the chest?"

"She says not. I even sneaked a look into the journal she keeps hidden under her pallet, and there is no mention of the chest."

"So how do you expect to unlock the chest if you can't get the key?"

"I'm hoping you'll help me find the way."

Harry was just beginning to become excited by the scent of a new adventure when they heard Abigail calling as she entered the house through the back door. The boys dove beneath the bed, Harry huffing and puffing to squeeze his portly frame under it.

"Shhhh!' said William as both of them tried to suppress their laughter.

"William? Harry? Are you in here? Come to the table. Dinner is ready."

Abigail opened the bedroom door, gave a quick glance around, and then left the house to search elsewhere.

Sneaking out the front door, William and Harry ran to join the feast.

# Chapter 22

## THE CHEST

Near the end of the last days of summer, the carpentry had been completed. The two houses were joined as one, with a doorway leading from the keeping room of the saltbox to the great room of the half Cape.

Sleeping arrangements were finalized to the approval of almost everyone. Joshua was a little upset that now he and Harry would have to share their bed with William. Anne complained the loudest, until she found that she and Abigail were to sleep in the newly attached house in the old woman's small former bedroom, with the old woman herself in the adjoining great room. She quickly became intrigued by the mystery of it all when Abigail convinced her to look upon it as an adventure.

Olivia Lyman Lyman was glad she had the entire great room of the Shore Street house to herself, happy that, on cold winter nights, she would be sleeping just a short distance from the fireplace. With the comfort of Kiah at her side, she loved her new bed, which was called a sleigh bed because of its large, curved, wooden headboard and footboard. She was a bit anxious that, while sitting up in the bed, she might not be able see her precious lacquered chest, which had guarded the foot of her bed for many years. It was difficult to admit to herself that she was adjusting to what she had formerly called an abomination. Yet she had no problem letting everyone know how miserable she still was.

By now, Harry had devised a plan to get the key and unlock the chest. As he and William lay in the straw in the loft of the barn, he explained his scheme, whispering even though he knew no one was anywhere near.

"Tonight," he said. "Tonight we will open the chest."

"Do you mean it? How? Why tonight? Tell me! What are we going to do?" William sat up and grabbed Harry's arm, shaking it as if by doing so all his questions would be immediately answered.

"Quiet! Slow down! Don't worry. I've taken care of everything. Here's what we'll do."

<hr />

A short while after the tall clock in the hall struck midnight, and with Joshua's steady snoring as a backdrop, the two boys crept down the stairs and into the keeping room, where coals glowed in the fireplace.

Harry shoveled up three coals and placed them in a small, metal firebox that sat nearby. They would use this to light a candle in the barn to give them light enough to see what was in the chest. He wrapped the handle of the box with the piece of leather used to carry hot iron cooking utensils and picked it up. They tiptoed across the room and slowly opened the door that now connected the keeping room in the Crooked Pond house to the keeping room in the Shore Street house.

Bright moonlight shone through the two front windows, illuminating the sleigh bed in which lay the sleeping old woman and casting an eerie glow on the lacquered chest that stood at the foot of the bed, as if it were mysteriously lit from within. It was not a very big chest, only of a size to store two folded bed quilts and more decorative than practical. Young Hezekiah Lyman had brought it back from his trips to the China Seas long ago as a gift for his wife.

On hands and knees, the boys crept up to the chest, Harry managing to do so by quietly sliding the metal fire box ahead of him on the piece of leather, one creep at a time. William also moved slowly, alert to make sure no sounds were coming from the next room where the girls now slept. At the same time, he kept his eyes on his great-grandmother, who lay quiet and still, flat on her back, with her stick at her side. As they reached the foot of the sleigh bed, they felt secure that the footboard would shield them from her view if she should awaken.

Harry raised his left hand to point to the table beside her bed, where a brass key on a gold chain gleamed in the moonlight. As he did so, the shift of his considerable weight to his right knee caused one of the pine floorboards to protest noisily.

"Hezekiah, is that you?" Like a specter rising from the grave, the pale, white-haired woman in her white nightgown lifted slowly from her white sheets and looked around with blinking eyes.

The boys stopped breathing and flattened themselves to the floor as quietly as they could. They froze until the old woman lay down, turned over to face the wall, and mumbled herself back to sleep.

William once again pointed to the key and then to Harry, indicating that Harry was to creep up to retrieve it. Harry shook his head no and pointed back to William and then the key. Terrified over just having nearly been caught, William took deep breaths, slithered on his stomach to the table, reached up, took the key, put it in his pocket, and slithered back to Harry, who knelt beside the chest.

According to plan, they each took one of the brass side handles. But to their surprise, they found it was much too heavy to lift and carry easily across the room. Looking around, resourceful Harry soon found a solution. He crept to the front door, leaving the metal firebox where it was, and returned with the small braided rug that lay inside the door. He and William lifted the chest just high enough to slide the rug under it and then, with one pushing and the other pulling, quietly slid it back to the front door. Leaving the rug in its original place, Harry picked up the firebox once more, and they carried the chest outside, closing the door behind them as quietly as possible. With much huffing and puffing and whispering, they moved to the barn as fast as they could, stopping now and then to relieve their arms of the strain of their heavy treasure.

Exerting great effort, they finally reached the barn. Upon entering, they stopped to rest once more, being careful not to disturb the horses, oxen, and goats, which filled the vast area with their shuffling, grunts, and snorts as they dozed and slept. Moonlight filtering in through the many panes in the small side windows made the floor look as if a patchwork quilt had been spread over it.

They carried the chest to a small room on the far side, where servants had once slept, unseen from the house. Closing the door, Harry emptied coals from the metal box into the small fireplace, threw some straw on top, and lit two candles from the flames.

As soon as William turned the key in the lock and opened the chest they were met with an unfamiliar and mildly unpleasant smell.

Harry covered his mouth and pretended to gag. "Phew! Whatever is in this chest to make it smell like that?"

William wrinkled his nose. "I have no idea. I guess it's just been closed up so long. Let's look."

The first things they saw were a leather-bound ledger and a bunch of old letters, brown around the edges and tied together with ribbons that had long ago been white.

"I hope we didn't go through all this trouble just to see some letters," said Harry. He leaned over the chest, lifted out the ledger and letters, and began to dig deeper.

A tall, narrow, brown ceramic bottle hid in one corner, its corked top peering out over four dark blue, velvet bags as if keeping watch. The bags slouched at the bottom of the chest, surrounding and snuggling up against a cannonball.

William went first for the cannonball. "This is the British ball from the *Nimrod* that rolled over Great-Grandmother's foot! Feel how heavy it is," he said, hefting the thirty-two-pounder over to Harry. "No wonder we could barely lift the chest."

Then William lifted out the velvet bags one at a time, noticing how they jingled as he placed them on the hearth. Pulling on the drawstring to open the first bag, he found it was filled with jewelry. Gold chains and bracelets and strings of pearls gleamed in the candlelight as he held them up for Harry to see. "Just girl things," he said, disappointed.

The next three bags were heavier than the first one. One held two handfuls of shining buckles for belts and shoes and a golden starburst with a red jewel in its center attached to a long, red ribbon. Nothing was there to interest the two boys.

But the third and fourth velvet bags were different. They each took one, lifted it up, felt it, and tried to guess what could be inside. Shaking his bag next to his ear, Harry knew immediately that it contained coins.

"Golden Eagles!" Harry exclaimed, as he untied his sack and poured the coins from hand to hand. "I have seen only one of these in my entire life! There must be fifty of them in here! Oh … wait … no, some of these are Half Eagles, but they are still all gold."

Harry replaced the coins, leaned over, and shook William's arm. "Well, don't just sit there, William. What is in your bag? Open it." He grabbed the sack from William and dumped its contents on the hearth.

"Oh, no more gold, just some silver and brass coins, but so many of them! William, Great-Grandmother must be very rich."

"She has shown us some like these and a couple of other strange coins from foreign lands that my Great-Grandfather traded with, but she never told us she had so many." William sat back and tugged on his hair, shaking his head in disbelief. "She always said they lost everything when the British took their ships."

"Why would she lie to you?"

"Great-Grandmother must have had a good reason, but we will never know what it is, because she must never know we found this treasure."

"Of course." Harry dismissed that thought. He was more curious about the variety of shapes and sizes of the silver and brass coins now clinking away as they slipped through his fingers.

"Well, we had best put all this away now and take it back to the house," said William, yawning. "I have to go to bed."

Before William could return the bags to the chest, Harry wanted to make sure nothing else remained inside. He noticed a loop of black ribbon that appeared to be sticking out on one side at the bottom. Lifting the tall brown bottle from the corner of the chest, he noticed that the odor they smelled was coming from the bottle. Holding it away from his nose he shook it, and decided it was empty and therefore not worth uncorking. He reached in and pulled on the loop at the bottom of the chest.

"Look! The chest has a false bottom." He removed it, and the boys peered in.

"Oh it's only some old books," said William. "Nothing as exciting as those bags of gold." He yawned again, totally bored at the sight of books.

Harry lifted one out. He was attracted to its worn, light brown leather cover, elaborately embossed in faded, gold lettering. Holding the book closer to one of the candles, he read the title, struggling to pronounce the strange first name. *"Ar-is-tot-le's Masterpiece."*

"What's that all about? What in the world is an aris—what did you call it?"

"I have no idea." Harry opened the book and began to leaf through the pages. As certain words caught his attention, he became more and more excited. Then he came across the woodcuts. "Look, William, pictures of naked women and naked men, and ... oh my goodness ... What would Great-Grandmother want with a book like this?"

Just then, they heard the barn door slide open, a light breeze sending straw to slide rustling along the floor. "Quick! Put everything back," William whispered, suddenly wide-awake. Within seconds they dropped the false bottom in place, repacked the chest, locked it, blew out the candles, and sat motionless, scarcely daring to breath.

The footsteps were slow. From under the door, they could see a light becoming brighter and brighter. They knew the footsteps were coming closer. But suddenly the footsteps stopped, as if someone were trying to listen. Just as William could hold his breath no longer, in less than a minute they resumed, seeming to grow fainter and the light dimmer, as if whoever was approaching had turned around to leave. The barn door slid shut.

"Who do you think that was?"

"I have no idea, Harry. You don't have any ghosts around here, do you?"

"Not that I know of—although, there was a legend that a white-faced, moaning demon roamed the lands not too far from here. They say it was tall and thin and flew about ten feet above the ground, scaring all the villagers into running to their houses and the sheep to leaping over the stone walls and disappearing."

Upon hearing this, William gasped, bit his lower lip, put both hands to his hot cheeks, and felt something terrible going on in his stomach.

"But that was long ago," added Harry, seeing the terror in his new friend's eyes. "Nothing to worry about now. Yet we should wait a little before going back to the house."

After a few minutes of quiet contemplation on the subjects of ghosts and demons, Harry said, "What about Great-Grandmother's calling out to her dead husband, Hezekiah? Do you think his ghost comes to visit her at night?"

William lashed out, close to tears, and punched Harry in the arm. "Stop talking about such things, Harry!"

"All right, all right, just calm down. We have plenty to worry about without your behaving like a scared rabbit."

---

When they thought they had waited long enough, the boys cautiously returned to the house. William barely watched where he was going as he searched every inch of the yard for signs of the white-faced demon. They slid the chest on the rug back to the foot of Great-Grandmother's bed, put the rug back in its place, returned her key to the night table, and crept to their room. Careful not to awaken Joshua, they sneaked back into the bed they shared with him.

William was almost asleep as soon as he stretched out, but Harry nudged him and whispered. "William?"

"Go to sleep."

"William, I have to tell you something."

"What?"

"I took the book."

"What book?"

"The one with the pictures."

"Harry!" William almost shouted, causing Joshua to turn over in bed and grunt.

"Shhhh!"

Harry turned on his side away from Joshua to get closer to William's ear. "When we heard the footsteps in the barn, I stashed the book inside my shirt, and then I was so afraid of being caught that I forgot about it until we had already packed up the chest. Then it was too late to take everything out again, so I kept it."

"Where is it now?"

"Right here." He shoved the book up against William's arm.

"Get it away from me! I don't want to touch it. You stole her book!"

"I just borrowed it. Tomorrow we can go up to the loft in the barn and look all through it at the pictures of the naked ladies. Then we can return it tomorrow night."

"Will you two be quiet? I'm trying to sleep." Joshua shook Harry's shoulder.

William waited a few minutes before whispering, "If Great-Grandmother finds out you took her book, you are going to be in big trouble, Harry."

"No, William, *we* are going to be in big trouble." Harry tucked the book under his nightshirt, hugged it to his chest, and rolled over on to his stomach to sleep on it, keeping it safe.

They slept for only a short time before the first rooster began to crow, a signal to the household that it was time to wake up and begin the daily chores. The crop of early corn had been harvested and dried, and this was the day for Joshua to drive it to Dexter's Mill on his way to work at the fullers on Five Mile River.

Much against their will, Harry and William struggled to wake up to finish the job they had started the day before, helping to load sacks of corn onto the wagon. No amount of grumbling relieved them of their chore. After all, they could not claim as an excuse that they had been up almost all night sneaking around and poking their noses into someone else's belongings. Each taking one end of a sack, they worked together to swing it up and heave it to Joseph, the Wampanoag farmhand who piled the sacks carefully in a row. By the time the job was done, they were exhausted.

Coming out of the barn and climbing on to the wagon, Joshua

called to the boys. "Why so tired this morning? Didn't get enough sleep last night?"

The boys looked at each other. Was it Joshua who'd almost caught them in the barn?

"Oh, no, we're fine." Harry turned to leave, nudging William to follow him. Then he noticed his brother was still sitting on the wagon, going nowhere.

"Just go, Joshua." Harry was now convinced his brother knew what they had done. Had he heard them whispering last night in bed? Had he also found out about the book?

He jerked William's arm. "Come on, William, I'll race you to the barn."

The two boys took off in a flash.

---

Joshua shook his head, laughed, and flicked the reins on the backs of his two oxen to start the wagon moving. Since the miller had so many bags to grind for the nearby farms, it would take all day before Joshua's corn would be ground. He would leave it at the gristmill, drive to his job at the nearby fulling mill, and return at the end of the day to pick it up on his way home.

---

Once they got up to the loft, Harry moved aside three wooden boxes to retrieve the book from where he had hidden it that morning. The boys gaped at the woodcuts showing naked human figures.

Most of this was well beyond the ken of Harry. But he had been brought up on a farm, familiar with life cycles of the animals. Being an avid reader with the physical urges of a typical thirteen-year-old, his curiosity was vigorously sparked. William, too, could read, although the vocabulary and concepts were difficult for him. Still, he could not tear his eyes away from the pictures, some beautiful and some quite disturbing.

"Harry? William? Are you up there?" It was Abigail calling them to the noon meal.

Harry slammed the book shut and hid it back under the boxes. Then they joined the family at the outdoor table, where Harry saw that a stranger had arrived and was seated next to the old woman whose private life he had just spied upon. He couldn't help but steal embarrassed glances at this person he now had to call Great-Grandmother. William could not look at her at all. Focusing on his bowl, he spooned up his chowder with one hand and tugged intermittently on his forelock with the other.

Olivia Lyman Lyman spoke up. "I would like us all to welcome to our new home my dearest friend from Falmouth, Mattie Burns, who will, I am delighted to discover, continue her visits to me once a month, even though we no longer live in her neighborhood." She glanced at her friend and raised her eyebrows, smiling as if asking her a question.

Mattie Burns smiled back with an affirmative nod.

A chorus of welcomes greeted the guest, a muscular, middle-aged woman who would have been called attractive except for a dark birthmark on the right side of her lower lip. William had once boldly asked her if it got in her way when she ate, a question which had rewarded him with three sharp blows from Great-Grandmother's stick and a reminder that it was a person's moral character, and not his or her physical attributes, that counted. Now, seated here, William had two people he could not bear to look at.

Situated outdoors between a large English oak tree and the covered well, the fully laden table provided an expansive view of the pond below. The hearty meal—of chowder; corned beef with cabbage, potatoes, carrots, and squash; baked beans; and brown bread—was soon devoured by the hungry family, guest, and field hands.

Benjamin, Titus, and Eben pushed back from the table to return to the fields with the other men. Jenny, Susanna, Abigail, and Anne began to carry dishes and bowls back to the keeping room. William and Harry knew they had to escape quickly. But just as they turned to go, they were confronted by the old woman.

"William, Henry, I should like to speak to you after my friend leaves. Please go to my room immediately and wait for me there, while I see her to her carriage."

"Yes, Great-Grandmother," William and Harry replied in unison, knowing immediately what they were in for.

Heads down and like two dogs who had just been scolded for chewing on a favorite slipper, they sulked their way to the old woman's room—the scene of last night's adventure, which had now turned into a terrible wrongdoing.

"Remember, William," said Harry, "admit to nothing unless we are absolutely certain she knows what we did."

# Chapter 23

## THE CONFIDENCE

It seemed to the boys like an endless wait, but finally Great-Grandmother joined them. They had seated themselves as far away from the chest as possible, on the other side of the room, in two straight-backed chairs. Harry picked at a callus on the palm of his pudgy hand while William fidgeted with his hair.

Without a word to either of them, the old woman removed her bonnet. Then she began to walk around the room, looking from side to side, looking from ceiling to floor, looking from window to window, looking from fireplace to door, *tap-tapping* her stick on the wide floor planks with every step as she continued her pacing.

After about five minutes of being ignored, Harry could stand it no longer. "You wanted to see us, Great-Grandmother?"

"Hush! I shall speak to you when I am ready."

She walked to her carved, wooden chair at the foot of her bed, inches away from the chest, and sat looking down at the chest. The boys froze.

Holding her stick in one hand and with closed eyes, she ran the fingers of the other hand up and down over the fox head, touching it lightly. Then she suddenly pounded her stick loudly on the floor, startling the boys, and turned abruptly to face them. "I have come to a decision. Come, stand here, both of you."

She waved her stick at them and then tapped it twice more on the floor, indicating exactly where she wanted them to stand, directly in front of her. Her tall, thin frame; curly, white hair; and otherwise fragile appearance contrasted sharply with the amount of noise Olivia Lyman Lyman could create whenever she desired to make her position clear.

Holding their breaths for as long as they could, the boys walked stiffly toward her, exchanging glances as if they knew they were about to receive the punishment they deserved.

She spoke slowly. "I have come to a difficult decision. I have decided to take both of you"—she paused, looking from one to the other just long enough for William to imagine she was going to take them into the woods and leave them there for the wolves or the white-faced demon to devour.

He had to blink to keep the tears from his eyes. His hands were shaking.

She continued. "I have decided to take both of you … into my confidence. Do you know what it means to be taken into one's confidence, William?"

"Yes, I think so. It means you are going to tell us something no one else knows?"

"That is correct. And if one is taking someone into one's confidence, she must believe certain things about that person. Am I correct, Henry?"

"Yes, ma'am."

"And how are you to address me?"

"I mean, yes, Great-Grandmother."

"What certain things, Henry?"

"She must believe she can trust the person to keep the confidence."

"Smart young man." She paused again, watching them squirm. "Do you understand that, William?"

"Yes."

"Yes, *what*?" She pounded her stick and frowned at him.

"Yes, Great-Grandmother."

"Fine. Now that we understand each other, I will proceed to take you into my confidence."

She unfastened the top three buttons of her dress, reached inside, and pulled out the brass key on the gold chain, holding it up before them.

"Do you know what this is, William?" She waited only a split second before continuing. "Of course you do not. How could you possibly know? It is the key to my locked chest here at the foot of my bed." She watched them for a reaction.

Harry pinched William's back to remind him to admit nothing until the moment doing so was absolutely unavoidable.

"As William knows, I have kept knowledge of the contents of this chest from the entire family. I have my reasons, but now I wish to engage the two of you to help me in recording the number and kind of these contents. William, will you please take this key and open the chest?"

William hesitated but a second before Harry lightly pinched him again, saying, "What an adventure this is, right, William?" And then to their elderly confidante, he added, "How fortunate we are to have you ask us for your help, Great-Grandmother." Playing the part of the innocent was nothing new to Harry.

Once the chest lay open, the old woman directed William to put aside the letters and the ledger, exposing the cannonball and the four blue velvet bags they had seen not too long ago. Both boys were startled to see that the strange-smelling brown ceramic bottle was missing. Harry's eyes darted around the room, coming to a jolting stop on the mantel. There the bottle sat, gleaming in the bright sunshine that dared to enter the same room, where a dark cloud of foreboding hung over the heads of the two boys.

"William, show Henry the cannonball that was fired into our cellar."

William hefted up the thirty-two-pounder and handed it to Harry, not chancing to look directly at him. "This is the ball that smashed into Great-Grandmother's ankle last January."

"Oh, really? We heard your house had been hit."

"Now I would like you both to help by counting the contents of the bags. I have an exact enumeration here and want to be sure everything is still in place." She held up the leather-bound ledger and opened it to a page in the middle of the book. "Go ahead, you first, William. Pour out the contents and then describe and count every piece aloud so I can compare it to my list."

They knew they had not taken any of the gold, silver, or jewelry, so this task, although tedious and nerve-racking, was accomplished without added worry. The difficult thing was that they were supposed to have never seen any of it before and had to remember to exclaim in surprise over the opening of each sack. In their anxiety, they lost the opportunity to ask where all the gold had come from.

Compounding all this was the lack of sleep the night before, causing both boys to perspire profusely, mopping their brows on their sleeves and dreading what her next request would be.

"Well, thank you, boys. Everything has been accounted for, right down to the last gold coin." Slamming the ledger shut, with enough energy to make both boys visibly jump, she leaned over the chest and peered in. "It seems that we have checked everything. Am I correct? Please look to see if we have left anything in the bottom of the chest."

They leaned over and studied the false bottom, their eyes catching on the loop of ribbon. "Looks empty to me," said Harry. "Does it look empty to you, William?"

"Oh, yes it certainly does." He rested back on his knees and wiped both eyes with the backs of his hands, as if to wipe the lies from them.

"So, now put everything back exactly as it was and then—" She stopped herself. "I forgot. Henry, would you please go to the mantel and bring me that tall brown bottle? I'd like to see if it will fit in the chest."

"Oh, it will fit, I … I … I mean it looks as if it will fit," William stammered. "Don't you think so, Harry?"

Harry gave him a look of exasperation. "We will *try* to fit it in." Taking the bottle from the mantel, Harry thought that now it felt quite heavier than it had last night when he had lifted it from the chest. Now it appeared to be full.

"Fine," said the old woman. "Please put it in, lock the chest, and give me the key."

Harry dared not give the bottle to William to replace, for he knew the youngster would try to put it back exactly where it had been last night. The woman was watching their every movement. First he pretended to try to lay the bottle down on top of the bags, but the cannonball got in the way. Then he tried a few other positions.

201

"I'm not sure it will fit."

"Try standing it up in the corner," she told him.

"Where?'

"Oh, try that corner over there." She pointed to the exact place where they had found it the night before.

"Thank you, boys, for helping me. But you must remember, the things you have seen and done here today are to be revealed to no one—not your parents or anyone else—no one. Do you understand?"

"Yes, Great-Grandmother," they answered in unison, relieved to be finally dismissed.

As they practically ran to the door to escape, she called out to them. "Wait!" She rose from the chair and raised her stick in the air.

"Here it comes," Harry muttered under his breath as they stopped in their tracks and slowly turned around to face the old woman, whose clutches they thought they had avoided.

"Before you leave, I want to invite you back here tomorrow, right after our noon meal. I have a very special book I would like to show you. I do believe you are both old enough to gain educational benefits from its contents. It is an illustrated book, and I should like to read certain passages to you, especially one about how little ones are really made. Now, run along and tend to your chores."

At a safe distance from the house, Harry said, "William, do you understand what she just said?"

"I think so. She is going to read to us."

"Yes, she is going to read to us *out of that Aristotle book*! We must return it tonight."

<hr />

Once the door was closed behind them, the old woman walked to her carved wooden chair, sat down, smoothed her skirts, and smiled. Holding the ebony shaft of her stick in one hand, she ran her fingers up and down the brass fox head and gazed down fondly at it.

"Oh, Kiah, how I love these crafty little boys." She drew the fox head to her breast. "I simply cannot wait until tonight."

Olivia Lyman Lyman smiled and held her stick close while sitting in her chair. She turned to look out the window at the field where corn shocks stood in straight rows, drying out before being carried to the barn. "Well, they will be too wet to be taken in tomorrow," she said to Kiah as a light rain began to fall. The sky gradually darkened, promising more. She unscrewed the fox head and took a sip.

———•◆•———

By midnight, gale force winds whipped through the fields, roaring around the house as if in some kind of competition with the rain, thunder, and lightning. Harry and William huddled down beside the closed door that led from the saltbox directly into the half Cape. They had been there for an hour, hoping the storm would pass so they could move the chest once more to the barn to replace the book. No parts of the storm were willing to give up. Neither wind, nor rain, nor thunder, nor lightning seemed willing to be the first to go.

"We have two choices, William. Either we do nothing and take our medicine tomorrow, or we go in there and replace the book in the chest right now where it sits at the foot of her bed."

"We can't do that! With all this noise from the storm, she is probably not even asleep."

"We'll have to take that chance. We must be brave like our men defending the town against the British … this time, I mean." His reference to the fact that his family now supported the fight against the British was lost on William. Harry reached up to the doorknob, only to have William pull his arm back.

"No!"

"Yes. We must. We can do it. Trust me. Now listen." He grasped William by the shoulders and looked straight into his eyes. "The thunder and lightning is the boom and flash of cannon. The wind is a ball flying by close enough to whisk our caps from our heads. And the rain is our good friend because it will put out any fire that may be caused by the cannonballs bursting into our house."

Harry let go, opened the door, and entered the half Cape. William, recalling that terrifying night last January when Great-Grandmother had herded them all into the cellar, was not going to leave Harry's side for one minute.

Hunching along across the floor on their bellies, both boys stopped and winced whenever the thunder crashed. The lightning flashed so frequently that the room was almost fully lit the entire time. A loose shutter banged mercilessly against the side of the small house. As they drew closer to the bed, Harry looked up and saw that the old woman was not sleeping on her back as she had been the night before. Now she was sleeping on her side, directly facing the door they had just sneaked through. If she opened her eyes, she would see them as clearly as if it were broad daylight.

They managed to slither to the foot of her bed, where they sat with their backs against the broad, polished mahogany. William panted with fear and sweated like a goose on a spit, while Harry delighted in the new sense of power he had over his young cousin.

Harry, as he had the night before, pointed to William and then jerked his thumb backward over his shoulder to indicate that William was to crawl around to the night table to retrieve the key. By this time, William had almost totally fallen apart. He scrunched closed his eyes and shook his head in terrified refusal.

"Baby," spat Harry to his sniveling cousin. Then he crawled around himself, only to practically fly back.

"The key is not there!" He had all he could do to keep his voice down.

"I don't believe you," William hissed. "You just want me to go and look and get caught."

"What difference does it make who gets caught? We're both here. I say the key is not on the table." Then he hissed at his cousin, "You go look for yourself."

Taking a deep breath and silently vowing that he would never again give Harry an excuse to call him a baby, William crept on his hands and knees as if in a trance, up to the table at the head of the bed. Harry was right. There was no key. Summoning all his courage, he took a deep breath and dared to turn to look at the face of his Great-Grandmother, no more than two feet from his own. Then he saw the key. It was on the chain draped around her neck, its weight having caused it to slide off her chest over the side of the bed and hang down to the point where it was dangling right under William's nose.

His loud gasp occurred just as the greatest flash of lightning lit the room and a clap of thunder rattled the windows and shook the floor, causing the old woman to sit bolt upright in bed. "Hezekiah?" she looked around the room. But fortunately for William, who lay flat as a flounder on the floor close to the bed, she did not look down.

"Oh dear," she said aloud. "I forgot to remove my key before getting into bed. Whatever was I thinking?"

She removed the chain from around her neck and dropped the key noisily on the night table. Then, turning her back to it, she lay down facing the wall, trying with all her might to push her pillow into her face to stifle her laughter.

If it were not for the trembling of his body, William might have fallen asleep on the floor before he deemed that sufficient time had passed to have let the old woman fall once more to sleep. He reached up, took the key, and slid back to where Harry was grinning.

"Well done, William! Good soldier! Now, let's get to work."

As the nor'easter finally moved out, leaving behind an eerie silence when it disappeared across the bay toward Providence, they began to lift the contents out of the chest one by one.

With the pile of velvet bags snuggled together on the floor beside them and William holding on to the cannonball, Harry reached under his shirt, took out *Aristotle's Masterpiece*, and pulled on the ribbon loop at the bottom of the chest to expose the false bottom.

"Damnation!" Harry swore, almost under his breath, and then both boys froze.

In the space where they were to replace the book lay another book, leaving not an inch for *Aristotle* to squeeze in. Harry opened the book. "It's a book of poems by someone named Blake."

William could do nothing but hug the cannonball with one hand as he clamped his other hand over his mouth; spread two fingers slightly; and, between them, quietly mutter the words, "Now what?"

Harry had only to think for a minute before the idea hit him. He leaned over and whispered into William's ear. "You say Great-Grandmother sometimes forgets things, right?"

"Right. You heard her call your sister Anne by the name of her dead daughter, Jane."

"Yes, and she also talks to her dead husband Hezekiah. So she probably forgets other things too, right?"

"Probably."

"All right. So here's what we'll do."

Harry lifted the new book out of the bottom of the chest and returned *Aristotle* to its former position. He then returned the false bottom, the velvet bags, the cannonball, the letters, the ledger, and the ceramic bottle, closed the lid, and locked it. He returned the key to the bedside table and then took Blake's poetry book and placed it on the mantel.

"There. If anything looks out of place, she will think she just forgot. Believe me, William, this will work."

# Chapter 24

## THE READING

The next day dawned as hot and sunny as the final day of summer should be. At the noon meal, the boys once more attempted to avoid the old woman's eyes, hoping that doing so would encourage her to forget her invitation to read to them after they had finished eating. William toyed with his food before attempting to actually place any of it into his mouth, hoping that, by the time they finished eating, she would grow tired of waiting.

Olivia Lyman Lyman did not forget; nor did she grow tired of waiting. The boys followed her solemnly into her room, their eyes communicating to each other words they dared not say aloud. After they were all inside, she locked the door behind them.

"Come now, William and Henry, sit down here on either side of me on the settee." She took one of each boy's hands in hers and held them on her lap.

"Now, do you remember yesterday when I spoke to you about a special book I have from which I wish to read certain passages to you?"

They shifted their bodies uncomfortably as they nodded their heads in unison.

"Well, let us begin. William, will you please go to the mantel and take down the book you see there?"

William could not believe his ears. He stood up and walked slowly across the room. He had thought for sure Great-Grandmother was going to ask him instead to open the chest and take out *Aristotle*. "You mean that poetry book over there?" He pointed to the mantel.

"William!" It was Harry who could not contain himself. "You do *not know* that's a book of poetry!"

William covered his face with his hands and began to sniffle.

"What is it, William? Come here." The old woman banged her stick on the floor. "Is there something you wish to tell me?"

"No!" said Harry, rising and rushing to his cousin's side. "You have nothing to tell her, right, William?"

By this time the younger cousin was sobbing. He pulled roughly away from Harry's grip. "It was all his idea!" He pointed to Harry. "He said we should—"

"Oh, no!" shouted Harry. "You're the one who told me about the chest in the first place!"

Olivia Lyman Lyman stood up. "Whatever are you two talking about? What is this nonsense with the chest? Come over here this minute!" She banged her stick on the floor once more.

Instead of obeying her command, William ran to the door, only to find that he had forgotten it was locked. He slowly sank to the floor and sat there with his back against the door, head on his bent knees, sobbing.

Harry stood with his back to both of them, looking down at his shoes, hands in his pockets. "Damnation *again*," he said to himself, kicking the floor

"William," the old woman demanded, "stop that crying this minute! You will both come over here and tell me what is going on!"

The boys looked at each other, and Harry raised his hands, palms up, and shrugged his shoulders in a gesture of resignation. He walked over to William and offered to help him up off the floor.

"Now, what is it you wish to tell me?"

They revealed their escapade, taking turns, each telling another step in their proceedings until the tale was told. When they got to the end, she had a question.

"Who do you think it was that came into the barn that night while you were hiding in the back room with the chest?"

William answered first. "I think it was Joshua. He has been acting very strange lately."

"Henry?"

"I think … I think … Was it you?"

"Yes. You see, I knew all along what you were up to since you first crept into my room."

"Then why didn't you say so?" Harry asked.

"Because I was waiting to hear you admit to it before I confronted you with the truth. It did take a bit longer for you to own up to your dishonorable behavior, and I hope the anxiety you experienced through all this will be a lesson to you. Are you both truly sorry for sneaking into my room to betray my trust in you?"

"Yes, Great-Grandmother. I am truly sorry for what we did."

"Me too," added Harry.

"Do you believe that your anxiety was enough punishment for your devious actions?"

"Oh yes! It was terrible!" Harry exclaimed.

"Yes, it certainly was!" William agreed.

"Well, I think differently." She unbuttoned the top of her dress, took the key, and handed it to Harry. "Please open the chest and take out the book you had stolen from me. William, please go to the mantel and take down the book that I saw Henry place there last night, the book you so rightly identified from a distance of ten feet as one of poetry."

"You saw me place the book there?"

"Of course."

They did what they were told and joined her on the settee once more. She held both books to her bosom. "From which would you like to have me read first?"

The boys exchanged furtive glances. "Oh, the poetry book will be fine—right, William?" Harry nodded his head as if eager to convince William that this was the best choice.

But William needed no convincing. "Oh yes, we both think the poetry will be just fine. We love to hear poetry, don't we, Harry? We love it. Please read the poetry."

With a smile of triumph, she opened William Blake's *Songs of*

*Innocence and of Experience* and began with "The Lamb": "Little lamb, who made thee? / Dost thee know who made thee?"

She interrupted herself. "Actually this poem is a fitting introduction to the information in the other book. Now what do you suppose the rest of this poem is about? Henry?"

"Um ... well ... ah ... Could it be about what the sheep ... um ... do before they can have the little lambs?" Being brought up on the farm, Harry knew that part, but his blood-red face gave him away as relating that experience to the human procreation lesson he dreaded hearing the old woman read from the other book.

"No, no, no, my child." She laughed and congratulated herself on procuring the exact response she'd hoped for.

"This poem is about Our Lord, Jesus Christ, who was meek and gentle, my dears. And it is the way you must learn to behave, instead of sneaking around in the middle of the night violating my privacy—the privacy of me, your great-grandmother, who should be treated with the utmost reverence. Listen."

She finished Blake's short poem and then put the book down. "Now, let us see what *Aristotle* has to offer. I assume you have already seen some of the illustrations. Am I correct?"

The boys darted looks at each other, each waiting to see who would be the first to lie.

"Well," she repeated in a louder voice, "am I correct in assuming you have already seen some of the illustrations in this book? Speak up."

"Yes, Great-Grandmother," they replied in unison.

She decided to prolong their discomfort. "So, William, what do you remember from the book?"

"Well ... um ..." William took a deep breath and then let it all out at once. "There was a scary picture and a story about a two-headed person with four arms born with his brother attached to his back. And they grew up, and the brother died, and he had to carry the dead body around until he died. And it said how the stench and weight of the dead body was what killed him." By the time he got to the end of this long description, he was choking on the words.

"Anything else, William?"

"Well." He blushed. "There were some nice pictures of naked ladies."

"Thank you William. Now, Henry. What do you remember?"

Not wanting to mention the "Act of Copulation" section, Harry quickly agreed with William. "That two-headed person." Then he put his head down, realizing that he had lied once more.

"Is that all you remember, Henry?"

"No, ma'am." He took a deep breath, deciding to tell the truth. "I remember reading a short section about ... about ... I guess it was called something like 'the body parts of women' ... or something like that."

"All right. You both have been honest, even though I can see it has been difficult and embarrassing for you. And I want to thank you for your honesty. Do not ever, *ever* again sneak around this house and violate the privacy of your family. Do you understand?"

"Yes, Great-Grandmother."

"Yes, Great-Grandmother."

"I purchased this book, this *Aristotle's Masterpiece*, three years before my son Titus was born. First published in 1759, it is meant to be a medical guide for midwives to aid in the delivery and care of babies. It is a manual filled with important information for young married men and women who are about ready to start having a family. It has a section of approved home remedies for certain ailments."

She leaned over and turned from side to side to look deep into the blinking eyes of each boy and then sat up straight once more to continue. "I shall not attempt to read the entire book to you. Once you attain an appropriate age, I shall call you in here so you may receive appropriate instruction. For now, you will listen while I read chapter sixteen, 'The Organs of Generation in Man.' You might as well know what your bodies were made for. Now, stop your fidgeting and listen."

They nodded, speechless.

"Oh, by the way, before I begin, this book has nothing whatsoever to do with that great Greek philosopher Aristotle. But I am sure neither of you has actually ever heard of him. Next week, I will summon you here again, and I will read to you some works by the *real* Aristotle.

"Now, on with 'The Organs.' You do know what I am saying when I read the words *penis* and *testicles*, do you not?"

They both could do no more than nod their heads in affirmation.

"I expect a *verbal* answer when I pose a question."

They replied in unison, "Yes, Great-Grandmother."

"Fine. I shall proceed."

Just before the boys were about to become physically sick with the knowledge their Great-Grandmother was sharing with them, she ended the chapter. She then gave them permission to leave her room, with a warning to tell no one what had happened there today or over the past few days. They promised, gratefully.

Flying out the front door, they rounded the house at a clip; ran stumbling down the hill to the banks of Crooked Pond; stripped off their clothes; and, with a whoop and a holler, jumped in.

---

As soon as they left the room, the old woman put both books down on the settee beside her and took up her beloved stick. "You know, my dear Kiah, I do believe living here is going to be almost as interesting as living in Boston. And much better than living in that small house on Shore Street. I must admit, it is a comfort not to have to worry about those British ships any longer."

She gazed thoughtfully out the window to see a flock of ducks land on the pond. "And once I finish with the boys and that moody Anne, I think I shall attempt to kindle a fire between my adorable Abigail and that darling cousin Joshua."

She rose slowly, walked over to the open chest, and lifted out the brown ceramic bottle, continuing to talk to her deceased husband. "And now that I have these captivating adventures ahead of me, I shall attempt to not need so much of this."

She uncorked the bottle, filled her stick with as much tincture of opium as it would hold, carried the bottle to the open window, and paused before emptying the contents into the grass below.

"On second thought, Kiah, I believe it is best that I keep this." She corked the bottle and returned it to the chest. "One never knows how long my friend Mattie Burns will continue her visits to replenish my supply."

As she positioned herself comfortably on the settee once more and opened her book of poetry, the smell of honeysuckle floated into the room on the warm summer breeze. Taking a deep breath, Olivia Lyman Lyman felt she was finally home.

---

The old woman, being obsessed with the practicality and common practice of marriages between distant cousins, was able, within three years, to bring about the marriage of Abigail and Joshua, sealed with the opal ring Joshua presented to his bride. This union might not have come about at all if she had not given *Aristotle's Masterpiece* to Joshua to read, once she had shared an appropriate amount of its contents with a squirming William and a blushing Henry.

Almost giddy with that success she also, eight years later, contrived to bring the petulant Anne (whom she still called Jane from time to time just to amuse herself when observing the family's reaction) to accept William's proposal. But there was no match she could make for Henry, for he had gone to sea on a whaler out of Nantucket.

Olivia Lyman Lyman passed away at the age of ninety-three, shortly after William and Anne's wedding. One bright morning, she simply did not wake up, having made up her mind that it was time to go—a decision she had most likely come to upon realizing she had nothing better to do. She could never bear being bored.

Susanna found her lying flat on her back in bed, still as stone. While one bony hand held the brass fox head to her chin, the other clutched the shaft of the ebony walking stick. It was then that Susanna found both sections to be hollow, a few small drops of liquid spilling out on to the blanket. There was a smile on the old woman's face. Kiah had finally taken her to join him.

# Part IV

# The Adventurer—Fall 1912

*Fortune does not change men, it unmasks them.*

*—Suzanne Necker, 1739–1794*

Daniel Lyman was born on Crooked Pond in 1879. He was the second son of the family's Civil War hero, Robert Lyman, who was the son of Joshua and Abigail. Daniel was a restless soul from the first day. Born in the middle of a howling hurricane, he also howled as he thrashed about in the small "borning room" off the keeping room in the Shore Street addition. He was such a wiggler and wailer as a child that he seemed destined to go on fighting and kicking his way through life. Unfortunately, his parents left his upbringing, as well as that of his siblings, to the stern housekeeper, Mrs. Kelley.

Daniel's older sister, Emily, was kind to him, but he was constantly teased and unmercifully tormented by his older brother—Charles. This brother's taunts focused on Daniel's slight frame (he called him "the runt of the litter"), his pale skin, and the scar on the right side of his face. When Daniel was seven, Charles had pushed him off the fence into the pigsty, where he had fallen on a small shovel, leaving him with a permanent scar on his cheek—a scar shaped remarkably like the letter *C*.

Charles was especially merciless in tormenting his little brother during the midday meal when the children ate in the kitchen with

Mrs. Kelley. The housekeeper never interfered when Charles would tease and ridicule Daniel until the poor boy was choking with tears. To escape, immediately after the meal, Daniel would run to the loft in the barn, flop down on the hay, and find solace in the only thing he loved—reading.

By the age of ten, Daniel had devoured the "rags to riches" novels of Horatio Alger, which his father had collected to inspire his older son with the message of the benefits of hard work. Alger's young boy heroes would overcome insurmountable odds; befriend a benefactor; and become successful, wealthy men. Daniel identified with the characters' powerful need to change their lives.

The fictional lads were saddened by poverty; Daniel was saddened by his feelings of worthlessness. He was frustrated by not knowing how to stop the verbal abuse and scorn—the oppressive mental and physical attacks heaped on him by Charles. At the age of twelve, he ran away from home, hoping to find his benefactor in Boston. But he returned after three days when he found there were also nasty people in Boston.

For the next few years, Daniel's daily life consisted of vacillating between angry shouting and quiet brooding, his mood-of-the-minute permeating every inch of any room he happened to be standing in.

In 1897, at the age of eighteen, he knew what he had to do, and he knew it was a difficult path he was about to take. Daniel stole $200 from his father's safe, which was hidden in a bookcase in the parlor, trudged to the West Falmouth depot, and booked a seat on the New York, New Haven and Hartford Railroad to New York. Once there, he paid forty dollars to travel to San Francisco.

In the ten days it took for him to cross the continent, riding third class in a train that also pulled freight cars, he reread the six Alger books he had taken with him—*Fame and Fortune*; *Luck and Pluck*; *Rough and Ready*; *Strong and Sturdy*; *Strive and Succeed*; and, his favorite volume, *The Young Adventurer*.

In this last book, a poor boy headed west in search of gold so he could help pay the family's mortgage. Daniel headed west in search of gold so he could feel important enough to no longer be bothered by the tormenting of his brother Charles. Upon reaching San Francisco, he worked his restless way north to search for that newly discovered, shiny, yellow mineral in the wilds of the Klondike region of British Columbia. Changing his name to Herb Allen, after the initials of his hero Horatio Alger, he became an honor student in what could be called "the Horatio Alger School of Success."

Through luck and pluck, he strived and succeeded in finding gold in the rivers near Dawson. Then, after a fire almost totally destroyed that town in 1899, he ventured west on a paddle wheeler down the Yukon River to the newly discovered gold in the sandy beaches of Nome, Alaska. His rough and ready determination to never be laughed at again helped him gain fortune and fame, though the latter would be better classified as infamy.

In 1906, for reasons not to be disclosed here, he sold the deed to his claim, and left Nome suddenly one night to hightail it back to San Francisco, one step ahead of the gold diggers who were pursuing him for breaking the law. As luck seemed to have it, he left San Francisco for New York City one day before the earthquake of 1906 destroyed nearly 80 percent of the city. The catastrophe obliterated almost all traces of evidence collected by those who were wishing to punish Herb Allen.

He returned to the East Coast on a train that took only four days to cross the country, riding in first-class luxury. He arrived in New York bearing a dark, secret memory, his once slender body now filled with muscle, his pockets, trunks, and two back teeth now filled with gold.

Daniel felt he was not yet ready to return home to Crooked Pond. He wanted to be sure that, when he did, he would have the confidence to stand up to Charles. He invested half his fortune in what would turn out to be two of the most successful businesses in the country—U.S. Steel and the Union Pacific Railroad.

Daniel became a gentleman. He absorbed the necessary practices, language, and manners, along with at least a semblance of patient self-control. These qualities, along with his considerable fortune, enabled him to meet and then marry a lovely young woman, Nell Dahlgren, who was whispered to be a distant cousin of the Astors. But then, weren't they all? With this accomplishment, Daniel felt he was finally ready to return home.

In his fifteen-year absence from Cape Cod, Falmouth had changed considerably. No longer the center of sheep, hogs, and guano, the town had now become known for its cranberry bogs and strawberry farms, its sandy beaches and gracious, shingle-style hotels. The wealthy of Boston saw Falmouth as a lovely resort where they would keep their summer homes for generations to come. Even the Robert Lymans no longer lived year-round on Crooked Pond, instead spending three seasons in their large brick house in fashionable Brookline. A caretaker and his wife, the Kelleys, lived full-time in a cottage Daniel's father, Robert, had built for them out behind the barn.

Robert had also extended the west side of the house with a half Cape addition, an exact reverse design of the small half Cape that had been moved from Shore Street and attached to the east side, back in 1814.

When the family gathered on Crooked Pond to welcome Daniel home, all wondered what he would be like.

# Chapter 25

## THE LETTERS

Daniel Lyman returned home with his bride in a 1912 Model T Torpedo Runabout, one of the first ever seen in these parts. The Ford was a marvel to behold. Its body and fenders sparkled with the bright summer blue of the sky over Buzzards Bay. The auto sported a convertible, dark blue leather roof, and the tufted seat was upholstered in the same blue leather. The front of the car's engine, its two headlights and two lanterns all gleamed with a brass so brilliant it looked as though Daniel had it made out of some of the gold he had discovered. At twenty miles to the gallon, it was quite the wonderful machine.

How handsome he was, hopping jauntily out of the car and grinning broadly as he pulled off his gloves. Removing his cap and goggles, he released a crop of dark, curly hair that fell casually—short enough to expose the C-shaped scar, which no longer embarrassed him. He ran around to the other side to help his beautiful bride of one week out of the car and out of her twill duster, hat, and goggles. Then he tossed off his own duster to reveal a fine, red jacket worn over a white shirt with a high, wide-band collar, bow tie, and brown knickers.

A pale, thin, sad, and angry boy had left home. A ruddy, confident, jolly young man with shining brown eyes returned. Apparently hard work had agreed with him. Finding a fortune had certainly helped.

While Nell stood smiling in a position of slender, formal elegance— her chin up, her back straight, her feet together, graceful in her fitted, dove-gray English wool day suit—she likely hoped no one would notice the nervous fidgeting of her hands.

Daniel laughed and hugged his mother and father, whom he now addressed fondly as Mamá and Papá, according to the custom of his stylish New York friends. He then playfully took up a fighting pose, punching the air while whistling and dancing around his former major tormentor, Charles, whom he now towered over. Although everyone laughed, it seemed that Charles did not appreciate the gesture. Or perhaps it was that he did not appreciate the positive attention being directed to the now very rich "little" brother he still despised.

Gladly noticing Charles's refusal to join in the fun, Daniel lifted his sister Emily by the waist to swing her in a circle. He laughed while singing a bawdy song he had heard in a bar back in Dawson.

His mother blinked joyful tears, and his father could not contain his surprised pleasure.

For the first time in the house on Crooked Pond, Daniel felt he was in control of his life. He felt worthy of the happy attention he was now given; he felt he was now an important member of his family. He immediately paid his parents back what he called his "two-hundred-dollar loan" with interest.

Daniel's parents were so proud of him and delighted with Nell that they decided to give Nell the opal ring Daniel's mother always wore—a ring that had been in the family for two hundred years. Brother Charles was more than a little angry about this, for he had always thought that, as the eldest, he would inherit the ring for his bride, if he ever found one. This made Daniel even more appreciative of the gift.

Daniel revealed his extensive plans to take his bride, the very next week, on a wedding cruise to Europe. To ensure a jovial time, he had generously insisted on taking along his two best friends from New York, Gilbert Rollins and his wife, Ethel, Nell's younger sister.

Before leaving, Daniel arranged with his father that he would take complete legal and financial control of the house and property. Robert was happy to agree, for he and Daniel's mother were spending more time in their house in Brookline. The rest of the family either lived miles away or could not afford the time or money to keep up the property.

Daniel and Nell would keep their luxury apartment in Manhattan and spend as many days as possible, plus all summer, at Crooked Pond.

The following week, promising to write his parents often to keep them up to date on his travels, he left with Nell, leaving the Model T in the barn. The couple took the train to Boston, met their friends, and boarded the RMS *Caronia* to Liverpool and then on to Naples and Rome.

—————

September 21, 1912
Savoy Hotel, Rome
Dear Papá and Mamá,

The cruise was wonderful. It took only ten days to Liverpool, but our favorite stop, once Nell and I got to this side of the Atlantic, was Gibraltar. We wish you could have seen it in the glorious moonlight. The glitter of lights on the town with the dark mountains behind was a sight we will never forget.

Our final stop on the cruise was Naples, which I thought to be the dirtiest major city I was ever in. It's no wonder the cholera and plague swept through here in the past. It is picturesque but filthy all the same.

The ride up here from Naples was quite pleasant. One would scarcely believe that the vegetation would change so quickly in about one hundred and fifty miles. We have entirely left the palms and orange and lemon and fig and olive groves. Up here it is about like home, as far as the trees go.

Rome is a delightful change from Naples in one way, for it is clean. Rome is modern, modern as can be, with finely paved streets and rows upon rows of beautiful houses and fine carriages and wonderful autos. The old ruins here are carefully preserved in among the modern things.

This afternoon, we had the fascinating experience of visiting Castello Maggiore, a twelfth-century marvel perched on a hill outside of town. A tall square tower with crenellated top stood on either end of the castle wall with a smaller, round tower in the center. We were amazed at the massive stonework. And inside, in the great hall, the walls and ceiling were painted with the most beautiful frescoes.

After visiting the wine cellar there, deep in the brick-arched underpinnings of the lovely, old castle, I have begun to seriously think of having a wine cellar of our own back home. I do have a friend who had one built in New York, and I shall ask him about it when we return.

The catacombs were all out along there, and we went down into one of the more famous ones, which has seven miles of galleries arranged in four levels. Most of the bodies are removed, but they have left a few heaps of bone and hair in glass boxes. How odd! We also saw a church where a lot of Capuchin monks live. They are all buried in the cellar when they die and, after a few years, are dug up and their bones used for ornaments.

We are all looking forward to more of the overland part of this trip. We will be in Florence and then Vienna, Budapest, Interlaken, and Paris and then on to Liverpool, from which we will sail for home on the twenty-fifth of October.

We were expecting to have a letter from you by now. I do hope one arrives before we leave here in three days, for this is the only address you have for contacting us before we reach Liverpool. We are having a most wonderful time. Nell and I send our best love to you both.

Yours aff'y,
Daniel

———◆———

Daniel went down to the lobby to post the letter to his parents and to inquire if there was any mail for him. The man at the desk handed him one with a big smile.

"I believe this letter for you is from a place in the States." He smiled, glancing at the envelope. "Brookline."

So delighted to find a dispatch from his parents' home, he quickly tipped the concierge in his usual excessive manor and then sprinted back up the stairs. He was sorry Nell had gone out for the day with Ethel and Gil. At first he thought to wait for her return before opening it to share it with her, but he could not wait. He tore open the envelope, without noticing it had not been addressed in his father's flourishing cursive script. He found the letter written in a hurried scrawl, the messy gathering of almost indecipherable words. The letter was from Charles.

---

September 10, 1912
Brookline, Mass.
Daniel,

Mother is dead. Our curtains are drawn, our clocks have been stopped, and our mirrors covered with crepe. We pondered for days whether to write to you or not, taking into consideration the fact that it would be impossible for you to get home in time for the funeral. I have gone against the wishes of Father and the rest of the family because I want you to know that our dear mother passed away just three days after you sailed. And I want you to know that I believe the excitement of your returning home after being gone so long out West was too much for her. Emily and Father insisted that telling you now would only spoil your wedding trip, but I want you to know, even if it does.

The funeral was held a week ago, and her painful death occurred in her bed in the room that will soon be yours in the house on Crooked Pond. She screamed and writhed in pain and left blood on the sheets and mattress, but certainly you can replace them. She has been buried in the family cemetery at the foot of the hill there.

Enjoy the rest of your stay. I'm sure with your newfound riches and high-society wife, you will continue to travel about in the grandest of style. Emily and I will be here in Brookline to console Father for another week, for he is terribly upset.

Charles.

Daniel slowly folded the letter, let both hands drop to his lap, and sat motionless, staring at the oriental carpet on the floor of the drawing room of their suite at the Savoy in Rome. Midmorning sunlight pouring in through the open casement windows caressed the rug, making its colors sparkle like jewels, an insult to his present state of shock.

Now he was glad he hadn't waited for Nell before reading the letter. He quickly realized this was a decision he needed to make alone, and he made it within minutes. He walked through the door to their bedroom, opened the large steamer trunk, and began to pack his clothes.

At three o'clock, Nell came bursting into the suite, flushed with pleasure. "Oh, Daniel, we have had simply the most glorious time! The castle was a complete ruin, but we were able to—"

"Stop. I want you to sit down. I have something to tell you."

"What is it?" And then, seeing his state of agitation, she added, "Are you all right?"

Taking both of her hands in his, he led her to the settee and sat down next to her. "I'm afraid I've had some very disturbing news from home." He took the letter from his pocket and handed it to her. "Please read it quietly to yourself. I cannot bear to hear his words again." He sat with his elbows resting on his knees, his head in his hands.

Nell had to read the letter twice to be sure she was not mistaking her impression of Charles's underlying intent. All she could offer were words of comfort. "I am so sorry, my darling. But you cannot hold yourself responsible. I hope you do know that."

"Of course. But *you* must understand. I am saddened by the loss of my mother. Yet at the same time, I am furious with Charles for writing the things he did."

Daniel got up and walked to the window, pulling it shut with a bang. His voice grew louder. "How in hell can he be so unkind? After all these years, he still wishes to torment me." He pounded his fist on the windowsill and then kicked a footstool to send it tumbling across the room. "Why? I thought all of that was behind us. I thought, since we were now adults, he would forget those childhood cruelties." He pounded his fist once more.

Nell was rendered speechless by this behavior, an anger she had never seen in her new husband. In the two years she had known him, Daniel had always been so mild mannered, so soft-spoken. She found her voice. "Daniel, perhaps—"

Not waiting for her to finish, he raised his eyes to the ceiling as if imploring a God he had not believed in for years. He practically screamed his words. "What does Charles want from me?"

He ran his fingers through his hair and clenched it as though he were going to pull it all out. Nell crossed over to him, wrapped her arms about his waist, and rested her head on his chest. "Hush, my darling. Please. The news of your mother's death is enough to deal with right now. Come. Sit down, and I shall call for some tea."

"*Tea?*" He threw her arms off and turned away. "I don't want any goddamned *tea*. I want another good, stiff drink!"

In five quick long strides, he was across the room at the small table that held three crystal bottles with embossed, sterling-silver labels hung around their necks. One was for scotch; one for gin; and, as a special Hotel Savoy token of appreciation for the American guests, one for Jack Daniel's Tennessee Whiskey. He refilled a crystal glass with it and tossed it down in two swallows. With difficulty, he regained a sense of composure, took a deep breath, and then gestured to his wife to join him again on the settee.

"There are some things I've not told you about Charles."

"You have said he was unkind to you."

"*Unkind* is the word a gentleman uses when trying not to offend any ladies who may be present. Charles was not just 'unkind'; he was

225

goddamned cruel, both physically and verbally. He constantly poked fun at me in front of the other kids at school and would either trip me or punch me or belittle me at home whenever he thought no one was looking."

"I'm so sorry."

Daniel leaned toward his wife until their faces were almost touching and pointed to his cheek. "See this? This scar on my face? The one I told you I got from a fall?"

"Yes, of course. You said you fell on a small shovel."

"Well, I fell all right, but it was because Charles pushed me off the fence into a pigsty when I was seven." He stood up and turned to her. "And, do you know what else? He tied me to a tree in the woods and left me crying there for hours! When I was ten and Charles had a bad cold, he blew his nose into his handkerchief and then rubbed his snot into my face and mouth!"

"Stop! That's enough! I don't want to hear any more. I understand." She covered her ears with her hands and turned her head so she would not have to look at his rage.

"Oh no, that's not enough." He roughly pulled her hands away and held them, forcing her to look at him. "On the playground at school once, he pushed me down into a pile of dog shit and then dragged me over to his bully friends to tell them I had soiled my pants. And then all the other kids gathered around and joined them, laughing at me."

He pointed his finger at her. "Do you know what if feels like to have all the kids you know laugh at you? No, of course not, because you were brought up in an atmosphere of gentility, where good manners and proper behavior were practiced by all."

He let go of her hands and dropped back onto the settee, holding his head in his hands. His voice was quiet. "And now he's into psychological cruelty. He's blaming me for my mother's death."

They sat in silence for a few moments, and then she gently rubbed his back. "What do you think we should do?"

"Think? I don't have to think. I've made up my mind. I know exactly what *I'm* going to do, and it's up to you to agree with me and head for home immediately. Or you may stay here with your sister and Gil and see the sights of Europe."

"Of course I'll go home with you. There is no question, if that's what you've decided."

He took her in his arms, trying to calm down. "Nell, thank you. I'm sorry for what I said about your upbringing. Gentility and good manners are what I have strived to attain."

"And you have, my dear, except for this outburst."

He kissed her lightly on the cheek. "I promise we'll return to complete our tour another time. I can't say when, but we will. Right now, I strongly feel that I've neglected my family responsibilities for too long." He thought for a moment before adding, "And this is the best time to finally set things straight with Charles. I believed that my success out west would be enough to silence him, but apparently it wasn't."

He held her at arm's length, as if attempting to keep her at a distance from the long-repressed anger he had felt. "I will never again allow his innuendos to torment me. Yes, we shall return to comfort Papá. But I am most assuredly determined to settle things with Charles once and for all." He continued, not realizing he was gently shaking her, "He cannot continue to throw these verbal barbs. He would have to be stupid to think I won't notice that he intentionally intends to agitate me. And I know damn well Charles is not stupid."

"Be careful of Charles, Daniel." Nell pulled away. "Even I, in the short time spent in his presence, have seen he has a vile temper. I thought he was actually going to strike you when you laughed over the wine he had spilled at dinner."

"Don't worry. I learned my lessons well on how to deal with vile tempers in those filthy, brawling bar rooms of Alaska. And I learned more civilized ways in New York." To himself, Daniel thought, *I just hope I can remember to curb my temper. If I am to become a true gentleman, I must.*

Nell turned away from him and walked across the room.

"Nell?"

"I am going to pack my trunk. We will talk with Ethel and Gil at dinner. I do think we should encourage them to stay."

"I agree."

"Daniel, you must calm down and see what you can do to arrange transportation home and then cable Father to let him know when to expect us to arrive."

"I have already done so. The concierge is arranging for the two of us to leave on the first train to Liverpool. The *Laconia* leaves there for Boston on the twenty-eighth. Once the reservations are made, I will cable Father at his office in Boston. Thank you, Nell," he paused, "for not asking me to cancel your tickets."

As she went to pack her trunk, she said, "I do believe you know me quite well, Daniel. I wonder if I know you as well."

# Chapter 26

## THE HOMECOMING

Upon debarking in Boston, Daniel and Nell had immediately gone to his father's house in Brookline. Robert and Daniel consoled each other for their loss that first night at dinner. But on the second night, Robert introduced them to an attractive dinner guest who had lost her husband a year ago.

"Elizabeth and her recently deceased husband, Gregory, were close friends with your mother and I for years," Robert explained. "And now we are able to comfort each other, recall all the good old days, and enjoy some new adventures together." He reached out and covered her hand with his as they smiled at each other.

Daniel had never seen his father smile at his mother this way.

The attractive woman with powdered face, bright red lipstick, and black eyeliner now patted their two hands with her free hand and then rested it there. She smiled at Daniel and Nell. "Oh, yes. And I am so pleased to finally meet you and your new wife, Daniel. I have already met your sister, the darling Emily, her husband, and your brother, Charles."

"Fine," said Daniel. "And how has Charles been lately?"

Nell gave him a cautionary glance.

"Oh, he is ... well, I believe."

Her hesitation made Daniel look at his father with raised eyebrows.

"Charles will always be Charles," Robert said with a shake of his head.

Elizabeth laughed and then pulled her hands away and clasped them together with a clap. "If I do say so, one must ask Mrs. Kelley, the housekeeper, if one wants to find out about Charles!"

"Elizabeth, please." Robert was briefly annoyed and then changed his tone. "My dear, we will have time later to discuss the family, but first we must find out more about the trip Daniel and his sweet wife took." He turned to his son. "Now, what was your favorite part?"

Seeing the way his father and Elizabeth looked at each other and hearing the plans they had for the next few days and weeks, Daniel could tell his father was neither lonely nor in any further need of his comfort. He and Nell left for Crooked Pond the next day.

Now that he was the new owner of the property, he was anxious to become more familiar with how it may have changed in the years he had been away. He began to think more seriously about making plans for a wine cellar.

———◆———

The caretaker of the house on Crooked Pond, Ian Kelley, had met Daniel and Nell at the West Falmouth Station with the carriage, and they were on their way home, all three longing to be sitting beside a crackling fire.

Oak leaves, ever reluctant to leave their branches until new buds would force them off, hung and quivered in their tired russet glory. The smell of wood smoke mingled with those of the pine and juniper on this chilled, foggy Cape Cod afternoon.

Riding up the long drive to the house, Daniel realized how he had loved and missed these woods, with the squirrels scampering about leaping from tree to tree, the osprey circling overhead, and the announcements of the crows. He knew the stories about how what was now a thick forest had, years ago, been acres and acres of open pasturelands and vast cornfields. Upon their first return home, he had hardly noticed anything, due to his excitement over showing the family his new bride, his new car, and his worldly success; and finally claiming his rights to a newfound respect in their eyes. This time, he was savoring the vital beauty of the place.

They had just climbed the low hill and rounded the last corner, bringing the house into view. "There she is," cried their driver. Although shrouded in fog, the house still asserted itself with its facade of perfect symmetry. Two half Capes clung to the sides of the tall saltbox like twin children hugging the skirts of a loving, protective mother. Huge English oak trees sheltered the house, running along the back from one side to the other and leaving the entire front of the house free to boast a wide, green lawn. Smoke billowed from all three chimneys, signaling to the two new occupants that they were welcome to sit at any fireside they chose. As they came within a hundred feet of the house, the dirt driveway changed to one of white, crushed clamshells that crunched under the wheels of the carriage.

Nell snuggled up to Daniel, holding on to his arm. "It is indeed such a lovely place, Daniel. And I am so looking forward to living the rustic life ... as long as we keep our place in Manhattan."

"Of course we will. And I must tell you, I am looking at it differently now that there isn't the passel of family members crowding about."

He leaned forward, reached out, and tugged on the back of the driver's jacket. "I must thank you, Ian, for taking such good care of the place," said Daniel as he looked around in admiration. "The lawn, the shrubbery, the walks, the fences are all in perfect shape. How do you ever manage to keep the leaves off this driveway?"

"Well, I don't do it alone, ye know." Ian laughed as he pulled the horse to a stop at the front door.

"Yes, that reminds me," said Daniel. "I'd like to talk to you about the help and other matters involving the management of the house and grounds, say ... in the library tomorrow at ten?"

"Yes. Sure an' I'll be more than happy to meet with ye there."

Daniel held out his hand to help Nell down as he continued talking with Ian. "Good. Now please take these trunks into the house. The other baggage should be arriving soon, hopefully before the rain." He looked around and shivered as the thickening fog began to leave a shine on their coats, and the first few drops of rain fell heavily on their shoulders.

Taking Nell by the arm, he quickly led her onto the pink granite front stoop. A flash of lightning, followed by a loud clap of thunder startled them just as the door opened. The caretaker's wife, an unsmiling Mrs. Kelley, grumbled a welcome. Daniel could never understand how Ian could remain so cheerful when married to a woman as sullen and mean-spirited as this.

As soon as they refreshed themselves from the long drive, Daniel took Nell into the parlor to show her a special surprise he had for her. Knowing it would contribute greatly to her contentment while spending time here on Cape Cod, Daniel had bought her an exact replica of the piano in their apartment in New York. It had been delivered by schooner to Falmouth Inner Harbor while they were on their cruise. Nell was delighted. She could sit and play for hours.

The next day's meeting with Ian brought bad news.

"Sure and 'tis not my wish to spoil yer first full day here, Daniel, but I wonder if ye had a chance to go out to the barn yet?"

"No, we were just settling in. And with yesterday's rain, I've not had the opportunity. What's out there that I should know about?"

"Come, I'll show ye." Ian led the way. The big barn door scratched and squeaked as he pulled it open. There stood Daniel's Model T, its right front fender crushed.

"What happened?" Daniel stood in shocked disbelief and then immediately came to a conclusion. "Wait. Let me guess," he said. "Charles?"

"I'm afraid 'tis so."

Daniel ran his hand lightly over the rough tangle of blue metal as he inspected the damage. "Damn him!"

Then, feeling his anger with Charles rise once again within him, he made a fist. "Damn him to hell!" He pounded the sharp edges of the crumpled fender, cutting his hand. "The bastard! Will he never stop?" He sucked the blood from the side of his hand before wrapping it in his handkerchief, immediately registering the thought that his anger was beginning to surface more frequently, now that Charles was back in his life.

Ever since reading Charles's letter in Rome, and especially now that he was back in his boyhood home, unpleasant thoughts and memories of his brother seemed to crop up everywhere. *Was it a mistake to move back here, even to live here only part-time?* Where was the anger control he'd worked so hard to achieve? And where was the gentleman he believed he was becoming?

Ian brought him back to Charles's latest act. "I tried to stop him, but he and an old friend from Falmouth insisted on taking it out every day and driving it around town the whole week after yer mother's funeral. Charles told me he had never even been in a motorcar before, let alone driven one. He not only used up all the gasoline but came home the day before he left for Brookline with this crushed fender. I'm sorry, Daniel. 'Twas a beauty."

Regaining his composure, Daniel said, "Well, you have nothing to be sorry for, Ian. It was not your fault. Nothing and no one can stop Charles from getting what he wants. Don't worry. It will take time, but the car can be repaired."

———

Daniel looked out over the pond. He'd come here upon leaving the barn with his damaged car. It occurred to him that, when he had said that no one could stop Charles, he had been wrong. *He* was going to stop Charles. But he wasn't going to just walk up and punch his brother in the face. No. Those days were a thing of the past. He would no longer let his temper dictate his actions. He was going to get even with his brother in a way that would prove he was now a gentleman, a way that would psychologically crush this hated sibling.

Knowing his brother's affinity for fine wines, Daniel would build an elaborate wine cellar, like the one he had seen in Rome. It would add a touch of elegance to what he would soon be calling his "country estate." He couldn't wait to see the look on Charles's face when he showed it to him. There was his revenge, his ultimate satisfaction—seeing Charles become insanely jealous. After he had shown it to Charles, he would tell him that he never wanted to see him again, that he was never to return to the house on Crooked Pond.

Daniel had already invited Charles; Emily and her husband, Willis; and Ethel and Gil to gather at Crooked Pond for his father's birthday on December 20 and stay through Christmas week—just two months away. Daniel wanted the wine cellar to be finished and fully stocked by the time everyone arrived. It would be a complete surprise and would solidify their new impression of him as a gentleman.

He would contact his good friend, Jiles Whitney in New York, for the name of the Italian brick mason who had built the wine cellar for Jiles's country home in Scarsdale. The mason's qualifications were excellent. Luigi Landucci had formerly built wine cellars of brick back in Italy but had immigrated to the States, along with hundreds of other Italian masons, to work on the Croton Dam. This huge stone-and-cement structure had been built about twenty miles north of New York City to supply the city with water. After the dam was completed in 1906, the mason and his family moved into the city, where Jiles had heard of Landucci's good work.

Daniel was sure he could secure the services of this man, for he would provide an excellent wage, plus housing for the mason and his wife. He was going to expand and renovate the old living quarters with the fireplace in the barn for them. The dozen or so able-bodied helpers needed for the brickwork and carpentry would be easily found among the young men of Falmouth, now that the summer tourist season was over, and no more fields needed tending.

But the number-one priority on Daniel's list, which would facilitate the implementation of the other two, was to have telephone service installed in the house. Already, telephone lines ran along the road leading past his driveway from West Falmouth to East Falmouth. Electric lights had been installed throughout the house, but apparently his father hadn't deemed it necessary to have a telephone line connected. All Robert had needed was one personal phone in his Brookline house and a couple of phones in his office in Boston. When spending summers at Crooked Pond, he had not wanted to be disturbed with a phone call. Daniel was not about to adopt such an isolated existence.

The day after he and Ian went over all the plans for the house and grounds, Daniel drove the carriage into Falmouth to request telephone service and arrange with a builder to immediately begin the work of making more room in the barn for the brick mason's family. He then cabled his friend Jiles in New York to set in motion the first steps in the construction of his wine cellar.

Within three days, the renovation of the small room in the barn had begun. By using wood from most of the twenty-four horse and ox stalls, which were no longer needed, the hired hands were able to quickly add on two rooms for sleeping quarters, as well as enlarge the original keeping room there.

Within a week, Luigi Landucci and his wife arrived from New York. The short, stocky man had big hands. His curly, black hair and sideburns were just starting to streak with gray, as if attempting to catch up with the full gray mustache that underlined and drew attention to his large, bulbous nose. His short, stocky wife was blessed with the most constantly cheerful expression Daniel had ever seen. The Landuccis were soon comfortably settled in their quarters in the barn, marveling over the best living conditions they had ever experienced.

---

While Daniel was occupied from dawn till dusk with supervising the outside work, Nell spent her days focused on the household help. Although accustomed to dealing with servants, she struggled with understanding the broken English of the cheerful Maria Landucci, who was to be their cook. Maria, who had years of experience in Italian restaurants in New York, was a most welcomed addition to the staff at Crooked Pond. For Nell, this language struggle was a joy compared to trying to understand the motives of the stern housekeeper, Mrs. Kelley, a thin Irish woman who could not seem to praise enough the virtues of Charles Lyman.

"Yes, that Charles, sure and he was as fine a young child as any mother could hope for," she said to Nell one morning, after being asked about her early days with the Lyman family. They were in the dining room, where Nell was sorting out the silverware that needed to be polished.

Mrs. Kelley continued. "Never cried for more than a minute or two at a time, that little darlin'. He was in my charge, of course, and as he was the firstborn, I allowed him to do most anything he wished. I still believe lettin' a boy have his own way helps him to grow up to be a true leader of men."

"And after the other children arrived?" Nell inquired. "Daniel seems to remember being teased mercilessly by his brother Charles."

"Well, that was Daniel. Daniel was the baby—and quite the angry, snivelin' weaklin', I must add. I didn't see any damage being done. Of *course* his brother teased him. 'Tis only natural."

Nell was not about to let up. "It seems you favored Charles over the others."

"Yes, I did. Was my favorite then, an' still is. I'll not pretend to feel differently, and that's not going to change. I'll always wait at the door for him to arrive. Now that he lives in Pittsfield, his visits are few and far between. But when he's here, my days are the happiest." She snatched up the pile of tarnished knives, forks, and spoons and headed for the kitchen.

———◆———

That evening, Nell and Daniel sat at the dinner table waiting for Maria to bring in one of her special Italian entrées. Luigi's wife of thirty years had simmered chicken with a tomato sauce from her own preserved tomatoes, grown in the rooftop garden she had kept above their small apartment in New York. Upon the move to Crooked Pond, cases of her preserved fruits and vegetables had come with her.

While finishing the last of their first course of beef consommé, Nell decided to share with Daniel the conversation she'd had with Mrs. Kelley that morning. But as soon as she mentioned Charles, Daniel held out his hand to stop her.

"Nell, please. I have enough to think about right now with all the construction going on. I do not want to discuss Charles. Just the mere mention of his name gives me a headache." He closed his eyes, shook his head, and continued. "I've told you, I will deal with him when he gets here in December, when the rest of the family arrives."

"Well, my darling, I am sorry. But I must know just one thing. Was Mrs. Kelley totally responsible for the care and upbringing of you children?"

"Yes, she was our nanny for as long as I can remember. Now that is all. No more questions. Please."

Nell persisted. "But what about your mother and father? While Mrs. Kelley saw nothing wrong with the way your brother treated you, didn't your parents notice?"

Daniel sat back in his chair and closed his eyes. He said quietly, "Nell, I will have no more of this. If we're going to live in this house, it'll be totally in the present, looking toward the future. I will not be reminded of my unhappy past within these walls."

Then his voice rose, becoming louder with each word. "I've told you time and again that I'll take care of this when I'm ready, and not a minute before. Do you understand?" He pushed his chair back, stood up, leaned toward her, and slammed his hand on the table. "I will have no more of this!"

His words flew out just as Maria entered the room bearing her steaming platter of chicken. Feeling deeply hurt that he did not like what she was serving, she turned around and headed back to the kitchen with tears dripping onto the chicken.

"Now look what you've done," Nell said to Daniel. Then she called to Maria, "We are sorry, Maria. Please, you may bring dinner to the table. Mr. Lyman was not talking about your cooking."

# Chapter 27

## THE CAVE

Luigi Landucci stood among the gravestones in the Lyman family burial grounds behind the house, at the bottom of the hill next to the pond. His bulbous nose was red from the chill, his muscular arms folded as he pondered his task. Being a man of precise calculations, he admired the way the graves were laid out facing the pond in five straight rows, ten to a row. While pondering the various ways his client's new wine cellar might be constructed, he walked among the stones, bending over to pick up small dead branches and twigs that had been blown down during last night's windstorm. He piled them carefully next to the road that led up to the house. He would gather them, on his way back to the barn, to use for firewood.

He looked again at the hill and then took from his pocket the sketches Daniel had made, drawn from his memory of one of the smaller cellars at Castello Maggiore. It was to be a circular brick shaft dug straight down from under the west wing of the house, with a spiral staircase leading to the bottom where his wines would be stored. Looking at the plan, Luigi laughed heartily, shook his head, and tore the paper into little pieces.

"Arrivederci," he said.

Tossing the bits of paper up with both hands to the light breeze, he watched as they blew out over the pond, scattering, and then swaying gently down to float on the surface of the water, much like the brown oak leaves would soon be falling to the ground in the adjoining woodlands.

He did not need these drawings. While living in Rome, he had been to the caves of Castello Maggiore many times to repair some of the crumbling brick archways there. He knew the place well, brick by brick.

When the last piece of Daniel's paper landed on the water, Luigi looked again at the steep bank of the hill and then up at the house. The ideas in his head were no longer arguing with each other. He now knew exactly what he wanted to do.

Instead of a hill covered with tangles of wild grape and cat's-claw briars, Luigi saw a heavy, arched wooden door with wrought iron hinges built into the side of the hill. This door would open into a magnificent brick cave he would create for storing the wine, and this wine cave would be his masterpiece. All he needed to do was convince Mr. Lyman that a man with an estate such as this one on Crooked Pond needed a far more glorious and extensive wine cellar than the one originally planned. He needed a wine cave as fine as the finest in Italy. This plan would keep the Landucci couple employed here for a long time.

Just then he heard the sound of a horse snorting as it trotted down the road. He looked to see Mr. Lyman coming to join him. He hoped his boss would not notice the pieces of paper floating on the pond.

Daniel dismounted. "Good morning, Luigi. I was hoping to find you somewhere on the grounds but didn't expect it to be here."

Luigi removed his hat and held it in his hands. "I like to take a look around before the men come, boss."

"Fine. And what have you discovered?"

"You say there's a bank of clay here under the house?"

"Yes. It was discovered years ago, when my father had the west wing built on. As the men dug the round cellar under the house, they found it was entirely of clay, and that's why I want you to dig down under that cellar to create my wine cellar. He swept his hand through the air in an arc that encompassed the entire cemetery. "Every time another family member was placed in a grave here, more clay was found." His eyes lingered on the most recent grave, its pink granite stone engraved with his mother's name.

Luigi followed his look and saw fresh flowers on the mound beside the stone. He could read the name engraved there. "I'm sorry, boss. This woman who died last month, your mama?"

"Yes. Thank you. Now, where are the plans I drew up for you?"

"If I may, boss"—Luigi turned the hat in his hands as if feeling the brim to see if the drawing were there and then shifted his weight from one foot to the other—"I have another idea you might like better."

"Go on," said Daniel. "And, Luigi, stop turning that hat. Put it on your head. It's cold out."

Luigi did what he was told. "Well, boss, I know you have plans to dig down from the cellar under the house to hollow out a place for your wine, but I think you will like it more if we also tunnel in from here to meet the shaft going down from the house. I have done this before. Your wine cellar will be an exact copy of the one at Castello Maggiore, only ... smaller."

"Go on." Daniel's interest was sparked.

"Just as you suggested, we'll start digging the opening in the clay floor of your bean pot cellar in the west wing. And we'll dig a round shaft about six feet in diameter but ... judging from what I see here"— he looked up the hill to the foundation of the house—"instead of going down ten feet like you said, we'll dig to about twenty-four feet deep."

"Isn't that a long way down to get a bottle of wine?"

"Yes, it is, but only when you have to go all the way to the bottom." Luigi's gestures with each idea painted a clear picture for Daniel. "My plan is to build shelves for bottles winding down the inside of the brick-lined shaft, with access from a spiral, wrought iron staircase. Oh, boss, bellissimo! It'll be beautiful!" He kissed his fingers and flung the kisses into the air.

Daniel smiled at the enthusiasm of the mason. "But why tunnel in all the way from down here?"

"I'm sure you're the kind of man who'll want to import cases of the best Italian wine." Luigi congratulated himself on remembering to flatter the man from whom he wanted to get something. "You'll have the cases delivered by having them driven down this road," he went on, "so they may be easily placed in the cellar through a door that'll enter the cave right about ... there." Luigi ran over to the side of the hill, where he outlined the future door with his arms, and then returned to where Daniel was standing.

"Boss, this wine cave will be the most beautiful one in this part of the world! In the cave, there'll be large arches of brick, with niches along the walls for storing the bottles. And the temperature will be just about perfect. Then, as the wine ages properly in the bottles, you have them moved up to the niches in the side of the shaft, to take their place in the wall with easy access from the house."

Daniel thought for a minute before speaking. "This is a much grander project than I had planned for. Although I believe it's a wonderful idea, I want my wine cellar completed before my family arrives, and I don't think your plans can meet this deadline."

Luigi's entire body sank with a deep sigh, as if it were going to melt into the ground. He had learned a lot about dramatic effect from a cousin who was an actor in Palermo. He looked out at the pond, squinted his eyes, and ran his hand through his graying hair as if scratching his scalp would solve the problem. He would need a much greater labor force if this project was to be accomplished on time, but he hesitated to ask for it outright. Luigi knew how to convince a rich man to spend his money without actually asking for it.

"You're right, boss. All I can promise is that the brick shaft with the shelves and the spiral staircase will be done by then. It will be beautiful, and you can have a few cases of your favorite wines stored there. With our limited workforce, I might be able to make a rough tunnel to connect the shaft to the outside here before your family arrives. But as for those grand arches in the cave, I'm sorry." He shook his head and stared at the ground. "There will not be enough time for such a glorious effort." He removed his hat again and waited, head down, twirling it once more in his hands. He glanced sideways to see if his boss was reconsidering.

"What if I'm able to contract with more laborers?"

Luigi broke into a big grin. "In that case, I'll try my best. I know I can contact at least six masons from New York who know the building methods used in Italy a thousand years ago. That's all I can promise, boss. I think we can do it. It's up to you to get the lumber for supports, the bricks, and the cement here."

"By tomorrow morning, Luigi, give me a list of everything you'll need. I'll see to it that everything gets here as soon as possible."

He clapped Luigi on the back. "I thank you for your idea to build the grand cave into the hill here. I'm sure you will have it completed in time." He mounted and was ready to ride up the hill when Luigi stopped him, knowing he had nothing to lose by asking for more.

"Oh … one other idea I have, boss. Your cave would truly be even more beautiful if you have its vaulted ceiling plastered and painted with frescoes, like you saw at Maggiore."

"And how do you expect to accomplish this? Are you an artist too?"

"Oh no, boss. But I have a younger brother in Rome who is an expert at it. If you could make arrangements to bring him here … I mean … the frescoes would not be completed right away. But he could stay in the barn with Maria and me and could help with the bricks too, before the ceiling was ready for him to paint." Luigi realized he was rambling on but just had to get it all out at once before his courage left him. "Just knowing Sal would be coming here to work with me would make my work go a lot faster, boss."

"All right, Luigi. Contact him, and I'll make the arrangements." Daniel laughed and shook his head, mounted his horse, and proceeded up the path.

Once Daniel was out of sight, Luigi fell to his knees, blessed himself, and clasped his hands in prayer. "Dear Blessed Virgin Mary Mother of God, I didn't really lie about finishing in time, you know. I'll try, but I do believe it's impossible. Please forgive me." He got up and then quickly knelt down once more. "Oh, one more thing. Please make Sal's trip across the ocean a safe one."

# Chapter 28

## The Shaft

Within a week, the Lyman property on Crooked Pond took on the appearance of a vast construction site as men began work on the wine cave. Tons of bricks packed in straw arrived in Falmouth by train from the Bridgewater Brickyard north of the Cape and were transported by ox-drawn wagons to the property. Lumber, to form supports for the cave and shaft, was also delivered by train and then by wagon. Daniel was able to rent two trucks, driven down from Boston, to help with all of this, resulting in a constant dust and din of creaking, clattering, chugging, clanging, scraping, and shouting that reminded him of his days of hard work and heavy drinking back in the Northwest.

Once enough materials had been delivered and the labor force assembled, the first project was to dig an entrance and ramp into the side of the bean pot cellar under the west wing. This was necessary so the movement of men and material could take place without their having to pass through the house. Daniel divided this workforce into three categories—diggers, carriers, and drivers. The diggers shoveled the soil into buckets, the carriers lugged the buckets out and emptied them into a wagon, and the drivers took it all to dump into a depression to the east of the property.

When the outside ramp was complete, excavation of the shaft and cave began. While six men worked on digging down and removing clay to construct the shaft, eight more started to tunnel into the hill by the graveyard. Daniel couldn't help but worry if Luigi's calculations were correct and whether the vertical shaft and horizontal tunnel would meet where Luigi said they would. But that was not his only worry.

One evening he and Nell sat together, wrapped in the warmth of a roaring fire that blazed in the large fireplace in the library of the main house. She snuggled up against him, a move that usually resulted in his putting his arm around her, but he sat motionless. He was exhausted. Trying to pull this project together so it would be completed on time was taking its toll. Everything annoyed him lately.

Nell lifted his seemingly lifeless arm and put it around her shoulders. He still did no more than stare at the fire.

"Daniel," she said, "please tell me. Is there another problem with the construction? There seems to be something new every day that carries you farther and farther away from me."

"No, no, I'm sorry. I know I've been neglecting you. It's just …" He paused and then decided to share his thoughts with her. "Now that we're about six weeks away from when the family is to arrive, I'm realizing how much more has to be done. The cellar *must* be finished before the family, and especially Charles, gets here."

"And why is that so important? I'm sure he will find something to criticize no matter how wonderful it is."

"Of course he will. But the more finished it is, the more his envy will be tearing his insides out. He loves wine. Remember how he boasted about his knowledge of the various vintages when we were here last?"

"Yes. He did go on so, as though he thought you knew nothing about wines at all. And I also noticed how surprised he was when he found out you did."

"Well, once he has turned sufficiently green over my marvelous wine cellar, I'll make it clear to him that his cruel behavior will not be tolerated. It's important to me that he be so envious he'll never want to return. But just in case, I'll tell him that, after this Christmas, he will never be welcomed here again."

"Even if he stops his nasty behavior?"

"Nell, the more I think of Charles, the more I'm certain he will never change. He didn't change in all the years I was away. Why should he change now?"

"Is he arriving on the nineteenth along with everyone else?"

"Yes. Even though Charles doesn't answer my letters or phone calls, Father assures me he has been in touch with him and that he will arrive on the same train as Emily and her husband."

"Well, Mrs. Kelley and I have been preparing the guest bedrooms to be sure everyone is as comfortable as possible."

"And I assume Mrs. Kelley is still lauding the merits of her dear Charles?"

"Well," said Nell, pausing before going on. "Just this morning, Mrs. Kelley and I had a major disagreement over which bedroom her dear Charles would have. She wanted to put him in the larger room over the east wing, which would leave a smaller room for Emily and her husband."

"I still don't see why she favors him." Daniel stood up, walked to the fireplace, placed both hands on the mantel, and stared into the fire. He could feel his level of control diminishing whenever his brother was discussed.

"If it weren't for the long time Ian has worked for the family, I would get rid of the Kelleys, but I hate to think about letting Ian go. He knows more about running this place than I do. Yet, he *is* getting on in years, and his painful leg seems to have gotten much worse since we saw him in September." Daniel thought for a moment and then added, "I simply cannot *begin* to think right now of training a new caretaker!" He kicked at a smoldering log.

Nell tried to soothe him. "Well, my darling, if Mrs. Kelley's only fault is her preoccupation with Charles, I believe we can tolerate that."

Daniel spun around, shooting her an angry, questioning look. "What do you mean she is preoccupied with him? Is she not doing her work? Really, Nell, I'm leaving the running of this household up to you. I have enough to do. I cannot be responsible for this too."

"I say she is preoccupied with him because she constantly talks about him. Every day, it's 'Charles used to do this' or 'Charles loved that' or 'I remember when Charles ...' whatever. It does get rather tiresome. Sometimes I think she is deliberately trying to provoke me. And she must be succeeding, because I find myself either trying to avoid her or to mollify her. I gave her a book from the Boston School of Housekeeping, which did nothing but insult her. She told me that Charles would not think her housekeeping needed improvement. I actually overheard her talking to him on the telephone the other day when she thought I was upstairs."

"What? He talks to our housekeeper? Why didn't you tell me?"

"Because I didn't want to upset you, like I obviously have just now." She stood up and put her hand on his arm. "Lately, you've been snapping at everyone, including me. You used to confide in me, sharing your dreams as well as your concerns. We used to laugh together. Now you shut yourself off and … you're different. I'm worried about you. You are not the man I married. Look at yourself … your hair, your beard, your constant disheveled appearance. I am beginning to wish you would forget about trying to finish this cursed wine cellar before the family arrives."

"Well, you're not going to get your wish!" He abruptly brushed away her hand and stormed out of the room, slamming the door. For the first time in years, Daniel felt like running to the loft in the barn to escape into the pages of a book.

---

Nell could not sleep. She lay alone in bed waiting for Daniel, but to no avail. Just after she heard the hall clock chime the hour of midnight, she heard him come up the stairs, walk down the hall, and then open and shut the door to one of the guest bedrooms. By the time she heard the two o'clock chime, she decided to give up trying to sleep.

Stepping softly to go down the hall past the room where she could hear Daniel's muffled snoring, she peered through the open door of one of the other bedrooms. Moonlight shone in through the window, brightening the colorful patchwork quilts on the twin beds, giving them a look of peaceful charm. This comforted her yet at the same time made her feel even sadder as she stood there. Before, every time she had looked into this room, she would imagine seeing their children one day snuggled up in these beds. Tonight, she was beginning to doubt it would ever happen. She returned to her empty bed.

The next morning's sunlight streamed through the two south-facing windows in the parlor. Nell walked about the room. She ran her fingers over her three favorite books, which were piled one on top of the other on one of the shelves, thinking fondly of the memories they brought. The beautifully bound small books had been a gift from her father seven years ago. She treasured these works of Tennyson, Shakespeare, and Longfellow, but reading Tennyson's poems was her favorite pastime. Now she longed for the peace of those days.

She sat down at her piano and halfheartedly tried to decide what to play. She shuffled through her music collection merely for suggestions, not for instruction, for she could play almost all without needing to read the music. She finally settled on Mozart. His twenty-first piano concerto laced slow, dark tones with the same sad, uneasiness she herself felt on this morning, twelve hours after her husband had walked out of the room, slamming the door. She had not seen Daniel since.

She placed the pile of music on the top of her new, cherished piano. It was an elegant mahogany upright with five arched panels of mythological paintings running along the front of the cabinet. As she began to play, swaying with the music, her eyes soon focused on the middle panel. Nell paused, placing her hands on her lap. How appropriate, she thought, reading the title under the painting, "The Judgment of Midas."

She sat, oblivious to the rumblings of the wagons and shouts of the workers outside, unmindful of the sweet aroma of Maria's bread baking in the kitchen. She recalled the story of Midas, the king who got his wish that everything he touched would turn to gold. How fine that was, until he touched a person he loved and she, too, turned to gold—gold that was bright and shining and valuable but, at the same time, hard and solid and silent.

As her fingers returned once again to the ivory keys, the major and minor notes woven throughout the music filled her with a sense of longing for the sweet, peaceful days back in the city when her husband's greatest concerns were about choosing when to attend the latest opera. By the time she had finished the piece, she knew what she had to do.

---

Nell waited until early that afternoon, when Ian left to drive his wife and Maria to the market in town. Standing at the window to watch the carriage pull out of the driveway, she entered the west wing and looked down into the cellar where the men were excavating at about halfway down the shaft. A cold blast of air rose from the ramp, which was open to the outside, sending shivers throughout her body as she breathed in the smell of the earth. She saw Daniel pacing back and forth on the dirt floor of the bean pot cellar, calling down to the men, telling them how to do what they already knew how to do. Feeling safe that she would not be disturbed, she moved quickly back to the library, picked up the telephone, and placed a call to New York.

---

That evening, she and Daniel sat across the dinner table from each other, with barely ten words passing between them. Finally Nell spoke up. "Daniel, I have decided to go away for a while."

"*What?*" His question was as curtly posed as she had expected.

"I am going to visit with my family in New York. I'll be staying in our apartment there. It will be good for me to spend some time with Father and Mother before the holidays begin. And I believe you'll be better off here without me while you tend to your project."

"You're leaving me?" He was surprised at how much the thought bothered him. "Do you know how much I count on you being here, sitting at the piano, filling the room with your Mozart and Beethoven and Chopin? I may not have taken the time lately to mention any of this to you, but you *must* know how important you are to me."

She took a sip of Chardonnay. "I'll only be gone for a few weeks. I'll leave next week and return a day before everyone arrives in December. This will give me time to make all the arrangements for the holidays, to leave instructions for Maria and Mrs. Kelley, and to obtain my train reservations."

"Look, Nell, if this is about last night—"

She raised her hand to stop him. "Of *course* it is. But it took last night to convince me that I'm just another burden for you to endure while you focus your attention on the completion of the wine cellar. This way, you'll have an entire month to do nothing but devote your time to getting the work done."

Putting down his fork, he pushed back from the table and went to her. Taking her hands, he gently pulled her to her feet. "I've never, ever thought of you as a burden."

"I know it was not intentional, but it was there," she said. "Daniel, I do realize just how important this project is to you. And because I can't understand why it is so, I truly believe the only way I can be of any help is to be away from it all."

"But, Nell—"

"You will get along just fine. It will only be for a few weeks. And then we will have a glorious reunion and a happy holiday with the family here. And your wine cellar will be a greatly admired surprise." She took his face in her hands, kissed him, and smiled.

# Chapter 29

## THE ARRIVALS

The wind screamed, banging the shutters with a sound that reminded Daniel of the shooting of guns in the gambling houses of Dawson. But that shooting noise had been purely for fun. This storm seemed bent on destruction. It was the beginning of December, unusually early for such weather on the Cape. The blizzard tossed heavy, wet snow, breaking branches and knocking down entire trees, some of which had grown on the property for more than a hundred years. Downed telephone poles left all of Cape Cod without its treasured new electricity and phone service. And as the snowstorm raged along the New England coast, all work, except emergency services, ceased from Providence to Portland.

It was evening when Daniel paced the floor in the candlelit parlor, clutching a glass of Jack Daniels, while the howling wind piled a foot of white wonder up against the front door with promises of more to come. Now all plans for completing his project had to be put on hold until the storm passed and cleanup efforts could begin. The roads and driveway would have to be passable to permit delivery of the final supply of bricks and the spiral staircase.

The family was due to arrive in sixteen days. Normally, that would have been enough time to get the work done. But with the storm, the loss of more than a few days' work would make it impossible. As he paced, Daniel realized that the cave would not be completed in time. He would have to abandon his great plan to surprise the family and get even with Charles. He gulped down his third whiskey and threw the hand-cut crystal glass into the fireplace, smashing it against the back wall.

He stumbled into the kitchen, thankful he had told both Maria and Mrs. Kelley they did not need to come into the house to wait on him. He could fend for himself until the storm was over. He was also thankful Maria had left a pot of rabbit stew simmering on the woodstove that afternoon, before the storm had gained full force. Its aroma calmed him. Taking an earthenware bowl from the kitchen cupboard he decided to sample it. Daniel missed Maria's cheerful banter but was relieved not to have to listen to Mrs. Kelley. Now that Nell was not here, Ian's wife had taken to enumerating the charms of her favorite Lyman son, Charles, on a daily basis, to Daniel. Just last week, he'd demanded that she stop mentioning Charles's name.

Then, as if just thinking about this despised woman was enough to draw her closer, the door to the kitchen suddenly flew open. It slammed against the wall, and a bundle of wool, snow, and ice blew in. Daniel dropped the bowl of stew to the floor as he rushed to push with all his might to close the door against the north wind. A storm-soaked Mrs. Kelley stood there with a letter for him. It was from Charles.

"Whenever did this arrive?" he demanded as she dripped in front of the stove.

"Yesterday, but I forgot to bring it over before the storm kicked up this afternoon, and by then, it was too late. But tonight I thought you might want to have it."

"You forgot to bring me a letter from Charles? You *know* all mail is to be brought immediately to the house here directly upon Ian's return from the post office."

"Well, you told me to stop talking about him, so I thought you might not be so interested in his letter." She rubbed her hands over the open stew pot to warm them.

Daniel took a quick, deep breath; thought for a moment; and then exhaled slowly. "That will be all, Mrs. Kelley. You may go back to your cottage."

She did not move but looked boldly at him. "Aren't you going to open it?

He was not surprised by the nerve of this woman. "Why? Do you expect me to read it to you? Or"—he waved the letter in her face as a thought crept into his head—"or have you already read it?" His voice grew louder. "You had plenty of time. What did your darling Charles have to say? Why don't you tell me?" He grabbed the wet scarf that was tied around her neck and pulled her face close to his. "Tell me!"

She stared emotionless into his bloodshot eyes. Then a slow smile curved her lips without affecting her eyes. She pulled away; turned her back on him; and left, leaving the open door to usher in another icy blast of snow.

After mopping and sweeping the snow, stew, and broken bowl from the floor, Daniel filled another bowl and sat at the kitchen table. He leaned over the bowl, inhaling deeply of the savory vapors, and then slowly allowed his eyes to shift to the unopened letter that lay straight ahead of him. Reaching across to the center of the table, he tilted up the potted geranium Maria was wintering over in the house and slid the letter underneath, making sure he could not see even one tiny part of it. He wolfed down the stew, retrieved the letter, and left the kitchen.

Back in the living room, Daniel threw two more long logs on the fire, lit the five candles that stood in a silver candelabrum, and placed it on a table beside his chair. Before opening the letter, he carefully examined the flap to see if he could see any signs that it had been tampered with. The wrinkles on the flap of the envelope left him convinced that the letter had, in fact, been opened and then resealed.

---

November 27
Pittsfield
Daniel,

Sorry to have to spoil your fun. I will not be able to gather at Crooked Pond with the family to celebrate Father's birthday on December 20 but will arrive on Christmas Day. I have left my position here at the GE plant and will be occupied with two new job interviews in Philadelphia. I will return to Crooked Pond on Christmas Day.

I hear from Mrs. Kelley that you are constructing a wine cellar under the west wing, and that you are so terribly involved and anxious over trying to complete the project before everyone arrives that your wife had to leave for the duration. I always thought your wife's city-bred ways would not last long in our isolated house on the Cape. Give dear old Mrs. Kelley my best.

Charles

<hr />

Dear old Mrs. Kelley. Daniel had given explicit directions to everyone working at Crooked Pond that the wine cellar was to be a surprise for the whole family. But with this letter, Daniel could see that Mrs. Kelley had told Charles about it and had, no doubt, also told him it was to be a surprise. Since she'd most likely read the letter, she knew that he knew she'd told Charles. He now understood why this woman, fifteen minutes ago, had stood there and sneered at him with the same disparaging look she had so often given him since he was a child. She had always taken great pleasure in his discomfort.

He would no longer stand for any of her flagrant insubordination. The Kelleys must go. After the holidays, he would break the news to Ian. Daniel could no longer tolerate Ian's wife, no matter how valuable Ian was to the estate.

For now, he would give them a week off before Christmas to return a day before Nell arrived. The Kelleys had traditionally been given the week after Christmas to spend with Ian's brother and their family in Boston. But Daniel was coming to realize that things need not always be done as they had in the past, a thought that offered him unexpected peace.

After the Christmas holiday, Charles and the Kelleys would leave, giving Daniel the satisfaction of never having to deal with either again. Daniel was about to toss the letter into the fire but changed his mind and tucked it into his vest pocket. He relaxed, stretched his feet before the fire, blew out the candles, and fell asleep listening to the roar of the storm.

———•———

Harsh fall weather on Cape Cod, no matter how late in the season, has a way of unexpectedly turning mild. So it was that the blizzard's three feet of snow had all but disappeared with a few days of rain and sunshine. Roads were cleared, power was restored, and the telephone was working once more.

By the end of an exceptionally wet day on December 16, workmen had completed the construction of half of the wine cave and the entire circular brick shaft. Before leaving late that rainy afternoon, the men removed all the scaffolding. Just a ladder remained, clamped to the curving wall of the inside of the shaft. The spiral staircase was due to arrive and be installed the next morning, the same day the Kelleys were to arrive back from their week off in Boston.

After dinner that night, Daniel bundled up in his heavy canvas work jacket and scarf; turned on the lights to the shaft; and climbed slowly down the ladder, running his hands along the series of arched wine bottle compartments winding down along the brick wall into the lower region. He pictured each compartment filled with bottles of his favorite wines and was pleased.

At the bottom, Daniel stepped off the ladder onto the hardpacked clay floor. He glanced up and imagined how it would look tomorrow, with the staircase in place. Each triangular, black, wrought iron step would be embossed with clusters of grapes and leaves. The spindles on the curved handrails, entwined with an iron grapevine, were designed to appear to curl upward from the first step on the bottom to the last at the top. Upon reaching the top, the handrail would partially encircle the opening to prevent anyone from stepping on the hatch of clear, thick glass. Daniel was constantly in awe of Luigi Landucci's design and skill. Tomorrow, when the three sections of the staircase were assembled and in place, he would reward Luigi with a huge bonus.

He lit a lantern and walked through the opening in the wall of the shaft leading to the cave. A door was yet to be put in place leading into the arched cave, according to Luigi's calculations. Moving into the unfinished section of the cave, Daniel held the lantern high to light his way. He stepped carefully around the wheelbarrows and shovels and pickaxes left behind by the workers. He closed his eyes for a second to breathe in the welcome scent of moist earth, enjoying it as much as Nell enjoyed her finest perfume.

Suddenly, he startled himself by almost tripping over the wrought iron dragon sculpture that he'd had a local blacksmith make. It was to hang, curving over the top of the door that led from the cave to the shaft. He had taken special delight in having the smithy design the flat metal piece to include a replica of the opal ring his parents had given Nell. The gold, circular basket of her ring was duplicated in wrought iron to surround the one eye of the fire-breathing, flying beast. Instead of an opal in the center, the smithy had attached a gleaming oval mound of sterling silver. Now, the dragon reminded Daniel of the extra pleasure he would take watching Charles's reaction when he saw it, as he knew how much his brother had coveted the ring for his own future wife.

Bumping up against the one of the support beams, he covered his head and ducked, fearing that the whole fifteen feet of unbricked tunnel was about to fall in on him. Then he laughed at himself, apologizing to the absent Luigi for lack of confidence in the mason's work. Only a few pieces of the clay wall came loose, and he quickly kicked them off to the side and then stomped them into the ground to hide his blunder from tomorrow's crew.

Upon reaching the finished part of the cave, Daniel looked with admiration at the brick arches running along the walls, the mosaic flooring, and the cement ceiling that would soon be painted with the loveliest of frescoes. Tying his scarf tighter around his neck, he shivered, but he could not yet leave the wonders of this place. A wooden bench offered him and his lantern a place to sit. It was damp and cold, but yet how wonderfully quiet it was. How still.

How removed this sanctuary was from the rest of the house, where every room he looked in brought memories of his brother's slights—echoes of Charles's mean laughter and degrading insults and the pains of being tripped, pinched, and punched. Daniel was not certain he could erase this blight with new coats of paint on all the walls and new furniture in all the rooms, but he was sure of one thing—this wine cellar would be the only place Charles had never spoiled with years of taunts and sarcasms, a place which would always belong completely to himself.

In a way, he was glad Charles would not arrive until days after the rest of the family. Their appreciation for the wine cellar, even though it was not finished, would have been overshadowed by Charles's snide remarks. This way, Daniel could at least feel the untarnished joy of pleasing his family. Then he would be ready to deal with Charles.

As he sat on the bench, he leaned back heavily against the wall, turned down the wick on the lantern, and thought about Nell. He missed her, almost to the point of desperation. Right now, if she were here, she would be playing the piano in the living room while he sat reading by the fire.

But he had no time for dreams. The Kelleys were returning tomorrow. Nell would be here the day after, and the rest of the family, without Charles, the next day. He still had work to do.

He walked back through the tunnel to the shaft and climbed up the ladder and then the stairs to the west wing. At three steps from the top, he heard eleven bells chiming the hour from the tall clock in the upstairs hall and then more sounds, sounds that seemed to be coming from the piano in the parlor. He quickly crossed to the door, his heart pounding. Then he stopped to let the music of Mozart pour out from the piano, like a fine wine just waiting to be tasted. Nell had come home two days early. He rushed into the living room.

"Nell? How did you ever—?" He froze. A dark figure sat leaning over the piano keys, drops of rain running off his oilskin coat and wide-brimmed hat.

Charles spun around. "No, my dear brother. It is not your darling Nellie. It is I, your beloved brother Charles."

"What the hell are you doing here? I thought you were in Philadelphia at a job interview."

"Yes, you *thought*. Well, I thought I would pay you an unannounced visit—a surprise, so to speak. You do like surprises, don't you?" Charles's voice was as slick and slippery as the oilskin raincoat he shrugged out of, his smile false. He dropped the coat; his wet hat; and his small, leather bag on a chair and then crossed the room to where Daniel was standing.

"How did you get here?" Daniel, his heart racing, looked out the window, expecting to see a carriage in the driveway. There was none.

"If you mean from Pittsfield, of course it was by train. You should know better than to ask a stupid question like that. As to how I got to the house, I preferred to come in secret ... so as not to spoil my ... surprise. I hired a carriage to take me just about to the end of Blacksmith Shop Road, and then I got out. You see, I didn't want any townsfolk calling you on the phone and telling you that your brother was about to arrive. Then I walked here through the woods in the rain. You do remember how we used to play in those woods, don't you?"

Daniel did remember how Charles had once tied him to a tree and left him there for hours. He refused to answer that question.

"How did you get in here? I had new locks put on all the doors, and I locked them myself tonight."

"Well, let's just say I have a friend who sent me a new key, just in case I should need one. Now, then, Daniel," he said, looking brazenly up at the face of the younger brother who stood a foot taller than he, "where are your recently discovered, yet superficial manners? I did have quite a trudge up here through the woods, you know. Aren't you going to offer me a glass of wine? Or must you go down to your wine cellar to find an appropriate one? Oh! That's right, your wine cellar is not finished yet!"

Daniel remained silent and motionless, staring at his brother in disbelief, his heart pounding.

"Well, it looks like I will just have to help myself." Charles walked to the liquor cabinet that had stood in the same corner for two centuries, filled two glasses with Glenfiddich, and then handed one to Daniel.

"What do you want here, Charles? I thought you were looking for a new job."

"Yes," he said, taking a big draft of the scotch, "that's what I told the family. You see, I wanted the family to believe I was not going to be here for Father's birthday for a good reason. But I actually came here to show you some things I have here in my bag—things we'll save for later. Daniel, no one knows I'm here, except you of course, not even Father. Or should I call him Papá?"

He drained the glass, filled it again, and continued. "Your darling wife is away, enjoying herself immensely, I hear, at parties in New York. The Kelleys are with family in Boston, and the lights in the Landucci apartment at the back of the barn have been out since nine this evening. So you see, Daniel, as I said, absolutely no one knows I'm here."

"You've been here since nine o'clock? What were you doing skulking around in the rain like that? Why all this secrecy? What were you looking for?"

"Just waiting for the best moment to come and visit you. That's all. Don't you remember what I said just a few moments ago? To surprise you. I did surprise you, didn't I, Daniel?" He leaned in so their faces were almost touching. "I also have two letters I want to share with you. You will love the contents."

Charles smiled, patted his breast pocket, and then walked back and forth in front of the fireplace, its glowing light sending his shadow across the room. He finally stopped right in front of his brother, hand still patting the pocket.

"Oh, by the way, do you know a man named … Herb Allen?" He stopped patting to look directly into his brother's eyes.

Daniel summoned all his strength to pretend he was trying to think whether he knew the name—the name he had not heard mentioned in six years. What did Charles know? "No, can't say I do." He lifted a log and threw it on the fire. "Who is he, a friend of yours?" He clapped the small pieces of bark from his hands and, in doing so, noticed they were beginning to tremble.

"No. Just someone I heard of who was wanted for murder in Alaska. And since you were there …" He let his voice trail off.

"Never heard of him. Alaska is a big territory, you know, Charles." Daniel jabbed at the logs with an iron poker, still hoping to calm his hands.

"Right. And probably a territory that's easy to escape from if one so wished. Don't you think, Daniel?"

"Wouldn't know about that." He still could not turn to face his brother, jamming his hands into his pockets and looking up at the portrait above the mantel.

"Oh, and another thing. I took a walk down to the family cemetery to have a look at the new wine cellar entrance. I heard that you could not manage the workers well enough to complete the job before Christmas. Am I right?" Charles moved up to stand close behind Daniel.

The smell of his cheap cologne almost sickened Daniel, bringing him to his senses. He was not going to take the bait. "Charles, I'm tired. I had a busy day. Take your things and go to bed, if you must stay. The room in the loft over the east wing is to be yours."

"Ah, but I am not the least bit tired. You may go to bed if you like. I'll just take a look around to see what magnificent work you've done with … our house. I believe I'll start in the west wing, where you have probably almost completed the brick shaft."

Daniel had had enough. He believed Charles had incriminating information in his pocket about his days in Alaska as Herb Allen. He also now knew his brother had knowledge of all the construction that had taken place in the house the last two months. As soon as this was apparent, Daniel forgot how tired he was. He would immediately implement his plan to make Charles seethe with jealousy before throwing him out of the house and telling him he was no longer welcome to return.

He smiled slightly as he gained confidence. "All right, I'll show you our work in the west wing. And just think. You will be here tomorrow when they install the spiral staircase. It is to be a beauty, the likes of which you have never seen. Come, Charles, let me show you my incomplete, yet fantastic wine cellar."

Daniel could not stop the name *Herb Allen* from crashing into his mind as though the words were bouncing off the walls. Just as he was about to open the door to the west wing, Charles stopped.

"Oh, I forgot something." He went back to the chair, where his hat, raincoat, and leather bag lay.

Daniel could see only his brother's back as Charles unbuckled the bag, took something out, and put it in his pocket.

"Just my cigarettes," he said, returning to the door.

Daniel wondered why a pack of cigarettes would make such a large bulge in Charles's pocket, but he let the thought pass. Charles struck a match to light one, blowing the smoke into the back of Daniel's neck as he followed him to the staircase in the room in the west wing.

"The first thing I would like to bring to your attention," said Daniel as they descended the stairs to the bean pot cellar and stepped out onto the brick floor, "is the magnificent circular brickwork in the floor here that radiates out from the edge all around the top of the shaft. I had it personally designed and installed by my talented stone mason." He paused to see if he was getting a reaction from Charles and saw a brief flash of interest that quickly passed.

Daniel continued, gesturing grandly. "Notice the perfect spacing of every brick, how each one is placed exactly the same distance apart from the adjoining ones. And be careful, watch your step. The hatch on the shaft has not yet been installed."

The dim light from above the staircase barely illuminated the room. All that could be seen was a dark, open circle in the middle of the brick floor.

"And now, my dear Charles," Daniel said, "feast your eyes on this." He flipped a switch and the entire shaft lit up from small hidden lights tucked into the tops of each of the arched wine bottle compartments that wound down the walls of the shaft. "Wonderful, no?"

Charles walked to the edge of the opening in the floor, peering over. "How thoughtful of you. I know Father signed the house and property over to you when you told him how your money would take care of it, Daniel, but … how wonderful of you to think of doing all this for us."

"What do you mean, for us? This is my house now, not yours."

"Well"—he took two steps back—"if something should happen to you, say … before you had any male children … the house would revert to me as the oldest son. It's in the deed. Haven't you seen it? The house must stay in the hands of male members of the family for as long as any survive."

"That's a lie. My wife inherits my estate. It's in my will."

"Oh yes, your money; your business investments; your gold; and your exciting Model T, which I admit is a joy to drive, but not this house. Really, my dear brother, I am surprised you are so ignorant of this legality. Yes, if you should die before I do, all this ... will be mine."

Charles let out with a small laugh and flicked his cigarette butt into the shaft. "The great youngest son has returned feeling so successful, yet he is still the dumb little shit he always was."

"You bastard!" Daniel lunged at Charles and tried to grab him by the neck, but Charles ducked out of the way, laughing.

"Ha! Missed me! I'll bet Herb Allen would not have been so clumsy!"

Daniel stood clenching his fists, panting with growing rage. "What do you know about Herb Allen?"

"Only this." Charles reached into his jacket pocket and pulled out one of the letters. He then took out of the envelope a copy of a newspaper clipping.

Daniel snatched it from his hands and moved to stand under the light so he could see more clearly. It was from the *San Francisco Chronicle*, dated July 20, 1898, one year before Daniel had left Dawson for Nome. The photo showed a close-up of three bearded men at a camp there, grinning broadly as they held up gold nuggets. The caption identified the men on the left and right as sons of a prominent San Francisco banker. It identified the man in the center as Herb Allen, a man who, if you cut his hair and removed his beard, would look just like Daniel Lyman, right down to the C-shaped scar on the right side of his face, which even a beard refused to cover.

"You see, Daniel, while doing a little investigating into your activities out West, I wrote to a friend in San Francisco. He had come across this clipping and thought the man in the middle looked remarkably like you. Don't you agree?"

Daniel stared at the picture, not able to move, not able to say a word.

"Oh, and look at this—another clipping, showing Herb Allen as being wanted for murder in Nome. Imagine that!"

Daniel slowly lifted his eyes from the paper and looked at his brother. Suddenly, he felt his childhood feelings of fear and helplessness turn to hatred and rage. He could see his new life about to be destroyed. All of his striving to succeed was going up in flames before his very eyes. He glared at Charles, who glared back with an arrogance Daniel well remembered.

With the quickness of an attacking cobra, Daniel slammed Charles against the wall and then kicked him between the legs and threw him down precariously close to the edge of the shaft. Charles lay on his side groaning in pain, but instead of trying to get up, he took a swipe at Daniel's legs, causing him to stumble and hit his head on a pile of scaffolding. For a split second, Daniel lost sight of where he was and what he was doing. Then, shaking his head to bring himself back to reality, he saw Charles struggling to get up off the floor and reaching into his pocket. Without waiting to see what Charles could possibly pull out of there, Daniel delivered another forceful kick, this time to his brother's stomach, sending him over the edge. His despised brother fell screaming twenty-four feet down the shaft, crashing into the hard clay at the bottom.

Daniel stood in shock, clasping his hands to his ears in an unsuccessful attempt to block out the scream that had already ceased. Then the realization of what just happened swept over him. He stuffed the newspaper clippings into his pocket, climbed down the ladder, and knelt at his brother's body. Charles's head was bent unnaturally to one side and his wide-open eyes seemed to stare directly at Daniel, his mouth posed in a silent scream, both legs twisted in gruesome positions.

As he felt for signs of life, Daniel discovered what Charles had been reaching for in his pocket. He lifted out a handgun and turned it over, trying to remember where he had seen it before. Suddenly that didn't matter. He had killed his brother. But had his brother come to kill him so he could inherit the house? Why else would Charles have made sure no one knew he was there? And who else had Charles told about Herb Allen?

He knelt down, breathing heavily, trying to control the thoughts that pounded through his head. What should he do? Tell everyone exactly what had happened and that it had been a mistake?

This wasn't the first time Daniel had leaned over the body of a man whose death he was responsible for. As Herb Allen, he had done the same six years ago in Nome. If Charles had told anyone else about Daniel's other identity, Daniel's story would be doubted. Who would ever believe a man could make two such mistakes? In his fear now, Daniel began to wonder if both really were mistakes after all. Was there possibly an evil streak within him? Or was he just responding to the evil in others?

The similarities between these two deaths were startling. Then, in Nome, a ridiculous fistfight had occurred over a precious bottle of whiskey he, as Herb Allen, had stashed in a pile of rocks beside the stream. One of the miners had found and consumed it, laughing in Daniel's face. Daniel had only meant to punish Jack, not to kill him. But his rage had become uncontrollable. Jack had fallen and hit his head on a rock. Now, Charles had fallen down the shaft.

In Jack's case, rumors had spread that Herb Allen had been seen digging a grave. He'd had to leave before the authorities caught up to him.

Shaving his beard, cutting his hair, and packing up his valuable gold, he left for San Francisco as soon as he could and assumed his original identity as Daniel Lyman.

——————

Daniel knew exactly what he had to do now. He had to bury the body. And he had to move quickly. In a few hours, the workmen would be arriving to install the spiral staircase. He dragged Charles's body off to the side, went into the tunnel, and carried back a pick and shovel. He would bury his brother in a narrow grave five feet deep at the bottom of the shaft, right where he had fallen. Tomorrow, the workers would install the spiral staircase, securing its wrought iron base into a twelve-inch layer of cement that would cover the entire floor of the shaft. No one knew Charles had come to the house on Crooked Pond, Daniel reasoned, so certainly no one would ever think to look for him here.

He rifled through Charles's clothes, finding his wallet, keys, coins, and the remaining letter. He stuffed everything into his own jacket pockets, along with the gun. It took about an hour with the pick and shovel to dig the narrow grave. After pushing his brother in, he reached into his pocket for the handful of Charles's change and hurled it with all his might on top of the body. He was not going to let something even as impersonal as his brother's coins remain in his possession any longer than necessary.

Wiping the sweat from his forehead, he filled the hole. Each shovelful wildly thrown in to splat upon the body was accompanied by a curse. And after Daniel had run out of all the curses and foul epithets he had ever learned, he threw in the last shovelful and stopped. Finally ridding himself of the entire burden of pent-up anger and fear he had ever felt toward his brother, he collapsed on the floor.

But he had one last job to do. Dragging himself up, he took the water-filled steel roller that was leaning against the wall of the unfinished tunnel. He strained as he pushed it back and forth, back and forth over the grave in all directions to compact the clay, until he was finally satisfied. The floor looked exactly the way it had when the workers had left that afternoon; it was ready to be covered with cement and to accept the spiral staircase.

Placing his left foot on the first rung of the ladder and grasping the side rails to begin his climb, Daniel closed his eyes, took a deep breath, exhaled, and then looked back over his shoulder at the smooth ground now covering his brother's body. Then he spit on the floor.

# Chapter 30

## THE STAIRCASE

At eight o'clock the next morning, Daniel was jolted out of his short, exhausted sleep by shouts coming from the driveway. He stumbled out of bed and looked through the window to see workmen arriving from town on the creaking wagon. In it, the three sections of his beautiful spiral staircase glistened in the bright sunlight. His excitement was short-lived, for not too far behind the wagon, he saw the Kelleys arriving in their carriage.

Suddenly he painfully remembered last night, and by the time he pulled on his boots he had another memory, one he cursed himself over for not thinking of before he went to bed. He had to get downstairs before Mrs. Kelley came into the house. Charles's raincoat, hat, and leather bag were still lying on the chair in the parlor.

He clambered shirtless down the stairs, crossed the room to the chair, and grabbed his brother's things. He was just about halfway up the stairs rushing back to his room when the door from the kitchen opened. He looked over the railing, relieved to see it was just Maria.

With a curt "Good morning, Maria," he bounded to his room.

Once there, he slid the bolt on the door, knowing Mrs. Kelley had a way of entering any room whenever she pleased. He collapsed on his bed, still clutching the coat, hat, and bag to his body. He lay there panting but slowly relaxed until he was able to regain his senses. The first sensation he experienced was that choking smell of cologne on Charles's coat. With one swift motion, he hurled it across the room yelling, "Get away from me."

A knock came on the door. "Daniel? Ian and I just got back, and I've come to clean yer room."

"Mrs. Kelley, go and clean somewhere else."

"Well, your room seems to be the only one up here that's been used since I left." She jiggled the doorknob.

"Will you go the hell downstairs and leave me alone!" He couldn't believe it. Charles and Mrs. Kelley were still tormenting him.

He listened for her footsteps going away and then picked up the hat, raincoat, and bag. Carefully checking to see no one was around, he walked down the hall to the door that led to the attic stairs. For now, he would pack Charles's coat and hat in an old trunk under a pile of long-forgotten clothing. Later, he would bury it somewhere on the property, far away from the house. He closed the lid on the trunk and was about to hide the leather bag deep within the clutter under the rafters when he thought he'd better open it first and see what was inside. But just then he heard footsteps in the hall below.

"Daniel?" It was Luigi, knocking on his bedroom door.

He quickly stashed the bag under a pile of old rugs and left the attic.

"Oh, there you are." Luigi said. "Boss, I thought you would like to come and see your new staircase being installed. The staircase is just like I told you. Bellissimo! Oh, we have a small problem, but we've just started taking care of it."

"Of course, Luigi, I'll be down as soon as I can." Without even a glance at the mason, he continued on into his bedroom and shut the door, sliding the bolt once more.

Daniel sat slouching on the bed, breathing deeply. He knew in the back of his mind there was still something wrong, but he was not able to bring it forward. He got up and walked to the closet. There, crumpled in a heap on the floor, was the clay-choked clothing he had worn last night. He snatched up the rumpled jacket and went through his pockets, pulling out his brother's handgun, the newspaper clippings, the two letters, and Charles's wallet and keys. He threw everything on the bed and stood staring at it all. His eyes lingered on the letters. Both were addressed to Charles. One was from Mrs. Kelley. His first instinct was to burn it in the bedroom stove, but he cursed himself for needing to read it. The second letter, the one holding the newspaper clippings, was from San Francisco.

There was no time now. He had to think of what to do with these incriminating possessions. Daniel knew he couldn't leave any of Charles's things in the room. Mrs. Kelley had been away a week, and she had to come in now and clean it before Nell arrived tomorrow. When Mrs. Kelley cleaned a room, nothing was left untouched. It was impossible to hide anything from her prying eyes.

He looked around and saw the mess he had created—clothes dropped, draped, stashed, and stored on every piece of furniture plus the floor. Mrs. Kelley would have to start this laundry and cleaning as soon as possible if the room was to be respectable by tomorrow. He needed to get out of there in a hurry. Daniel finished dressing quickly, pulling on a clean shirt and a clean canvas work jacket. Stuffing the gun, the letters, the wallet, and the keys, into his pockets, he knew the only way to keep them hidden for now was to secure them on his own body. He rushed down to the west wing to supervise the installation of the spiral staircase.

Near the bottom of the stairs to the bean pot cellar, vivid images of the previous night slashed into his mind, overcoming him, forcing his knees to weaken. The memory of his brother's twisted, broken legs and neck and the grotesque look on his dead face sickened him.

He fell back to sit on the stairs and caught his breath. He had to concentrate on keeping his mind on the task at hand. There would be plenty of time to reflect on those horrors later.

From where he sat, he could see that the workers had already attached a pulley to the ceiling so they could lower two sections of the spiral staircase to fit into the one section they would fix into the cement floor at the bottom of the shaft. He gazed at the two round, wrought iron staircase sections that lay near him. Side by side on the red brick floor, they looked like sleeping black giants. Then he moved to the opening and looked down, shocked at what he saw.

"What in hell are you doing?" he shouted to the men at the bottom. With picks and shovels, they were digging into the clay. "Stop that digging! Stop it at once." He practically slid, rather than climbed, down the ladder to confront Luigi.

"What the hell is going on down here? I thought you were to be laying a cement floor to anchor the bottom section of the staircase."

Luigi removed his hat and twirled it in his hands. "Well, you see, boss, remember I told you we had a slight problem? We ordered three eight-foot sections, but they delivered three ten-foot sections." He shifted his weight back and forth. "It's no big problem. Don't worry. All we have to do is dig down six more feet and then install some steps to have the bottom come up even with the floor of the cave."

"You will not dig down!" Daniel had to wipe the sweat from his eyes.

"But, boss—"

Daniel grabbed Luigi by the collar, pulling his face closer. "You will *not* dig down! Do you understand?"

"Sure, boss, but ...?"

"But nothing!"

Daniel let go and paced the small area, avoiding two wheelbarrows and the three men who stood there with puzzled looks, leaning on their shovels and picks. He realized how insane he sounded, but he could not help himself. He stopped in front of his brick mason.

"Look, I'm sure you can think of some other way to solve this problem." He paced, looking up the shaft and then back at the bottom section of the staircase that lay waiting in the tunnel. He suddenly remembered a job he had handled out west in the mines.

"All right. Here's what you will do. Instead of digging down, you will fill in this shaft with clay that you removed and left piled up outside."

"Boss! You want us to fill in the entire shaft?"

"No, not entirely, listen to me. You will fill it in four feet to bring it up to twenty feet deep. Then you will have to use only two of the three ten-foot sections of staircase. You will build a set of stairs leading from the newly filled bottom section down into the finished part of the cave."

Luigi fought back tears. "You want me to bury some of the fine brickwork we did along the walls here?" He looked at Daniel as if he were asking him to give up his grown children.

"Yes. Fill in enough so that the top section of the two pieces of staircase comes out level with the brick floor above. That's exactly what I want you to do."

"And you want us to have finished all this by tomorrow?" Luigi was shaking his head no even as he asked the question.

Daniel turned his back from Luigi and stood with both hands leaning against the wall. Head down, he gathered his thoughts. It was no longer necessary to impress Charles. The rest of the family would be pleased with seeing whatever had already been done. They would also be pleased with being told what the finished wine cellar would soon be like. They would look forward to being invited back to see the project as soon as it was completed.

He took a deep breath, suddenly able to feel relieved of his great burden, relieved of his relentless obsession with taking revenge on Charles, relieved of whatever it was Charles had found out about Herb Allen. It no longer mattered that he was responsible for his brother's death. What mattered was that he was now free. He opened his arms and gave the startled Luigi a big hug. "My friend, you may take as long as you need."

He climbed the ladder, knowing that he was finally going to be rid of the great albatross he had worn around his neck for as long as he could remember.

That evening, once the staircase was in place, and the workmen had left, Daniel returned to the shaft through the entrance to the cave down by the pond. He knew better than to chance putting his weight on the still drying cement by climbing down the spiral staircase. Walking through the cave, he held his lantern high, admiring the fine masonry. At the back of the cave he climbed the temporary wood stairs to the new bottom of the shaft. There he knelt on the wooden platform at the entrance. He took a small stick from his pocket and leaned in, hovering over the wet cement surface of the floor of the shaft, being careful not to lose his balance. With a great feeling of satisfaction he carved R. I. H. into the floor, next to the edge where it met with the curving brick wall.

He left with three last words to his brother. "Rest in hell, Charles."

# Chapter 31

## THE OAK

The next day, right after breakfast, Daniel found Mrs. Kelley in the midst of tossing his dirty clothes into the laundry basket. He wanted to tell her to get out but knew the room had to be cleaned. As he was about to leave, the housekeeper spoke.

"How did ye do this past week with Ian and me gone?"

"Very well, actually."

"Have any visitors?"

He stopped, halfway out the door, suddenly feeling he was about to be trapped. He thrust his hands into the deep pockets of his jacket, fingers unconsciously closing around Charles's gun.

"No. Why do you ask?"

"Oh ye know. It being the holiday season, I thought maybe someone might drop in on ye unexpectedly."

Daniel stood, still facing the door, with his back to her, speaking to the ceiling. "Mrs. Kelley, no one was here." It took all his strength to move to the stairs in what he hoped was a casual manner.

Had Charles told her he was coming? He immediately thought of the two envelopes he had taken from his dead brother, the letters Charles said he wanted to read to Daniel. They now sat in Daniel's breast pocket, pressing against his chest. He had seen the newspaper clippings about Herb Allen but had yet to read the letter accompanying the clippings and the one in the other envelope. He could not read them here in the house.

270

Going to the barn, he looked longingly at the now repaired Model T, promising to take it for a spin as soon as he could. He saddled his horse, and out they went, down the driveway. With a quick glance back at the house, he thought he caught a glimpse of someone standing at his bedroom window, the curtains suddenly being drawn closed.

Something about a certain curve in the drive about a quarter mile from the road made him pull his horse to a stop. He tugged on the reins to urge the beast off to the left and into the woods. A few hundred yards in, he remembered what had drawn him to this particular spot. There, on the crest of a small hill, stood the great English oak tree Charles had tied him to. After that frightening experience, Daniel had never again ventured onto this part of their property, but now he felt compelled to urge the mare up the hill. Winding along through the low bushes, Daniel felt drawn closer to the tree that had once terrified him.

He dismounted, stood at the base of the tree, and looked up at the lichen-covered branches. He remembered Charles telling him they were going on an adventure to build a wonderful swing from a very special, secret tree deep in the woods. He remembered being afraid of going so far away from the house but being assured by Charles that he would take care of him. He remembered Charles tying him to the tree with what he thought was going to be the rope for the swing. He remembered begging his brother not to leave him. He remembered Charles laughing as he left, telling him he was going to die there because no one in the entire world knew about this secret place in the woods, and even if he screamed as loud as he could, no one would hear him.

Daniel's mind was made up. Here is where he would bury Charles's leather bag, along with his coat, hat, keys, and empty wallet. The letters he would burn in his bedroom stove. But he had yet to read the letters in his pocket or go through the contents of Charles's bag in the attic. He reached in, took out the letters, and leaned against the tree. The first letter was from Mrs. Kelley.

November 20, 1912
Crooked Pond
Dearest Charles,

I hope to find you in the best of health and no longer so upset by the demands of your position at GE.

Things here are unbearable. Your brother is in a wild frenzy planning and supervising his so-called secret mission to build a fancy wine cellar before you all arrive in December. I've already told you how much I disapprove of these activities. He is so involved that his wife has decided to leave him and return to her family in New York. She said it is only for the duration of the construction, but I wonder. He is beginning to neglect himself to the point where even a slovenly barmaid would not want to take up with him.

I'll never quite understand how your father could have turned the estate over to Daniel. From what he led me to believe, it would all go to you as eldest son, and Ian and I would be able to live out our lives here happily serving you. Instead, we are now going to have to serve Daniel and endure missing you. You know what a hard time I have being in this place without you, my dear Charles. And you do know my attachment to you.

Please, try to do anything you can to reverse the direction we are heading in with Daniel in charge. Anything, I repeat, anything you may do will be deeply appreciated and held in secret, close to my heart. Maybe we will still be able to live here together one day, forever.

I love you and will always keep your best interests at heart.

Love,
M
PS. You should soon receive the package you asked for in the mail.

Daniel felt his legs buckle beneath him as he slowly slid his back down the trunk of the tree and sat on an exposed root at its base. He closed his eyes. So this was the information Charles wanted to share. Why was she so attached to Charles? And why had she signed her name "M"? Although Mrs. Kelley was never addressed by any other name, everyone in the family knew her first name was Irene. And what could have been in the package Charles was to expect?

He folded the letter and returned it to his breast pocket and then, suddenly feeling the chill of the strengthening wind, thrust both hands into the pockets of his jacket. He drew out the gun and stared at it. He had known from the moment he had found it last night that he'd seen it before. But where?

The steel barrel and chambers of the Colt pistol gleamed with the standard dark blue, but its carved ivory handle was unique. He closed his eyes once more and could picture, as if in a dream, the same gun lying in a drawer. It was the top drawer of a tall dresser. He was too short at the time to see into the drawer, but Charles had picked him up to show the gun to him. Then they had both left the room, sneaking out through the back door of the barn.

Then it came to him. While Daniel still lived at home, the Kelleys had lived in the apartment in the barn where the Landuccis now lived. Once all the Lyman children had grown and left the house, the Kelleys had moved out of the barn and into the cottage. The gun belonged to Ian Kelley. Daniel was convinced this gun had been in the package from Mrs. Kelley—the package Charles was to look for. Why had she sent him the gun?

He opened the second letter—the one in the envelope with the clippings of Herb Allen. Addressed to Charles, it had a San Francisco return address. Looking more closely, Daniel could see it was from a Harvard College classmate of Charles's—one Daniel had met before he'd left for the West Coast—Matthew Stone.

Reading the letter, he could see that Matthew had seen the posters showing Herb Allen as being wanted for murder. Matthew was inquiring if indeed this was Charles's brother.

——•◦•——

Urging the old mare to run faster than either of them thought she could, Daniel was soon back at the house. He rushed up the stairs to his room, finding the cleaning finished and no one at all on the second floor. Opening the door to the wood stove, he took the two letters from his pocket and thrust them into the fire. Ripping the newspaper pictures of Herb Allen to shreds, he threw them in and then slammed the door shut.

Picking up a neatly folded, empty laundry bag, he raced to the attic, stuffed the leather bag, the raincoat, and hat into it, and carried it all out to the barn. Grabbing a small shovel, he mounted his waiting horse and, within minutes, was on his way back to the oak tree. He had to bury everything before Nell arrived, and it was already midafternoon. In another hour or so, it would be dark.

After digging a hole at the base of the tree, Daniel gathered Charles's possessions together in a pile on top of the opened oilskin raincoat. As much as he wanted to get this task over with, he could not resist first finding out what it was that Charles had wanted to show him. He dumped the contents of the leather bag onto the opened raincoat.

Four things fell out—a book by Oscar Wilde, *The Picture of Dorian Grey*; a linen bag filled with angular objects; and two heavy brown envelopes.

The first heavy, brown envelope contained five old photographs on cardboard—formal, dark, and shiny—taken by a professional photographer. One showed a young, almost attractive Mrs. Kelley holding a newborn baby, the woman beaming into the camera with a smile Daniel had never seen. Daniel did not remember her and Ian having had any children.

Next, he found a photo of her with a young boy about five years old, the boy holding a small, intricately carved, wooden horse—a toy Daniel clearly remembered. Three more photos comprised the collection, taken at about two-year intervals, all of Mrs. Kelley with the same boy, the boy Daniel now recognized as Charles.

In each photo, Charles was holding a different carved wooden toy; all were toys Daniel remembered from childhood, toys he'd wanted to play with but had been forcefully forbidden to do so by both his brother and Mrs. Kelley. The horse, the lamb, the whale, and a magnificent osprey with wings outspread had all been lovingly hand carved by Ian for his wife to give to her favorite young boy. Glued to the back of the envelope, a note written in what Daniel recognized as Mrs. Kelley's handwriting stated, "Property of Mrs. Ian Kelley, Crooked Pond, Falmouth, Massachusetts."

The linen bag languished on the oilskin coat, almost demanding that Daniel open it. Its hidden contents, poking up from within, seemed to be struggling to get free. But its drawstring, pulled tight and knotted, prohibited such an adventure. When Daniel finally untied the bag, four carved, wooden toys tumbled out. He could barely bring himself to touch them.

The second brown envelope was marked "tickets." Inside, Daniel found a train ticket with today's date from Falmouth to Boston and a round trip ticket between Boston and Philadelphia, returning the day before Christmas. Daniel now was convinced of Charles's diabolical plan. He sank to his knees as he worked it all out.

Charles was going to let the family believe he couldn't make it to Father's birthday on the twentieth because he had quit his job at GE and was going to be looking into two job offers in Philadelphia. He had come to make Daniel squirm at the thought of Matthew Stone's inquiry and then to kill him. Charles had the perfect alibi. Everyone thought he was elsewhere. No one knew he was at the house. He had the motive. With Daniel out of the way, Charles would inherit the house and a magnificent wine cellar. When Charles showed up on Christmas Day, he would be met by a grieving family. He would act shocked that Daniel had been killed by an intruder when no one else was home. He would act sad that he would inherit the house because of his brother's death. Charles would move in, and Mrs. Kelley would have her wish come true. Had the two of them really collaborated on this plan? What was the seemingly deep connection between them, a connection only amplified by the photographs? Daniel would have to ask his father.

With only a moment's hesitation, Daniel wrapped everything, including the gun, tightly in the oilskin raincoat, stuffed it all in the laundry bag, and dropped it into the hole. Thinking again, he lifted it all out, removed the photographs and tucked them in his breast pocket, and then rewrapped and returned everything to the hole. As he filled it in, he could not believe it was just last night that he had also been shoveling dirt, that time on top of his brother's grave. He put the fact that he was responsible for his brother's death completely out of his mind. Daniel had no time to feel remorse for a terrible act, if it had good consequences. He thumped the dirt down with the back of the shovel and then covered it all with a pile of dead leaves and pine needles, rolling two heavy rocks over them to mark the place.

Riding back to the house, it came to him that he was thankful for one truth Mrs. Kelley had written in the letter. He had let himself go. Now he knew he had to clean up, bathe, shave, trim and clean his fingernails, have Maria cut his hair, and do everything else necessary to welcome his wife back late the next afternoon. He knew he had not been very congenial in their telephone conversations while Nell was gone. He had neglected to accept her loving attempts to comfort him. He had preferred to dwell, mired in his distrust of Mrs. Kelley and his anxious desire to complete the wine cellar, thereby exacting revenge upon his brother. In Nell's absence, Daniel had unconsciously built a wall between them, a wall made of bricks, each one indelibly stamped with the name of either *Charles* or *Mrs. Kelley*.

Now, with Charles out of the way and Mrs. Kelley soon to leave, he was ready to return to his new personality, the Daniel Lyman his dear Nell had married. He would have to become a gentleman once again—well groomed, well spoken, and well mannered. He only hoped he could.

# Chapter 32

## THE ADMISSION

To Daniel, the next day seemed to move along as slowly as sap oozing from the trunk of a pitch pine. Nell's carriage was due to arrive. He paced back and forth between the parlor window and the piano. That morning, he had cut a few sprigs of holly from the yard and placed them in a vase on top of her piano to welcome her home. Now he could not stop himself from constantly rearranging them. The red berries, standing out in lively independence from the sharp and shiny green leaves, lent a cheerful holiday glow to the room. Yet every time he adjusted one of the sprigs, another berry or two fell off.

As he picked the fallen berries from the top of the piano and stuffed them into his pocket, he was startled to notice Mrs. Kelley standing half-hidden behind one of the wingback chairs, watching him. Her arms were folded in front of her, the frown upon her face a permanent fixture ever since she had arrived the day before, her eyes seeming to accost him from under her heavy brow. He had no idea how long she had been standing there. Before he could say a word, she left the room.

Just then, the clatter of hooves on the clamshell driveway called to Daniel. He flew to the door, and was out in the freezing cold air in a flash. Helping his wife down from the carriage and quickly into the warmth of the house, he hugged and kissed and hugged and kissed her. Holding Nell at arm's length, he looked her up and down, absorbing her lovely presence. How grand she looked, dressed in her mink coat and hat. Holding her close once more, he breathed deeply of her scent as though he needed to use all of his senses to believe she was truly there. Her smiling eyes and lilting voice told him she was glad she was.

That evening, sitting close together by the fire as they waited for Maria to call them to dinner, she enthusiastically told him all the adventures she had had in New York. Then, with a quieter tone to her voice, she added, "My dearest Daniel, I suspected something before I left here for New York. And this was one of the reasons I thought it best to go."

"What did you suspect?"

"Well, the dust billowing in from the west wing, the noise, and the constant activity were all getting on my nerves."

"I was afraid I was the only thing getting on your nerves." Daniel hugged her again.

"I must admit you were quite beastly at times." She nestled against his chest, playfully punching him in the arm.

"Now, listen to me," she continued. "I suspected I may be pregnant and—"

"What? Why didn't you tell me?"

"Hush, husband. As I was saying, if I were pregnant, all the dust, noise, and my shattered nerves would not be good for the child. Then I saw my doctor in the city, and he confirmed it. You, my darling, are going to be a father."

Daniel's reaction changed rapidly from joyous surprise to worrisome doubt. The look on his face was not at all the one Nell had expected.

"Are you not happy to hear this?" She pulled away from him.

"Of course I am. I am delighted. But should you have returned now? The wine cellar is not yet finished as I thought it would be before you arrived. There has been a delay, and there will continue to be dust and noise because the workmen are still busy."

Nell stood up and moved closer to the fireplace, the chill in her voice almost enough to block the warmth from the fire. "So. It's the wine cellar again. You cannot even share my happiness with the news that I'm carrying your child, because of your concern with that almighty wine cellar!"

"Nell, I'm sorry. You're right. I'm still being a beast over this project.

I was only worried for you and the baby. Please forgive me." He went to console her.

She buried her head into his chest. "I never want to hear one more word about that cellar until it is finished. Do you hear me? I am beginning to wish you could fill it all in."

That thought sent a memory shivering through Daniel. "I won't speak of it again if it upsets you so, my love. I promise you. It's impossible to measure how happy I am right now with you and our child here beside me." He gently kissed her eyes and then held her close so she could not see the pain in his.

Tomorrow morning he would tell Luigi that the workers could leave immediately. There was no longer any rush to complete the wine cellar.

———◆———

By next evening, the house was all aflutter as the newly arrived family gathered around the dining room table. Set with Nell's antique Lowestoft china, their finest crystal, and silverware, the white damask tablecloth beamed in proud delight. Fifteen bayberry candles set in three magnificent candelabra cast a warm glow, their scent mixing with the aroma of juniper sprigs that danced down the middle of the table. Daniel rose and raised his wineglass in a hearty welcome.

"To our wonderful family. Nell and I are so pleased to be able to welcome you to Crooked Pond to celebrate our father's birthday and the Christmas season." He paused to smile with a nod to each. "To Papá; to Emily; to her husband, Willis; and to my new in-laws, Nell's sister, Esther, and her husband, Gilman, usually known as just plain Gil," he added with a chuckle. "We count ourselves fortunate to be once again in your most delightful company. Cheers to all and a happy birthday to Papá."

After a chorus of cheers and birthday wishes filled the room, Daniel spoke once again. "I would like to have us all raise our glasses once more, this time to my dear wife, Nell, who, near the end of next summer, will be presenting us with a new addition to the Lyman family tree."

Congratulations flew about as Emily rose and ran to the other side of the table to kiss both her brother and his bride. At that moment, Daniel could see that all the difficult choices he had ever made since returning to Crooked Pond had been the right ones.

Robert Lyman rose, tapping his glass with his silver knife to gain the attention of the boisterous group. "As the esteemed patriarch of this fine family," he said, pausing, "I would like to take a moment for us all to quietly think of those family members who could not be here this evening."

Daniel cringed internally.

"We do expect Charles to join us in a few days, but Mother will never again be here at this table. May we all bow our heads briefly in quiet remembrance."

Little did they know, thought Daniel, this was as close to a graveside sermon as Charles was ever going to get. With all heads bowed, Daniel lifted his head a bit to sneak a look around. Maria stood at the door to the kitchen, her head down, crossing herself in Catholic piety. Next to her stood Mrs. Kelley, hands on her hips, head up, staring straight into Daniel's eyes. He clenched his fists to keep his hands from trembling.

After dinner, when the exhausted travelers and the tired mother-to-be had all gone to sleep, Daniel sat alongside Robert on the leather sofa beside the fire in the library.

"Papá," he began, "I need to talk to you about two things that have been bothering me."

"Well? What is it?" Robert lit his pipe and began to puff away, the smoke blending in with the wild, white hair on his head and the bushy, white muttonchops running down along the sides of his cheeks.

Knowing he had to present his questions in just the right way, Daniel began. "All right. First of all, when you deeded this property to me, I believed I would will it to my wife. But ... in a letter ... from Charles, he said the property would go to him as eldest son, and that it was recorded in some seventeenth-century land deed. Is this so? Is it still legal and binding?"

"Oh, that! I remember it. It's so ancient that I doubt it will still hold up in court over an up-to-date will. It's merely a tradition."

Daniel took no comfort in his father's words. "But Charles was convinced he would inherit Crooked Pond if anything should happen to me."

"Why does this worry you so? I know Charles has always wanted to live here. He loves the place. But he had to move to where his job took him in Pittsfield. He was actually very upset when I told him you were returning and I was going to turn the place over to you. He said he had always planned on living here."

"All right." In an instant Daniel digested the information, saying not another word on the topic.

"Now, Papá, what is this deep affection Mrs. Kelley has for Charles? She constantly talks about how wonderful he was … I mean … is. She always favored him when we were growing up and still does. She cannot wait until she can see him again on Christmas Day and has constantly treated him as if her were her own son. What's going on here?"

"Really, Daniel, are you thinking that I fathered a child with our housekeeper? I am ashamed of you for even letting the thought cross your mind." Robert got up as if to leave the room, but Daniel grabbed his arm.

"Wait. I'm not accusing you of anything. But since you brought it up, is Mrs. Kelley really Charles's mother?"

Robert, the family's decorated Civil War veteran, appeared to grow shorter before his son's eyes. "All right, I'll tell you. Sit down and listen. And never, ever bring up this subject again. Do you hear me? The honor of this family must be preserved." He pushed Daniel into the closest chair and stood leaning over him.

"Wait, Papá. Preserving the honor of a family does not always involve the truth, although I believe we both know it should."

"I'm glad you understand that. Remember, what I'm about to tell you is in complete confidence. I now trust you more than I ever have, out of respect for the way you have grown and changed and returned to us successful and confident for the first time ever."

Robert pulled up a chair so he could directly face his son, their knees almost touching. He drew deeply on his pipe, inhaled, and leaned forward, his shoulders sinking.

"I returned from the Civil War to marry your mother and bring her home here to Crooked Pond. Your grandfather had just taken on the Kelleys as caretakers. Even though I respected your mother highly, when Irene Kelley forced herself upon me, I … shall we say … strayed. I admit I was weakened by her beauty after having just come from spending two years in the army with only male company, and those friends losing their lives at an alarming rate. I had all the urges of a young man—urges that could not be met by my new wife. Soon, both your mother and Irene found themselves to be pregnant—both, I believed, with a child that was mine."

"Why did you think Mrs. Kelley's child was not Ian's?"

"We were not sure. But in our most passionate embraces Irene and I wished that the child she was carrying were mine."

Daniel leaned back in his chair, looking up at the ceiling. "So?"

"Irene Kelley and your mother were both due to give birth at about the same time, and indeed they did. Irene's child was stillborn. Your mother, after giving birth, was very ill for a while and went into a deep depression. Irene took it upon herself to care for Charles, even to the point of becoming his wet nurse. From that time on, she became obsessed with the belief that Charles was her child."

"So that explains these." Daniel reached into his pocket and pulled out the photographs of Charles with his carved toys and the woman who wanted to believe he was her son. He spread them out on the nearby tea table.

"Where did you get those?" Robert jumped up and clapped on his spectacles to look closer at pictures he had not seen in decades.

"From Charles," Daniel said, not daring to explain any further.

"Irene promised me she would never let them be seen by anyone."

"Apparently *Irene* changed her mind." Daniel felt strange calling Mrs. Kelley by her first name for the first time in his life.

"How long have you had these?"

Daniel thought for only a split second. "Oh, Charles mailed them to me. I picked them up myself at the post office a few days ago." Then he added, "I guess he wanted … I mean … I guess he wants me to show them to the family when he arrives at Christmas."

"You will not show these to the family." In one quick motion, Robert gathered the five pictures together and tossed them all into the large opening of the fireplace. As the last one fluttered down to the flaming logs and curled to a shiny black, Daniel could see Charles proudly holding up above his head a carved wooden osprey with outspread wings.

"Papá," said Daniel, not sure this was the best time to tell his father, after seeing his fury over the photographs, but then feeling it had to be done, "I have decided to let the Kelleys go."

Robert stood facing the fire, not moving a muscle. Daniel waited for a reaction. Finally his father spoke. "Ian has been a good and faithful caretaker of this property for forty-three years. I am truly sorry that I have wronged him and your mother, but that cannot be changed. We must learn to live with the decisions we make and take full responsibility for the consequences of these errors."

Daniel let this sink in. "Thank you. You can't know how much hearing you say that means to me. I too am sorry for what has happened, but Ian is getting on in years. His leg is getting worse, and I can no longer tolerate his wife's presence. I will give them a good severance pay, enough for them to live comfortably for the rest of their lives." He paused, avoiding his father's eyes. "But they must live elsewhere."

Robert was silent for a long time before he spoke. "So be it then. But promise you will do me the favor of not telling them until I have left after Christmas. It will be easier for all of us that way."

"I promise."

"And one more thing." Robert put down his pipe, walked to his son, and placed both hands on Daniel's shoulders. "Please do not reveal any of this conversation to Charles when he arrives on Christmas Day."

"Yes, Papá. I will say absolutely nothing to Charles."

———•———

Most of the family was concerned over Charles not showing up on Christmas Day. But they had a grand time anyway. The next day, amid a flutter of hugs and kisses, they all left the house on Crooked Pond.

Mrs. Kelley continued to grumble and glare at Daniel, as if she thought he might be responsible for the disappearance of her darling Charles. But that did not bother Daniel. He knew she would soon be gone.

One week after Christmas, on the day they were to leave, Mrs. Kelley told Ian to wait a few minutes for her as he sat in the wagon holding the reins of the two horses Daniel had given them. With one glance at the wagon piled high with the possessions they had accumulated over their years at Crooked Pond, she returned to the cottage.

Upon entering she wrote something on a blank piece of paper and placed it in the middle of the kitchen table. Then, taking an ax from the woodpile at the back door, she drove it with all the force she could muster through the paper and into the table. Mrs. Kelley walked out, slammed the door, and climbed up on the wagon to sit beside her husband. Ian clicked the reins, and the two caretakers left the house on Crooked Pond. On the paper in the cottage, the name Herb Allen was almost cleft in two as it remained impaled there in the table, the ax handle still quivering from the blow.

Watching them drive their cart down the driveway for the last time, Daniel felt a great relief. There was nothing that could now stop him from going back to the peaceful life he wished to live with Nell. He decided to take a look around the cottage the Kelleys had just vacated. As soon as he walked in, he saw the ax in the table.

Soon after the Kelleys left, Daniel drove his repaired Model T to Boston to pick up Luigi's brother, Sal, who was coming from Italy to paint the frescoes on the ceiling of the wine cellar.

---

At the beginning, there was a bit of a buzz about the whereabouts of Charles, but he had no close friends who might persist in looking for him after his family had searched for three years. Finding no leads, the family gave up their obligation to continue the search.

Daniel maintained an office in New York. He and Nell and their children returned weekends and entire summers to enjoy their house on Crooked Pond. His spectacular, five-hundred-bottle wine cellar became the talk of New York society as more and more of their friends were invited to spend summer days and nights there. They all greatly appreciated Maria's fine gourmet cooking, and Luigi was even better at managing the property than Ian had been. Daniel and Nell's family grew, steeped in the manners of what was deemed to be proper Lyman behavior. And so, along with his expertise in safe investments, the family prospered.

Ian did appreciate the Boston "retirement" compensation he and his wife had received from Daniel. He had happily imagined spending the rest of his years living near his brother, Brian Kelley, in the Boston house Daniel had bought for them. Shortly after they'd left Crooked Pond, though, Mrs. Kelley had been found dead late one foggy night in the middle of Commonwealth Avenue. A lone witness claimed she had been hit by one of those fancy new automobiles. The driver was never found.

In 1932, on the afternoon of November 5, Daniel Lyman was found in the cottage by the house on Crooked Pond with a bullet in his head. Beside his body lay a Colt revolver with a carved ivory handle.

# Part V

# The Author—Winter–Spring 2014

*Courage is found in unlikely places.*

—*J. R. R. Tolkien, 1892–1973*

In but a short time the whole ordeal had brought Abby Jenkins and Stan Kelley closer than either of them could ever have believed. He loved her practical approach to a difficult situation. She loved the way his sense of humor could make her see more clearly the possible outcomes of a difficult situation.

One week was left for her to make her decision. Would she take the offer of Joshua Lyman, her newly discovered biological father, move into the house on Crooked Pond as his daughter, and write the Lyman family story?

# Chapter 33

## THE DECISION

Abby and Stan sat at the kitchen table in her studio apartment, sharing boxes of Chinese takeout. Stan dipped a hot egg roll into some soy sauce. "So?"

"I know what I'm going to do. My mind is made up. But first, what do you honestly think I should do?"

"Even though this guy is your father, he's certainly unstable. Can you really trust him to stay away from the house until he's invited? You have to consider that. I don't think you should move into the house alone, even though there will be a guard."

"It does make me worry a little."

"You say Gladys and Tom are not willing to move in with you there?"

"Right. My father wants to stay close to the rehab center he's been going to in Chatham, even though I've told him about the excellent facilities available here in Falmouth. My mother supports his position."

"And?"

"I really think he's so upset over this whole revelation that he just can't deal with moving into the house owned by the man who betrayed him. He has been my dearest daddy, dad, and father for all these years. He was my safety net. He is the father I will always love. Linton, I mean, Joshua, can never take his place."

Abby began to choke on her words as she continued. "My dad feels deeply hurt by the man who had sworn to him to never reveal his paternity. And he also feels he's losing me, even though I've assured him that would never be the case."

"And your mother?"

"We've never really been that close. And now I can see why. Think of how she must have felt when Dad insisted they move to the Cape to escape her parent's insistence that they would tell me when I turned five. Now I can see why we never truly connected as mother and daughter. Yet she does love the prospect of seeing the Lyman house entirely renovated."

"So?"

"After we finish the article for the *Star* on Linton's war memorabilia, writing about the family I've never met now seems even more interesting. I can't wait to get to work on stories about this family. Can you imagine what's in that collection of letters and journals? I'm excited to try my hand at writing an historical fiction account. I'd like to publish it as a series, telling the tales of a few Lymans at a time. That way, I can incorporate all the research Nils has done with all the research I can do and then add my own ideas about what probably happened."

"But will you feel safe there?"

"Somehow I feel, deep down inside, that maybe he's sincere. And if he is, then how can I turn him away?"

"You feel he's sincere because ...?"

"I completely understand his need to feel like he's part of a family, his need for belonging. He's already shown some good signs. He got rid of that ridiculous wig and beard, so he doesn't look so creepy. And once he assumes his original identity, as Joshua Lyman, he's going to finance a scholarship at the community college and contribute to the local cat rescue service. I'm going to take a chance and accept his offer."

Stan pushed back from the table and stood looking out the window. "Abby," he said, with his back still toward her, "I also have an offer to make to you. Hopefully, it will help you feel more comfortable about living there."

"What?"

"Now that I know about the connection my great-great-uncle Ian Kelley and his wife once had to the house, I've come up with an idea.

Since Linton says he's going to renovate the cottage along with the rest of the place, and since my lease where I live now is about to expire, what do you think about renting the cottage to me so I could move in there?"

He hesitated a moment and then continued, not yet facing her. "That way, I'd be seconds away if you ever needed to call for help at night. The guard will only have to cover the property during the day while I'm at work. What do you think?"

He stood, still as a stone.

Abby got up and walked over to stand close to his back. She put her arms around him, resting her head against the soft warmth of his plaid wool shirt. She was no longer afraid of possibly spending the rest of her life with a man she could love.

"I daresay," she said with a grin, "I shall seriously consider your offer, kind sir." Then she hugged him closer. "I'll let you know in about … three seconds."

# Epilogue

Joshua Lyman kept his promise. He hired an armed guard and caretakers. He restored the run-down portions of the house and the cottage behind the barn. The barn itself was restored to hold his wartime material until Joshua could find an appropriate museum to permanently house the collection.

The last renovation Joshua wanted to complete was in the wine shaft. He had his workmen dig the wine shaft deeper so the bottom of it could come out even with the floor of the ossuary. Yet, in order to install the new spiral staircase Joshua had ordered, they had to dig a few feet deeper to allow for a substantial base of new concrete to be laid. They were shocked at what they found. Not knowing the true identity of the bones, yet not wanting to cast any aspersions on the family, Joshua, knowing the men could lose their licenses by not reporting what they had uncovered, silenced them with cash. He told them the bones probably belonged to someone who had died in the original construction of the shaft. The bones of Charles Lyman were placed in a box on the shelf beside those of Daniel Lyman. The word "Unknown" was engraved on the brass label.

Abby published her article on John Linton's wartime collection, with Stan's photographs, and it was a great success, stirring up a storm of inquiries about the former actor's current whereabouts. It was at this time that John Linton's true identity as Joshua Lyman became public, along with the news that his daughter would be writing a story about their Lyman family. The press was excited.

On the fifth day of April, Joshua signed the deed to the house over to Abby, with guarantees that he would continue to offer his financial support of the buildings and grounds. Abby moved into the house and Stan into the cottage. Her new father visited her, each time upon invitation and each time leaving both her and Stan more confident in his sincerity that he wanted to build a family relationship.

---

On a warm evening in June, with the rhododendrons in full bloom, the spring peepers singing on the pond, and the scent of lilies of the valley drifting in through the open window, Abby Lyman Jenkins sat at her desk in the library of the large house that had been lived in by her ancestors for more than three hundred years.

After extensive historical research to add to the work of Nils Swanson; after having read through sixteen diaries and journals written between 1709 and 1989; and after having investigated more of the family artifacts stored in the attic, closets, and cellar, she was ready. There were so many stories to tell. She had to make a choice. Which stories would she select to write about in the first book of her series on the Lyman family?

She'd had to struggle to accept the fact that her parents were not the ones she had believed them to be and to summon the courage to accept her new identity. She chose three ancestors who'd also had to summon the courage to endure oppressive circumstances.

Abby had found in the journals of Quaker Tacy Swift Lyman that, in 1712, her ancestor had been forced to embark on an unwanted future as the wife of an unpleasant man. She had discovered that Olivia Lyman Lyman, in 1814, had needed to summon the courage to endure living with a part of the family she had been taught to detest. And Daniel Lyman had found the courage to leave home and venture west to find his fortune so he could return in 1912 to take a gentleman's revenge on an older brother who had constantly abused him. When Abby thought about the disappearance of Charles Lyman and the box in the ossuary filled with "unknown" remains, she began to wonder if Daniel's revenge was not one that would have been taken by a gentleman.

As she sat there, thinking about how to begin, a strange sensation crept over her. She looked up at the "summer beam," the largest beam to be put in place when the house was first built in 1685. She wondered how it must have once looked as a tall oak growing near the edge of a pond. She felt as though she could hear it talking to her, telling her tales about what it had witnessed in the lives of these three Lymans—tales that could not be found in her research. She began to compose her story, the keyboard on her computer clicking away as though she were playing a bit of Mozart on the beautiful antique piano that still stood in what was now her living room, in her house on Crooked Pond.

"Be careful what you say as you walk through the forests of Cape Cod," she wrote. "The trees are listening."